PENGUIN BOOKS
FROG

Mo Yan was born in 1955 in Gaomi County in Shandong province, China. He is the author of various novellas and short stories, as well as numerous novels including *Red Sorghum*, *The Republic of Wine*, *Big Breasts and Wide Hips*, *Life and Death Are Wearing Me Out* and *The Garlic Ballads*. In 2012 he was awarded the Nobel Prize in Literature.

Howard Goldblatt is the award-winning translator of many works of contemporary Chinese into English. He has been awarded the National Translation Award from the American Literary Translators Association and a Guggenheim Fellowship.

D1422133

MO YAN
Frog

Translated from the original Chinese edition by
HOWARD GOLDBLATT

PENGUIN BOOKS

PENGUIN BOOKS

UK | USA | Canada | Ireland | Australia
India | New Zealand | South Africa

Penguin Books is part of the Penguin Random House group of companies
whose addresses can be found at global.penguinrandomhouse.com.

First published by Shanghai Art and Literature Publishing House 2009
This edition first published by Penguin Group (Australia) in association with
Penguin (Beijing) Ltd 2014
First published in Great Britain by Hamish Hamilton 2014
Published in Penguin Books 2015
009

Text copyright © Mo Yan, 2009
Translated from the original Chinese by Howard Goldblatt
Translation copyright © Penguin (Beijing) Ltd, 2014

The moral right of the copyright holders has been asserted

Printed and bound in Great Britain by Clays Ltd, Elcograf S.p.A.

A CIP catalogue record for this book is available from the British Library

ISBN: 978-0-241-96732-4

Dramatis Personae

Tadpole and Gugu's family

GUGU, *or* WAN XIN, *midwife*

JIN XIU, *cousin of Xiaopao, business partner of Xiao Xiachun*

LITTLE LION, *Gugu's medical intern*

WAN KOU, *aka Eldest Brother, brother of Xiaopao, father of Wan Xiangqun*

WAN LIUFU, *father of Gugu, soldier and doctor, founder of the Xihai Underground Hospital*

WAN MAN, *sister of Xiaopao*

WAN XIANGQUN, *air force pilot, nephew of Xiaopao, son of Wan Dakou*

WAN ZU, *or* XIAOPAO *or* TADPOLE, *nephew of Gugu*

WUGUAN, *cousin of Xiaopao*

YANYAN, *daughter of Xiaopao*

Chen Bi's family

AILIAN, *mother of Chen Bi*

CHEN BI, *classmate of Xiaopao*

CHEN E, *father of Chen Bi*

CHEN ER, *daughter of Chen Bi*

CHEN MEI, *daughter of Chen Bi*

Other Characters
(in alphabetical order)

TEACHER CHEN

DU BOZI, *a villager/fisherman*

FAN, *carpenter*

FANG LIANHUA, *Wang Jiao's wife*

FLATHEAD, *rafter, son of old classmate of Xiaopao*

GAO MEN, *village beggar*

GENG XIULIAN, *wife of Zhang Quan*

HAO DASHOU, *the clay-doll maker*

HUANG JUN, *aka Melon Huang, hospital director, the son of Huang Pi from Hexi Village*

HUANG QIUYA, *doctor at health centre, enemy of Gugu*

DOCTOR LI

POLITICAL COMMISSAR LI

LI SHOU, *son of Teacher Yu, younger schoolmate of Xiaopao*

CHIEF LIU, *Armed Forces Bureau*

LU HUAHUA, *village beggar*

LU MAZI, *civil administration clerk*

LÜ YA, *brigade commander*

POSTAL DIRECTOR MA

NING YAO, *commune security chief*

QIN HE, *brother of Qin Shan, beggar/actor, boat pilot, clay-doll maker*

QIN SHAN, *commune Party secretary, brother of Qin He*

QIU, *commune Party secretary (and Qin Shan's successor)*

SESAME TWIST, *wife of Yuan Sai*

DIRECTOR SHEN, *Bureau of Health*

COMMANDER SUGITANI, *Japanese Army*

SUGITANI AKIHITO, *mentor to Xiaopao*

TIAN GUIHUA, *old midwife*

WANG DAN, *daughter of Wang Jiao, twin of Wang Gan, classmate of Xiaopao*

WANG GAN, *son of Wang Jiao, twin of Wang Dan, classmate of Xiaopao*

WANG HUAN, *the bean curd peddler*

WANG JIAO, *owner of a horse and cart, father of Wang Dan and Wang Gan*

WANG JINSHAN, *aka* OLD WANG, *the school cook*

WANG RENMEI, *daughter of Wang Jinshan, wife of Xiaopao*

WANG XIAOTI, *Gugu's fiancé, Air Force pilot, traitor*

WANG XIAOMEI, *a seventeen-year-old girl from Wang Village, Director Huang's lover*

SECRETARY WU, *commune Party secretary, 1980s*

WU JINBANG, *school principal*

XIAO BI, *office manager of bullfrog farm, sculptor*

XIAO SHANGCHUN, *stretcher-bearer in the Eighth Route Army, commune granary watchman, Windstorm Rebel Corps Commander, enemy of Gugu, father of Xiao Xiachun*

XIAO XIACHUN, *classmate of Xiaopao, son of Xiao Shangchun, entrepreneur*

XIE BAIZHUA, *restaurant owner*

XIE XIAOQUE, *the son of Xie Baizhua*

COMMANDER XU, *Eighth Route Army*

TEACHER XUE

YAN, *assistant director of the commune*

YANG LIN, *county Party secretary*

CHAIRWOMAN YANG XIN, *family-planning committee*

YANG XIONG, *county chief, son of Yang Lin*

TEACHER YU

YUAN LIAN, *village Party secretary*

YUAN SAI, *son of Yuan Lian, classmate of Xiaopao*

ZHANG JINYA, *Party secretary of Dongfeng village*

ZHANG QUAN, *from Dongfeng village*

BOOK ONE

BOOK ONE

Dear Sugitani Akihito sensei,

It has been nearly a month since we said goodbye, but I can relive virtually every moment of our time together in my hometown as if it were yesterday. With no concern for age or physical frailties, you crossed land and sea to come to this out-of-the-way spot and engage in literary conversations with me and with local fans of literature; we were deeply moved. On the second morning of the year, you favoured us with a presentation in the county guesthouse auditorium that you called 'Literature and Life'. With your permission, we would like to publish a transcription of the taped lecture in the local publication Frog Calls, *so as to make available to those who were unable to attend in person a chance to appreciate and learn from your use of language.*

On the morning of the first day of the year I accompanied you on a visit to my aunt, an obstetrician for more than fifty years, and though she spoke too quickly in her accented Chinese for you to grasp everything she said, I am sure she left a deep impression on you. In your talk the next morning you cited her often in support of your views of literature. You said you came away with an image of a doctor racing across a frozen river on a bicycle; another of her with a medical kit slung over her back and an open umbrella in one hand, trouser cuffs rolled up, as she forces her way through a mass of croaking frogs; yet another of a doctor laughing joyfully as she holds a newborn infant in her hands, her sleeves spattered with blood; and finally one of a doctor with a care-laden face, a cigarette dangling from her lips, clothing rumpled . . . you said that all these mental pictures sometimes come together into a single image and at other times split into discrete fragments, like a series of carvings. You urged local literature fans to create poignant works of art out of my aunt's life, either in fiction, in verse, or in drama. Sensei, your encouragement has produced a creative passion in many of us. An associate at the county cultural centre has already begun a novel about a village obstetrician, and though my understanding of what my aunt accomplished is much greater than his, I do not want to enter into a competition and will leave the writing of a novel to him. What I want to do, sensei, is write a play about my aunt's life. On the night of the second, when we were talking as we sat on the kang at my house,

I experienced an epiphany thanks to your high praise and detailed analyses, as well as your unique insights into the plays of the Frenchman, Sartre. I want to write, I feel I must write librettos as fine as The Flies *and* Dirty Hands, *with the audacious goal of becoming a great playwright. With your instruction as a guide, I will proceed slowly, without forcing the issue, as patient as a frog on a lily pad waiting for insects to come its way. But when I put pen to paper, it will be with the speed of a frog jumping up to snatch an insect out of the air.*

When I was seeing you off at the Qingdao airport, you asked me to send you in letters the story of my aunt's life. Although she is still alive and well, I could describe her life using such potent metaphors as 'surging forth magnificently' and 'rife with twists and turns'. There are so many stories, and I don't know how long this letter ought to be, so with your indulgence, I will put my meagre talents to use by simply writing until the time has come to stop. In this age of computers, writing a letter with pen and paper has become a luxury, but a pleasurable one, and I hope that as you read this, you enjoy a taste of olden times.

While I'm at it, I want to tell you that my father phoned to say that on the lunar twenty-fifth, red blossoms burst onto the tree in our yard, the one whose unique shape prompted you to call it a 'talented' old plum. Many people came to witness our blooming plum, including my aunt. My father said that a feathery snow fell that day, saturated with a redolence of plum blossoms that cleared the head of anyone who smelled it.

Your student, Tadpole
21 March 2002, in Beijing

1

Sensei, an old custom in my hometown dictated that a newborn child is given the name of a body part or organ. Nose Chen, for instance, Eyes Zhao, Colon Wu, Shoulder Sun . . . I haven't looked into the origin of this custom, but I imagine it embodied the outlook of 'those who are badly named live long'. Either that or it evolved from a mother's thoughts that a child represented a piece of her body. The custom is no longer followed, as young parents have no interest in naming their children in such an unusual way. Local children these days are endowed with elegant and distinctive names of TV characters in dramas from Hong Kong, Taiwan, even Japan and Korea. Most of those who were named the earlier way have adopted more conventional names, most but not all. We still have Chen Er (Ears) and Chen Mei (Brow).

Chen Er and Chen Mei were the daughters of Chen Bi (Nose), my classmate and my friend. We entered Great Sheep's Pen Elementary School in the fall of 1960. That was during the famine, and nearly all my strongest memories of the time deal with food. I've told the story of eating coal. Most people think I made that up, but I swear on my aunt's good name it's true.

The coal was part of a ton of high-grade ore from the Longkou Coal Mine, so glossy I could see my face in it. I've never seen the likes of it since. Wang Jiao (Foot), the owner of a horse cart, transported the coal over from the county seat. Wang, a man with a square head, a thick neck and a bad stammer, had a bright look in his eyes when he spoke, his face flushed from the effort. He had a son, Wang Gan (Liver), and a daughter named Wang Dan (Gallbladder). They were twins, and both were my classmates. Wang Gan was tall and well built, while his sister never grew to full size and remained a tiny thing – to be unkind, a dwarf. Everyone said she was so small because her brother had sucked up all the nutrition in their mother's womb. After school was out, we ran over with our backpacks to watch Wang Jiao shovel the coal to the ground, where it landed crisply on a growing pile. He stopped to wipe his sweaty neck with a blue cloth he'd wrapped around his waist, and when he saw his son and daughter, he shouted: Go home and mow the grass.

Wang Dan turned and headed for home, struggling to keep her balance as she ran, like an infant learning how to walk; a lovely sight. Wang Gan backed up but did not run. He was proud of his father's occupation. Children these days, even those whose fathers are airline pilots, are not as proud of theirs as he was of his. Wang drove a horse cart whose wheels threw up dust as it rumbled along; an old branded warhorse said to have distinguished itself by once towing an artillery piece was between the shafts, while a bad-tempered mule was up front in a harness, a mean animal known to kick and bite. That aside, it was astonishingly powerful and could run like the wind. No one but Wang Jiao could control it. Though many villagers admired his line of work, they kept their distance from the mule, which had already bitten two youngsters: Yuan Sai (Cheek), son of Yuan Lian (Face); and Wang Dan, who had been bitten and picked up by the head while playing in front of the house. We were in awe of Wang Jiao, who stood over six-two, with broad shoulders, and the strength of an ox. He could lift a stoneroller weighing two hundred jin over his head. But what really wowed us was his skill with a whip. That time the crazy mule bit Yuan Sai, Wang pulled back the brake and, with one foot on each of the shafts, brought the tip of his whip down on the animal's rump with a crack that drew blood. The mule reacted by kicking out, but then began to quake as its forelegs buckled and its head hit the ground, mouth in the dirt, rump raised ready for another hit. It was Yuan Sai's father, Yuan Lian, who came to its rescue. It's okay, Old Wang, he said, sparing the animal further anguish. Yuan was our village's ranking official, the Party secretary. Not heeding his word was not an option for Wang Jiao. After the crazy mule bit Wang Dan, we eagerly awaited another good show, but instead of striking out with his whip, Wang Jiao scooped up a handful of roadside lime and pressed it against the girl's head as he carried her inside. The mule did not taste his whip this time, but his wife did, just before Wang kicked his son.

That crazy mule was one of our favourite topics of conversation. Skinny as a rail, the indentations above both eyes were so deep they could accommodate hen's eggs. Its eyes emitted a sorrowful gaze, as if it were about to howl. How a skinny animal like that could exert such strength was a mystery. We were talking about that as we drew up to the mule. Wang Jiao stopped shovelling coal and glared menacingly, backing us up terrified. The pile in front of the school kitchen grew higher and higher, the load of coal on the cart kept getting smaller. We sniffed in unison at the strange aroma in the air, a bit like burning pine or roasting potatoes. Our sense of smell drew our gaze to the pile of glistening coal as Wang Jiao flicked the reins and drove his cart out of the schoolyard. This time we didn't chase it out of the yard, as we usually did, even risking the bite of Wang's whip when we tried to climb aboard to satisfy our desire for a ride. No, we kept our eyes glued to the pile of coal as we shuffled forward. Old Wang, the school cook, wobbled over with two buckets of water on his shoulder pole. His daughter, Renmei, was also a classmate who, much later, would become my wife. She was one of the rare children not burdened with the name of a body part, and that was because her father had attended school. As the one-time head of a commune animal-husbandry station, a careless comment had cost him his job and sent him back to his village. He observed us with a wary eye. Did he think we were planning to raid his kitchen? Go on, you little shits, get out of here! There's nothing here for you to eat. Go home and suck your mothers' teats. We heard him, of course, and even considered what he'd said. But he was just mouthing off. Already seven or eight years old, we were way past nursing at our mothers' breasts. Even if we hadn't been, our half-starved mothers, with their flattened chests, had nothing to give us. But we weren't interested in arguing with Old Wang. Instead, we stood in front of the pile of coal, heads down and bent at the waist like geologists who have discovered an unusual rock formation. We sniffed the air like dogs searching for food in a rubbish pile. At this point I need to first thank Chen Bi and then Wang Dan. It was Chen who first picked up a chunk of coal and sniffed it, crinkling his brow as if pondering a weighty question. His big, high-bridged nose was a source of laughter for us. After a thoughtful pause, he smashed the coal in his hand against a much larger piece, like shattering glass, releasing a strong aroma into the air. Both he and Wang Dan picked up shards. He licked his to taste it and rolled his eyes as he looked our way. She copied him by tasting hers and looking our way. They exchanged a glance, smiled, and as if on cue, cautiously took small bites; they chewed briefly before taking bigger bites and chewing like crazy. Excited looks burst onto their faces. Chen Bi's big nose turned red and was beaded with sweat. Wang Dan's little nose turned black with coal dust. We were entranced by the sound of coal being chewed and shocked when they swallowed it. They'd actually swallowed coal! It's good, guys, he said softly. Eat up, big brother! she cried out shrilly. Wang Gan picked up another piece and really started to chew, while she grabbed a large chunk and handed it to him. So we followed their lead, smashing the coal into smaller chunks and nibbling it at first to see how it tasted. Though it was sort of gritty, it wasn't half bad. Chen Bi picked up a large chunk. Eat this kind, guys, he said helpfully, it tastes the best. He pointed to some slightly transparent, amber-like pale yellow coal. That was the source of the pine aroma. From our nature study class we'd learned that coal formed over millennia from buried forests. Our teacher for that class was our principal, Wu Jinbang. We hadn't believed him or what the textbook said. How could green forests turn into black coal? We'd thought he and the textbooks were lying. But the smell of pine trees changed our minds. Our principal and the textbook were telling the truth. All thirty-five students in our class, except for a few absent girls, picked up chunks of coal and started chewing, crunching away, slightly mysterious looks of excitement on our faces. It was like improvisational theatre or a strange game. Xiao Xiachun (Lower Lip) turned a piece of coal over and over in his hand, but chose not to eat it, a superior look on his face. He didn't eat it because he wasn't hungry, he said, and that was because his father was the commune granary watchman.

Old Wang the cook came out, his hands flour-dusted, and was stunned by what he saw. (My god, that's flour on his hands! In those days, the only people who ate in the kitchen were the principal, our political instructor, and two locally stationed commune cadres.) What are you kids doing? Old Wang cried out in alarm. Are you . . . eating coal? Who does that? Wang Dan picked up a piece and, in a tiny voice, said, It's delicious. Here, Uncle, try it. Old Wang shook his head. Wang Dan, he said, why is a nice little girl like you acting like these wild kids? She took a bite. It really is delicious, Uncle, she said. A red evening sun was setting in the west. The two privileged commune cadres rode up on their bicycles. We got their attention, as Old Wang tried to shoo us away with his shoulder pole. The fellow named Yan – I think he was the assistant director – stopped him. With a disdainful wave of his hand and a sour look on his face, Old Wang stormed back into the kitchen.

The next day in school we nibbled on coal while listening to Teacher Yu's lesson, our mouths smeared black, coal crumbs in the corners. The boys weren't the only ones either. Wang Dan taught even the girls who'd been absent the day before how to eat it. Old Wang's daughter, my future wife, Renmei, enjoyed it more than anyone. Now that I think about it, she probably had a gum disease, since her mouth bled as she chewed. After writing several lines on the blackboard, Teacher Yu turned back to the class and asked her son, Li Shou (Hand): What are you kids eating? It's coal, Ma. Want some, Teacher Yu? called out Wang Dan, who sat in the front row, a lump of coal in her hand. Her voice was like that of a kitten. Teacher Yu stepped down from the podium and took the lump from Wang Dan, holding it up to her nose either to smell it or get a closer look. She didn't say anything for a moment then handed it back. Today we're on lesson six, class, 'The Fox and the Crow'. The crow found a piece of meat and was proud of herself, perched high up in a tree. From under the tree, the fox said, Crow, you have such a beautiful singing voice you put all the other birds to shame. Swooning over the flattery, the crow opened her beak to sing and, ha, the meat fell right into the fox's mouth. The teacher led us in reading the story aloud, which we did with our black-as-crow mouths.

Teacher Yu was an educated, out-of-towner who followed the local custom by giving her son the name Shou (Hand), using his father's surname, Li. Li Shou did well enough in the exams to be admitted to medical school. After graduation he returned to the county health centre as a surgeon. When Chen Bi lost four fingers while cutting hay, Doctor Li was able to reattach three of them.

2

Why did Chen Bi have a big nose that was so different from everyone else's? Probably only his mother can answer that question.

His father, Chen E (Forehead), with the style name Tianting (Middle of the Forehead), was the only man in the village with two wives. A well-educated man, he came from a family that had farmed a hundred acres of prime land, run a distillery, and owned a business in Harbin before the establishment of the People's Republic. Chen's first wife, a local, had borne him four daughters. He fled north just before Liberation, but was brought back from the northeast in the custody of Yuan Lian and a pair of militiamen around 1951. He had fled alone, leaving his wife and daughters at home in the village, but brought another woman back with him. This woman, who had brown hair and blue eyes and looked to be in her early thirties, was called Ailian. She carried in her arms a spotted dog, and since she and Chen E had married before Liberation, it was perfectly legal for him to have two wives. Poor, unmarried village men were upset that Chen had two wives and half jokingly asked him if they could share one of them. Chen could only grin in response, a look somewhere between laughing and crying. The two Chen wives lived in the same house at first, but since they fought like cats and dogs, Chen received permission to put his junior wife up in two rooms next to the school, given that the school buildings had once housed his family's distillery, which meant that the two rooms counted as his property. He reached an agreement with the women that he'd divide his time between them. The dog the light-haired woman had brought with her was tormented to death by village mongrels, and not long after Ailian buried it she gave birth to Chen Bi. People liked to say that he was a reincarnation of the spotted dog, which might explain his ultra keen sense of smell. By that time, my aunt had returned from the county seat, where she'd gone to learn the newest methods of midwifery. She became the first professional midwife in the entire township. That was in 1953.

In 1953, villagers were adamantly opposed to new midwifery methods, thanks to rumours spread by old midwives, who said that children born through these methods were prone to be arthritic. Why would they spread such rumours? Because once the new methods caught on, they'd be out of work. Delivering a baby at the mother's home meant a free meal, a pair of towels, and a dozen eggs. Whenever these women entered the conversation, my aunt – Gugu – ground her teeth in anger. She could not begin to calculate how many infants and pregnant women had died at those old witches' hands. Her descriptions of their methods were chilling: they grew long fingernails, their eyes emitted green will-o'-the-wisp-like glimmers, and their breath stank. She said they pressed down on the mother's belly with rolling pins and stuffed rags in their mouths to keep the foetuses from coming out there. They knew nothing about anatomy and were totally ignorant of a woman's biological make-up. When they encountered a difficult birth, according to Gugu, they crammed their hands up the birth canal and pulled with all their might, sometimes actually wrenching the womb out along with the foetus. For the longest time, if I'd been asked to compile a list of people most deserving to be lined up and shot, I'd unhesitatingly say: the old midwives. Gradually I came to understand why Gugu was so prejudiced against them. Crude, ignorant old midwives certainly did exist, but experienced old midwives who, through their own experience, had a keen grasp of the secrets of a woman's body, existed as well. Truth be told, my grandmother was one of those midwives, one who advocated a policy of interfering as little as possible into the process. Her approach could be characterised as 'the melon will fall when it is ripe'. In her view, the best midwives simply offered encouragement as they waited for the foetus to emerge, then cut the umbilical cord, sprinkled on some lime, wrapped the child, and that was that. But she was not a popular old midwife, considered by some to be lazy. Those people seemed to prefer women whose hands were constantly busy, who kept running in and out of the room, shouting and carrying on; those old midwives perspired as much as the woman in labour.

My aunt was the daughter of my great-uncle, who had served as a doctor in the Eighth Route Army. He'd entered the army as a specialist in traditional Chinese medicine, but then had been taught Western medicine by the Canadian Norman Bethune, whose subsequent death from blood poisoning hit him so hard he fell desperately ill. He told his superior he wanted to see his mother before he died, a request that was granted so he could recuperate. Gugu's grandmother was still alive at the time, and the minute he walked through the door he was greeted by the familiar smell of mung bean soup. His mother had washed the pot and started a fire to make the soup, and when her daughter-in-law came up to help, she pushed her away with her cane. My great-uncle sat in the doorway waiting impatiently. Gugu said she was old enough then to remember such things, and when she was told to greet her father, she ran behind her mother to peek at him from there. She'd often heard her mother and grandmother talk about her father, whom she was now meeting for the first time, and to her he was a stranger. She told us how he sat in the doorway, sallow-faced, his hair long, fleas crawling up his neck, tufts of cotton wadding peeking out through tears in his tattered lined coat. Gugu's grandmother – my great-grandmother – was in tears as she worked at the stove. When the soup was finally ready, Great-Uncle eagerly picked up a bowl and began slurping, despite the mouth-burning heat. Son, his mother said, slow down. There's more in the pot. Gugu said his hands were shaking. He ate a second bowl, and his hands stopped shaking. Sweat ran down the sides of his face. Signs of life showed in his eyes as the colour returned to his face. Gugu said she could hear his stomach rumble, the sound of a millstone turning.

An hour or two later, Gugu said, her father went to the outhouse, where he emptied his bowels, almost taking his intestines along with the loose mixture. That's when his recovery began, and within two months he was his old, vigorous self again.

I told Gugu I'd read something like that in *The Scholars*. The what? she asked. I told her it was a famous classical novel. She glared at me. If things like that happen even in classical novels, that proves it was true.

Now that he was fully recovered, my great-uncle made preparations to rejoin his troops on Mount Taihang. Son, his mother said, I can't live much longer. Wait to go till after my funeral. And there was another matter his wife found hard to bring up, that was left to Gugu. Father, she said, Mother doesn't mind if you go, but she'd like you to leave me a little brother before you do.

Soldiers from the eastern Shandong military district of the Eighth Route Army showed up at Great-Uncle's house to recruit him, as a follower of Norman Bethune, reminding him of his fine reputation. I already belong to the Shanxi-Chaha'er-Hebei arm, he said. But we're Communists, just like they are, the Shandong representative said. It doesn't matter where you work. We really need someone like you, Old Wan, and we'll do whatever is necessary to keep you here. Commander Xu said if an eight-man sedan chair won't do the trick, he'd hogtie him and take him under escort to a banquet in his honour. That is how Great-Uncle wound up staying home in Shandong, where he founded the Xihai Underground Hospital.

The hospital had underground passages that linked the wards and other rooms, including a sterilisation room, a treatment room, an operating theatre, and a recovery room, all of which remain in Zhu Family Village, which is part of Yutong Township in the Laizhou Municipal area, and are still well maintained. An old woman of eighty-eight, Wang Xiulan by name, who was Great-Uncle's nurse back then, is still alive and well. Several of the recovery rooms lead directly to a well. One day back then, a young woman went to the well for water, and was surprised when her bucket stopped before reaching the bottom. She looked down, and there in a hollow in a wall, a young, wounded

Eighth Route soldier looked up and made a face at her.

Talk of Great-Uncle's superb medical skills quickly made the rounds. It was he who removed the shrapnel lodged near Commander Xu's scapula. He also managed to save both Political Commissar Li's wife and her child during a difficult birth. Word had even spread to Pingdu city, which was under the command of an officer named Sugitani, whose warhorse had stepped on a land mine during a mop-up operation. He had taken off on foot, leaving the horse behind. Great-Uncle performed surgery on the horse, and after it recovered it became the mount for Regimental Commander Xia. But before long, the horse was so homesick it bit through its tether and ran back to Pingdu. Sugitani was so happy to see his horse again, with its wounds healed, he told his Chinese collaborators to find out what had happened. He learned that the Eighth Route Army had established a hospital right under his nose, and that the medical skills of its director, Wan Liufu, were responsible for saving the life of his horse. Commander Sugitani, who himself had received medical training, was impressed by Great-Uncle's skills and summoned him to surrender. To do so, Sugitani adopted a scheme from the classical novel *Three Kingdoms*, which was to secretly infiltrate our hometown to kidnap my great-grandmother, my great-aunt, and my aunt, and take them back to Pingdu, where he sent a letter to Great-Uncle, telling him they were being held hostage.

After reading Sugitani's letter, my great-uncle, a dedicated Communist, wadded it up and threw it away. The hospital commissar retrieved the letter and delivered it to district headquarters. Commander Xu and Commissar Li wrote a joint letter to Sugitani, denouncing him as a petty man and threatening to throw the entire weight of the Shandong Eighth Route Army against him if he harmed a hair of any of the three members of Wan Liufu's family.

Gugu said that she and her mother and grandmother were well treated during the three months they spent in Pingdu. According to her, Sugitani was a fair-skinned young man who wore white-framed glasses and had a moustache. Quiet and bookish, he spoke fluent Chinese. He called my great-grandmother Aunt, called my grandmother Sister-in-law, and called Gugu Niece. She did not have a bad opinion of him. Of course, she only said that privately to members of the family. To others she said that all three were victims of Japanese brutality, subjected to coercion and bribery, though they remained steadfast.

Sensei, I could talk about my great-uncle for three days and nights and never exhaust the subject. We'll continue this some other day, but I must tell you about how he died. Gugu said he was gassed while performing surgery in the underground hospital. That is how his death is listed in historical documents prepared by the county consultative congress, but a private source claimed that he rode his mule into Pingdu with eight hand grenades on his belt, determined to single-handedly rescue his wife, his daughter and his ageing mother, but unfortunately struck a land mine placed by the Zhao Family Trench militiamen. The source of this account was Xiao Shangchun (Upper Lip), a stretcher-bearer for the Xihai Hospital. A quirky individual, Xiao served as the commune granary watchman after 1949, where he invented a pesticide that was a potent rat poison, for which he was extolled in the local newspaper, which changed his name from the *chun* that meant 'lip' to the one that meant 'purity'. Later it was discovered that the main ingredient of his rat poison was a banned highly toxic pesticide. He and Gugu were bitter enemies, which makes his account highly unreliable. He once said to me that my great-uncle disobeyed orders by neglecting his patients in favour of playing the hero, and that he'd fortified himself before setting out by drinking two jin of potato liquor, winding up so drunk that he stumbled on one of their own land mines. A gloating Xiao Shangchun flashed a yellow-toothed grin as he continued: Your great-uncle and the mule he was riding were blown to bits, both carried back to the hospital in boxes, bones and hooves all mixed up, and dumped into a coffin. Not a bad coffin, though, one confiscated from a wealthy family in Lan Village.

When I repeated his story to Gugu, her eyes grew wide and she gnashed her silver teeth. One of these days, she said, I'm going to cut that bastard's balls off!

Boy, she said staunchly, you can forget about everything else, but the one thing you must believe is that your great-uncle was a hero of the resistance and a revolutionary martyr! His body rests in a mausoleum on Martyrs Hill, his scalpel and leather shoes are part of the display in Martyrs Hall. They are English shoes, bequeathed to him by Norman Bethune on his deathbed.

3

Sensei, I rushed through the story of my great-uncle so I could take my time telling Gugu's story.

She was born on 13 June 1937, the fifth day of the fifth lunar month, which is Duanyang, the day of the Dragon Boat Festival. They called her Duanyang until she started school, and was then called Wan Xin (Heart). Great-Uncle named her, showing respect for local tradition while investing her name with a message. Not long after Great-Uncle's death, his mother died of natural causes in Chengdu. Members of the Shandong military district launched a large-scale rescue mission to free Gugu and her mother from their captivity, and once they were in the liberated zone, Gugu was enrolled in the Resistance elementary school and her mother was sent to a factory to make soles for cloth shoes. After Liberation, the future for descendants of martyrs like Gugu could not have been brighter, but her mother hated the idea of leaving her hometown and Gugu hated the idea of leaving her. Officials at the county level asked her what she would like to do; when she said she'd like to carry on her father's work, she was admitted to the prefectural medical school. She graduated at the age of sixteen and was assigned to the township health centre, where she undertook a training course for modern birthing methods organised by the county health bureau. Gugu forged an unbreakable bond with the sacred work of obstetrics. According to her calculations, from the fourth day of the fourth month of 1953, when she attended her first birth, till the spring of last year, she delivered around ten thousand babies, counting two as one when working with someone else. She told you this in person. I assumed she'd inflated the number somewhat, but there had to have been seven or eight thousand at least. She had seven interns, one of whom she called 'Little Lion', a young woman whose hair was never combed, who had a flat nose, a square mouth, and a face full of zits. She was so devoted to Gugu that if she'd been told to kill someone, she'd have picked up a knife and done it without asking why.

We've already seen how, in the spring of 1953, women in my hometown resisted modern birthing methods, including the old midwives, who spread all sorts of rumours. Gugu was only seventeen at the time, but with her unconventional experience and privileged background, she was already an influential young woman who was held in high esteem. Admittedly, her good looks played a role in that. Putting aside head, face, nose, and eyes, her teeth alone are worth mention. Our water was so heavily fluoridated that everyone, young and old, had black teeth. But after spending her youth in the liberated areas of eastern Shandong and drinking spring water, not to mention being taught to brush her teeth by Eighth Route soldiers, Gugu's teeth were spared of that noxious effect. Hers were the envy of all, especially the girls.

Chen Bi was the first baby Gugu delivered, a fact that caused her a lifetime of regret – her first ought to have been the son or daughter of a revolutionary, not a landlord's mongrel. But at the time, the necessity to start something new and do away with old birthing methods would not allow her to take such issues into consideration.

When Gugu learned that Ailian had gone into labour, she jumped on her bicycle (a rarity at the time), a medical kit over her back, and rushed home, covering the ten li from the health centre to our village in ten minutes. Village secretary Yuan Lian's wife, who was washing clothes on the bank of the Jiao River, watched her race across the narrow stone bridge, so scaring a puppy playing on the bridge it fell into the river.

Medical kit in hand, Gugu burst into Ailian's room, only to find that the old midwife Tian Guihua was already attending to her. The old woman, with her pointed mouth and sunken cheeks, was in her sixties; by now, thankfully, this torchbearer for the obstructionists is feeding worms. When Gugu entered, Tian was straddling Ailian and pushing down on her bulging belly with all her might. As Tian was suffering from chronic bronchitis, the sound of her laboured breathing merged with the hog-butchering screams of her pregnant victim, producing a tragically heroic aura in the room. Chen E, the landlord, was in the corner on his knees, banging his head in supplication on the floor, over and over, and mumbling incoherently.

As a frequent visitor to Chen's house, I knew its floor plan well. Two cramped rooms with hanging eaves faced west. The first thing you encountered after entering was the stove, which was backed by a two-foot-high wall. The sleeping platform, the kang, was behind that low wall. So Gugu witnessed the scene the moment she walked in, and was livid with anger; in her own words, 'the flames were thirty feet high'. She dropped her medical kit, ran up and, with her left hand on the old woman's left arm and her right hand on her right shoulder, yanked her off the kang. The old woman's head banged into the bedpan, splashing its contents all over the floor and filling the air with the smell of urine. Dark blood oozed from a head wound. It wasn't a serious injury, but you wouldn't have known that by her shrieks of agony. Most people, hearing such pitiful wails, would go dumb from fright. But they had no effect on Gugu, who had seen a thing or two in her life.

She took her place next to the kang, donned rubber gloves, and spoke sternly to Ailian: No more crying, no more screaming, since neither of those is helpful. Listen to me if you want to come out of this alive. Do exactly as I say. That had the desired effect on Ailian, who knew all about Gugu's background and her uncommon experiences. You are a little old to be having a child, Gugu told her, and the position of the foetus is wrong. Babies are supposed to come out headfirst, but yours wants to come out hand first, his head still inside. In years to come, Gugu often teased Chen Bi by saying he wanted to emerge with an outstretched hand to ask the world for something. To which, Chen always remarked: I was begging for food.

It was her first case, and yet she was calm and composed, not a hint of panic, someone whose techniques produced better than expected results. Gugu was a natural genius as a woman's doctor. What her instincts told her, her hands put into practice. Women who witnessed her at work or those who were her patients absolutely revered and admired her. My mother said to me more than once: Your aunt's hands are different than other people's. Most people's hands are cold some of the time, hot at other times, sometimes stiff, and sometimes sweaty. But your aunt's hands were always the same, whether in the cold of winter or the heat of summer: soft and cool, not spongy soft, more like . . . How can I describe them? My educated elder brother said: Like a needle tucked into cotton, supple yet firm? That's it, Mother said. And the coolness of her hands was never icy. I can't find the words . . . Again my brother came to her aid: Can we call it outer heat and inner coolness, like cool silk or fine jade? That's it, Mother said, that's it exactly. All she had to do was lay her hands on a sick person for that illness to retreat at least 70 per cent. Gugu came close to being deified by the women in our township.

Ailian was a lucky woman; she'd been a smart one to begin with. As soon as Gugu's hands touched her belly, she felt a sort of vigour. She often told people she met afterward that Gugu had the bearing of a general. Compared to her, the woman lying on the floor in a puddle of piss was a clown. In the inspiration and power derived from her scientific approach and dignified demeanour, Ailian saw brightness and gained the courage to deliver; her gut-wrenching screams and pain were greatly reduced. She stopped crying and did as Gugu said, working in concert with Gugu's movements to bring Chen Bi safely into the world.

Chen wasn't breathing when he emerged, so Gugu held him by his feet and smacked him on the back and chest until he produced a kitten-like cry. How is it the little imp has such a big nose? Gugu wondered. He looks like one of those Americans. She was as happy as she could be, like an artisan who has just completed the first project. And a smile spread across the face of the exhausted mother. Though Gugu was imbued with strong class-consciousness, class and class struggle were completely forgotten as she helped the infant emerge from the birth canal. Her elation constituted the pure essence of happiness.

When he heard that it was a boy, Chen E stood up. Feeling helpless, he threaded his way back and forth in the narrow space behind the stove, strings of tears dripping like honey from his dried-up eyes. He was incapable of describing the joy he felt. (There were terms like male heir and patriarchal clan, but from a man like him they would have been offensive.)

The boy has such a big nose, Gugu said, why don't you just call him Chen Bi – Nose Chen?

She was just teasing, but Chen E nodded and bowed to her, taking her words as if they constituted an imperial edict: I thank Gugu for favouring him with a name, he said. Nose it is. We'll call him Chen Bi.

Swathed in Chen E's insistent thanks and Ailian's tears of joy, Gugu packed up her kit and was on her way out when she spotted Tian Guihua sitting in the corner against the wall, the broken bedpan on the floor in front of her. She actually appeared to be asleep. Gugu could not say when this transformation had taken place or when her hair-raising shrieks had stopped. She thought the woman might be dead, but light in her cat-like eyes proved her wrong. Waves of anger surged through her mind. What are you hanging around for? she said. I did half the work, the woman said, and you did the other half. By rights I should get one towel and five eggs, but my head is injured, thanks to you. For the sake of your mother, I won't report you to the authorities, but you have to give me your towel to wrap the wound and your five eggs for my health.

That reminded Gugu that the old midwives always demanded a fee, and the thought disgusted her. Shame on you! she said through clenched teeth. Shame, shame on you! What do you mean, you did half the work? If I'd let you finish, there would be two corpses lying on that kang. You witch, you think a woman's birth canal is like a hen's rectum, that all you have to do is squeeze for an egg to pop out. You call that a delivery? What it is is murder. And you want to report me? Gugu aimed a flying kick on the woman's chin. You want a towel? And eggs? Another kick followed, this one on the woman's backside. She then grabbed her medical kit with one hand and the tight bun of hair on the woman's head and dragged her out into the yard. Chen E followed them out, wanting to make peace. Get your arse back in there! Gugu demanded angrily, and take care of your wife!

It was, Gugu told me later, the first time she'd ever struck anyone. She'd never thought herself capable of such a thing. But she kicked her again. The old woman rolled over and sat up, pounding the ground with both hands. Help! she shrieked. She's trying to kill me . . . Wan Liufu's bandit daughter is trying to kill me!

Evening is when that occurred. The setting sun, a colourful western sky, light breezes. Most of the villagers were taking their dinner out in the streets, rice bowls in hand, and they came trotting over to see what all the commotion was about. The village Party secretary, Yuan Lian, and Brigade Commander Lü Ya (Tooth) was among them. Tian Guihua was a distant aunt of Lü Ya, close enough to be considered family. Wan Xin, he said to Gugu, aren't you ashamed to hit an old woman?

Who did Lü Ya think he was, scolding me like that, a creep who battered his wife to make her crawl around the house?

Old woman? Gugu said. Old witch is more like it. A demon! Ask her what she was doing here.

I don't know how many people have died at your hand, but if a woman like me had a gun, she'd happily put a bullet in your head. Gugu pointed her finger at the old woman's head. She was all of seventeen at the time. The crowd tittered at her use of 'a woman like me'.

There was more Lü Ya wanted to say in Tian Guihua's defence, but he was cut short by Yuan Lian: Doctor Wan did nothing wrong. Old witches who play games with people's lives deserve to be severely punished. Tian Guihua, stop the phoney act. You got off lightly with only being struck. You ought to be sent to prison! From now on, Doctor Wan is to be called when any woman is about to have a child. Tian Guihua, if you ever again show up to do what you do, I'll rip those dog fingers right off your hands!

Gugu said that Yuan Lian was not an educated man, but he could see which way tides ran and knew the importance of justice. He was a good cadre.

4

Sensei, I was the second child Gugu delivered.

When my mother's time came, my grandmother did what tradition called for her: she washed her hands, changed clothes, and lit three sticks of incense, which she stuck in a burner in front of the ancestral tablets. Then she bowed three times, rapping her head against the floor, and sent all the males in the family outside. It was not my mother's first child: two boys and a girl had preceded me. You're an old hand at this, my grandmother said to her, you don't need any help. Just take your time. Mother, my mother replied, I don't feel good about this one, there's something different. My grandmother would not hear of it. How different can it be? she said. You're not expecting a unicorn, are you?

My mother's feeling did not betray her. My brothers and sister had all come out headfirst. Me? Leg first.

My grandmother was scared witless when she saw my tiny leg emerge. There's a popular saying in the countryside that goes: If a leg is foremost, then you owe a ghost. Owe a ghost? What does that mean? It means that in a previous life someone in the family had an outstanding debt, and the person owed had returned as a newborn baby intent on making things difficult for the woman in labour. Either both woman and child die together, or the child hangs around till a certain age, then dies, leaving the family destitute and devastated. So Grandma tried her best to appear calm. This one, she said, is born to be a runner – someone who runs errands for an official. Now, don't worry, she said, I know what to do. She went out into the yard, where she picked up a copper basin, carried it inside, then stood at the foot of the bed, and beat it like a gong with a rolling pin – *Bong! Bong!* Come out, she shouted, come out now! Your father wants you to deliver an urgent message, and you're in for a whipping if you don't come out right this minute!

Sensing that something was indeed seriously wrong, Mother tapped on the window with her bed whisk and shouted to my sister, who was waiting anxiously in the yard, Man – my sister's name – go fetch your aunt, and hurry!

Quick-witted as always, my sister ran to the village administrative office, where she asked Yuan Lian to phone the township health centre. I later put that ancient hand-crank telephone away as a keepsake. You see, it saved my life.

It was the sixth day of the sixth lunar month, a day when the Jiao River overflowed its banks and submerged the local bridge, although waves crashing over the stones made it easy to see where it stood. Du Bozi – Du the Neck – who had been fishing in the river, saw my aunt speed down the opposite bank on her bicycle, sending sprays of water at least three feet into the air as she crossed the bridge. The way the river had turned into rapids, if she'd fallen into the water, well, sir, I'd never have made it into this world.

Gugu rushed in dripping wet and took charge.

Mother later said that seeing Gugu walk in the door put her mind at ease. She told me that the first thing Gugu did was take Grandma aside and say, with unmistakable sarcasm, Auntie, how would he dare come out with you making all that racket? With a lame attempt at defending herself, Grandma said, Children crave excitement, so why *wouldn't* he want to see what the noise was all about?

Well, Gugu said she grabbed hold of my leg and yanked me out like pulling a radish out of the ground. I knew she was joking. After bringing Chen Bi and me into the world, our mothers became her volunteer propagandists. They showed up everywhere to spread the word, while Yuan Lian's wife and Du Bozi told everyone about Gugu's incredible bike-riding skills. The speed at which her reputation spread matched the drop in interest in the old midwives, who were relegated to the status of historical relics.

The years 1953 to 1957 saw a rise in China's rate of production, creating a period of vigorous economic activity. The weather was good, producing bumper crops every year. With plenty to eat and good warm clothing, the people's mood was one of wellbeing, and the women were eager to get pregnant and have a child. Gugu was a busy woman in those days. The tyre tracks of her bicycle were visible on every street and in every lane of all the eighteen villages of Northeast Gaomi Township, her footprints in most people's compounds.

From 4 April 1953 to 21 December 1957, she performed 1612 deliveries, bringing a total of 1645 babies, six of whom died. But of those, five were stillborn, the sixth died of a congenital illness. This remarkable achievement approached perfection.

Gugu joined the Communist Party on 17 February 1955. That occurred on the day she delivered her one-thousandth baby. The child was our classmate Li Shou.

Gugu said that Teacher Yu, Li Shou's mother, was her most nonchalant patient ever. While she was busy down below, Teacher Yu was preparing for class, a textbook in her hand.

In her later years, Gugu often thought back to this period – modern China's golden age, and hers as well. I don't know how many times I saw her eyes light up as she said longingly: I was a living Buddha back then, the local stork. A floral perfume oozed from my body, bees swarmed in my wake. So did butterflies. Now, now nothing but goddamn flies . . .

Gugu also came up with my name: in school I was known as Wan Zu (Foot), but I was Xiaopao – Jogger – as a toddler.

I'm sorry, Sensei, I should have made myself clear: Wan Zu is my true name, Tadpole is just a pen-name.

Gugu had reached marrying age. But she was a salaried professional, a public servant who ate marketable grains and enjoyed an enviable background, which kept the local boys from entertaining any hope of being the one for her. I was five at the time, and often heard my great-aunt and my grandmother talk about my aunt's marital prospects. Wan Xin's aunt, I heard Gugu's mother say, her voice laden with anxiety, Xin is twenty-two. Girls born the same year as her already have two children of their own, but not a single proposal has ever come her way. There's no reason to be concerned, my grandmother said. A girl like her, who knows, she could marry into the royal family and wind up as Empress. When that happens, you'll be mother-in-law to the Emperor, and we'll all be royalty, enjoying reflected glory. Nonsense, Great-Aunt said. The Emperor went out with the revolution. We're a republic now, with the Chairman at the helm. Well, if that's the case, Grandmother replied, then we'll have Xin marry the Chairman. You might live physically in the modern world, Great-Aunt said impatiently, but your mind is stuck in pre-Liberation days. I'm different than you, Grandmother said. In all my life I've never left Heping. But you've been to the liberated areas and spent time in Pingdu city. Don't talk to me about Pingdu city, Great-Aunt said. Just hearing the name makes my scalp itch. I was kidnapped by those Jap devils, taken there to suffer, not to enjoy myself.

The longer the two sisters-in-law talked, the more their conversation sounded like an argument. The way Great-Aunt stormed off angrily, you'd have thought she never wanted to see my grandmother again. But she was back the next day. Whenever my mother witnessed the two of them talking about Gugu's marital prospects, she had to stifle a laugh.

I recall one evening when our water buffalo calved. I don't know if the mother modelled herself after my mother or the calf modelled itself after me, but it started coming out leg first, and got stuck. The mother's bellows gave testimony to her agony. My father and grandfather were so distressed they could only wring their hands, stomp their feet, and pace the area in tight little circles. A farmer's life revolves around a buffalo, and this particular one had been sent to us by the production team to tend. There'd be hell to pay if it died. My mother whispered to my elder sister: Man, I heard your aunt coming in. My sister took off. My father glared at his wife and said: Don't talk like an idiot. She works with women. The principle's the same, Mother replied.

Gugu walked in the door and raged: You people are going to kill me from exhaustion. Delivering human babies has me running all day, and now you want me to deliver a cow!

With a smile, Mother said: Like it or not, Sister, you're a member of this family. Who else should we ask for help? Everybody says you're a reincarnated bodhisattva, and bodhisattvas are supposed to deliver all living creatures from torment, to save the lives of all sentient beings. A water buffalo may not be human, but it's a life, and I can't imagine you letting it die without lifting a finger.

It's a good thing you can't read, Auntie, Gugu said. If you knew how to read a couple of handfuls of characters, our village would be too small to hold you.

If it had been eight handfuls, not two, I'd still be no match for even your little toe.

Annoyance still showed on Gugu's face, but the feeling behind it was fading. Night had fallen, so Mother lit all the lanterns in the house, turned up the wicks, and carried them out to the barn.

When the birthing mother saw Gugu come in, she bent her front legs and knelt on the ground. The sight nearly caused tears to spurt from Gugu's eyes.

Ours were not long in following.

Gugu made a quick examination of the mother's body. Another leg-first, she said in a sympathetic, but slightly mocking tone.

Gugu sent us out into the yard so we wouldn't be upset by what we might see. By the sound of her commands, we could picture what she was telling Father and Mother to do. It was the fifteenth day of the lunar month; as the moon hung in the southeast corner of the sky, illuminating the earth below, we heard Gugu shout: Good, it's out!

With whoops of delight we ran inside, where we saw a little sticky-coated creature on the ground behind its mother. Wonderful, Father announced excitedly, it's another female!

Isn't it strange, Gugu seethed, how men pull a long face when a woman gives birth to a girl baby, but grin happily if a cow does the same thing.

When this calf matures, she'll have calves just like her, Father said.

What about humans? Gugu countered. When a girl matures, she'll give birth to girls, also just like her.

That's different, Father said.

Different how?

Seeing that Gugu was about to lose her temper, Father stopped talking.

The mother turned her head to lick the sticky substance that covered her calf's body. Her tongue appeared to have miraculous powers, for every spot she licked clean seemed to be strengthened. The sight overwhelmed us. I sneaked a glance at Gugu, whose mouth hung open and whose eyes radiated love, as if she were the one being cleaned and groomed by the cow's tongue, or it was her tongue that was cleaning the calf. When the sticky substance was nearly all gone from its hide, the calf wobbled onto its legs.

Someone brought a basin and filled it with water. A bar of soap materialised, and a towel, so Gugu could wash her hands.

Grandma sat in front of the stove using a bellows. Mother stood at the kang making noodles.

I'm starved, Gugu said after washing her hands. I'll eat here tonight. This is your home, isn't it? Mother said.

Of course it is, Grandmother said. It wasn't long ago when we all ate out of the same pot.

On the other side of our compound wall, Gugu's mother shouted for her to come home for dinner. I can't work for them for nothing, Gugu shouted back. I'm going to eat here. Your aunt has lived on a tight budget, Great-Aunt replied. If you eat even one bowl of her noodles, she won't forget that for the rest of her life. My grandmother picked up a poker and ran over to the wall. If it's food you want, come in and have a bowl. If not, then go home! I'm not interested in eating anything you've got, Great-Aunt said.

When the noodles were ready, Mother filled a bowl and told my sister to take it to Great-Aunt. (Years later I learned that in her haste, my sister stumbled, spraying the soupy noodles everywhere as she dropped the bowl and broke it. To keep her from getting yelled at back home, Great-Aunt took a bowl from her cupboard, and told my sister to take it home with her.)

Gugu loved to talk, and we loved listening to her. After she'd eaten her noodles, she sat on the kang, leaned back against the wall, and started the chatter. By appearing in just about every house in the area, she'd met all sorts of people and heard many interesting things, and was not above spicing up her accounts like a professional storyteller. In the early 1980s, when we watched the serialised TV stories told by Liu Lanfang, Mother would say, That could have been your aunt. If she hadn't become a doctor, she had what it took to be that kind of storyteller.

That night she began telling us about her battles of wits with Commander Sugitani in Pingdu city. I was seven at the time. She looked at me and said: I was just about Xiaopao's age when I went with Great-Grandma and your great-aunt to Pingdu city, where we were shut up in a dark room with two ferocious guard dogs outside the door. The dogs were fed human flesh every day and drooled whenever they saw a child. Great-Grandma and your great-aunt cried all night long. But not me. I went to sleep as soon as my head hit the pillow and I didn't wake up till the next morning. I don't know how many days and nights we spent in that room until they moved us to a separate compound, where there was a lilac tree that smelled so good it made my head swim. A gentleman from the countryside in a long robe and formal cap came to invite us to a banquet hosted by Commander Sugitani. Your great-grandma and your great-aunt wept and did not dare accept the invitation. The gentleman said to me: Young lady, tell your grandmother and your mother there's no need to be afraid. Commander Sugitani has no desire to harm you. All he wants is to be friends with Mr Wan Liufu. So, Grandma, Mother, I said, you can stop crying. It doesn't do anybody any good. It won't help you sprout wings, will it? Can you bring the Great Wall down with tears? The gentleman clapped his hands. Well spoken, young lady, you're a smart one. You're going to be someone special when you grow up. At my urging, your great-grandma and great-aunt stopped crying, and we all followed the gentleman over to a large wagon pulled by a black mule. After countless twists and turns, we entered a compound with a high gate, flanked by two military guards, a Chinese collaborator on the left and a Japanese soldier on the right. It was an enormous compound, with one courtyard after another as we went deeper and deeper, with no end in sight. Finally, we came up to a large reception hall in the middle of a garden, with sandalwood armchairs and windows framed by wooden carvings. Commander Sugitani was dressed in a kimono, slowly folding his fan in and out, the cultured man. After greeting us with some formal gibberish, he offered us seats around a large table overflowing with fine food. Your great-grandma and great-aunt wouldn't even pick up their chopsticks, but I wasn't shy, not about eating the little prick's food. His pointed chopsticks were hard to use, so I dug in with my meat hooks, cramming food into my mouth. Sugitani held his wine cup and watched me eat, smiling the whole time. When I'd had all I could eat, I wiped my hands on the tablecloth and started to doze off. Would you like your father to come here, little girl? Sugitani asked. I opened my eyes. No, I said, I wouldn't. Why not? My father is Eighth Route, you're Japanese, and the Eighth Route fights the Japanese. Aren't you afraid that's what he'll come to do?

Gugu paused and rolled up her sleeve to check her watch. There couldn't have been more then ten wristwatches in all of Gaomi Township at the time, and Gugu wore one of them. Wow! my eldest brother exclaimed. He was the only member of the family who'd ever seen one before. He was enrolled in the county middle school, where he studied Russian, taught by a returnee from the Soviet Union, who also wore a wristwatch. My brother's 'Wow!' was followed by a second exclamation: A wristwatch! My sister and I joined in: A wristwatch! we shouted.

Gugu rolled down her sleeve, feigning indifference, and said, It's only a watch. What's the big deal? That casual comment – intended as such – intensified our interest dramatically. My brother spoke up first: Gugu, I've only seen teacher Ji's watch from a distance . . . can I take a look at yours? Please, Gugu, show it to us, we joined in.

She smiled. You little rascals, it's just an old wristwatch, not worth looking at. But she took it off her wrist and handed it to him.

Be careful! Mother said.

My brother accepted the watch timidly, cradling it in his palm at first, and then put it up to his ear. When he was finished, he handed it to my sister, who handed it to my second brother when she was finished. He didn't even have time to hold it up to his ear before Eldest Brother snatched it away and handed it back to Gugu. I showed how unhappy I was by crying.

Mother was quick to scold me: When you grow up, Xiaopao, you'll run far enough away to have a watch of your own.

Him? Eldest Brother snapped. His own watch? I'll draw one on his wrist tomorrow.

People cannot be judged by appearance alone any more than the ocean can be measured by bushels, Gugu said. Don't be swayed by how ugly our Xiaopao is. He could grow up to be someone special.

If he becomes someone special, my sister said, then the pigs out in the sty can turn into tigers.

What country is this from, Gugu? Eldest Brother asked. What brand is it?

It's Swiss, an Enicar.

Wow! he exclaimed. Second Brother and Sister echoed him.

Warty toads! I hissed angrily.

What's it worth, Little Sister? Mother asked her.

I don't know. It was a gift from a friend.

What sort of friend gives something that valuable? Mother said as she gave Gugu a searching look. Are we talking about a new uncle?

It's almost midnight, Gugu said as she stood up. Bedtime.

Thank heavens my little sister is spoken for, Mother said.

Now don't you go around saying things, Gugu said, giving us all a stern look. We haven't even exchanged the horoscope for our birth dates. I'll tan your hides if you do.

The next morning, maybe because he was feeling guilty for not letting me see Gugu's watch the night before, my brother drew one on my wrist with a fountain pen. It looked like the real thing; it was beautiful, and I took pains to keep it that way. I kept it dry when I washed my hands and covered it up in the rain. Whenever it started to fade, I borrowed my brother's pen to add ink. It stayed on my wrist for three whole months.

6

The man who gave Gugu the Enicar wristwatch was an air force pilot. In those days that was something to be excited about – an air force pilot! When they heard the news, my brothers and sisters croaked like an army of frogs, while I turned somersaults in the yard.

This was a joyous event for more than our family; the elation spilled across the township. Everyone considered a pilot the perfect match for Gugu. Cook Wang from the school kitchen, who had fought in the Korean War, was of the opinion that they were made of gold. Can you make a person out of gold? I asked him, filled with doubt. In front of the teachers and the commune cadres, who were eating their dinner, he said: How stupid can you be, Xiaopao Wan? What I mean is, the cost of training an air force pilot to the nation is the equal of seventy kilograms of gold. Oh, my, Mother said when I told her what Wang had said. How in the world are we supposed to treat your new uncle when he comes to the house?

We youngsters spread all sorts of fanciful talk about pilots. Chen Bi said his mother had seen a Soviet pilot when she lived in Harbin. They wore deerskin jackets, high-topped leather boots, had gold inlays in their mouths, wore gold wristwatches, ate black bread and sausage, and drank beer. Xiao Xiachun (Lower Lip, the characters later changed to summer and spring), son of Xiao Shangchun (Upper Lip), the granary watchman, said that China's pilots ate better than their Soviet counterparts, and even created a menu, as if he were going to cook for them. Breakfast: two eggs, milk, four oily fritters, two steamed buns, and a chunk of pickled tofu. Lunch: braised pork, a whole croaker, and two large corn cakes. Dinner: roasted chicken, two pork buns, two mutton buns, and a bowl of millet congee. Fruit, of course, after each meal: bananas, apples, pears, grapes . . . whatever they couldn't eat they could take home. Pilots' leather jackets had two large pockets. What for? For carrying fruit. What people said about the pilots made us drool. We all dreamed of one day becoming air force pilots and living a magical life.

When the air force announced that they were coming to our county's Number One High School to recruit pilots, my eldest brother signed up excitedly. Our great granddad had worked as a landlord's hired hand, was a tenant farmer, and served the People's Liberation Army as a stretcher-bearer. He'd fought in the battle of Mengliang Mesa and was one of those who'd carried the body of Zhang Lingfu down the mountain. My maternal grandmother's family was also dirt poor. Add to all that the fact that my great granddad was a revolutionary martyr, and our family background and social status were above reproach. One day my brother, who was a high school sports star, a discus thrower, came home for lunch and feasted on a fat lamb's tail. Back at school that afternoon, he had energy to burn, so he picked up a discus and flung it over the school wall into the field beyond. It so happened that the farmer was ploughing his field at that moment, and the discus hit his water buffalo's horn, slicing it off. All this is to say that my brother's background was unimpeachable, his grades in school were excellent, he was especially fit, and his aunt was going to marry an air force pilot. Everyone naturally assumed that even if they only picked one candidate from our county, it would surely be him. He wasn't chosen. The reason: a scar on his leg from a childhood boil. Our school cook told us that scars were immediate disqualifiers, because the pressure of high-altitude flying would cause them to rupture. Even a set of uneven nostrils would squelch one's chances.

In sum, from the time my aunt began a romantic relationship with the pilot, we were alert to anything having to do with the air force. I'm now in my fifties, and still haven't shaken off the essence of vanity or my penchant for showing off, someone who would blare all over town the news that he'd won a hundred yuan in the lottery. Just think, I was only in elementary school and had a future uncle who was an air force pilot. You can imagine how insufferable that made me.

The Jiaozhou airport was fifty li south of our village; the Gaomi airport was sixty li to the west of us. Aeroplanes flying in and out of the Jiaozhou airfield were big, black, and very slow – bombers according to what the adults told us. Aeroplanes that used the Gaomi airfield were swept-wing, silvery aircraft that left contrails and could make spectacular manoeuvres. Eldest Brother said they were Jian-5s, modelled after Soviet MIG-17s, elite fighter planes, the ones that shot the shit out of US jets during the Korean War. Needless to say, these were the planes our future uncle flew, at a time when war fever was at its peak, and training manoeuvres filled the skies over the Gaomi airfield every day. They swept over the township, opening up a site for dogfights. Three more planes arrived one moment, then six, one plane nipping at the tail of another. Suddenly one plane went into a steep dive, pulling up just before crashing into a pine tree at the head of our village and soaring back into the sky like a sparrow hawk. One day there was a thunderous explosion in the sky – Gugu told us she was assisting an older woman who was experiencing convulsions from anxiety, preparing to use her scalpel, when the explosion startled the woman, breaking her concentration; the convulsions stopped, and with one push, the child emerged. The explosion tore the paper window coverings in every house in the village. Shocked by the sound, we couldn't move for a moment, until our teacher led us outside, where we looked up into a clear blue sky and saw several aeroplanes chasing one that was towing a tubular object. We saw puffs of white smoke emerge from the tubular object, followed by earsplitting explosions. But these bursts of cannon fire weren't nearly as powerful as the blast that had pounded our eardrums just a moment before, the second most powerful explosion I've heard in my entire life. Not even a lightning strike powerful enough to split a willow tree in half made that much noise. It seemed as though the fliers did not want to bring the target down, since the puffs of white smoke appeared near but not on the tubular object. Even as it disappeared from view, it had not suffered a direct hit. Chen Bi rubbed his nose, which had earned him the affectionate title of 'Little Russian', and sneered: China's flyboys can't hit a damned thing. If those had been Soviet pilots, one burst would have brought that target down! I knew his comment stemmed from jealousy towards me. Born and reared in our village, he'd never seen a Soviet dog, let alone one of its air force's top guns.

At the time we kids, who lived in an out-of-the-way village, had no idea that Sino-Russian relations were deteriorating. Chen Bi's unflattering comparison of Soviet and Chinese fliers made us all – especially me – unhappy, but no one's thoughts went beyond that. Years later, at the beginning of the Cultural Revolution, when we were in the fifth grade, our classmate Xiao Xiachun exposed this incident from the past, not only causing trouble for Chen Bi, but leading ultimately to the deaths of his parents. The Soviet novel *A Real Man*, about a Soviet Air Force hero who returned to active duty after both feet were amputated, was discovered in his house. Based upon a true story, this novel of revolutionary inspiration was proof to the mobs that Chen Bi's mother, Ailian, was the Soviet hero's lover and that Chen Bi was their bastard offspring.

While the Jian-5 fighter planes were training, the Jiaozhou airfield aircraft were not idle. They went out at night, every night around nine o'clock, which was about the time the nightly local broadcast was coming to an end. Airfield searchlights abruptly lit up the sky, their broad beams beginning to break up in the sky above our village, though they sent shivers through us anyway. I was always saying stupid things at the worst possible moment. Wouldn't it be great if I had a flashlight like that! I remarked. Stupid! Second brother said as he rapped my head with his knuckles. Of course, since we were about to gain a special uncle, my second brother had become a sort of expert in flying affairs; he'd committed to memory the names of all the volunteer pilots and could recite the details of their heroic achievements. He was also the one who told me once, when he asked me to check him for fleas, that the explosion that ripped the paper in our window coverings was called a sonic boom, caused by a plane breaking the sound barrier. What does that mean? I asked. It means going faster than the speed of sound, you dope. When the Jiaozhou bombers flew training missions, the mesmerising searchlight beams were the only things worth talking about. Some people said they weren't for the sake of training, but were intended to guide lost planes home. The beams swung back and forth, crossing in places, moving together in others, occasionally capturing a bird in mid flight and throwing it off balance, like a fly caught in a bottle. In the end, after a few minutes of watching the searchlights, we heard the roar of an aeroplane engine, and then spotted the outline of a big black object in the sky, its outline visible because of the lights on its nose, tail and wingtips. It gave the impression of sliding down a beam of light to its nest. Aeroplanes have nests, just as chickens do.

7

In the second half of 1960, that is, not long after our coal-eating incident, word spread that Gugu would soon be marrying the air force pilot. Her mother came over to our side of the wall to discuss a dowry with Mother, and together they decided to cut down the hundred-year-old catalpa tree on the other side of the wall and have a man named Fan, the finest carpenter in the township, make a set of furniture from it. I saw Father and Fan come over to measure the tree, which shook so hard from fright as it anticipated its death that leaves fell to the ground, as if the tree were crying.

In the end, nothing came of the plan, and Gugu was away a long time. I ran over to Great-Aunt's to see if there was any news, for which I got a taste of her cane. That's when I discovered that she was older than those old midwives I'd heard about.

On the morning of the season's first snowfall the sun shone bright red. On our way to school in our hempen sandals, our hands and feet were half frozen. We were running around the playground, whooping and hollering to keep warm, when suddenly we heard a frightening roar in the sky. We looked up, mouths agape, and spotted an enormous object – dark red – trailing black smoke – a pair of staring red eyes – gigantic white teeth – shuddering in the sky – coming right at us. Aeroplane, damn, it's an aeroplane! Was it going to land on our playground?

None of us had ever seen an aeroplane so close before, so close its

wings blew feathers and dead leaves off the ground to swirl in the air.
Just think how great it would be if it could land on our playground! We
could walk up and get a good look, we could touch it, and if our luck held,
we'd be allowed to climb into its belly and have a great time. We might
even be able to talk the pilot into telling us war stories. Maybe he was
one of my future uncle's comrade-in-arms. No, my uncle-to-be flew a
Jian-5, which was much better looking than this dark thing. My uncle-
to-be wouldn't have a comrade-in-arms who flew something this big
and slow. But, how should I put it, anyone who could fly anything was
pretty impressive, don't you think? Anyone who could get something
this big, made of steel, up into the air had to be a hero. I couldn't see
the pilot's face, but years later, lots of my classmates swore up and down
that they saw it through the windshield. The aircraft, which we thought
was going to land in our midst, veered to the right almost reluctantly
and scraped its belly on the top branches of a poplar tree on the eastern
edge of the village before crash-landing in a wheat field. We heard a
thunderous explosion, louder and deeper than a sonic boom, and we felt
the ground shake. Our ears rang and we saw spots in front of our eyes.
A pillar of dense smoke and fire blasted into the sky, immediately
turning the sunlight a deep scarlet and releasing into the air a strange
smell that made it hard to breathe.

It took us a long time to snap out of our stunned state. We started
running to the head of the village, and when we reached the road, we
were nearly overcome by heat. The plane lay in pieces, one of its wings
stuck in the ground like a gigantic torch. The field was on fire, filling
the air with a burnt leather odour. Then a second explosion sent shock
waves through the air. Wang the cook, who had plenty of experience,
screamed, Hit the deck!

We did as he said and, following his lead, began to crawl.

Crawl fast, there are bombs under the wings!

We were later told that the aircraft was outfitted for four bombs, but
only carried two that day. If there had been four, none of us would have
made it out alive.

Three days after the crash, Father and other village men carried remnants of the destroyed aeroplane and the body of the pilot to the airport on their carts and wagons. They had barely returned to the village when Eldest Brother came running up out of breath. Our champion athlete had run all the way home from County High without stopping. Fifty li, just short of marathon distance. The moment he entered the yard, he sputtered a single word – Gugu – and simply collapsed, foaming at the mouth, eyes rolled back into his head. He was out.

Everyone rushed to his side. Someone pinched the spot over his upper lip, someone else pinched the spot between his thumb and finger, and a third person thumped him on the chest.

What about Gugu?

Finally, he came around. His mouth twisted and he burst into tears.

Mother rushed up with water in a gourd and poured some into his mouth. The rest she flung into his face.

Out with it. What about your aunt?

Gugu's pilot defected with his aircraft . . .

The gourd fell out of Mother's hand and smashed to pieces.

Defected to where? Father asked.

Where else? My brother wiped his face with his sleeve and clenched his teeth. Taiwan! The traitor, the turncoat flew to Taiwan to join Chiang Kai-shek!

What about your aunt? Mother asked.

Taken away by county security agents, Eldest Brother said.

Tears fell from Mother's eyes. Do not tell your maternal grandmother, not a word, she commanded. And don't talk about this outside.

What good will that do? Everyone in the county already knows about it, Eldest Brother said.

Mother went into the house and came out with a large pumpkin, which she handed to my sister. Come with me, she said, we're going to see your great-grandma.

My sister came running back breathlessly before too long. Grandma, she called out the minute she stepped inside, Mother wants you to go over there right away. Something's wrong with Great-Aunt!

8

Forty years later, my eldest brother's son, Xiangqun, was recruited into the air force. There had been many changes in the world in all that time, and lots of things that had once seemed so sacred they could cost you your head had turned to jokes; professions that had once made people sit up and take notice had become the work of the lower classes. But being recruited into the air force was still a joyous development that excited families and made neighbours green with envy. And so, my brother, who had retired as head of the Bureau of Education, returned to the village to host a celebratory banquet for family and friends.

The meal was served in my second brother's yard. An electric wire was strung from the house for a light bulb that lit the yard up like the sun. Two tables were put together to accommodate a couple of dozen chairs, on which we sat shoulder to shoulder. The meal was catered, with delicacies of every kind, meat and foul and fish, dish after colourful dish of tasty food. In her heavy Yantai accent, Eldest Sister-in-law said: I hope you enjoy these meagre offerings. Hardly, Father said. Think about the 1960s, when even Chairman Mao could not have eaten a meal like this. My soon-to-be flyboy nephew said: Those days are over, Grandpa.

After three rounds of toasts, Father stood up and said: Our family managed to produce an air force pilot. Back when your father applied to be one, a scar on his leg was all that kept him out. Now Xiangqun has made our dream come true.

What's the big deal about being a pilot? Xiangqun said with a bit of a scowl. If you want to really make it big, become a high-ranking official or a millionaire.

Hogwash! Father said, holding out his cup, draining it, and banging it back down on the table. An airman is a dragon among men, he said. Your great-aunt had a man way back then, Wang Xiaoti, who was a towering tree standing and a brass bell seated. He took vigorous strides when he walked, and if he hadn't foolishly flown over to Taiwan, he could be air force commander-in-chief today . . .

Are you kidding me? Xianqun exclaimed. I thought Great-Aunt's husband made clay figurines. Where did that airman come from?

That's ancient history, Eldest Brother said. Let's drop the subject.

No, Xiangqun said. I'm going to ask her. Wang Xiaoti flew his plane to Taiwan. That's wild.

Don't you go looking for that kind of excitement, his father said anxiously. People need patriotism, especially in the military, and that goes double for air force pilots. A man can steal, he can rob, he can commit murder and arson . . . what I mean to say is, you cannot become a traitor. They leave a tainted name forever, and are doomed to a bad end . . .

That's really got you scared, hasn't it? Xiangqun said scornfully. Taiwan is part of the motherland, so what's wrong with flying over there to have a look?

I'll have none of that! his mother exclaimed. If that's the way you think, then you have no business becoming a pilot. I'll go phone Chief Liu of the Armed Forces Bureau.

Don't get excited, Ma. I'm not *that* stupid. I wouldn't sacrifice my family for my own pleasure. But don't forget, the Nationalists and Communists are all members of the same family. If I flew over there, they'd have to send me back.

That's the way to uphold our family's moral standing, Elder Brother said. Wang Xiaoti was a son of a bitch who ruined your aunt's life.

Did I hear my name mentioned? Gugu broadcast her arrival as she squinted in the bright light. She turned and put on a pair of sunglasses, looking quite cool, if slightly comical. Do you really need that bright a light? Like Great-Grandma always said, You won't stuff food up your nose even if you eat in the dark. Electricity requires coal, coal has to be dug by miners three thousand feet underground, hell on earth, corrupt officials, crooked bosses, the miners' lives as worthless as the dirt above them. Every lump of coal is stained with blood. With her right hand on her hip, she held her left hand out in front, the thumb and outer two fingers curled inward, her index and middle fingers pointing ahead; she was wearing a 1970s-vintage Dacron military uniform, sleeves rolled up. Overweight and greying, she had the look of a commune cadre from the Cultural Revolution. Seeing her provoked mixed emotions in me. This is what Gugu, who had once been pretty as a lotus fresh out of the water, had become.

Eldest Brother and his wife had gone round and round trying to decide whether or not to invite Gugu to the celebration meal. So they'd asked Father, who had thought long and hard before saying, Better not. Now she's . . . she doesn't live in the village anyway . . . we'll tell her later . . .

Her arrival created an awkward situation. We all stood, at a total loss.

What's this? After spending most of my life on the road, I come home to find there's no seat for me. There was an edge to her voice.

That woke us up. Mass confusion followed, as we all stepped back to offer her our seats.

Eldest Brother and his wife rushed to explain: You were the first person we planned to invite. The Wan family seat of honour is always reserved for you.

Bah! Gugu sat down next to Father. She chided Eldest Brother. Do you really expect me to take the seat of honour while your father is alive, Dakou? Or, for that matter, after he dies? When a daughter marries, it's like spilled water, isn't it, Eldest Brother?

You never were an ordinary daughter, Father said as he pointed to each of us. Your contributions are greater than anyone's. Is there a single one of these youngsters you didn't bring into the world?

A hero is silent about past glories, Gugu said. Back then . . . what's the point of dredging up the past? Let's drink! What's that? I don't have a glass. Well, I've brought my own. She reached into her oversized pocket and brought out a bottle of Maotai, which she banged down on the table. Fifty-year-old Maotai, she said. Given to me by an official in the city of Tinglan whose mistress – twenty years his junior – wanted nothing more than to give him a son, and since she'd heard that I had a secret formula for changing the sex of a foetus from female to male, that's what she wanted me to do. I told her that was just a quack doctor's trick, but she didn't believe me. She cried and refused to leave, all but getting down on her knees to beg. She said the man's wife had given him two daughters, and if she could produce a son, the man would be hers. His head was filled with feudal ideas like favouring boys over girls, not the sort of thing you'd expect from someone so important. Hell, Gugu spat out angrily, those people's fortunes are all ill-gotten, so whom should I take advantage of if not the likes of him? So I made up nine packets of herbal concoctions, with things like angelica, Chinese yam, rehmannia and licorice, stuff you can buy for ten cents a bunch, no more than thirty yuan in total, and I asked her for a hundred for each packet. She was so happy she sort of waddled as she climbed into a red car and drove off, leaving a trail of exhaust fumes. This afternoon the official and his mistress came to see me with their pudgy little baby boy and gifts of fine tobacco and liquor to thank me. If not for my miracle prescription, they said, they wouldn't have such a wonderful son. Ha ha! Gugu laughed loudly, grabbed the glass my brother was respectfully holding out to her, and drank it down in one swallow. I can't tell you how happy I am! she said as she smacked herself on the thigh. I ask you, how could a high-ranking official, someone who's supposed to be educated, be such a simpleton? Changing the sex in the womb! If I could do that, I'd have won the Nobel Prize for Medicine a long time ago. Pour me another. She held out her empty glass. Don't open the Maotai. Save that for Eldest Brother. No, no, no, my father said. Putting something that good into my stomach is a waste. But she stuffed the bottle into his hand and said, This is from me, so you drink it.

He fingered the red ribbon at the top. How much does something like this cost? he asked gingerly. At least eight thousand, Elder Brother's wife said. The price has gone up recently. My god! Father exclaimed. That's not liquor. Dragon slobber and phoenix blood aren't worth that much. Wheat sells for eighty cents a jin. Can one bottle of liquor be worth ten thousand jin of wheat? I could work like a dog all year and not be able to afford half of one of these bottles. He handed the bottle back to Gugu. You keep it, he said. I can't drink liquor like this. I'm afraid it'd shorten my life.

I gave it to you, so you drink it, Gugu said. It didn't cost me anything. You'd be crazy not to enjoy it. Like back in Pingdu city. I'd have been crazy not to eat the spread the Japanese devils prepared. Don't be crazy. Drink it.

I understand what you're saying, my father said, but I ask you, can a bottle of peppery liquor really be worth that much money?

Eldest Brother, you don't get it. Nobody who drinks this stuff ever pays for it. People who have to pay for their liquor can only afford to drink this – Gugu held out her glass and drained it. You're over eighty years old, she said. How many more years do you have to enjoy a good drink? Patting herself on the chest, she said dramatically: I'll make you a crazy offer in front of all these members of the younger generation: I will supply you with Maotai from today on. What's there to be afraid of? I used to be scared of my own shadow, and the more scared I was the worse things got. Pour some more! Do you people have no vision? Feel sorry for the liquor?

Of course not, Gugu, Father said. It's for you to drink.

How much do you think I can manage? she said, a note of melancholy creeping into her voice. Back then, I held my own with those bastards from the People's Commune. A bunch of guys who figured they could easily make a spectacle of me wound up under the table barking like a pack of dogs – come on, you youngsters, down the hatch.

Have something to eat, Gugu.

Something to eat, you say? Your great-uncle could drink half a jug of sorghum liquor with only a leek to go with it. Real drinkers don't need food. You people are eaters, not drinkers.

Warming up from the alcohol, Gugu unbuttoned her blouse and patted Father on the shoulder. If I tell you to drink, Elder Brother, you have to drink. You and I are the only two left from our generation. We should be eating and drinking anything we want. What's the point in saving money? Money is just paper until you spend it. I have a skill, so I'm not afraid I'll ever be short of money. You can be an official, high or low, but you'll still get sick, and then you'll have to come see me. Besides, Gugu roared in laughter, I have that special talent to change a foetus's gender. People would happily shell out ten thousand for the complicated technique of turning a female foetus to male.

But what if they still got a baby girl after taking your gender-bending potion? Father asked anxiously.

You don't get it, Gugu said. What's traditional Chinese medicine anyway? All practitioners of traditional medicine are adept at fortune-telling, and fortune-tellers are adept at going round and round when telling someone's fortune without ever getting themselves tangled up.

Xiangqun managed to slip a question in when Gugu paused to light a cigarette. Can you talk about the pilot, Great-Aunt? Maybe one day on a whim I'll fly to Taiwan to see him.

Stop that nonsense, my elder brother said.

You're out of line, his wife said.

A seasoned smoker, Gugu puffed away, sending clouds of smoke up through her uncombed hair.

When I think about that now, Gugu said after draining the liquor in her cup, I can say he destroyed me, but he also saved me.

She took a couple of deep puffs before flicking the butt away with her middle finger. It described a dark red arc before landing on a distant grapevine trellis. I've had too much to drink, she said. The party's over and it's time to go home. She stood up, looking stoutly clumsy, and swayed her way towards the entrance. We hurried over to steady her. Do you really think I'm drunk? she asked. You're wrong. I can drink a thousand cups without getting drunk. At the gate, Hao Dashou, the clay-doll maker who'd recently been named a county folk artist, was waiting patiently for her.

9

Sensei, the next day my nephew, curious to learn more about Wang Xiaoti, came home on his motorcycle and asked my father to take him to see Gugu. You don't want to do that, my father said. She's nearly seventy and she's had a difficult life. I'm afraid you'll upset her by bringing up the past. Besides, she'd find it hard to talk about that in front of her husband.

Xiangqun, I said, listen to your grandfather. Since you want to hear what happened, I'll tell you what I know. Actually, all you have to do is go online to get most of the details.

I've long planned to write a novel based on Gugu's life – now, of course, that's changed into a play – and Wang Xiaoti will figure prominently. The work has been twenty years in preparation. Relying on connections, I've interviewed many people from that time, made special trips to the three airfields where Wang had served, visited his hometown in Zhejiang, interviewed one of his squadron comrades-in-arms as well as his commander and deputy commander, actually climbed into the cockpit of his Jian-5, and interviewed the one-time head of the county security bureau's anti-espionage unit, and the one-time security division head at the county health department. I don't mind saying that I know more than anyone else; my only regret is that I never got to meet Wang Xiaoti himself. But your father got Great-Aunt's OK to sneak into a theatre before they arrived to see a movie. He saw Wang and Gugu enter hand-in-hand. He was sitting close enough to Wang to be able to describe him for us: Five-nine, maybe a bit taller, fair skin, a long, gaunt face, eyes on the small side, but alert. Sparkling white, even teeth.

Your father said they were showing a Soviet version of Ostrovsky's novel *How the Steel Was Tempered*. He was watching Wang Xiaoti and your aunt's movements and gestures until he was drawn to the love and revolution themes of the movie. In those days, many Chinese youngsters had Soviet pen pals. That included your father, who was writing to a girl named Tonia, the same as the girl in the movie. He got so caught up in what was happening on the screen that he neglected his vital mission. That isn't to say the scheme was a total failure, since he was able to get a look at Wang before the movie began and could smell the sweets on Wang's breath when they were changing reels (back then theatres had only a single projector). Naturally he also smelled and heard the sunflower seed and peanut eaters in front and behind. Back then you could eat almost anything in theatres, resulting in a thick layer of wrappers, melon seeds and peanut shells on the floor. When the movie was over, in the bright lights at the lobby entrance, Wang pushed his bicycle up to ride your great-aunt back to the health centre dormitory (she had a temporary assignment at the health centre). Wang Xiaoti, she said with a little laugh, I want to introduce you to someone. Your father was hiding in the shadows behind a column in the entrance. Wang looked all around. Who? Where is he? Wan Kou, come over here. Your father stepped shyly out from behind the column. He was about Wang's height back then, but skinny as a rail. All that talk about hurling a discus over the school wall and slicing off an ox's horn was just that – talk. His hair looked like a magpie's nest. This is my nephew, Wan Kou, your great-aunt said by way of an introduction. Aha! Wang slapped your father on the shoulder. A spy, I see. Wang Kou, that's a good name. Wang reached out his hand. Nice to meet you, pal. I'm Wang Xiaoti. Apparently overwhelmed by the attention, your father grabbed Wang's hand with both of his and shook it spiritedly.

Your father said he went to look up Wang at the airfield after that, and was treated to a casual air force meal of braised prawns, spicy chicken nuggets, eggs and day lily, and as much rice as he could eat. His description of the meal made us green with envy. For me, there was pride as well. Not just because it was Wang Xiaoti, but because I had a brother who'd eaten in the air force mess.

Wang Xiaoti also gave your father a harmonica, a very expensive one. Your father characterised Wang as multi-talented. He wasn't a bad basketball player, who could shoot from all angles, and as well as the harmonica, he could play the accordion; he was also a fine calligrapher and painter. He had tacked a sketch of his onto the wall, a portrait of Gugu. There wasn't a blemish in his family background. His father was a high-ranking Party cadre, his mother a university professor. Why would someone like that fly to Taiwan and go down as a thoroughly reviled defector?

Wang's squadron commander said he'd defected after secretly listening to enemy propaganda broadcasts. He had a short-wave radio capable of receiving broadcasts from Taiwan, in particular a KMT station announcer with a sweet and highly alluring voice who called herself 'Night Air Rose'; a real killer, she was, he assumed, and what ultimately turned Wang into a defector. Did that mean my aunt wasn't attractive enough for him? The doddering former squadron commander said: Your aunt wasn't bad, with an excellent family background, good-looking, and a Party member. By standards of that time she was an ideal catch, and we all envied Wang Xiaoti. But your aunt was too revolutionary, too principled, and not appealing enough for someone like Wang, who had fallen for the poisonous appeal of bourgeois thinking. Afterward, the security division examined Wang's diary, in which he had given your aunt the nickname 'Red Blockhead'. It was a good thing they had his diary, his squadron commander said, for it left your aunt in the clear. Without it, she could not have recaptured her good name even if she'd jumped into the cleansing waters of the Yellow River.

Sensei, I told my nephew that his great-aunt wasn't the only one who nearly met destruction by Wang's hand. The authorities investigated your father several times, I said, and that harmonica was confiscated as evidence of Wang Xiaoti's corruptive influence on the young. He'd

written in his diary: *Red Blockhead introduced her dumb nephew to me,
another Red Blockhead, and he had a goofy name: Wan Kou, Wan Mouth!*
Again, it was that diary that saved your father.

Maybe Wang did all that on purpose, my nephew said.

Your great-aunt came to that conclusion later. She believed that
Wang had left his diary behind to protect her. That's why last night she
said that he'd ruined her, but he'd also saved her.

Sensei, my nephew was mainly interested in how Wang Xiaoti
managed to defect. He especially admired Wang's flying skill. He said
the slightest miscalculation while flying eight hundred kilometres an
hour no higher than five metres above the water could have sent his
Jian-5 plunging into the ocean. It was a skillful, gutsy performance,
according to the youngster. There's no denying his cockpit mastery,
regardless of weather conditions. Before his defection, every time he
flew a training mission over our village, he'd wow us with his aerobatics.
We used to say he could fly down to the watermelon patch on the
eastern edge of the village, pluck a melon out of the ground, and, with a
wing wave, soar back up into the clouds.

Did they really reward him over there with five thousand ounces of
gold? my nephew asked.

Maybe, I said. But even ten thousand ounces wouldn't be worth it.
You mustn't envy him, Xiangqun. Money and beautiful women are as
transient as floating clouds. Country, honour, and family are the only
true treasures.

You must be joking, Third Uncle, he said. Who says things like that
in this day and age?

10

In the spring of 1961, after Gugu came out from under the cloud of the Wang Xiaoti incident, she returned to work at the obstetrics ward in the health centre. Over a two-year period, however, not a single infant was born in any of the more than forty villages that made up the People's commune. The reason? Famine, of course.

Hunger disrupted women's menstrual cycles. Hunger turned men into eunuchs. The obstetrics ward included only Gugu and a middle-aged doctor named Huang. Dr Huang was a graduate of a prominent medical school, but because of a questionable family background and her own history as a rightist, she'd been exiled to a rural health centre. Every time she mentioned the woman's name, Gugu could barely contain her anger. The woman had a strange disposition. Some days she might not say a word to anyone, on other days she'd be bitterly sarcastic, talking a blue streak. She could give a lengthy speech to a spittoon.

Gugu stopped going home so often after her mother died, but whenever there was something special on the table, Mother had my sister send some over to Gugu. One day my father got his hands on half a rabbit in the field, probably the remnant of a hawk's meal. Mother went out and picked half a basket of wild greens and cooked them together with the rabbit. She wrapped up a bowlful of the meat and told my sister to take it over to Gugu. When she said she wouldn't do it, I volunteered. You can go, Mother said, but don't sneak some of it for yourself on the way. And keep your eyes open while you're walking. I don't want you breaking that bowl.

The health centre was about ten li from our house. I started off trotting, wanting to get there while the rabbit meat was still warm. But my stomach began to growl at the same time as my legs began to ache, and I was sweating and light-headed. In short, I was hungry. The two bowls of porridge with greens I'd eaten that morning had passed through my stomach and the smell of the cooked rabbit was seeping through the wrapping. A debate, soon to develop into an argument, between me and myself broke out. Have a bite, one me said, just one bite. No, the other me countered, you have to be an honest boy and do what your mother said. My hand came close to undoing the wrapping more than once, but the image of Mother's face flashed into my mind.

Mulberry trees lined both sides of the road from our village to the health centre, all stripped bare of leaves by famine victims. I broke off a branch and began gnawing on it, finding its sharp, bitter taste hard to swallow. But then I spotted a cicada that had just emerged from its cocoon, a nice soft yellow, its wings not yet dry. Ecstatic, I flung down the mulberry branch, scooped up the cicada and popped it into my mouth. Cicadas were a nutritious delicacy to us, but only after they were fried. By eating this one raw I saved on fuel and time. It had a fresh taste and, I was willing to bet, was more nutritious than if it had been fried. I searched all the trees as I walked along, but found no more cicadas. I did, however, find a fancy coloured handbill showing a young man with a glowing face holding a lovely young woman in his arms. The text read: *Communist Air Force pilot Wang Xiaoti has left the dark side and flown into the light, where he is now a Nationalist Air Force Brigadier General. He has received five thousand ounces of gold, and is the glorious mate of the famed songstress Miss Tao Lili.* My hunger abruptly forgotten, I experienced a strange and powerful emotion. I felt like screaming. In school I'd heard that the Nationalists sent reactionary handbills across the Strait by balloon, but I never thought I'd actually see one or that it could be quite so flashy. And I had to admit that the woman in the photograph was better-looking than Gugu.

Gugu and Dr Huang were having a heated argument when I walked into the ward. Dr Huang wore a pair of dark glasses over a hooked nose, thin lips, and exposed, badly stained teeth – in future years Gugu would often remind us that staying single was preferable to marrying a woman whose teeth showed when they talked – there was a gloomy cast in her eyes that sent chills down my back. I heard her say, How do you get off telling me what to do? You were still in nappies when I was in medical school!

Gugu gave her tit for tat: Don't think I don't know that you, Huang Qiuya, are a capitalist's daughter and were the campus queen in med school. Did you wave a flag to welcome the arrival of the Japanese into the city? Did you dance cheek to cheek with Japanese officers? Well, when you were dancing with them, I was in Pingdu engaged in a battle of wits with the Japanese commander there.

The woman sneered. Got any witnesses? I'd like to know who saw you have your battle of wits with the commander.

The mountains and rivers are my witnesses.

I couldn't, I mustn't, under any circumstances let Gugu see that handbill, not now.

What are you doing here? she asked unhappily. And what's this?

A reactionary handbill, one of the KMT's reactionary handbills. My voice quavered with excitement.

Gugu barely looked at it, but I saw her body tense, a spasm like she'd been shocked. Her eyes grew wide, the blood fled from her face. She flung the handbill away as if it were a snake – no, a frog.

When she had regained her composure and bent down to retrieve it, she was too late.

Huang Qiuya had already picked it up and examined it. She looked up, glanced at Gugu, and took another look at the handbill. A green glare emerged from behind those dark glasses. That was followed by an icy laugh.

Gugu sprang at the woman to snatch the handbill back, but Huang spun around to prevent that. So Gugu grabbed the back of Huang's smock and shouted, Give me that!

Huang lurched forward to free herself, and we heard her smock rip, exposing her back, which was the white of a frog's belly.

I said give me that!

Huang turned around, but held the handbill behind her back; she was shaking as she moved slowly towards the door.

Give it back? she said with a sinister, smug look. Hah! You dog of a spy, defector's woman. The defector took all he wanted from you, you slut! Scared, are you? Have you quit selling the stink of your so-called martyr's descendant?

Gugu, maddened by the comment, charged Huang.

Huang ran into the corridor. We've got a spy! she cried. Come catch the spy!

Gugu followed her into the corridor, where she grabbed her by the hair; even with her neck bent back, Huang thrust the handbill out in front, her cries even more shrill. Treatment rooms were in the front of the health centre, offices in the rear. Everyone heard her cries and came into the corridor to see what was happening. Gugu had by then pushed Huang to the floor and was straddling her as she fought to retrieve the handbill.

The director, a bald, middle-aged man, ran up. He had bags under his long, narrow eyes and blindingly white false teeth. Stop that! he shouted. What's going on?

Gugu fought harder to pry open Huang's fingers, apparently not hearing the director. By this time Huang Qiuya's screams had turned into tearful wails.

Stop that, Wan Xin! the director demanded angrily. And you people, he said loudly to the rubberneckers, have you all gone blind? Pull those two apart!

Two male doctors went up and, with difficulty, pulled Gugu off Huang.

Two female doctors picked Huang up off the floor.

Huang's dark glasses had fallen off and there was a trickle of blood from her gums. Cloudy tears poured from her sunken eyes. But she was still clutching the handbill. Director, she bellowed, you have to back me on this!

Gugu's clothes were pulled this way and that, and her face was ashen. A pair of bloody gouges marred her cheeks, obviously from Huang Qiuya's nails.

What's this all about, Wan Xin?

Gugu's face wore a desolate smile; tears fell from her eyes. She threw the torn pieces of the handbill in her hand to the floor and, without a word, walked unsteadily back to the ward.

Like someone who has performed heroically under brutal circumstances, Huang Qiuya handed the crumpled remains of the handbill to the director and then got down on her hands and knees to feel around for her glasses, which she found and put back on, holding them to her face since one of the arms was broken. When she saw the torn pieces Gugu had thrown away, she frantically scooped them up, as if she'd found hidden treasure.

What's this? asked the director as he smoothed out the handbill.

A reactionary handbill, said Huang as she handed him the torn fragments, as if they were treasured gifts. Don't forget these, they're the rest of what the defector Wang Xiaoti sent to Wan Xin.

The curious doctors and nurses were transfixed.

Suffering from a case of far-sightedness, the director held the handbill out at arm's length so he could read it. The doctors and nurses crowded around him.

What are you people looking at? What's there to see? Get back to work, he scolded as he put away the handbill. Come with me, Dr Huang.

The doctors and nurses wasted no time in sharing their views of the incident as Huang followed the director to his office.

Gugu's heart-rending wails erupted from the obstetrics ward, and I was suddenly aware of what a destructive thing I'd done. I stepped nervously into the ward, where I saw Gugu sitting with her head down on a table, crying and pounding her fists on the tabletop.

Gugu, I said, Mother sent me over with some rabbit for you.

She ignored me, just kept crying.

I laid my bundle down on the table, opened it, and placed the bowl of rabbit meat next to her head.

Gugu swept the bowl off the table with her arm. It shattered on the floor.

Get out of here! Go! Go! She raised her head to scream at me. Get out of my sight, you little bastard!

11

It wasn't until later that I realised just how terrible the thing I'd done was.

After I fled from the health centre, Gugu slit her left wrist, then dipped her right index finger in the blood and wrote: *I hate Wang Xiaoti! I have always been a Party member, and I will die a Party member!*

When Huang Qiuya returned triumphantly to the ward, Gugu's blood had seeped all the way to the door. Huang shrieked before crumpling to the floor.

Gugu was saved, and placed on probation by the Party. The reason was not that her relationship with Wang Xiaoti remained suspicious, but that she had tried to use suicide to show the Party what she was capable of.

12

Northeast Gaomi Township enjoyed an unprecedented harvest from its thirty thousand acres of sweet potatoes in the autumn of 1962. After putting us through three abominable years, soil that had refused to grow anything regained its bountiful generosity and its innate ability to nourish. Each acre produced a record of more than ten thousand jin of sweet potatoes that year, and the mere recollection of that year's crop made me sense a stirring for some reason. A rich yield of sweet potatoes lay beneath the ground. The largest potato unearthed in our village came in at thirty-eight jin. A photo of Yang Lin, the county's Party secretary, holding it appeared on the front page of *Masses Daily*.

Sweet potatoes are wonderful, truly wonderful. It was not only a bumper crop in terms of quantity, but the potatoes were rich in starches, they cooked up with a perfect texture, and they tasted a bit like chestnuts, delicious with high nutritional value. Sweet potatoes were piled in every family's yard, wire was strung along every wall to hang slices of drying sweet potatoes. We had enough to eat, finally enough to eat. No more days of eating grass or the bark of trees; the days when people starved to death were gone, never to return. Before long our legs stopped suffering from oedema; the skin around our middle thickened, and our bellies flattened out. A layer of fat began forming under our skin, light returned to our eyes, and our legs no longer ached when we walked; we started to grow, to really grow. At the same time, women's breasts swelled and their periods returned to normal. Men's torsos straightened, whiskers reappeared above their lips, their sex drive was reawakened. After two months of eating their fill of sweet potatoes, all the young women in the village were pregnant it seemed. In the early winter of 1963, Northeast Gaomi Township experienced the first baby boom in the history of the People's Republic. Two thousand eight hundred sixty-eight babies were born that year in the fifty-two villages incorporated in our commune alone. According to Gugu, this crop of babies was known as the 'sweet potato kids'.

The health centre director had a good heart. He came to see Gugu after she returned home to recuperate from her failed suicide attempt. As the nephew of my maternal grandmother on her husband's side, he was a shirt-tail relative, what we call 'melon-vine kin'. He criticised Gugu for being foolish and hoped she could lay down her ideological baggage and return to work. The Party and the people are blessed with bright-seeing eyes, he told her. Under no circumstance would they treat a good person unjustly or make allowances for a bad one. He urged her to trust the organisation and prove her unsullied record through positive actions in order to be reinstated into the Party as quickly as possible. You're different from Huang Qiuya, he said privately. Her character is essentially bad, while your roots are red and your limbs are straight. Though you have made missteps, if you work hard you can have a bright future.

The director's words made Gugu cry bitterly once more.

His words made me cry bitterly as well.

Gugu regained her footing in a pool of blood and threw herself into her work as if on fire. At the time, even though every village was equipped with trained midwives, many women chose to have their babies in a health centre. Gugu put aside her resentment and worked closely with Huang Qiuya, in the capacity of both a doctor and a nurse. She might not shut her eyes once for days at a time, caught up in the business of pulling birthing mothers back from the gates of Hell. Over a period of five months, they delivered eight hundred and eighty babies, eighteen by caesarian section, at a time when the procedure was extremely complicated, and the fact that a small commune health centre obstetrics ward dared to even attempt it caused a sensation. Even someone as ambitious and proud as Gugu had to admire Huang Qiuya's surgical skill. She was in debt to that one-time enemy for her fame in Northeast Gaomi Township as an obstetrician with both local and foreign skills.

Huang Qiuya was what was known as an old maid. She'd likely never tasted romance, which might explain why she had such an odd disposition. In her later years, Gugu often spoke to us of her old adversary. For the daughter of a Shanghai capitalist and the graduate of a top university to be sent down to Northeast Gaomi Township to work was a case of 'a fallen phoenix is not the equal of a common chicken'. And who was the chicken? In a tone of self-ridicule, Gugu answered her own question. That would be me. A chicken that pecked at a phoenix. A chicken that beat a phoenix into submission. She shuddered when she saw me, Gugu said emotionally, like a lizard that's swallowed a hunk of tar. Everyone was crazy in those days. It was a nightmare. Huang Qiuya was a magnificent obstetrician. She could be beaten bloody in the morning and show up in surgery in the afternoon, so focused and composed that not even an opera being performed right outside the window would have had an effect on her. What a pair of hands she had! Gugu said. With them she could create a flower on a pregnant woman's abdomen . . . Gugu always enjoyed a hearty laugh at this point; she'd laugh till tears spilled from her eyes.

13

Gugu's marital situation had become a family obsession. The grown-ups weren't the only ones who worried about her; even teenagers like me were deeply concerned. But we didn't dare broach the subject with Gugu since that made her unhappy.

In the spring of 1966, early on Qingming, grave-sweeping day, Gugu came to the village to perform routine exams on girls who had reached child-bearing age. She was accompanied by the apprentice we knew only by her nickname: Little Lion. Eighteen years old, short and stocky, she had a pug nose surrounded by pimples, eyes too wide for her face and dishevelled hair. When they'd finished their exams, Gugu brought Little Lion home with her for dinner.

Wheat cakes, hard-boiled eggs, yellow onions and fermented bean sauce.

We'd already eaten, so we watched Gugu and Little Lion eat.

The girl was so shy she wouldn't look us in the eye. Her pimples stood out like red beans.

Seeming to take to the girl, Mother asked her one question after another, moving increasingly close to the marriage question. That's enough questions, Sister-in-law, Gugu said. You're not looking for a daughter-in-law, are you?

You must be joking, Mother said. How could a village woman like me aspire that high? Little Lion is on the national payroll. There isn't one among your nephews who's worthy of her.

Little Lion's head drooped lower; her appetite seemed to have left her.

My classmates Wang Gan and Chen Bi came running up at that moment. Wang Gan was so focused on the inside of the house he stepped on a bowl of chicken feed and smashed it.

You clumsy oaf, Mother scolded. Why don't you look where you're going!

Wang Gan just rubbed his neck and sniggered like an idiot.

How's your sister, Wang Gan? Gugu asked. Has she grown some?

About the same.

Tell your father when you get home – she swallowed a bite of wheat cake and wiped her mouth with her handkerchief – that your mother mustn't have another child. If she tries, her uterus will come right out of her.

Don't talk to them about women's health, Mother said.

Why not? Gugu replied. I want them to know how hard it is to be a woman. Half the women in this village have a descended uterus, the other half have inflammations. His mother's uterus has torn loose and hangs there like a rotten plum. But Wang Jiao wants another son. The next time I see him . . . and you, Chen Bi, your mother isn't well either —

Mother cut her off and turned to me: Scram, she scolded. You and your knucklehead friends go play outside. I don't want you goofing around in here.

Out in the lane, Wang Gan said, Xiaopao, you have to treat us to some roasted peanuts.

Why's that?

Because we have a secret, Chen Bi said.

Tell me, I said.

First treat us to some peanuts.

I don't have any money.

What do you mean, you don't have any money? Chen Bi said. You stole a piece of cast-off copper from the state-run farm and sold it for one-twenty. Did you think we didn't know?

I didn't steal it, I jumped to my own defence. They threw it away.

Whether you stole it or not doesn't matter. You did sell it for one-twenty. Your treat, come on. Wang Gan pointed to the swing set next to the threshing square, where people had gathered around an old man who sold roasted peanuts amid the back-and-forth creaks of swings.

After I divided thirty cents' worth of peanuts into three portions, a dreadfully earnest Wang Gan said, Xiaopao, your aunt is going to marry the county Party secretary to be his second wife.

Like hell! I said.

Once she's married to him, Chen Bi, said, your family will be in a much better position. Before you know it your brothers and your sister, even you, will be moved into the city, where you'll get jobs, eat marketable rice, go to college, and become Party cadres. Don't forget your friends when that happens.

That Little Lion is quite the looker! Wang Gan blurted out.

14

When the 'sweet potato kids' were born, the household heads could register them with the commune and receive coupons for sixteen and a half feet of cotton and two jin of soybean oil. The amounts were doubled for twins. The receivers' eyes would be moist and their hearts would swell as they gazed upon the gold-coloured oil and the cotton coupons, printed with sweet-smelling ink. What a wonderful new society! Gifts for the newborn. The nation needs people, Mother said. The nation needs workers; it values people.

The masses were grateful for the gifts received and silently vowed to repay the nation with even more children. The wife of the granary watchman, Xiao Shangchun, who was the mother of my classmate Xiao Xiachun, had already given my friend three kid sisters, the youngest still nursing, and she was pregnant again. On my way home from tending our ox, I often saw Xiao Shangchun coming down off the little bridge on his rickety bicycle. He'd put on so much weight his bicycle strained audibly under its burden. Old Xiao, villagers liked to tease, how old are you now? Do you have to go at it every night? No, he'd say with a grin, but I have to labour hard to produce people for the nation.

In late 1965, the population explosion was a source of considerable pressure on the leadership. As the first family-planning policy in New China peaked, the government proposed: One is good, two is just right, three is too many. When the county film unit came to town, before the movie started, family-planning slides went up on the screen. Enlarged images of male and female genitalia produced queer shrieks and wild laughter from the viewers in their seats. We youngsters contributed mightily to the commotion as many young hands – boys and girls – came together on the sly. The birth control propaganda acted like an aphrodisiac. The country drama troupe split into a dozen small teams that went into the villages to perform the short play *Half the Sky*, that criticised favouring boys over girls.

By then Gugu had been promoted to director of the health centre's obstetrics department and deputy head of the commune's family-planning steering committee. The Party secretary, Qin Shan, was listed as committee head, but he was a figurehead, leaving the actual responsibilities of leading, organising and implementing family-planning policy for the whole commune to her.

Gugu had put on a bit of weight; her teeth, whose whiteness had been the source of so much envy, had begun to yellow as her work schedule hardly even allowed time to brush her teeth. A male-like hoarseness crept into her voice, as we heard over the loudspeakers on a number of occasions.

Gugu's announcements invariably opened in the same way: People do what they're best at and peddle the goods they have. I'll stay with mine, so today I want to talk to you about family planning . . .

The prestige she'd once enjoyed was on the decline during those days; even village women who had benefited from her counsel and attention began to cool towards her. She worked diligently in the service of family planning, but with meagre results. In the village she became isolated.

One day the county drama troupe came. When the female lead sang out, The times have changed: boys and girls are equal. Wang Gan's father, Wang Jiao, shouted out from beneath the stage, Bullshit! Equal? How dare you say they're equal! His outburst was echoed by those around him – catcalls and unfriendly shouts. Then came the missiles – chunks of brick and roof tiles – that were hurled onto the stage, sending the actors scurrying like scared rats. Wang Jiao had finished off a half jin of liquor that day – courage in a bottle – and his wild nature surfaced. Pushing people out of his way, he jumped up onto the stage, wobbling unsteadily as he stated his case with unrestrained gestures: You people can govern heaven and earth, but who says you can govern common people about having kids? Get some twine and sew up women's openings if you think you're up to it. That was greeted by roars of laughter, which further energised him; picking up a broken roof tile, he took aim at the bright gas lantern hanging from a railing in front of the screen and hurled it. The lantern went out, leaving the area in darkness. Wang Jiao spent the next two weeks in lockup, but was unrepentant upon his release. If you're man enough, he railed at just about everyone he met, just try to cut off my dick!

Gugu had drawn large enthusiastic crowds upon her return home years before. But now, on the rare visit, she was shunned by nearly everyone. Gugu, Mother once asked her, this family-planning business, was it your idea or were you following orders?

What do you mean, my idea? Gugu replied testily. It's the call of the Party, a directive by Chairman Mao, national policy. Chairman Mao has said: Mankind must control itself, people must learn to embrace viable population growth.

Mother just shook her head. Since the beginning of time, having children has been governed by nature. During the Han dynasty, the Emperor issued an edict that girls were to marry when they reached the age of thirteen. If they were not married, their fathers and elder brothers were held responsible. If women didn't have children, where would the nation get its soldiers? Every day we hear that America is planning to attack us and that we must liberate Taiwan. If women can't have babies, where will the soldiers come from? And with no soldiers, who wards off the American attack and who liberates Taiwan?

Don't bother me with those platitudes, Sister-in-law. Chairman Mao is a bit smarter than you, don't you think? And Chairman Mao has said: We must control our population! With no organisation and no discipline, at the rate we're going, mankind is doomed.

Mother was ready: Chairman Mao also said that more numbers means more manpower, and more manpower means more things can be achieved. People are living treasures. The world requires people. He also said: It is wrong to keep rain from falling and to keep women from raising children.

You are putting words into Chairman Mao's mouth, Sister-in-law, Gugu said, not knowing whether to laugh or cry. In olden days, you'd lose your head for falsifying an imperial edict. We've never said that women cannot have babies, but that they should not have too many. In other words, planned pregnancies.

How many children a woman bears in her life is controlled by fate, Mother said. Who needs your planning? To me you people are like a blind man lighting a candle, just wasting wax.

As Mother said, Gugu and the others were wasting their effort and money and creating a bad name for themselves. They began by giving free condoms to the heads of women's associations in every village to pass out to women of childbearing age and ask their husbands to wear them. The condoms wound up in pigpens or were blown up like balloons, some even painted, for children to play with. Gugu and the others went door to door to distribute birth control pills, but met with resistance from women who complained about side effects. Even if they forced them to take pills in front of them, as soon as they left, the women would stick their fingers or chopsticks down their throats to regurgitate the pills. The resistance eventually led to a call for vasectomies.

Word quickly spread throughout the villages that Gugu and Huang Qiuya were the inventors of vasectomies. People even went so far as to say that Huang created the concept, while Gugu put it into practice.

They aren't normal, two old maids who are green with envy whenever they see a married couple, Xiao Xiachun said assertively, which is why they came up with their plan to make every family childless. He told us that Gugu and Huang had first experimented on young male pigs, then on monkeys, and finally on ten death-row prisoners. When the experiment was called a success, the men had their sentences reduced to life imprisonment. Naturally, it didn't take us long to discover that Xiao did not know what he was talking about.

Back then, Gugu's voice often came to us through loudspeakers.

Brigade cadres, hear this: In the spirit of the eighth meeting of the commune's family-planning steering group, all men whose wives have borne them three or more children and any male with a total of three children are to report to the commune health centre to undergo a vasectomy. They will receive a bonus of twenty yuan to help them recuperate and will be given a week off with no deduction of work points.

Men got together to complain. Shit, they griped, you neuter a pig, you castrate a bull, and you geld horses and mules, but since when did they start cutting off a man's balls? We're not candidates for palace eunuchs, why go after us? But when the family-planning cadres explained to them that a vasectomy only . . . Well, they glared and they protested: That sounds fine now, but when you put us up on the bed and get us all numb, we doubt you'll stop with our balls. They'll probably cut our pricks off at the same time. Then we'll have to squat to pee, like women.

Good for the women, it was a simple procedure with extremely rare after-effects for the men, but it met with inflexible resistance. Gugu and her helpers prepared a room in the health centre and waited. No one showed up. The county headquarters called daily for a report on numbers, and were openly dissatisfied with Gugu's lack of progress. The Party secretary called a special meeting, which led to two resolutions: 1) Vasectomies will be performed on males beginning with the commune leadership and spread to Party cadres and regular workers. In the villages, brigade cadres will take the lead, followed by the masses. 2) Men who resist the procedure and those who initiate and spread rumours will be subject to the dictatorship of the proletariat; all those who qualify for vasectomies but refuse to undergo the procedure will have their right to work revoked until they do so; if that doesn't prevail, their grain ration will be reduced. Cadres who resist will be removed from office, workers who resist will lose their jobs, and Party members who resist will have their membership revoked.

Party Secretary Qin Shan made a personal address over the PA system in which he said that family planning was an issue of paramount importance to the national economy and the people's livelihood, and that commune departments and production brigades were to attach the greatest importance to it. Qualified male cadres and Party members were to lead the way in undergoing the procedure to set a positive example for the masses. Then, abruptly changing to a more relaxed, everyday tone, Qin said: Comrades, take me for instance. My wife has already undergone a hysterectomy due to an illness, but in order to allay men's fears, I plan to have a vasectomy performed on me tomorrow morning.

In his address, Secretary Qin asked the Communist Youth League, the Women's Association and school authorities to get behind the campaign and publicise it aggressively in order to reach peak participation. As in previous movements, Teacher Xue, the school's most talented literary figure, composed a clapper-talk lyric, which we quickly memorised. Then, organised into groups of four and armed with homemade paper or tin-plate megaphones, we went up onto rooftops and climbed trees to spread the word:

> *Commune comrades be not afraid,*
> *Commune comrades be not delayed.*
> *Vasectomies are the simplest things,*
> *No gelding attempts will ever be made.*

> *The tiniest cut, half an inch long,*
> *Fifteen minutes, you can't go wrong.*
> *No blood and no sweat,*
> *Back to work that day, just as strong.*

Over that special spring, according to Gugu, a total of 648 vasectomies were performed at the commune, only 310 by her hand alone. All that was really needed, she said, was a clear explanation of the rationale behind the policy; then, with the senior personnel taking the lead, followed by men at every level, the masses would respond reasonably. The majority of procedures she personally performed were on village cadres and organisational heads who came willingly. Only two cases involved troublesome men who were openly hostile and required coercion. One was our village carter Wang Jiao, the other was Xiao Shangchun, the granary watchman.

Wang Jiao, whose family background was politically ideal, acted with reactionary arrogance. He was no sooner released from detention than he began to rant that anyone who tried to force him into undergoing a vasectomy would know what it meant to see a knife go in clean and come out red. My friend Wang Gan, who had fallen hard for Gugu's assistant, Little Lion, was on Gugu's side emotionally. He tried to get his father to get a vasectomy, for which he was rewarded with two resounding slaps. Wang Gan fled from his house, his father on his heels, whip in hand. When they reached the pond at the head of the village, a coarse argument bridged the water.

Wang Jiao: You fucking dog, how dare you try to get your father to have a vasectomy!

Wang Gan: I'm a fucking dog? Okay, I'm a fucking dog!

Wang Jiao stopped to think. Calling his son names was the same as calling himself those same names. He renewed the chase; father and son began circling the pond, like turning a millstone. The curious stopped to look and added fuel to the generational fire with provocative shouts and raucous laughter.

One day Wang Gan stole a deadly sabre from his house and turned it over to the village's branch secretary, Yuan Lian, telling him it was a lethal weapon that his father had said he'd use on anybody who tried to make him have a vasectomy. Yuan Lian did not waste a minute, running off to the commune with the sabre to report to Party Secretary Qin Shan and my aunt. He's not on our side, Qin roared as he pounded his desk. Sabotaging our family-planning campaign is a counter-revolutionary act! Letting Wang Jiao get away with this will make our job harder, Gugu said. You're right, Qin agreed, knowing that village males in line to get vasectomies were watching to see what happened with Wang Jiao.

Arrest the hoodlum, Qin ordered.

Ning Yao (Waist) from commune security, pistol on his belt, led a group consisting of the Party secretary, the Women's League chairwoman, the militia commander and four of his men; they burst unannounced into Wang's yard.

Wang's wife was on a stool in the shade of a tree, a nursing infant in her arms, making a braid out of grass. She threw her handiwork down at the sight of the intruders, sat down on the ground, and wailed.

Wang Gan was standing under the eaves, not making a sound.

Wang Dan was sitting on the front door threshold, gazing at her small face in a tiny hand mirror.

Come out here, Wang Jiao! Yuan Lian shouted. The first time was a request, this time it's a demand. Commune Security Chief Ning is here. You might get away today, but there's always tomorrow. Be a man and do this on your own.

The Women's League chairwoman turned to Wang Jiao's wife. Stop crying, Fang Lianhua, and tell your man to get out here.

Not a sound from inside the house. Yuan Lian glanced at Security Officer Ning, who waved the four militiamen into the house, ropes in hand.

From where he stood under the eaves, Wang Gan pointed his chin at the pigpen for Ning's benefit.

Even though one of Ning's legs was longer than the other, he was fast on his feet. He hightailed it to the pigpen, unholstered his pistol, and shouted at the top of his lungs, Come out of there, Wang Jiao!

Wang Jiao crawled out of the pigpen, sporting cobwebs on his head, and was immediately surrounded by the four militiamen. He wiped his sweaty face. Cripple Ning, he fumed, what are you shouting at? Who do you think you're scaring with that rusty piece of steel?

I'm not trying to scare you, Ning said. Come quietly and there'll be no problem.

And what if I don't? You going to shoot me? He pointed to his crotch. If you've got the balls go ahead and shoot me in mine. I'd rather lose my balls to a bullet than to a bunch of old biddies with scalpels.

Wang Jiao, the Women's League chairwoman said, Don't be so

stubborn. All they do is tie off that little tube . . .

They ought to sew up that thing of yours, Wang Jiao retorted crudely, pointing at her crotch.

As he waved his pistol, Ning gave the command: Tie him up!

I'd like to see you try, Wang Jiao threatened as he reached behind for a shovel, then held it out in front of him, eyes blazing. I'll lop off the head of anyone who comes close!

The diminutive Wang Dan chose this moment to stand up, still holding her mirror. She was thirteen at the time, but stood only two and a half feet tall. Though extraordinarily small, she wasn't misshapen, and was like a lovely Lilliputian. She shone rays of blinding sunlight into Wang Jiao's face with her mirror and giggled with girlish naivety at the sight.

The militiamen took advantage of Wang's temporary blindness to rush him, wrench the shovel away, and yank his arms around behind him.

As they started to wrap their ropes around him, he burst into loud wails. There was such agony in his howls that rubberneckers sprawled atop his wall or gawking at his gate were pained by what they heard. The four men stood there helpless, ropes hanging from their hands.

Are you a man, Wang Jiao, Yuan Lian asked, or aren't you? How can a little procedure like this put such a fear in you? I already did it, and it hasn't affected me at all. If you don't believe me, have your wife ask my wife.

That's enough, Wang Jiao sobbed. I'll go with you.

That bastard Xiao Shangchun set a bad example at the commune, Gugu said. His rationale for opposing the vasectomy campaign was his trifling service as a stretcher-bearer for an Eighth Route Army underground hospital. But when research determined that he was to be removed from his public office and sent back to his village to work the land, he rode his rickety bicycle up to the health centre and insisted that I personally perform the procedure. A notorious lecher, he was a filthy-mouthed hooligan. As he climbed onto the operating table he said to Little Lion: Here's what puzzles me. There's a saying – 'When the essence reaches fullness, it will flow on its own.' But if you tie off my tube, where will my essence flow to? Will my belly swell to bursting?

She looked at me, red-faced from embarrassment. Prepare him for surgery.

I hadn't expected him to have an erection while she was prepping him. She'd never seen anything like that before; she dropped the scalpel and cowered in a corner. Clean up your thoughts! I demanded. My thoughts are perfectly clean, he said shamelessly. It got stiff on its own, and there's nothing I can do about that. All right, then, Gugu said as she picked up a rubber mallet and, with a nonchalant tap, put an end to his erection.

I swear to the heavens, Gugu said, I took scrupulous care in carrying out the procedure on both Wang Jiao and Xiao Shangchun, with total success, but afterward, Wang Jiao walked around bent at the waist, complaining that I'd cut a nerve, and Xiao made a pest of himself at the centre, complaining to county officials that I'd made him impotent. Of those two, Wang Jiao was probably emotionally unstable, while Xiao was nothing but a troublemaker. During the Cultural Revolution, as head of a Red Guard faction, he raped more women than you can count. If we hadn't performed a vasectomy on him, he might have retained some scruples out of a fear that he'd impregnate someone and suffer serious consequences. But tying off his tubes freed him from all that.

15

Winter, 1967

So many people turned out for the rally to denounce Party Secretary Yang Lin that the revolutionary committee head, Xiao Shangchun, came up with the ingenious idea of moving the site to the retarding basin on the northern bank of the Jiao River. It was the dead of winter. As people looked out over the ice-covered river, they were treated to a vista of glazed beauty. I was the first villager to learn that the rally was to be held there. One day I was ice fishing beneath a floodgate bridge over the basin when I heard loud voices above me. One of them was Xiao Shangchun. I could have picked his voice out of ten thousand. Damn, he said, what a great setting. We'll hold the rally here. We can put the stage here on the bridge.

A floodgate had been built above the Jiao River Dam to protect the lower reaches. Every year, when summer turned to autumn, the Jiao River crested and the floodgate was opened, transforming marshland into a lake. Northeast Township residents were unhappy with what was done, since marshland was still land, and the only crop that could be planted in the marsh was sorghum. But who were we to take issue with the needs of the nation? This was one of my favourite hangouts when I skipped school, a place where I could sit and watch water rushing through twelve sluice holes. After the water was let out, the

former marshland became a lake some ten square li in size, where fish
and shrimp were plentiful enough to bring hordes of fishermen and,
increasingly, fishmongers. They tried setting up their stalls on the bridge,
and when that didn't work, they moved to the eastern bank, under a
row of willows. During the busy season, a line of stalls would stretch at
least two li. Once they formed a market, the local marketplace moved
from the commune to the eastern bank of the river. The vegetable
peddlers came, the egg sellers came, the oil cruller peddlers came, and
with them came other marketplace denizens: thieves, hooligans and
beggars. Members of the commune's armed militia turned out several
times to clear the area, and their arrival sent undesirables scurrying; the
militiamen's departure witnessed a probing return of the same people.
A combination of legal and illegal commerce thus came into being. I
loved looking at fish: carp, silver carp, crucian carp, catfish, snakehead
fish, eel, and, while I was at it, crabs, loaches and clams. The biggest fish
I ever saw there weighed a hundred jin and had a white belly; it looked a
little like a pregnant woman. The old fishmonger stood cowering behind
the fish, as if he were in possession of a deity. By then I was palling
around with those sharp-eyed, keen-eared fishmongers. Why sharp-
eyed and keen-eared? Because agents from the tax bureau often came
to confiscate their fish, not to mention the idlers in the commune who
pretended to be from the tax bureau to trick them out of their wares.
That huge fish was nearly taken away by two men in blue uniforms,
cigarettes dangling from their lips, and black satchels in their hands. If
the fishmonger's daughter hadn't come running up crying and making
a fuss, and if Qin He hadn't exposed the two men's real identities, they'd
have carried that fish off with them.

Qin He wore his hair with a side part and dressed in a blue
gabardine student's uniform, with a Doctoral brand fountain pen and
a New China two-colour ballpoint pen clipped to his breast pocket;
he looked like a college student reduced to begging during the May
Fourth period. His face was deathly pale, his expression gloomy, his
eyes moist, as if he were forever on the verge of tears. Yet he was an
eloquent speaker of standard Mandarin, his every utterance stage-play

quality. He exerted considerable influence on my later decision to try my hand at being a playwright. He was never without his enamel mug, emblazoned with a five-pointed red star and the word 'Prize'. Standing in front of the fishmongers, he'd say emotionally: Comrades, I'm a man who's lost the ability to work. And you might say: You're too young to be a man who's lost the ability to work. Well, I tell you, comrades, what you cannot see is that I have a serious heart condition, caused by a stabbing. Any physical exertion could cause my damaged heart to rupture, and I'd bleed to death. Won't you give me one of those fish, comrades? It doesn't have to be a big one, a small one, even a tiny one will do . . .

He was always successful, and then he'd rush down to the riverbank, clean his bounty with a penknife, find a spot protected from the wind, gather some kindling, and stack a couple of bricks; then, after placing his water-filled enamel mug on top, he'd make a fire and start to slow cook. I often stood behind him to watch him cook his fish and breathe in the aromatic steam emerging from his mug, which soon had me drooling. Oh, how I envied him and his lifestyle . . .

Qin He, who'd been one of the most talented students at the Number One High School, was the younger brother of Qin Shan, the commune's Party secretary. According to some, the reason Qin He was like he was stemmed from his insane infatuation with my aunt, which became so serious that he tried, but failed, to kill himself with his brother's pistol. The injury left him in that state. At first people laughed at him, but after he helped the old man hold on to that giant fish, the fishmongers' view of him changed. To me he was like a magnet. I tried very hard to understand him. The look in his moist eyes cried out for sympathy.

Late one afternoon, after the fishmongers had left for home, I saw him walking into the sunset, trailing a long shadow; so I fell in behind him, hoping to discover his secret. When he realised he was being followed, he stopped, turned, and greeted me with a deep bow. Please don't do this, dear friend, he said. In an imitation of his voice, I said, I'm not doing anything, dear friend. What I mean, he said in a forlorn voice, is please don't follow me. You're walking, I replied, so am I. I'm not following you. He shook his head and murmured, Please, my friend, show some pity for a man of misfortune. He turned and continued walking. I fell in behind him again. He started loping, taking long, high-stepping strides, his body nearly floating as he rocked from side to side, sort of like a paper cutout. I kept up with him at about half-speed, until he stopped to catch his breath, his face the colour of gold foil. Friend . . . his face was tear-streaked . . . I beg you, let me go. I'm terribly disabled, a severely wounded man . . .

Moved by his plea, I stopped and let him continue alone, my eyes filled with the image of his back, my ears to the sound of his sobs. I hadn't meant to bother him; I'd just wanted to know a bit about how he lived, like, for instance, where he slept at night.

As a teenager I had exceptionally long legs and big feet – size 40 shoes – which caused my mother no end of worries. Our gym teacher, Mr Chen, was a one-time track and field star athlete, and a rightist. Like a buyer of livestock, he squeezed my legs and feet and pronounced me to have the wherewithal to be a star, with the right training, of course. He taught me how to run, to breathe correctly, and to use my strength to best advantage. I proudly took third place in the three-thousand-metre race in the youth category at the all-county elementary and middle school track meet. My skipping school to run to the fish market to see what was happening became an open secret.

That incident initiated a friendship between Qin He and me. He always greeted me with a friendly nod. It was a pan-generational friendship, since he was more than ten years older than me. In addition to Qin, two other beggars camped out in the fish market: Gao Men was a broad-shouldered man with big hands, someone you'd peg as a man of considerable strength. Lu Huahua, who had suffered from jaundice, for some reason had been given a girl's name. One day Gao and Lu, one with a willow club, the other with a worn-out shoe, ganged up on Qin He and gave him a severe beating. Qin did not raise a hand to defend himself. Beat me to death, he said, and I'll be eternally grateful. But don't eat any frogs. Frogs are our friends, and you mustn't eat them. They have parasites that will make you stupid if you ingest them . . .

I saw green smoke spiralling into the air from a bonfire under a willow tree, and deep in the fire some half-cooked frogs; next to the fire burnt frog skins and bones gave off a foul, nauseating stench. That's when I realised that Qin He had been beaten for trying to keep them from cooking and eating frogs. The sight of him being beaten brought tears to my eyes. Everyone ate frogs during the famine, though my family vehemently opposed the practice. We'd have rather starved than eat a frog. From that angle, Qin He was our ally. I picked a piece of burnt wood out of the bonfire and used it to poke Gao Men in the butt and Lu Huahua in the neck. Then I took off running down the riverbank with the two beggars hot on my heels. I kept them at a comfortable distance to have some fun, and each time they stopped chasing me, I shouted insults or threw objects at them.

That was the day commune members from forty-eight villages streamed down roads or across the frozen river, waving red flags and beating gongs and drums and pots and pans, as they dragged village miscreants to the retarding basin, where a rally was to be held to subject Yang Lin, the county's number one capitalist roader, and bad people from all commune departments to public denouncements. We made our way across the river ice, some on homemade skateboards. Gym teacher Chen, who had been such a generous tutor, was wearing a paper dunce cap and a pair of straw sandals, a goofy smile on his face, as he followed the scowling school principal, who also wore a dunce cap. Xiao Shangchun's son, Xiachun, was driving them along with a javelin. His father was the head of the commune revolutionary committee, while Xiachun himself was the leader of our school's Red Guard brigade. He was wearing the white Warrior brand sneakers he'd taken off Teacher Chen's feet. A double-bang starting pistol I'd have loved to get my hands on, and which was supposed to have been public property, now hung from Xiao Xiachun's belt. From time to time he drew the pistol, added gunpowder, and fired it into the air: *Pow pow!* White smoke followed the explosions, saturating the air with the pleasant odour of nitrate.

I'd wanted to join the Red Guards when the revolution began, but Xiao Xiachun wouldn't let me. He called me a black model promoted by Teacher Chen the Rightist. He called my great-uncle a traitor, a false martyr, and said that my aunt was a Nationalist secret agent, a turncoat's fiancé and a capitalist roader's paramour. To get even, I picked up a dog turd, wrapped it in a large leaf, and hid it in my hand. I walked up to him and said: Xiao Xiachun, how come your tongue is black? He opened his mouth, just as I'd planned. I crammed in the dog turd and took off running. He hadn't a chance of catching me, since the only person in the school who could outrun me was Teacher Chen.

Watching him strut smugly along in Teacher Chen's shoes, javelin in hand, starter pistol on his hip, gave rise to hateful jealousy – he needed fixing in the worst way. I knew he was deathly afraid of snakes, but there'd be no snakes in late autumn, so I scrounged up a length of rotting rope under a mulberry tree by the river, coiled it and held it behind my back. As soon as I was right behind him, I collared him with the rope and screamed: A venomous snake!

With a blood-curdling scream, he threw down the javelin and tore the thing off of his neck. When he saw it was only a piece of rope, he slowly gathered his wits, picked up the javelin and said through gnashing teeth: Xiaopao Wan is a counter-revolutionary!

Death! He pointed the javelin at me and charged.

I ran.

He chased me.

On the frozen river I lost my speed advantage, and sensed that a blast of cold air was catching up to me. I was terrified that I'd be run through by his javelin. I knew the guy had honed the tip on a grinding wheel, I also knew that he was mean enough to stick me with it. He'd already shown that by stabbing tree trunks and scarecrows, and had even killed a pig mating with a sow. I kept looking back as I ran. His hair was standing straight up, his eyes were open as far as they'd go, and if he caught me I was a goner.

I ran around people, I threaded my way through people, and when I slipped on the ice, I rolled and crawled to get away from his javelin thrust. He missed and struck the ice, sending chips flying. Then he slipped and fell. I scrambled to my feet and started running again. He got to his feet and was chasing me once more, banging into people right and left – men, women . . . Who the hell do you think you are! Hey – help! Murder —

I crashed into a line of people banging gongs and drums, sending them stumbling in all directions and causing dunce caps to fly off the heads of the miscreants. I bumped past Chen Bi's father Chen E and his mother Ailian – I bumped into Yuan Sai's father, Yuan Lian (he'd been labelled a capitalist roader), and crashed into Wang Jiao on my way past. I saw the look on Mother's face and heard her horror-struck scream – I saw my good friend Wang Gan – I heard a thudding sound behind me, followed by a screech – Xiao Xiachun's voice. I later learned that Wang Gan had stuck out his foot and tripped Xiao Xiachun, who'd cut his lip when his face hit the ice, and was lucky he hadn't lost a tooth. When he got to his feet, he turned on Wang Gan, but was kept from getting even by Wang's father. Xiao Xiachun, you little bastard, Wang Jiao growled, if you so much as touch my son I'll gouge out your eyes! Three generations of our family have been tenant farmers, he said. Other people might be afraid of you, but you're looking at one man who isn't!

The meeting site was a sea of people, all gathered in front of an impressive stage made of wood and reed mats. At the time, the commune boasted a group of skilled workers who specialised in building stages and bulletin board kiosks. Dozens of horizontal red flags adorned the stage along with red banners with white lettering. When we arrived, four loudspeakers mounted on a pair of corner posts were blaring 'A Song of Quotations': Marxist thought has thousands of threads that come together in a single remark: To rebel is justified! To rebel is justified!

The place was in an uproar. I attempted to muscle my way up front, my eye on a spot at the foot of the stage. People I shouldered out of the way responded churlishly with feet and fists and elbows. But after all that hard work – my clothes were soaked and my body was black and blue – I not only didn't make it to the front, I was actually manhandled to the edge of the crowd, where I heard the sound of cracking ice, and had a bad feeling in my bones. Just then a man whose voice sounded like a duck's quack, burst from the loudspeakers: The public denouncement session is about to begin. All you poor and lower-middle-class peasants, please quiet down . . . in the front rows, please sit down, sit down . . .

I made my way over to the three storage sheds for gate boards on the western edge of the sluice gate. By wedging my toes in the spaces between bricks and grabbing hold of the eaves, I pulled myself up until I made it onto one of the roofs, all the way to the central ridge, from where I could see throngs of people and more red flags than I could count. I was nearly blinded by sunlight off of the river ice. Dozens of people were hunched over just west of the stage, all with their heads lowered. I knew who they were: the commune's evil ox-ghosts and snake-demons waiting to be hauled up on the stage to be hounded by the masses. Xiao Shangchun was bellowing into a microphone. The one-time down-on-his-luck granary watchman could never have dreamed that such a position would one day be his. But at the beginning of the Cultural Revolution, as rebel leader, he had created a title for himself: Windstorm Rebel Corps Commander.

He was wearing an old army uniform turned white from too many launderings and made whole with dark patches; a red armband circled his bicep. His hair was so thin the scalp glistened in the sunlight. He affected the speech of big-shot characters we'd all seen in movies: drawing out his words, one hand on his hip, the other making all sorts of gestures. The loudspeakers made his voice loud enough to burst eardrums, overlaying the sound of waves crashing onto a rocky shore created by the masses, and caused by disturbances here one minute, there the next. I began to worry about the safety of my mother and other oldsters who were there. I tried to spot them in the crowd, but the glare from the ice was too bright. Bitter winds cut through my tattered coat and chilled me to the bone.

Xiao Shangchun waved his hand, and a dozen hulking men with clubs and sporting Security bands around their arms came out from behind the stage. They jumped down and began to quiet the boisterous crowd with clubs that had red cloths tied to the ends, making them look like torches. One young fellow, who was hit over the head, angrily tried to take the club away, and received a nasty poke in the ribs for his effort. Wherever these ruthless crowd controllers wielded their clubs, the people meekly made way, as Xiao Shangchun's shrill voice sliced through the loudspeakers: Sit down, everyone! Sit down! Drag out the troublemakers.

The young man targeted by one security enforcer was yanked out of the crowd by his hair . . . the masses finally quieted down, some on their haunches, others seated, but no one on their feet. Like scarecrows in the field, the enforcers stood evenly spaced amid the crowd of people.

Bring the ox-ghosts and snake-demons up on the stage! Xiao Shangchun commanded. The miscreants' feet never touched the ground as they were bundled up onto the stage.

I saw Gugu among them.

She did not go meekly. Every time one of the men pushed her head down, she defiantly raised it as soon as the hand was taken away. Her defiance only increased the pressure the next time, and in the end she was knocked to her knees; one of the security men put his foot on her back. Some members of the crowd hopped up onto the stage to shout slogans, but they evoked no echoing response from the people below. Finding their shouts ineffective, the sloganeers slipped back down into the crowd. Just then, a piercing wail exploded from somewhere in their midst. It was my mother's howl of anguish: My poor suffering sister . . . have you horrid beasts no conscience at all . . .

Xiao Shangchun ordered his men to take all the other ox-ghosts and snake-demons off the stage and leave Gugu alone up there. The enforcer kept his foot on her back and struck a valiant pose. This was a demonstration of the popular slogan: Knock the class enemies to their knees and step on them when they're down. When I saw that Gugu wasn't moving, I worried she might be dead. My mother's howls had faded away, and I thought she might be dead too.

The remaining ox-ghosts and snake-demons were herded over to a large poplar tree, where they were guarded by a security team armed with rifles. The detainees sat on the ground, heads lowered, unmoving as clay statues. Huang Qiuya's head was resting against a brick wall, half of it shaved to make her not only ugly, but terrifyingly so. I'd been told that during the early days of the movement, Gugu had been one of the founders of the Norman Bethune Combat Brigade in the local health system. Like a fanatic, she'd shown no kindness to the director who had once been her protector, and she had treated Huang Qiuya with unprecedented cruelty. I knew this had been a survival measure, like a night traveller whistling past a graveyard out of fear. The old director, a decent man who'd found the bullying and humiliation intolerable, had killed himself by jumping down a well. Huang Qiuya, on the other hand, had responded to the imprecations of her antagonist by producing evidence of Gugu's concealed relationship with the turncoat Wang Xiaoti, revealing that she had often cried out his name in her sleep at night, and divulging that when she came off duty one night, she discovered that her colleague, Wan Xin, was not in the dormitory; she wondered where an unmarried young woman could be that late. As she was weighing the possibilities, she saw three red signal flares soar up out of a grove of willow trees on the bank of the Jiao River and heard the roar of an aeroplane engine high overhead. Not long after that, a figure slinked back into the dormitory, and she recognised who it was – Wan Xin. Huang said she reported the incident to the director, but the capitalist roader was in cahoots with Wan Xin and suppressed her report. There was no doubt, she said, that Wan Xin was a secret agent for the Kuomintang, and this incident was serious enough to cost her her life. But she wasn't finished. She also said that Gugu had engaged in trysts with the capitalist roader Yang Lin in the county seat, resulting in a pregnancy that Huang herself had aborted. The masses were a repository of rich creativity, but also a repository of evil imagination. Huang Qiuya's revelation of Gugu's two major crimes easily satisfied the people's emotional needs; Gugu's refusal to admit to any of it and her steadfast defiance further guaranteed fireworks at every denouncement session, and constituted a monstrous episode in the history of Northeast Township.

I gazed down from my rooftop perch at Huang Qiuya's weird half-bald head and my loathing was tempered by sympathy, confusion, fear and grief. I picked up a shard of tile and took aim at that head. I could have hit it with ease. But I hesitated, and in the end did not throw it. Years later I told Gugu what I'd thought of doing. I'm glad you didn't, she said. That would have made things even worse for me. In her later years Gugu believed she'd been guilty of terrible, unforgiveable things. I thought she was being too hard on herself, convinced that she was no worse than anyone who lived during those times. You don't understand . . . The note of sorrow in her voice was palpable.

Yang Lin was dragged up onto the stage. The man whose foot was on my aunt's back moved away so they could pick her up and stand her next to Yang, where their heads were pushed down, they were forced to crouch, and their arms were yanked behind them, a contrived position to resemble the wings on Wang Xiaoti's Jian-5 aircraft. I looked down at Yang Lin's exposed scalp. Six months earlier, he had been the next thing to a god, someone who had reached unparalleled heights, and we had entertained hopes that he and Gugu might marry someday, even though he was more than twenty years older, and even though she would be a replacement for his recently deceased first wife. But he was the Party secretary, a high-ranking cadre with a monthly income of over a hundred yuan, a big shot who visited the villages in a green Jeep, accompanied by an assistant and bodyguards.

I only met him once, Gugu said years afterward. I found his big belly – easily the size of a pregnant woman in her eighth month – repulsive and was turned off by his foul garlic breath – he was as rustic as they come – but I'd have married him. For all of you, for the family, I'd have married him. The day after she met Yang in the county seat, she said, the commune Party secretary, Qin Shan, made an inspection tour of the health centre and, in the company of the director, came to the obstetrics ward, all smiles and honeyed words, a living, breathing slave. In the past, she said, Qin Shan had strutted around, high and mighty, but he had abruptly turned into the man she was looking at now, and she didn't know what to make of that. I'd have married the man to spite all those petty people, if not for the Cultural Revolution.

A squat, stocky female Red Guard walked up with two pairs of worn-out shoes and draped one around the neck of Yang Lin, the other around Gugu's neck. I could bear up under the labels of counter-revolutionary and special agent, Gugu said, but not harlot, not ever. It was an insult they concocted to disgrace me. She reached up, took the shoes off, and flung them away. As if they had eyes, they landed at the feet of Huang Qiuya. The Red Guard jumped up, grabbed a handful of Gugu's hair, and pulled her head down. Gugu jerked her head back up to defy the girl. Lower your head, Gugu, I warned silently. If you don't, she might rip your hair out and take some of your scalp with it. That girl has to weigh a hundred kilos or more. She's holding onto your hair with both hands, actually hanging from you. Gugu shook her head like a wild horse tossing its mane, and the girl, who held onto the hair, lost her balance, bringing Gugu down to the stage floor with her, a tuft of loose hair in each hand. Gugu's head started to bleed – she still has a pair of coin-sized scars there – the blood running down her forehead and into her ear. She held her body rigid. The crowd was deathly silent. A mule hitched to a wagon raised its head and split the air with a loud bray. I didn't hear Mother howl; my mind was a blank.

As that was happening, Huang Qiuya picked the worn shoes up off the ground in front of her, trotted over, and went up onto the stage. I assumed she didn't know what had just happened, because she wouldn't have done what she did otherwise. She froze when she saw the scene in front of her, dropped the shoes, and backed up, mumbling something. Xiao Shangchun strode up onto the stage. Wan Xin, he bellowed, how arrogant can you be! With wild gestures, he tried leading the people in shouted slogans to change the atmosphere. But no one below the stage joined in. The fat girl flung away the two handfuls of hair, as if they were snakes, and began to blubber as she stumbled off the stage.

Stay where you are! Xiao ordered Huang Qiuya, who was slowly backing up. He pointed at the worn shoes. You, he said, put those around her neck.

The blood had run down Gugu's ear onto her neck and past her brows into her eyes. She rubbed her face with one hand.

Huang picked up the shoes and walked unsteadily up to Gugu, where she stopped and looked into her face. With a garbled shriek, she began foaming at the mouth and fell backward.

Red Guards rushed up and dragged her off the stage like a dead dog.

Xiao Shangchun grabbed Yang Lin by the collar and pulled it back to straighten him up.

Yang's arms hung loose at his sides, his legs buckled, and he went limp. If Xiao let go, he'd have collapsed in a heap.

Being stubborn is Wan Xin's road to Hell, Xiao said. She won't come clean, so you do it. Leniency to those who confess, severity to those who refuse! Tell us, did you and she have an adulterous affair?

Yang Lin held his tongue.

Xiao waved a hulking man up to join him and give Yang a dozen vicious slaps across the face, loud cracks that reached the tips of the trees. Some white things landed on the stage; I guessed they were teeth. Yang began to lurch and would have fallen if the man hadn't grabbed his collar to hold him up.

Did you or didn't you? Speak up.

Yes . . .

How many times?

Just once . . .

The truth!

Twice . . .

You're lying!

Three times . . . four . . . ten . . . many times . . . I can't recall . . .

With a spine-tingling screech, Gugu jumped up and threw herself at Yang like a lioness taking down her prey. Yang fell heavily to the floor, where Gugu scratched his face relentlessly. Several ferocious security men had to work hard to pry her off of Yang's body.

At that moment, strange noises on the lake emerged as the ice began to crack, and people fell into the freezing water.

BOOK TWO

BOOK TWO

Dear Sugitani Akihito sensei,

Your willingness to spend so much of your valuable time reading a long letter it took me two months to finish so I could save money on postage and then to offer so much encouragement and positive feedback has both moved and made me feel guilty.

What caused a welter of feelings was learning that Pingdu Garrison Commander Sugitani during Japan's invasion of China was your father. Because of that, you represented your deceased father by apologising for his offences to my aunt, my family, and the people of my hometown. Your attitude in facing up to history and assuming responsibility for certain actions moved us deeply. Apparently, you too were a victim of the war. In your letter you wrote about how you and your mother suffered fearful pangs of anxiety throughout the war and debilitating cold and hunger when it was over. If you want the truth, your father was a victim too. As you have said, if there had been no war, he would have been a surgeon with a brilliant future. The war changed all that; his life and his nature would never be the same again. A one-time saver of lives, he became a taker of lives.

I read your letter to my aunt, to my father, and to many of the people here who lived through the war. They reacted emotionally, even tearfully. You were no more than four or five years old when your father was the Pingdu Garrison Commander, and you are not culpable for his crimes. But you shouldered his crimes and demonstrated a willingness to expiate them for him. By doing so, you have endeared yourself to us, for we know how precious that sort of attitude is. It is an attitude too seldom seen in today's world. If all people could reflect on history and on their own lives, mankind would not display so much idiotic behaviour.

My aunt, my father, and my fellow townspeople are eager to welcome you again as a guest to Northeast Gaomi Township. My aunt would like to accompany you on a visit to Pingdu city. She took me aside to tell me that she harbours no ill will towards your father. There is no denying that there were many cruel, vicious, and ill-mannered Japanese officers who participated in the invasion of China, the sort we see in movies about the war, but there were also cultured officers, like your father, who treated people with courtesy. My aunt judged your father this way: He was far from the worst of the lot.

I returned to Gaomi in June, more than a month ago. While here I've done a bit of research for the play I plan to write, focusing on my aunt. I've also continued relating the story of Gugu's life in letter form, as you asked me to do, and, as you requested, included in those letters as many of my own experiences as possible.

My aunt and my father have asked me to pass on their regards to you and your family.

Northeast Gaomi Township welcomes you!

Tadpole
July 2003, Gaomi

1

Sensei, 7 July 1979 was my wedding day. I married a classmate from elementary school, Wang Renmei. With our long legs, we looked like a pair of cranes. Just the sight of her legs made my heart race. We met at the well one day when I was eighteen. When one of her buckets fell into the well, she walked around in circles, not knowing what to do. So I jumped up onto the wellhead and fished her bucket out for her. I was in luck that day, snatching it on my first try. Hey, Xiaopao, she said admiringly, you're a master bucket fisherman. A substitute PE teacher at the elementary school, she was tall, had a long thin neck and a relatively small head, and wore her hair in braids. Wang Renmei, I stammered, I want to tell you something. What? she asked. Did you know that Wang Dan and Chen Bi like each other? She froze briefly, then broke out laughing. Xiaopao, she said between laughs, you don't know what you're talking about. Wang Dan is so little, and Chen Bi's as big as a horse. They are a terrible match. She stopped, seemed to think about something, and started laughing so hard she actually bent over; and she was blushing. I'm not lying, I declared solemnly. If I was, I'd be a dog. I saw them with my own eyes. What did you see? she asked. You can't tell anybody what I'm about to say. Last night after leaving the work points office, I heard some sounds in a haystack on the threshing floor. I went up to see what it was, and I heard Chen Bi and Wang Dan whispering things to each other. Don't worry Brother Chen Bi,

Wang Dan was saying, I might be small, but I have everything a girl's supposed to have, and I promise I'll give you a son. Wang Renmei bent over laughing yet again. Do you want to hear what I have to say or don't you? I said. Yes, she replied, but hurry up. Then what happened? What did they do after that? I think they kissed. Nonsense! she insisted. Tell me how they kissed. I'll give it to you straight, I told her. They kissed the way they're supposed to. Chen Bi took Wang Dan in his arms, like he was holding a baby, and they kissed the way they felt like it. Wang Renmei blushed again. Xiaopao, she said, you're a little hooligan! And so is Chen Bi! Wang Renmei, since Chen Bi and Wang Dan are dating, do you think you and I could become friends? Again she froze, and again she laughed. Why do you want us to be friends? You have long legs and so do I. My aunt says that if we got married, our child would have nice long legs, and we could train the kid to be an international champion athlete. You've got quite an aunt, she said, still laughing. Not only is she good at performing vasectomies, she's a matchmaker as well. Wang Renmei picked up her water buckets and walked off. Her carrying pole rocked up and down with each long stride, nearly sending the buckets on the ends flying into the air.

Years later, after leaving home to join the army, I heard that she and Xiao Xiachun were engaged. He was teaching language and writing as a substitute teacher in the agricultural school. One of his essays, 'An Ode to Coal', which was published in the newspaper *Masses Daily*, created a stir in our hometown. I had quite an emotional reaction to the news, because those of us who had actually eaten coal did not write any odes to coal, while Xiao Xiachun, who hadn't eaten it, did. Renmei, it seemed, had chosen a mate wisely.

When Xiao Xiachun was accepted into college, his father set off three strings of 'thousand head' firecrackers out on the street in celebration and hired a movie company to erect a screen on the school grounds to show three movies, one after the other. It was a display of arrogance the likes of which we'd never seen.

As a decorated soldier returned from the Sino-Vietnamese Conflict who had received a commission as an officer in the regular army, I was visited by a host of matchmakers. Xiaopao, Gugu said, I've found the right girl for you. I guarantee you'll approve. Who is it? Mother asked. My apprentice, Little Lion. She's thirty if she's a day, Mother said. Exactly thirty, Gugu confirmed. Xiaopao is only twenty-six. The older the better, Gugu said. They know enough to be caring.

Little Lion's fine, I said, but Wang Gan has been gaga over her for more than a decade. I can't steal a girl from a friend.

Wang Gan? Gugu remarked. He's the proverbial toad wanting to taste the swan's flesh. If there's anyone Little Lion *won't* marry, it's Wang Gan! His father hobbles over to the health centre every market day, bent at the waist, cane in hand, to make a scene and blacken my name. And for years, mind you! He's gotten no less than eight hundred yuan in nutritional expenses from the centre.

That Wang Jiao, Mother said, is pretty good at faking things.

Pretty good? Gugu railed. He's a master of the art. He takes the money he extracted from me to the market to feast on braised meat and strong liquor until he's drunk, at which time his back is straight and he zips around the market. Tell me why I've bumped into scoundrels like that all my life. Then there's that bastard Xiao Shangchun, who damn near killed me during the Cultural Revolution, and now struts around like a lord and master, waving his palm-leaf fan as he enjoys the good life at home. I hear his son has tested into college. Is that right? What happened to the old saying that 'good is rewarded with good, evil with evil'? The good people suffer, the rotten eggs live like kings, that's what. People still get what's coming to them, Mother said. It just takes time. How much time? Gugu asked her. My hair has already turned white!

After Gugu left, Mother said, Your aunt has not had an easy life. Someone said Yang Lin came to see her after what happened, I said. That's what she told me, Mother confirmed. By then he'd been promoted to the position of district commissioner, and arrived in a chauffeured sedan. He apologised to your aunt and told her he was willing to marry her to make up for his behaviour during the Cultural Revolution. Your aunt sent him away.

As we were sighing over Gugu's misfortunes, Wang Renmei came barging in the door. Aunty, she said to Mother, I hear that your Xiaopao is searching high and low for a wife. How about me?

I thought you were spoken for, young lady.

I broke it off, she said. He's a latter-day Chen Shimei, the storybook character who deserted his wife when he became a high official.

Mother said, How could he drop you just because he's going to college?

He didn't drop me, Renmei said, I dropped him. So he's going to college. What's the big deal? Firecrackers, movies, I've never seen such insolence! Xiaopao's better than that. He's an army officer without having to blow his own horn. As soon as he came home, he went into the field to work.

You're too good for Xiaopao, young lady, Mother said.

I guess we're going to have to ask Xiaopao what he thinks, Aunty. Xiaopao, what do you say – I'll be your wife and present you with a champion athlete son.

You're on! I said, gazing at her legs.

2

The weather was bleak on my wedding day. Dark clouds gathered as thunder rumbled. When the thunder ended, a downpour followed.

Yuan Sai said he'd picked a fine, auspicious day for you to get married, Mother complained, but what we got was flooded streets.

At ten o'clock Wang Renmei arrived during a cloudburst in the company of two female cousins. In their raingear they looked like dike control volunteers. A plastic tent with a stove inside had been thrown up in our yard. I was on my haunches stoking a fire with a bellows to boil water. My cousin Wuguan (Facial Features), who was known for speaking his mind, said: What's a hero of the self-defence-counterattack conflict doing crouched down by a stove to heat water when his bride-to-be has arrived? Then come take my place, I said. No, your mother put me in charge of the firecrackers, which will require all my skills in this rain-squall. Wuguan, Mother called from the doorway, stop the idle chatter. It's time for the firecrackers. He reached under his coat and removed a string of firecrackers wrapped in plastic. After he lit the fuse, he held the string in his hand – no pole for him – opened an umbrella, and leaned out into the rain to set them off. The pounding water kept the gunpowder residue from spreading beyond him. Wuguan, kids cried out as they clapped their hands and stomped their feet, all soaked to the skin, Wuguan, you're turning green! What are those pathetic excuses for children shouting? Mother remarked.

This is how it was supposed to happen: the bride was to say nothing as she entered the house and went straight to the wedding chamber, where she sat on the kang to wait, what's known as 'sitting in bed'. But Wang Renmei stopped as soon as she was in the yard to watch Wuguan do his thing. His face was blackened by the firecracker residue, as if he'd stepped out from a stove. That made her laugh. She ignored the tugs on her sleeves by the bridesmaids. Her high-heeled plastic shoes made her taller than ever, tall and straight as a tree. Wuguan looked her up and down. Anyone who wants to kiss you, good Sister-in-law, will have to stand on a ladder! he quipped. Be quiet, Wuguan, Mother demanded. You're a moron, Wuguan, Wang Renmei said. Wang Dan and Chen Bi don't need a ladder when they kiss! Hearing the bride trading quips with her soon-to-be brother-in-law in the yard had the older women whispering among themselves. I emerged from the tent with my coal shovel. Our hero has emerged! the clapping, stomping kids cried out. Here's our hero!

I was wearing a new uniform, with a Merit Third Class medal pinned to my chest, my face as black as soot, coal shovel in hand, looking like a freak of nature. Wang Renmei doubled over laughing. I was so confused I didn't know whether to laugh or to cry. She seemed to be losing her mind. Take her inside this minute! Mother insisted. Madam, I said to Renmei with dripping sarcasm, the wedding chamber awaits. It's too stuffy in there, she said. It's nice and cool out here. Ao! Ao! Ao! the clamouring kids shouted. I ran inside, grabbed a gourdful of sweets, then stood in the doorway and flung them down the lane. When the kids swarmed over to fight for them in the mud, I grabbed Renmei by the wrist and pulled her inside, unfortunately banging her head with a loud thump as she went through the low door. Ouch! she complained. Damn you, you've cracked my head open. The older women laughed so hard they were rocking back and forth.

The room was too small for so many people. We could hardly turn around. The three young women took off their dripping raingear, but the only place they could hang it was over the door. The floor was wet to begin with, and the muddy soles of their shoes had made a real mess.

Piled high at the head of a kang barely two square metres were four new quilts, two bed mats, two woollen blankets, and two pillows, all from Renmei's family; they nearly touched the ceiling. The moment Renmei sat down, she shouted, Damn, this is no bed, it's a frying pan!

This comment so incensed Mother that she banged her cane on the floor. Frying pan or no, you sit there! We'll see if it manages to cook your butt.

That too made Renmei laugh. Xiaopao, she said under her breath, your mother has a great sense of humour. But if my butt really does get cooked, how will I give you your champion athlete?

I was so mad I was getting dizzy. But I couldn't show it on such an auspicious day, so I reached out to touch the bed surface. It burned my finger. All the aunts and grannies in the family were expecting to eat, so the stove never had a chance to cool down – steaming buns, stir frying vegetables, boiling noodles – until the bed mat nearly melted. I took one of the quilts from the pile, folded it into a square, and laid it on the bed against the wall. Madam, I said, please take your seat. She giggled. Xiaopao, she said, you're a riot, calling me madam. Follow local customs and call me daughter-in-law or, like you used to, Renmei. I didn't know what to say. With a crazy bride like her, what *could* I say? My sarcasm in calling her madam had gone right over her head, and she didn't realise I was unhappy with her. All right, I said, Daughter-in-law Renmei, please take your seat. With help from the two bridesmaids, I took off her shoes and her soaked stockings so she could climb up onto the bed. She immediately stood up, her head nearly touching the ceiling. In that cramped little room, she looked taller than ever, so tall the calves of her crane legs seemed to disappear. And her feet – they were almost as big as mine – two large, bare feet dancing on a little kang. By custom, the bridesmaids were supposed to sit next to the bride, but there was no room, so one of them stood by the wall, the other sat on the very edge of the kang. To show off, Renmei stood on tiptoes to see if she could touch the ceiling with her head. It was all a game to her – walking on tiptoes in circles and jumping up and down to bump the ceiling with her head. With her hand on the doorframe,

Mother stuck her head in. Daughter-in-law, she said, if you ruin the kang, where will you sleep tonight? If it's broken, she giggled, I'll sleep on the floor.

At sunset Gugu came over for dinner. Gugu's here, she called out as she walked in the door. Isn't anyone going to welcome me?

We ran out to greet her. We didn't think you'd be coming with all that rain, Mother said.

She had come with an oil paper umbrella, her pant legs rolled up, and bare feet, shoes tucked under her armpits.

You couldn't keep me away from the wedding of my nephew the hero if knives fell from the sky, Gugu said.

I'm no hero, Gugu, I said. I'm only a commissary officer, in charge of cooking. I've never laid eyes on an enemy soldier.

Commissary officers are important. Men are iron, food is steel. If a soldier doesn't get enough to eat, how's he going to face an enemy charge? Now get me something to eat, so I can get back in time. The river's swelling and if it swamps the bridge I'll be stuck.

That'll give you a chance to rest here a couple of days, Mother said. It's been a long time since we've had a chance to talk. You can tell us stories tonight.

Not tonight, Gugu said. The Political Consultative Congress is meeting tomorrow.

Xiaopao, did you know your aunt received an official promotion as a member of the standing committee?

Did you say official? Gugu said. More like adding rotten goji berries to a plate just to fill it up.

Gugu walked into the western room, sending all the people into a flurry of activity. The ones sitting on the kang tried squeezing together to make room for her. Stay where you are, she said. I'm leaving right after I have a few bites.

Mother told my sister to make a plate of food for Gugu, who went over, took the lid off a pot on the stove, and took out a corn muffin. It was so hot she sort of hissed as she tossed it from hand to hand. Finally she split it open, put some steamed pork with rice between the two halves, folded them back, and took a bite. Um um, she said. I don't need a plate, she said, or a bowl. This is the way I like to eat. Ever since I've been working at this job I haven't eaten more than a few real sit-down meals.

Let's have a look at the wedding chamber, she said as she ate.

Renmei was sitting on the windowsill – the kang was too hot for her – reading a children's book by light coming in through the window. She was giggling.

Gugu is here, I said.

Renmei jumped down and took Gugu's hand in hers. Just the person I've been looking for, she said. And here you are.

What is it?

Renmei lowered her voice. I hear you have some kind of drug I can take to make me have twins.

Where did you hear that? Gugu said with a frown.

Wang Dan said so.

A nasty rumour, Gugu managed to say as she choked on the muffin. She coughed, her face turned red, and she drank the water my sister rushed to hand her. She thumped her chest a couple of times. There's no such drug, she said, but even if there were, I wouldn't hand it out to anyone.

Wang Dan said a woman in Chen Family Village took a pill you gave her and had twins, a boy and a girl, Renmei said.

Gugu stuffed the half-eaten muffin into my sister's hand. Damn, that makes me mad! she cursed. I can't tell you how hard it was to get a baby out of that little witch Wang Dan, and she has the nerve to go around spreading rumours. I'll split that shitty mouth of hers the next time I see her.

Don't get mad, Gugu. I nudged Renmei's leg with my foot. You just shut up! I said under my breath.

Ouch, damn you! Renmei said with excessive drama. You almost broke my leg.

You can't break a *dog's* leg! Mother said angrily.

You're wrong, Mother, Renmei said insistently. Xiao Shangchun broke the leg of my second uncle's dog with his steel trap.

Xiao Shangchun, who had returned home after his retirement, spent most of his time brutalising living creatures. Arming himself with a fowling piece, he went around shooting birds, all kinds of birds, even magpies, which the villagers considered harbingers of good luck. He'd put up a mist net, with holes so tiny even inch-long fry could not get through, to catch them. And he'd set powerful steel traps in the woods or in the graveyard to catch badgers and weasels. A dog belonging to Renmei's second uncle had its leg broken when it carelessly stepped into one of his traps.

Gugu's face darkened when she heard the name Xiao Shangchun. That evil man, she said through clenched teeth, deserves to be struck by lightning. But no, he lives the good life, with fine food and drink. He's healthy as an ox, which just goes to show that even the heavens are afraid of that louse.

The heavens might be afraid of him, Gugu, Renmei said, but I'm not. If you need a wrong revenged, I'll do it for you.

That made Gugu happy. She laughed. I'll tell you the truth, I was opposed to my nephew marrying you at first. But I changed my mind when I heard that you broke off your engagement with Xiao Xiachun. She's got spunk, I said. So he's going to college, so what? The Wan family children will all go to college, and not just any college, but Peking University, Tsinghua University, Cambridge, and Oxford. And not just undergraduate degrees either, but MAs, even PhDs. They'll be professors and scientists and champion athletes!

Then give me the drug that'll let me have twins, Gugu. That way I can double my contribution to the Wan family's legacy. The news will probably kill Xiao Xiachun!

My goodness! They all say you're on the slow side. Well, they're wrong. You ambushed me! Then she turned deadly serious. You youngsters need to obey the Party, walk the Party line, and not veer from the straight and narrow. Family planning is national policy, and is of paramount importance. With Party secretaries in command, all Party members must get to work, leading the way as exemplars to strengthen scientific research, improve techniques and implement procedures. They must mobilise the masses and never let up. One child per couple is set in stone for the next fifty years. China is lost if she does not control her population. You're a Party member, Xiaopao, a revolutionary soldier, so you must set an example.

Just give me the drug on the sly, Gugu, and I'll take it right away. No one will ever know, Renmei said.

Child, I'm afraid that you might be as slow as they say, after all. I repeat, there is no such drug, and even if there were, I wouldn't dare give it to you. Gugu is a member of the Communist Party, a member of the Consultative Conference standing committee, and deputy head of the family-planning group. How could you expect me to be the first to break the law? I want you all to know that even though I suffered unjust treatment, my heart is as red as ever, and will never change. Alive I'm a Party member, dead I'll be a Party ghost. I go where the Party sends me. Xiaopao, your wife's thinking is a problem. She can't tell which is hot, the ashes or the fire. You need to be clear on matters and not get any crazy ideas. People have begun calling me the 'Living Queen of Hell', and I couldn't be prouder. I'll take a bath and burn incense before delivering babies for those who follow family-planning policy, but I'll deal mercilessly with those who go beyond one pregnancy – every last one of them! She made a chopping gesture.

3

On the twenty-third day of the twelfth lunar month, the day the kitchen god is sent off, my daughter was born. Cousin Wuguan brought us home from the commune health centre on his tractor. Before we left, Gugu said to me: I inserted an IUD in your wife. Wang Renmei ripped the scarf off her head and confronted her: How could you do that without my permission? Gugu put the scarf back. Keep that on, so you won't catch cold. Inserting IUDs right after birth has been ordered by the family-planning group. No exceptions. If you had married a farmer and your first child was a girl, you could remove the IUD eight years later and have a second child. But you married my nephew, an army officer, for whom the rules are more stringent. A second child means immediate dismissal and a return to the farm. So don't ever think about a second child. There's a price to be paid for the opportunity to marry an army officer.

Renmei sobbed like a baby.

With our infant wrapped tightly in my overcoat, I climbed onto the tractor. Let's go, I said to Wuguan.

We chugged down the pitted country road, black smoke puffing from the exhaust pipe. Renmei lay in the cab, covered by a quilt, her sobs punctuated by each bump in the road. Who said she could insert an IUD . . . no permission . . . how come I can't have more than one . . . who says so . . .

Stop crying, I said. She was trying my patience. It's national policy. That only made her cry harder. She stuck her head out from under the quilt; her face was pale, her lips blue, and there were flecks of straw in her hair. Who says? It's something your aunt dreamed up. They're not this strict in Jiao County. Your aunt is just looking for commendations and a promotion. No wonder people rage against her.

Shut up, I said. If you've got something to say, wait till we get home. If you cry and carry on the whole way, people will laugh at us.

She threw off the quilt and sat up. Glaring at me, she snarled: Who will laugh at me? I'd like to see who has the guts to laugh at me.

Bicycles kept passing us. We were pummelled by a cold north wind, with frost on the ground as a red sun climbed into the sky. Steam from the riders' mouths frosted their eyebrows. The sight of Renmei, with her dry, chapped lips, dishevelled hair, and staring eyes was nearly unbearable, and I had to say something kind. No one's going to laugh at you, now lie back and cover up. Getting sick during the first month is no laughing matter.

That doesn't scare me. I'm like a pine tree atop Mount Tai, fighting the bitter cold and warding off the wind and snow. I have a morning sun in my chest.

I forced a smile. I know all about you, I said, you're a mighty hero. Aren't you insisting you want a second child? Well, that won't happen if you ruin your health with this one.

Suddenly there was life in her eyes. You agree we'll have a second child, she said excitedly. You just said so, I heard you. Did you hear that, Wuguan? You're my witness.

Okay, I'm your witness, Wuguan said in a soft, muffled voice up front.

She lay back down compliantly and drew the quilt up over her head. You'd better be true to your word, Xiaopao, her voice came from underneath. You'll have me to deal with if you don't.

When our tractor reached the head of the village, we saw two people arguing on the bridge, and blocking our way.

My classmate Yuan Sai was having an argument with the villager who made clay figurines, Hao Dashou (Big Hand).

Hao Dashou was holding Yuan Sai by the wrist.

Let me go! Yuan Sai was yelling as he tried to break free. Let me go!

His struggles weren't working.

Wuguan got down off the tractor and walked up to them. What's going on here, guys? Who gets into a fight this early in the morning?

I'm glad you're here, Wuguan, Yuan Sai said. You can talk some sense into him. He was pushing his cart in front of me, and I wanted to pass him on my bicycle. He was bearing to the left, so I went to the right. But when I got up right behind him, he shifted his arse and moved to the right. Fortunately, I've got good reflexes. I let go of the handlebars and jumped onto the bridge. I could have been dumped into the icy river with my bicycle. If it didn't kill me, it would have crippled me. But Uncle Hao blames me for his cart winding up under the bridge.

Hao said nothing in rebuttal; he just held onto Yuan Sai's wrist.

So I stepped down off the tractor with the baby in my arms. When my foot hit the ground, a sharp pain shot up my leg. Damn, it was cold that morning.

I hobbled up the bridge, where I saw a bunch of coloured clay dolls. Some were smashed, others were fine. A beat-up old bicycle lay on the icy surface of the eastern side of the bridge, a little yellow flag curled up alongside it. I knew without looking that the words 'Little Immortal' were embroidered on the flag. Yuan Sai, different from other people, had been odd even as a child. He could draw nails out of a cow's belly with a magnet, he could geld pigs and dogs, and he was proficient in physiognomy, feng shui, geomantic omens, and the eight trigrams of the *Book of Changes*. Complimented by some people as the 'Little Immortal', he affixed an apricot yellow flag embroidered with those words to the rear rack of his bicycle, where it snapped in the wind. At the market, he planted the flag in the ground. His business flourished.

A wheelbarrow lay tipped over on the icy surface to the west; one handle was broken, as were the two willow baskets it had been carrying, the contents – dozens of clay dolls, most of them smashed – strewn across the ice. A tiny few remained whole and undamaged. Everyone was in awe of Hao Dashou, a true eccentric. Holding a lump of clay in his large, skillful hands, he'd fix his eyes on you and, in hardly any time, produce a remarkable likeness. He didn't stop making his dolls even during the Cultural Revolution. Both his father and grandfather had made fine clay likenesses of children, but his were better than theirs. He made his living creating and selling human dolls only. He didn't have to. He could also have made simple figurines of dogs, monkeys and tigers, which were popular with children, who were the primary customers for such artisans. Adults would not spend money on something their children did not like. But Hao Dashou made only children. He lived in a large house with five main rooms, two side rooms, and a big tent out in the yard; all were filled with clay figurines. Some were finished, with powdered faces and all the features in the right places; others were awaiting the application of colour. There was only enough empty space on his kang for him to lie down; the rest was cluttered with clay figurines. A man in his forties, he had a ruddy face and grey hair that was combed into a braid at the back. Even his beard was grey.

Neighbouring counties had figurine artisans too, but their dolls came from a single pattern and were identical. His were all made by hand, every one unique. People said: He made all the dolls in Northeast Gaomi Township. People said: Every resident of Northeast Gaomi Township can see what he looked like as a child. People said: He only went to market to sell dolls when he was out of rice. He sold his dolls with tears in his eyes, as if he were selling his own children. I could barely imagine the pain all those shattered dolls caused him. Why *wouldn't* he hold Yuan Sai by the wrist?

I walked up, holding my baby in my arms. I'd been in the army so long, it would have felt unnatural to be in civilian clothes, so I'd accompanied Renmei to the hospital in uniform. A young military officer carrying a newborn infant had plenty of authority. Let Yuan Sai go, Uncle, I said. He didn't mean to do it.

Yes, that's right, Uncle, I didn't mean it, Yuan Sai sobbed. Be forgiving. I'll find someone to fix your wheelbarrow and baskets, and I'll pay for the broken dolls.

For my sake, I said, and for the sake of my daughter and her mother, let him go so we can cross the bridge.

Renmei poked her head out from the cabin. Uncle Hao! she shouted. Can you make me an identical pair of boy dolls?

Popular wisdom in the township had it that if a woman bought one of Hao Dashou's dolls, tied a red string around its neck, laid it at the head of the kang, and made offerings to it, she'd have a baby exactly like it. But Hao would not let people choose the dolls they wanted. Artisans in other counties laid their wares out on the ground for people to choose. Hao Dashou kept his in covered willow baskets. After sizing up the buyer, he'd reach into one of his baskets to take one out, and that would be the only one he'd sell you. If you complained it wasn't attractive enough, he would not exchange it. With a sad smile on his lips, though he'd say nothing, you could almost hear him saying, Are there really parents who complain that their children are ugly? The more you look at the doll in your hand, the more it appeals to you, and the more alive it becomes, like a living breathing child. He won't bargain with you, and if you don't offer him money, he won't ask for any. No one ever heard him say thanks when they did pay, and people gradually came around to feeling that buying one of his dolls was much the same as ordering a real child from him. The talk kept getting stranger. If the doll he sold you was a girl, they'd say, when you went home, you'd have a girl; if it was a boy doll, that's what you'd have. And if he took out two, you'd go home and have twins. This was a totally mystical arrangement, one that held up as long as you didn't talk about it. People like my wife were impossible to reason with, and no one but she would blatantly try to get a pair of boys out of him. By the time the mysterious talk about Hao Dashou first reached our ears, she was already pregnant. It only worked before a woman was pregnant.

For my sake, Dashou let go of Yuan Sai, who rubbed his wrist and sobbed, This has been a terrible day for me. I walked out the gate and saw a bitch piss in my direction, and, sure enough, I walked into trouble.

Hao bent down to pick up the broken doll pieces and tucked them into his jacket. Then he moved to the side of the bridge to let us pass.

There was frost on his beard and a solemn look on his face.

What did she have? Yuan Sai asked.

A girl.

No problem. The next one will be a boy.

There'll be no next one.

Don't you worry, Yuan Sai said with a conspiratorial wink. I'll think of something when the time comes.

4

My daughter was nine days old on the first day of the year of the dog. According to local custom, this was a day of momentous significance, and friends and relatives arrived to help celebrate. We asked Wuguan and Yuan Sai to come over the day before to help us borrow all the tables and chairs, teapots and cups, glasses, plates, and chopsticks we'd need. A rough calculation came up with about fifty people. That meant two tables each in the eastern and western side rooms for the male guests, and one table in Mother's room for the women. I produced a menu with eight cold plates and eight hot dishes per table, in addition to a soup. Yuan Sai took one look and laughed. This won't do, my friend. Your guests are all farmers. They've got stomachs like bushel bags. What you have there is an appetiser for them. Listen to me, he went on. Forget all the variety and just pile on the meat. That and a big bowl of strong liquor counts as a feast for farming people. You're being too fancy, and their chopsticks won't be moving long before it's all gone; then they'll wait for more – which won't be forthcoming. You'll lose face, big time. I knew he was right, so I had Wuguan go to town for fifty jin of pork, half lean and half fat, and ten braised chickens, the kind with plenty of meat on their bones. Then I went out and ordered forty jin of tofu from Wang Huan, the bean curd peddler, and told Yuan Sai to buy ten Chinese cabbages, ten jin of bean noodles and twenty jin of liquor. Renmei's family sent over 200 hen's eggs, and when her father, my father-in-law, saw the preparations, he had a satisfied look. Son-in-law, he said, now you've done it. People have always laughed at your family for being cheap, but this lavish arrangement will change that when you send everyone home with a full belly. People who accomplish big things need to do everything in a big way.

About half the guests had arrived when it dawned on me that I'd forgotten to buy cigarettes. So I told Wuguan to go to the co-op to get some just as Chen Bi and Wang Dan arrived with their baby. Wuguan pointed to the gift they'd brought. No need to buy cigarettes, he said.

Chen Bi had done well in recent years, becoming one of the village's rich men, what we called a 'ten-thousand-aire'. He'd gone to Shenzhen and brought back some digital watches, which he'd sold to fad-crazy young people. Then he went to Jinan where he bought cigarettes from a wholesaler he knew and had Wang Dan sell them in the marketplace.

I'd seen her peddling them. She'd hung a well-designed device around her neck – a carrying case folded up and a display rack when let down. She'd dressed in a form-fitting blue jacket, with her baby strapped to her back in a cotton poncho, so only her nose showed. Whether they knew her or not, everyone who passed by took careful notice of her. The locals all knew she was the wife of the cigarette merchant Chen Bi, and the mother of the chubby little one on her back; outsiders took pity on the pretty girl who was out selling cigarettes with her baby sister on her back. Folks usually bought her cigarettes out of sympathy.

On this day Chen Bi was wearing a stiff pigskin leather jacket over a cable-knit turtleneck sweater. His face was red, his chin freshly shaved – big nose, sunken eyes with grey irises, hair curled.

Moneybags is here, Wuguan announced.

Moneybags, my eye, Chen Bi said. A small-time entrepreneur is more like it.

Tovarisch, Yuan Sai said. Your Chinese is pretty good, comrade.

Chen Bi raised the package he was holding. I'll give you a taste of this! he threatened.

Cigarettes? Yuan Sai shouted. Just what everyone's been clamouring for.

Chen Bi flung the package at Yuan Sai, who caught it and opened it to find four packs of Rooster cigarettes.

A true businessman, he said. How generous.

With that mouth of yours, Yuan Sai, Wang Dan said in a tiny voice, you could make a dead man dance disco.

Aiya, Sister-in-law, pardon my lack of manners, but how come he isn't holding you in his arms?

I'll split your lip! she said as she raised her hand threateningly.

Pick me up, Mama . . . It was Chen Er, who came around from behind her; she was now nearly as tall as her mother.

Chen Er, I said as I bent down and picked her up. How about letting your uncle hold you?

She started to cry, so Chen Bi took her from me and patted her bottom. Don't cry, Er-er. I thought you wanted to see your uncle the army officer.

Chen Er reached out for Wang Dan.

She's shy around strangers, Chen Bi said as he handed her to her mother. A moment ago she was fussing about wanting to see her uncle the army officer.

Just then, Wang Renmei smacked her hand against the windowsill. Wang Dan, she shouted, come here!

Carrying her daughter like a big toy in a puppy's mouth, a sight that was both comical and earnest, Wang Dan waddled over like a cartoon animal, her daughter's legs wrapped around her.

What a lovely little girl, I said. Like a doll.

How could a Soviet girl *not* be lovely? Yuan Sai said with an exaggerated wink. Brother Bi, everyone says you're hard-hearted, that you don't give your wife a moment's rest.

Shut your mouth! Chen Bi said.

Go easier on her, Yuan Sai persisted. She's still going to have to give you a son.

Didn't I tell you to shut your mouth? Chen Bi gave him a kick.

Okay, already, Yuan Sai said with a laugh. I'll shut it. But I want you to know how much I envy you. Married all these years, and still enjoying a good hug and a kiss. There's your proof that love marriages and arranged marriages are nothing alike.

Everybody's got troubles, and you, for one, don't know what the hell you're talking about, Chen Bi said.

I gave Chen Bi's belly a friendly pat. I see you've got a general's paunch.

Life is good, he said. I never dreamed I'd one day enjoy such a good life.

You can thank Chairman Hua for that, Yuan Sai said.

I'd rather thank Chairman Mao, Chen Bi said. If the old fellow hadn't up and died, everything would be the same as before.

More guests had arrived and were standing in the yard listening to our conversation. Even those who had gone inside were coming out to see what the commotion was all about.

My cousin Jin Xiu approached Chen Bi, looked up at him, and said, Elder Brother Chen, you're like a god in our village.

Chen took out a pack of cigarettes, handed one to Jin Xiu, and lit one for himself. Then with his hands thrust into his pockets, he said proudly, So, tell me, what do they say about me?

They say you flew to Shenzhen with only ten yuan in your pocket, Jin Xiu said as he scratched his neck, and that you fell in behind a delegation of Russians. The girls who worked there all thought you were part of the delegation and bowed to you. You responded with Harasho – very good. They say you checked into that fancy hotel with the Russian delegation, that you ate and drank like a king for three days, and that you received a lot of gifts that you turned around and sold on the street, making enough to buy twenty digital watches, which you sold here. You used what you earned to make more money, and it didn't take long to get rich.

Chen Bi stroked his big nose. Go on, he said, keep the story going.

They say you went to Jinan and roamed the streets until you saw an old fellow wandering aimlessly, and when you asked him why he was crying, he said he'd gone out for a walk and now couldn't find his way back. You saw him home. The old fellow's son was the head of the Jinan

Supply and Marketing Department, and he rewarded your good deed by declaring himself to be your sworn brother. And that is how you were able to acquire cigarettes wholesale.

Chen had a big laugh over that. Are you writing a novel, young man? he said when he finished laughing. Now I'll tell you the real story. I've flown on aeroplanes many times, and I've bought my own ticket for every flight. I do have friends at the Jinan tobacco plant, and they sold me cigarettes at a slim discount, enough for me to make three fen per pack.

No matter what you say, you're someone who knows how to get things done, my cousin said with heartfelt admiration. My dad wants me to become your apprentice.

The one who really knows how to get things done is right here, Chen Bi said, pointing to Yuan Sai. He's conversant with heavenly principles and earthly truths. He knows everything that happened five hundred years ago and half of what will happen five hundred years from now. He's the master you're looking for.

Elder Brother Yuan is a great man too, my cousin said. He set up his fortune-telling stand back home in the Xia Village marketplace, where we know him as the Little Immortal. When an old hen in my aunt's house went missing, Elder Brother Yuan curled his fingers and said, Ducks on the river, chickens in the grass. Go see if there's a grassy nest. Well, that's exactly where we found it.

He's not just a diviner, Chen Bi said. He can do lots of things. If he taught you even one of them, you'd have enough to live on for the rest of your life.

Kowtow to the master, Wuguan said.

No, the things I do are appropriate only for someone in the lower walks of society who's eking out a living. You need to follow your cousin by going into the army and becoming an officer. Or take the college exam and go to school. Those are the paths to a bright future as a leading member of society. Yuan Sai first pointed to himself and then to Chen Bi. We, including him, are not engaged in lines of work that are on the up and up. We do what we do because we have no choice. But you, you're still young, so don't follow in our footsteps.

No, my cousin insisted stubbornly, you're the ones with real skills and abilities. That's not the case with the army or college.

Good for you, young man. You think for yourself, that's good. In the future, we can work together, Chen Bi said.

Where's Wang Gan? I asked Wuguan.

I'll bet you anything he's posted himself at the health centre.

That guy's possessed, Chen Bi said. A team of horses couldn't pull him away from it.

The problem is his house, Yuan Sai said mysteriously. The front door is in the wrong place, so is the toilet. I told your father-in-law more than a decade ago that he had to make changes to his front door and to move the toilet; if not, someone in his family would go batty. He thought I was putting a curse on him and picked up a whip to use on me. So what happened? What I warned against came true. Every chance he gets he picks up a cane, bends at the waist, and goes to the health centre to put on a shameless act. If that isn't batty, I'd like to know what is. Wang Gan's no better, a farmer with petty bourgeois ideas who's gone gaga over that pimply Little Lion. In other words, batty.

All right, everyone, forget Yuan Sai's eyewash and come inside, I said. Come inside, all of you.

The feng shui of our commune is no good, either, Yuan Sai said. Since olden days, the yamen, the official residence, has always faced south. But the gate of our commune faces north, and is directly opposite the slaughterhouse, where knives go in clean and come out red all day long, with blood and guts everywhere, and a grisly atmosphere. When I went to complain they accused me of propagating feudal superstitions and barely fell short of locking me up. So what happened? The old Party Secretary Qin Shan suffered a paralytic stroke and his brother, Qin He, has been crazy for years. When Qin's replacement, Secretary Qiu, took a dozen people down south on an inspection tour, there was a traffic accident that killed or injured every one of them. Feng shui is of vast importance. No matter how unyielding a fate you have, it's never greater than that of the Emperor, and not even he is immune to the power of feng shui.

Take your seat, I said again as I gave Yuan Sai a tap on the shoulder. Feng shui is important, good master, but so are eating and drinking.

If they don't do something about the commune main gate, more people will go batty, and more major incidents will occur. You can believe me or not, Yuan Sai said. It's up to you.

5

Wang Gan's one-sided infatuation with Little Lion led to many strange occurrences that were the talk of the village. He was a laughing-stock, but I never laughed at him, for he had both my sympathy and my respect. He was, in my view, a uniquely talented individual who had been born in the wrong time and place. A devoted lover, if chance had allowed, he could have composed a sentimental love poem that would be sung for millennia. During our childhood, when we were ignorant of what romantic love was all about, Wang Gan was in the first bloom of love for Little Lion. I recall how years before he had said: Little Lion is so pretty! By any standard, she was not a pretty girl, not even attractive. My aunt had once thought of introducing her to me, and I'd declined with the excuse that she was the girl of Wang Gan's dreams. To be perfectly honest, her looks were a turn-off. But in his eyes, she was the most beautiful girl in the world. In elegant terms, it could be a case of a lover seeing in her the classical beauty Xi Shi; less elegantly, it could be seeing a green bean through the eyes of a turtle – the size and colour make a perfect match.

After posting his first love letter to Little Lion, Wang Gan was so excited he dragged me down to the riverbank to pour out his feelings. That was in the summer of 1970, soon after our graduation from the rural middle school. Grain stalks and dead critters were being swept along by raging waters over which a solitary gull flew quietly past. Wang

Renmei's father was sitting on the riverbank fishing in the calmer water close by. Li Shou, a schoolmate younger than us, was crouched down watching him.

Want to tell Li Shou?

He's just a kid, he wouldn't understand.

We climbed an old willow tree halfway down the riverbank and sat side by side on a branch that reached out over the water. The tip actually broke the surface, creating a series of ripples.

What do you want to tell me?

You have to promise not to tell anyone.

Okay, I promise. If I breathe a word of what Wang Gan tells me, let me fall into the river and drown.

Today I . . . I finally dropped a letter to her in the postbox . . .

Wang Gan had turned pale and his lips quivered as he spoke.

To who? The way you're acting, it sounds like you wrote to Chairman Mao.

Why would you say that? What does Chairman Mao have to do with me? No, I wrote to her. Her.

Who is 'her'? I started to tense up.

You promised to never tell anyone.

I promised.

She's as far as the ends of the earth, yet right in front of your eyes.

The suspense is killing me!

Her, she . . . A strange look came into Wang Gan's eyes. With a tone of longing, he said, She's my Little Lion.

Why write to her? Want to marry her or something?

You and your practical view of things! Wang Gan said emotionally. Little Lion, my dearest Little Lion, the one I want to love with all my youth, with my very life . . . my love, my true love, please forgive me, for I have already kissed your name a hundred times . . .

Cold chills and goose bumps were my only reaction. Wang Gan was obviously reciting his letter as he wrapped his arms around the trunk, face pressed tightly against the bark of the tree, tears in his eyes.

. . . I fell under your spell the first day I saw you at Xiaopao's house. From that moment till this very day, till the end of time, this heart of mine belongs to you only, and if you wished to eat it, I would unhesitatingly dig it out for you . . . I've fallen in love with your bright pink face, your lively nose, your soft lips, your fluffy hair, and your sparkling eyes; I've fallen in love with your voice, your smell, and your smile. Your laughter makes me dizzy, makes me want to fall to my knees, wrap my arms around your legs, and gaze up at your smiling face . . .

Fisherman Wang jerked his pole backward; beads of water dripped from the flashing brightness of his line, glistening like pearls in the sunlight. At the end of his hook a soft-shelled beige turtle the size of a tea bowl crashed to the ground, and was probably dizzy from the fall, lying on the ground looking skyward, its white underbelly exposed, four legs pawing the air, sad but awfully cute.

A turtle! Li Shou shouted gleefully.

Little Lion, my dearest, I am lowborn, the son of a farmer, while you are a doctor whose table is graced with top quality food. There's a chasm between our social standings, and you may not care to even take notice of me. After you finish my letter, only laughter will emerge from your lovely mouth before you tear it to shreds. Or maybe when it reaches you, you will toss it into a wastepaper basket unread. Nevertheless, I want to say to you, my dear, my dearest one, if you will accept my love, like a tiger with wings or a fine steed with a carved saddle, I will acquire unprecedented power and, as if boosted by an injection of blood from a young rooster, my spirit will be invigorated. There will be bread and milk; with your encouragement, I will improve my social status to stand with you as someone who, like you, subsists on marketable grains . . .

Hey, what are you two doing up there, reciting passages from novels? Li Shou shouted when he spotted us up in the tree.

. . . If you won't accept me, my dear, I'll not retreat, not give up, but will quietly follow you, trail you wherever you go, going down on my knees to kiss your footprints, I will stand outside your window to gaze at the lamplight inside, from first light to last – I want to turn into a candle and burn for you until there is nothing left of me. My dear, if I spit up blood and expire, I will be content if you favour me by coming to my gravesite for a brief look. If you can shed a tear for me, I will die with no regrets – your tears, my dear, a magic elixir that will bring me back from the dead . . .

The goose bumps on my arms were gone, and I was starting to be moved by his recitation of infatuation. I'd never dreamed he could fall for Little Lion and fall *that* hard, or that he had the literary talent to write such a plaintive letter. At that moment I felt that the doorway to adolescence was rumbling open for me, and that Wang Gan was leading the way. I knew nothing about love, but its splendour would draw me dashing recklessly towards it, like a moth to the flame.

The way you love her, I said, she has to love you back.

Do you think so? He gripped my hand, his eyes blazing. Will she really love me?

She will, absolutely. I gripped his hand back. If it doesn't happen, I'll ask my aunt to act as matchmaker. Little Lion will do anything she says.

No, he said, no, no, no. I don't want to rely on anyone else. A melon won't be sweet if you yank it off the vine. I want to win her heart with my own effort.

Li Shou looked up. What goofy stuff are you guys up to? he asked.

Fisherman Wang grabbed a handful of mud and threw it at us. You're scaring the fish with all that jabbering.

A motorised red and blue boat chugged towards us from downstream, the sound of its engine instilling in us a hard-to-describe sense of anxiety, panic even. The boat was straining against the rapid flow, its bow throwing up whitecaps and ploughing thin ridges right and left that filled back in little by little. A layer of blue mist floated atop the surface of the river, the smell of diesel fuel spread to our lips. A dozen seagulls glided along behind the boat.

The boat belonged to the commune's family-planning group, that is, Gugu's boat. Little Lion was aboard, of course. County officials had assigned the boat to Gugu to aid her in keeping residents from exceeding the family-planning quotas through illegal pregnancies and other unanticipated problems, and to keep the bright family-planning banner flying even when passage across the swamped stone bridge was interrupted during flood season. The small cabin had a pair of faux leather seats; a twelve-horsepower diesel motor was attached to the stern and loudspeakers were mounted on the bow to broadcast a lilting popular Hunan song, a paean to Chairman Mao that was soft on the ear. The bow turned towards our village and the music ended. A brief moment of silence intensified the motor noise. Then: The Great Chairman Mao has instructed us, Gugu announced hoarsely, that humanity must proceed with planned population growth . . .

Wang Gan went silent at the moment Gugu's boat hove into view. I saw that he was shaking, that his mouth hung open, that his moist eyes were fixed on the boat. As it passed by us it listed to one side, drawing a cry of alarm from Wang Gan. He tensed, and it seemed to me he might jump into the river. Farther up in the slow current, the boat turned and sped lightly towards us, the sound of its motor settling into a rhythmic hum. Gugu had arrived. So had Little Lion.

The boat was piloted by a familiar figure – Qin He. In the latter days of the Cultural Revolution, his older brother had been restored to the post of commune Party secretary, while he had been reduced to begging in the marketplace; no matter how civilised his begging methods were, he was as an embarrassment to his brother. We'd heard that he had asked his brother to assign him to work in the obstetrics ward at the commune health centre – You're a man, how can you work in an obstetrics ward? – There are lots of men in obstetrics wards – You have no medical skills – What do I need those for? – and so Qin He was made pilot of the family-planning boat. In the weeks and months that followed, he hardly ever left Gugu's side. On days when a boat was required, he went out onto the river; on other days he sat idly in the cabin.

His hair was parted down the middle, like the young men in movies set in the May Fourth period, and even in the dog days of summer he wore his blue gabardine student uniform, still with two pens in the breast pocket: a fountain pen and a two-colour ballpoint pen. His face seemed darker than the last time I'd seen him. He manoeuvred the boat slowly towards the riverbank, up near the twisted old willow. The motor slowed, ramping up the loudspeaker volume, making our ears ring. The commune had built a temporary pier west of the willow tree for the exclusive use of the family-planning boat. Crossbars had been fixed with wire to four thick posts in the water and overlaid by planks. After securing the boat to the pier, Qin He stood at the prow. The motor shut down and the loudspeakers went silent, reintroducing us to the splash of the river and the cries of gulls.

Gugu was first out of the cabin. The boat rocked, so did she. Qin He reached out to give her a hand but she pushed it away. She jumped onto the pier; though now on the heavy side, she was nimble as always. A bandage on her forehead emitted a harsh light.

Little Lion was next. Short and squat to begin with, she was dwarfed by the oversized medicine kit on her back. Though much younger than Gugu, her movements were clumsier. It was she who caused Wang Gan to wrap his arms tightly around the branch, his face pale, his eyes filling with tears.

Huang Qiuya was the third person to emerge. In the years since I'd last seen her, she'd become noticeably stooped; her head was thrust forward, her legs were no longer straight, and her movements were laboured. She rocked with the motion of the boat, arms in rapid motion to keep from losing her balance. All that kept her from crossing to the pier were legs that seemed incapable of leaving the boat. Qin He watched her impassively. No helping hand was offered. So she leaned forward and reached out to embrace the structure with both hands, like an orangutan, but stopped when Gugu said gruffly, Old Huang, why don't you stay aboard? Without even turning her head, she continued, Watch her carefully. Don't let her run off.

Gugu's order was directed at both Qin He and Huang Qiuya, since Qin immediately bent down to look inside the cabin. The sound of a woman's sobs soon emerged.

Once ashore, Gugu strode quickly along the riverbank heading east, Little Lion trotting to keep up with her. Blood had stained the bandage on Gugu's forehead. Her face was set, her gaze intense, her expression unrelentingly firm, almost menacing. Naturally, Wang Gan was not looking at Gugu; no, his gaze followed Little Lion. He was muttering something under his breath. I sort of felt sorry for him, but more than that I was moved. I could not understand how a man might lose his head over a woman.

We later learned that Gugu's injury had come as a result of being clubbed by a man who's wife was pregnant with their fourth child in Dongfeng Village, the birthplace of many bandits in the pre–Liberation era. The man, Zhang Quan, who had bovine eyes and a solid family background, was feared by all the men in the village. Every woman of child-bearing age in Dongfeng Village who had given birth twice had had their tubes tied off if one of them had been a son. If they'd had only girls, Gugu said she'd taken village customs into consideration, and chosen not to force the women to have their tubes tied; however, they were required to insert IUDs. After a third pregnancy, even if they were all girls, the tubes had to be tied. Zhang Quan's wife was the only woman in any of the more than fifty commune villages who had neither had her tubes tied nor used an IUD, and she was pregnant again. Gugu's boat had travelled to Dongfeng Village during a downpour expressly to get Zhang Quan's wife to go to the health centre for an abortion. While Gugu was on her way, Party Secretary Qin Shan phoned the branch secretary of Dongfeng Village, Zhang Jinya, ordering him to take all steps and use any force necessary to deliver Zhang Quan's wife to the health centre. When Gugu reached the village, Zhang Quan was standing guard at his gate with a spiked club; eyes red, he was shouting almost insanely. Zhang Jinya and a team of armed militiamen were watching from a distance, not daring to get close. Zhang's three daughters were kneeling in the doorway, noses running, tears flowing, as they cried out in what seemed to be practised unison: Merciful elders and uncles, mothers and aunts, brothers and sisters, spare our mother . . . she has a rheumatic heart. If she has an abortion she will die for sure – if she dies, we will be orphans.

Gugu said that the effects of Zhang Quan's sympathy-seeking ruse were excellent – many of the women watching were in tears. Of course, some were resentful. As women with two children and IUDs, or three without a son, had had their tubes tied, they had no sympathy for Zhang Quan's wife. A bowl of water must be carried level, Gugu said, and if we let Zhang Quan's wife have a fourth child, those women would skin me alive. If Zhang Quan prevailed, the red flag would be lowered, but that would be nothing compared to a halting in the progress of family planning. So I gave the signal, Gugu said, and walked up to Zhang Quan with Little Lion and Huang Qiuya. Smart, courageous, loyal Little Lion, moved in front of me in case Zhang used his club. I pulled her back behind me. The petty bourgeois intellectual, Huang Qiuya, was fine for a bit of technical help, but when push came to shove, she was so scared she nearly fell apart. Gugu strode straight up to Zhang. The language he used on me, she said, was worse than you could imagine, and if I repeated it, the words would dirty your ears and my mouth. But my heart was hard as steel then, and my personal safety was not a concern. Go ahead, Zhang Quan, call me any insulting thing you want – whore, bitch, murderous devil – I don't care. But your wife is going with me. Going where? To the health centre.

With eyes fixed on Zhang's savage face, she walked right up to him. His three daughters rushed up to her, cursing like their father, the two smaller ones holding on to Gugu's legs, while their oldest sister rammed her head into Gugu's midsection. All three were on her like leeches, and she tried to fight them off. A sharp pain in her knee, she knew, meant she'd been bitten. Another head to her midsection knocked her flat on her back. Little Lion grabbed the oldest girl by the neck and flung her to the side; but the girl came right back at her, driving her head into Little Lion's midsection, where her belt buckle hit her on the nose, which started to bleed. Seeing the blood on the back of her hand a moment later produced a mixture of terror and dread. As Zhang rushed to club Little Lion like a raving maniac, Gugu ran up and put herself between them. The club hit her forehead. She fell again. Are you people dead? Little Lion screamed at the onlookers. Zhang Jinya and his militiamen ran up and wrestled Zhang Quan to the ground, pinning his arms behind him. His daughters looked like they wanted to come to his aid, but they too were wrestled to the ground by Party women. Little Lion and Huang Qiuya wrapped a bandage from the medicine kit around

Gugu's head; blood seeped through the wrapping almost at once. They wrapped it some more. Gugu's head was spinning and her ears rang; she saw stars and everything took on the colour of blood; people's faces were as red as a cockscomb, even the trees seemed to blaze like torches.

Hearing what was happening, Qin He came over from the river and froze when he saw Gugu's injury. Then a howl burst from his lips, followed by a mouthful of blood. When people rushed up to help him, he pushed them away and staggered forward as if drunk, picking up the club, now stained with Gugu's blood, and raised it over Zhang's head. Put that down! Gugu shouted as she struggled to her feet. You're supposed to be watching the boat. What are you doing here? Making things worse. With a sheepish look, Qin He dropped the club and walked slowly back to the riverbank.

Gugu pushed Little Lion away and walked up to Zhang Quan, while Qin He was still howling as he walked towards the riverbank – Gugu was too focused on glaring at Zhang Quan to look behind her. The man was still cursing, but there was fear in his eyes now. Let him go, she said to the militiamen who held him by the arms. When they hesitated, she repeated herself. Let him go!

Give him back his club! she demanded.

One of the militiamen dragged the club up and tossed it down in front of Zhang.

Pick it up! Gugu said with a sneer.

Zhang mumbled, I'll fight anyone who tries to end the Zhang family line!

Fine! Gugu said. You're a brave man. She pointed to her head. Hit me here, she said, right here! She took a couple of steps closer. Me, she shouted, Wan Xin, this is the day I put my life on the line! Back when a little Japanese soldier came at me with a bayonet, I wasn't afraid, so why should I be afraid of you today?

Zhang Jinya came up and shoved Zhang Quan. Apologise to Chairwoman Wan!

I don't need his apology, Gugu said. Family planning is national policy. If we don't control our population, there won't be enough to feed and clothe our people, and a failure in education will lower the quality of our population, keeping the country weak. Sacrificing my life for national family planning is a small price to pay!

Zhang Jinya, Little Lion said, get on the phone and send for the police.

Zhang Jinya kicked Zhang Quan. On your knees! he demanded, and ask Chairwoman Wan for forgiveness.

Forget it! Gugu said. Zhang Quan, you could get three years in prison for hitting me, but I won't lower myself to your level, and I'm willing to let you go. There are two paths open to you now. You can have your wife go with me to the health centre for an abortion, where I will personally perform the procedure and guarantee that she comes through it safely. Or I can turn you over to the police for punishment; then, if your wife goes with me willingly, fine. If not – she pointed to Zhang Jinyan and the militiamen – they will take her there.

Zhang Quan was in a crouch, holding his head in his hands and sobbing. Three generations have had only one son each. Will I be forced to see that line ended? Open your eyes, Heaven . . .

Zhang Quan's wife walked out of the yard; she was weeping, and had straw in her hair. Obviously, she'd been hiding in a haystack.

Chairwoman Wan, be kind, forgive him. I'll go with you.

Gugu and Little Lion were heading east on the riverbank behind our village, probably to make a report at brigade headquarters. But as they entered the lane that would take them there, the woman on the boat – Zhang Quan's wife – came out of the cabin and jumped into the river. Qin He dived in after her, but since he did not know how to swim, he sank to the bottom. He managed to come up for air, but sank again. Help! Huang Qiuya screamed. Save them!

From our perch in the tree, we watched as Gugu and Little Lion turned back and ran to the river.

Wang Gan jumped nimbly into the river. Growing up on the banks of the river, we learned how to swim at about the same time we learned how to walk. The willow tree might as well have been set there for us to practise diving. I hoped that Little Lion had witnessed Wang Gan's beautiful dive. I followed him into the river. Li Shou dived in from the riverbank. We should have tried to save the pregnant woman first, but she was nowhere in sight. Poor Qin He was right there in front of us, thrashing in the water, like a fritter rolling in bubbling oil.

Grab his hair, Wang Gan's father alerted us, and watch out for his arms!

Wang Gan swam up behind him, reached out and grabbed him by the hair. He had a great head of hair. Wang Gan later said it was like a horse's mane.

Wang Gan was a better swimmer than any of us. He could ford the river holding his clothes over his head and reach the other bank without a drop of water on them. Being able to demonstrate his swimming skills in front of the woman of his dreams was a wonderful opportunity. Li Shou and I helped him, one on each side until Qin He was safely on the bank.

Gugu and Little Lion came running up.

You idiot, Gugu fumed. What were you trying to do?

Qin He was spread out on the ground, coughing up water.

Zhang Quan's wife jumped into the river, Huang Qiuya sobbed. He tried to save her.

Gugu paled. She turned her eyes to the river. Where is she?

She hit the water and disappeared, Huang Qiuya said.

I told you to watch her, didn't I? Gugu angrily jumped onto the boat. You might as well be dead, she said. This is on you! Start the boat, she ordered.

Little Lion was all thumbs as she tried to start the motor, but failed.

Qin He, Gugu shouted, get back here and start this thing!

Qin He got shakily to his feet, but bent over and threw up all the water inside him. He fell back to his knees.

Xiaopao, Wang Gan, try to save her, Gugu said. I'll reward you handsomely.

We looked over at the river and scoured it with our eyes.

The surface, broad and murky, carried foam and loose grass. Li Shou pointed at a watermelon rind on top of the water. Look over there, he said.

The rind glided along, occasionally rising out of the water on soggy strands of hair atop a head and neck.

Gugu sat down heavily on the side of the boat and breathed a sigh of relief. Then she burst out laughing.

Before we could dive in to make the rescue, she shouted, No hurry!

Can you swim? she asked Little Lion.

Little Lion shook her head.

Apparently, serving as a family-planning worker not only required being hit with a club, but swimming as well. She laughed as she pointed to the watermelon rind. See what a good swimmer she is? She's using the technique the guerrillas employed against the Japanese.

Qin He came on board, bent at the waist. He was soaked, his hair was a mess, his face was ghostly white, and his lips were blue.

Start the boat! Gugu ordered.

He turned the crank. Still woozy, he swayed and coughed a couple of times before spitting out a bubbly mouthful.

We let go of the ropes.

Climb aboard, Gugu said.

I could imagine what was going through Wang Gan's mind as he sat on the side near Little Lion. His hands were on his knees, all ten fingers quivering. I could see his heart beating under the wet undershirt stuck to his chest, like a caged rabbit banging against the bars. His body was so tense not a hair moved. Chubby Little Lion was oblivious to what was beside her, for her eyes were glued to the floating melon rind.

Qin He turned the bow away from the pier and the boat slipped forward, hugging the bank, its motor purring. Li Shou stood beside him studying his movements like an apprentice.

Go slow, Gugu said. That's right, now even slower.

When the bow was about five metres from the melon rind, the motor was slowed to just above the point of shutting down. Now we could all see the head of the pregnant woman under the melon rind.

She's good, Gugu said. Five months pregnant and still swimming that well.

Gugu sent Little Lion into the cabin to use the loudspeaker. The girl got up and slipped into the cabin at a semi-crouch. A void seemed to open up next to Wang Gan; a look of agony and loss showed on his face. What was he thinking at that moment? Had Little Lion already received the letter that showcased his prodigious talent?

My thoughts were all over the place when the loudspeaker erupted, scaring me, even though I'd known it was coming: The Great Leader Chairman Mao tells us we must control our population . . .

The pregnant woman pushed the melon rind off and showed her head. Startled into turning to look behind her, she quickly dove back under the surface. With a smile, Gugu told Qin He to keep the speed down. I want to see, she said softly, just how good a swimmer this Dongfeng Villager is. Little Lion emerged from the cabin and went up to the bow to gaze anxiously, and heaven answered Wang Gan's wish, as she moved close to him. I actually felt a tinge of jealousy. His skinny frame was right next to her. All that prominent solid flesh. I could imagine what he was feeling, sure that he could sense the warmth and softness of her body, that he could . . . With this thought my heart began to thump wildly, and I felt nothing but shame for having such dirty thoughts. I quickly looked away from them, thrust my hands in my pockets, and angrily pinched myself on the leg.

Her head! Little Lion shouted. There's her head!

The woman broke the surface about fifty metres from the boat and looked back as she stretched out and began swimming fast along with the current.

Gugu gave a sign to Qin He, who increased speed and began catching up with the pregnant swimmer. Gugu took a flattened pack of cigarettes from her pocket, removed one and stuck it between her lips. Then she thumbed her cigarette lighter until it lit. With her eyes half closed, she blew out a mouthful of smoke. A wind blew across the river, raising a series of turbid waves. I knew that no one could swim faster than a boat with a twelve-horsepower motor. A Hunan folk song in praise of Chairman Mao spewed from the loudspeaker: The Liuyang River bends nine times for ninety li to the River Xiang . . .

Gugu flipped the cigarette butt into the river; it was almost immediately snapped up by a gull that flew away with it.

The loudspeaker died out; the record had finished. Little Lion looked at Gugu, who said there was no need for more.

Geng Xiulian, Gugu shouted, do you think you can swim all the way back to the East China Sea?

No answer from the woman, who kept churning her arms, though she had slowed down considerably.

I wish you could be a little understanding, Gugu said, and come aboard so we can take care of things.

Stubborn resistance will get you nowhere, Little Lion steamed. Even if you *can* swim to the East China Sea, we'll be right behind you.

At that the woman began to cry, her arms still churning, her movements getting slower and slower.

Worn out? Little Lion laughed. Go ahead, swim if you're up to it. Kingfishers dive, frogs leap . . .

The woman's body was getting lower and lower in the water, and a stench of blood seemed to rise in the air with each breath she released. Gugu leaned down to get a good look. Uh-oh, she shouted. Hurry, get past her, Gugu ordered Qin He. Then she told us to dive in. Hold her up!

Wang Gan was first in the water, Li Shou and I were right behind him.

Qin He leaned the boat into the space beside her.

Wang Gan and I swam up to her. When I grabbed her left arm, she swung it over like an octopus tentacle and pushed my head under the water. I tried to shout and swallowed water. Wang Gan caught her by the hair and began towing her towards the bank. Li Shou grabbed her shoulders and lifted her up so I could come up for air. Everything was a blur as I was racked by violent coughs. The boat was just ahead of us. Qin He slowed down. My shoulder bumped against the hull; so did the woman's body. Gugu and the others leaned over the side, either catching hold of her hair or her arms, while we pushed her up by her bottom and legs. Everyone was shouting, and together we managed to get her into the boat.

Her leg was bleeding.

You boys don't need to come up. Just swim over to the bank. That said, Gugu spun around and said to Qin He, Quickly, turn this thing around and get moving. Fast!

In spite of the best medicines and finest treatment, Geng Xiulian died at the health centre.

6

The brigade leadership sent me an urgent telegram, informing me that Wang Renmei was pregnant again. I was told in no uncertain terms that as a Party member and a cadre, and with a certificate proving that my one child was a daughter, for which I received a monthly subsidy, my wife should not be pregnant with a second child. The news hit me like a bombshell. I was ordered to return home without delay and make sure the pregnancy was terminated.

My unanticipated appearance at home shocked everyone. My two-year-old daughter hid behind her grandmother and looked at me fearfully.

What are you doing here? Mother asked anxiously.

I'm on assignment and this was on the way.

Yanyan, this is your papa, Mother said as she pushed the girl towards me. Day in and day out you say you want your papa to come home, and now that he's here, you're afraid of him.

I reached out for her arm to hold her, but all that did was make her cry.

Mother sighed. We've been in constant fear, she said, and we tried to hide it. But the truth came out anyway.

How did it happen? I asked unhappily. Wasn't she fitted with an IUD?

She didn't tell me until she began to show, Mother said. When she knew you were coming home for a visit last time, she went to Yuan Sai and had him remove the device.

That bastard Yuan Sai! I cursed through clenched teeth. Doesn't he know that's against the law?

Don't report him, Mother said. Renmei begged him over and over, and even sent Wang Dan to plead her case, before he'd do it.

What a chance she took! Yuan Sai castrates animals. How could he have the nerve to remove one of those? What if something had happened?

He does it for lots of women, Mother said, keeping her voice low. Your wife said he was very skillful, that he plucked it right out with a metal hook.

Shameless, that's what it is!

Don't be so sensitive, Mother said. Wang Dan went with her, and Yuan Sai wore a surgical mask, dark glasses, and rubber gloves. He sterilised the hook first in alcohol and then by a flame to make sure it was safe. Your wife said she didn't even have to take off her pants. He just cut a little hole in the crotch, and that was it.

That's not what I meant.

Xiaopao, Mother said sadly, your two older brothers both have sons. You're the only one who doesn't, and that worries me. Why not let her have the baby?

I'd be willing to let her go through with it, but what if it isn't a boy?

It looks like a boy to me, Mother said. When I asked your daughter if her mother was carrying a little sister or a little brother, she said, A little brother! Words from a toddler are prophetic. Besides, even if it's a girl, she could be a help to you after Yanyan grows up, and you'll be protected if something should happen to her. I'm getting old, and once my eyes close for the last time, I won't know a thing. I'm just thinking about you.

Mother, I said, there are rules in the army. If I have a second child, I'll lose my Party membership and my army commission, and I'll be sent home to tend fields. I struggled for years to leave the village, and having a second child isn't worth giving all that up.

Are Party membership and a commission more precious than a child? It takes people to make a world. If you have no one to carry on the line, what good does it do to become a high official, even if you're second only to Chairman Mao?

Chairman Mao has been dead for a long time, I said.

Do you think I don't know he's dead? I was just making a point.

The door opened with a bang. Ma, Yanyan shouted, my papa's home!

I watched the girl totter on tiny legs up to her mother. Renmei was wearing the grey jacket I'd worn before going into the army. She was definitely showing. A red bundle, from which bits of coloured cloth peeked out, hung from the crook of her arm. She bent down and picked our daughter up. Well, now, Xiaopao, what are you doing home? she asked with an exaggerated smile.

Can't I return to my own home? You've really done it this time, I said testily.

Her face, covered with dark 'pregnancy spots', paled, then immediately turned bright red. What have I done? she asked, raising her voice. I'm out in the field during the day and take care of our daughter at night. I haven't done anything I shouldn't have.

Don't start splitting hairs. Why did you go see Yuan Sai behind my back? Why didn't you say anything to me?

Traitor! Turncoat! Renmei put down the child and stormed into the bedroom, nearly tripping over a stool, which she sent flying with her foot. Who betrayed me by telling you?

Our daughter was wailing outside.

Mother was sitting by the stove weeping.

Stop bawling and cursing, and go with me to the health centre to take care of this, and that'll be the end of it.

Don't even think it! she yelled as she flung a hand mirror to the floor. It's my child, in my belly, and I'll hang myself from the door of anyone who tries to harm it.

Xiaopao, why not forget about Party membership and being an officer, and come home to work the field? There's no more people's commune, so we can work our own land and have more food than we can possibly eat. You'll be free. I think you should come home . . .

No, absolutely not!

Renmei was tossing things around in the bedroom, making a racket.

This isn't only about me, I said. Our unit's reputation is at stake.

Renmei came out of the room with a large bundle. I stopped her. Where do you think you're going?

None of your business!

I tugged on her bundle to keep her from leaving. She whipped out a pair of scissors and pointed them at her abdomen. Her eyes were red. Let go of that! she demanded shrilly.

Xiaopao! Mother yelled.

I knew what Renmei was capable of.

Go, then, I said. You might be able to get through today, but not tomorrow. One way or the other, that's coming out.

Bundle in hand, she rushed out the door. Our daughter tried to follow her, arms spread out in front, but tripped and fell. Renmei ignored her.

I ran outside and picked the child up. She fought me and cried for her mother. With a welter of thoughts running through my mind, my tears began to fall.

Cane in hand, Mother hobbled out into the yard. Let her have the child, Son, she said. If you don't, I don't know how we'll get through the days . . .

7

That night my daughter cried for her mother and nothing I did could pacify her. Check out Grandma's house, Mother said, so I carried the girl over to my in-laws' house and knocked on the door. Wan Xiaopao, my father-in-law said through a crack, my daughter became a member of *your* family when she married you. Who are you looking for here? If something has happened to my daughter, I'll be your worst enemy.

I went to see Chen Bi. His gate was locked and the yard was pitch-black. Next I went to see Wang Gan, and pounded so long at the door the puppy on the other side set up a frenzy of barking. A light went on, and Wang Jiao came out to stand at the gate, his club dragging on the ground. Who are you looking for? He sounded angry.

It's me, Uncle.

I know it's you. Who are you looking for?

Where's Wang Gan?

Dead! He slammed the door shut.

Wang Gan wasn't dead, I knew that, but then I recalled that on my previous visit home, Mother mumbled something about Wang Jiao kicking his son out of the house, and that he was reduced to roaming the area, occasionally seen in the village, though no one knew where he was living.

My daughter cried herself out and fell asleep in my arms. I held her as I walked the streets, unable to dispel my glum feeling. Two years earlier the village had been electrified, and a streetlight had been installed alongside a pair of loudspeakers high atop a concrete pole behind the headquarters of the village committee. Several youngsters were standing around a pool table with a blue velvet surface under the light, noisily enjoying a game. A five- or six-year-old boy was sitting on a stool nearby, playing a basic keyboard. A glance at his face told me it was Yuan Sai's son.

Not long before, a broad gate had been built in front of Yuan Sai's house across the street. After some hesitation, I decided to go talk to him, but the thought of him removing Renmei's IUD made me very uncomfortable. If he'd been a real doctor, I'd have had nothing to say. But . . . damn!

He was surprised to see me. Sitting alone on the edge of his kang, he was drinking and snacking on small plates of peanuts and dried anchovies, plus a large plate of fried eggs. Barefoot, he jumped to the floor and told me to sit by him, and wouldn't take no for an answer. He called to his wife for more food. Another classmate of ours, she had a face marked by light pocks, and we all called her Sesame Twist.

Not a bad living you've got here, I said as I sat down. Sesame Twist reached out to take my sleeping daughter and lay her down at the head of the kang. I demurred briefly before letting her take her.

His wife scrubbed the wok and lit a fire to fry a ribbonfish to go with the liquor. None for me, I said, but the oil was already crackling, filling the air with its fragrance.

Yuan Sai insisted that I take off my shoes and climb up onto the kang. I made the excuse that it would be too much trouble since I was only going to stay a minute. But he insisted, so I gave in.

What brings you here, my esteemed friend? he asked after pouring me a glass. What are you now? Battalion commander? Regiment commander?

Shit, I said. A crummy company commander. I picked up the glass and drained it. And I won't be that for long. I'll be back ploughing a field pretty soon.

What does that mean? He too drained his glass. You're the classmate with the brightest future. Xiao Xiachun and Li Shou might be in college – that asshole Xiao Shangchun parades up and down the streets bragging about how his son has been given a job with the State Council – but neither one is your equal. Xiao Xiachun has broad cheeks and a narrow forehead and his ears are pointed, the spitting image of a yamen runner. Li Shou is good-looking, but good luck isn't in the cards for him. But you, you've got long legs and powerful arms, and eyes like a phoenix or a dragon. If not for the mole beneath the right eye, you'd have the look of an emperor. Have that removed by laser, and though you might not make it to general or minister, you'll go at least as high as a division commander.

That's enough, I said. You can BS people in the marketplace if you want, but stop talking like that to me.

Those are prophetic signs, I'm telling you, knowledge that's been passed down by our ancestors, Yuan Sai said.

Like I said, that's enough bullshit. I'm here to get even for what you did to me.

What did I do? I've never done anything to you.

Who told you to remove Wang Renmei's IUD without my knowledge? I forced myself to keep my voice down. Some busybody sent a telegram to my unit, which ordered me back home to take her in for an abortion. If I don't, I'll lose my commission and my Party membership. Now, Renmei has run away, so what do you recommend?

Who fed you that line? Yuan Sai rolled his eyes and spread his hands. When was I supposed to have removed Wang Renmei's IUD? I'm a fortune-teller who calculates fortunes by numbers, yin and yang, good and evil, and feng shui. That's what I do. Why would an ageing man like me get involved in removing IUDs? What you're saying might not seem inauspicious to you, but it is.

No more games, I said. Everyone knows that Little Immortal is a man of many talents. Feng shui and fortune-telling may be 'what you do', but you have time left over to geld animals and remove IUDs. I'm not going to take you to court for what you did, but I'm not going to let you off the hook either. Before you removed Wang Renmei's IUD, you should have checked with me.

I'm innocent, this is slander! Yuan Sai insisted. Bring Wang Renmei here to face me, and we'll see what she says.

She ran off, and I don't know where she's gone. Besides, would she admit it? Would she rat you out?

Xiaopao, you son of a bitch, you're not just anybody, you're an army officer, and you have to stand by what you say. How dare you accuse me of removing your wife's IUD. Got any proof? You've besmirched my reputation, and I'll sue you if you make me mad enough.

All right, what it's come down to is . . . I'm not blaming you. What I'd like from you is advice. The way things are now, what do you think I ought to do?

Yuan Sai shut his eyes, rubbed his fingers together, and began to mutter. Then his eyes snapped open. Worthy brother, he said, great joy!

How's that?

Your wife's pregnancy is the reincarnation of an important individual in the last dynasty. Since great secrets must not be divulged, I cannot tell you the individual's name, but I can give you four lines you mustn't forget: When the child is born, one, he'll have a fine physique; two, he'll accomplish great deeds; three, he'll rise to unprecedented heights; and four, he'll be invested with all the trappings of authority!

Weave your fairytales, I said, though what I heard filled me with a hard-to-describe happiness. Yes, indeed, if she could bear a son like that . . .

Yuan Sai had no trouble reading my mind. With what appeared to be a smile, he said, Heaven's will cannot be transgressed.

I shook my head. But if Renmei has the baby, my days are over.

There's an old saying: Heaven always leaves a door open.

So tell me.

You send a telegram to your unit saying she's not pregnant, that it was a rumour begun by someone who has it in for you.

Is that what you consider a foolproof plan? I said with a sneer. Do you think you can carry paper in fire? Once the child is born, what about registering for residence? How about school?

Why think so far ahead, good brother? Just having the child is a victory. Policy enforcement is strict around here. Other counties are rife with 'bootleg kids'. There's no more collective and everyone has plenty to eat. Go ahead and raise the kid. We're all citizens of the People's Republic of China, and you can't tell me that the country will declare him a non-citizen.

But if word gets out, won't that be the end of my career?

Then there's nothing I can do for you. Only one end of the sugar cane is sweet.

Damn that bitch, she needs a serious beating. I finished what was in my glass and got down off the kang. She's the cause of all my rotten luck.

Don't say that, good brother. I've looked at both your fortunes, and I tell you, Wang Renmei was born to help her husband achieve great things. Your successes will come from her.

Help her husband? Ruin her husband is more like it. I smiled coldly.

The worst that can happen is for Wang Renmei to have the child and you give up your career to come home and tend your field. What's wrong with that? In twenty years, your son will rise high in the world, and you'll live the enviable, comfortable life of a gentleman farmer. Isn't that something to look forward to?

I wouldn't be so upset if she'd told me beforehand, I said, but how am I supposed to swallow this sort of deceit?

No matter what you say, Xiaopao, the child in Wang Renmei's belly is yours, and whether it lives or dies is up to you.

You're right there, it is up to me, and I want to remind you that all walls have holes. You need to be careful.

I took the sleeping child from Yuan Sai's wife and started walking out. As I was saying goodbye to her, she said softly, Let her have the baby, good brother. I'll help you find a secret place to do it.

A Jeep was parked outside Yuan Sai's gate. A pair of policemen got out and stormed through the gate. Sesame Twist tried to stop them, but they pushed her out of the way and swooped into the house. Smacking sounds and Yuan Sai's screams emerged, followed a few minutes later by Yuan Sai himself, handcuffed and wearing his shoes with the backs stepped on, in the custody of the police.

Why are you arresting me? he protested, his head cocked to look at one of his escorts. What did I do?

Knock it off, the policeman ordered. Why are we arresting you? You know better than anybody.

Xiaopao, you have to get me out. I haven't broken any laws!

A heavy-set woman stepped out of the car.

Gugu!

She removed her hospital mask and said coldly, Come see me at the health centre tomorrow.

8

Let her have the baby, Gugu, I said sadly. I no longer want my Party membership or my commission . . .

She banged the table with her hand, sending water splashing over the sides of the glass in front of me.

What a misfit you are, Xiaopao! This isn't just about you. For three years the commune has not had a single case of exceeding the birth quota. Are you going to be the one to ruin our record?

But she's tried to kill herself more than once, I said with difficulty. What if she goes through with it?

With a cold look, she said, You know local policy where that's concerned? Don't hide the bottle if they want to take poison, give them a rope if they want to hang themselves.

That's cruel!

You think that's what we want? You don't need cruelty in the army, and you don't need it in the cities; you especially don't need it in foreign countries – all foreign women want is to enjoy themselves. They don't have children in response to government encouragement, not even if they're rewarded for having them. But this is rural China and we're dealing with peasants. We can reason with them, we can talk about policy, we can wear out shoe leather and talk ourselves hoarse, and will they listen to us? No. So what do we do? We have no choice but to control population growth, carry out national policy, and meet our superiors' goals. So what do we do? Those of us involved with family planning are reviled during the day and are the targets of missiles when we're out walking at night – even five-year-old children jab our legs with awls. Gugu rolled up a pant leg to show me a large purple scab. See that? A cross-eyed little bastard in Dongfeng Village did that to me a few days ago. You haven't forgotten what happened with Zhang Quan's wife, have you? – I shook my head, recalling the incident in the surging river a decade or more before – she jumped into the river and we pulled her out, but Zhang Quan and his fellow villagers insisted that we pushed Geng Xiulian into the river, where she drowned. They wrote a letter, signing it in blood, that went all the way to the State Council, and in the end we were forced to sacrifice Huang Qiuya.

Gugu lit a cigarette and puffed so hard her sad features were swathed in a cloud of smoke. She'd gotten old, with deep wrinkles at the sides of her mouth, bags under her eyes, and a clouded look – we did everything humanly possible to save Zhang's wife, including giving her some of my own blood, but she had a heart condition. In the end, we gave Zhang Quan a thousand yuan, which was a lot of money at the time. But even after taking the money he wouldn't let us off the hook. He carried his wife's body on a flatbed cart, followed by his three daughters in funeral hemp, to the offices of the county Party committee when the provincial head of the family-planning committee was in town on an inspection tour. The police sent a beat-up old Jeep to deliver Huang Qiuya, Little Lion and me to the county guesthouse. The police were surly and crude, and the way they manhandled us, you'd have thought we were criminals. The county officials wanted to talk to me, but I stiffened my neck and refused, saying I'd only talk to the provincial authority. So I walked unannounced into the visitors' room, where he was reading a newspaper in an easychair. One look and I knew, it was Yang Lin! Now a fair-skinned deputy governor with a healthy complexion. I was furious, and the words came out like machine-gun fire – *pow pow pow pow*. You people up there send down your orders, and we down here run our legs off and talk till our lips split open. You want us to be civilised, talk policy, and work on the ideological state of the masses . . . while you stand there giving orders, suffering no back pain and, since you don't bear children, you don't know how a woman hurts! Why don't you come down and see what's happening, see how we work like dogs so we can be cursed, beaten black and blue, our heads bloodied, and then, if some little problem arises, instead of backing us up, you take sides with hooligans and shrews! You cast a chill over us – here pride crept into Gugu's monologue – other people might shy from talking to high officials, but not me! When I see a high official I really start talking – it's not that I'm a great talker, but that I've got a bellyful of bile. I was crying the whole time I talked to him, and I stopped to show him the scar on my head. Did Zhang Quan break the law when he hit me with his club? Did jumping into the river to save his wife and giving her my own blood count as doing everything called for by humanity and duty? By then, I was really bawling. Go ahead, send me to a re-education camp, throw me in jail, but I'm through! Tears were welling in Yang Lin's eyes. He got up to pour me some water and went to the bathroom to get me a moist, hot towel. Work at the grassroots level is hard, he said. Chairman Mao said: Educating the peasant masses is critical. You have suffered, Comrade Wan. I know that, and so do the county officials. We have a high opinion of you. He came over and sat beside me. How would you like to come work for me in provincial headquarters, Comrade Wan? I knew exactly what he was getting at, but when I thought back to all those terrible things he'd said at the public denouncement rally, my heart cooled. No, I said firmly, that's not for me. I'm needed here. In a somewhat rueful tone, he said, Then how about a move to the county health centre? No, I said, I'm staying put. Maybe I should have gone with him, Gugu said, just up and left. What you can't see doesn't bother you. If people want babies, let them go ahead and have them. Two billion, three billion, when the sky falls, the tall people can hold it up. Why should I worry about any of this? I've suffered all my life from being too compliant, too revolutionary, too loyal, and too serious about things.

It's not too late to come to your senses, I said.

What the hell does that mean? she spat angrily. Come to my senses? I've just been venting to a member of my own family, a little private bitching. Your aunt is a steadfastly loyal Communist who did not waver when she was being brutalised during the Cultural Revolution, so why would she now? No, family planning is absolutely essential. If we let people have all the babies they want, that's thirty million a year, three hundred million a decade. At that rate, in fifty years the Chinese population alone would flatten the earth. So we must lower the birth rate, no matter what it costs. That will be China's greatest contribution to humanity.

I understand what you're saying, Gugu, I said, but my immediate problem is, Renmei has run off . . .

She can run but she can't hide. Where could she go? She's hiding in your father-in-law's house.

Renmei has a stubborn streak, and if she's pushed too far, I'm afraid she might do something stupid . . .

You can stop worrying. I've come up with a plan. I've fought it out with women like her for decades, and I know exactly how they think. They're all talk, and she won't kill herself. She likes living too much. It's the quiet ones who might hang themselves or take poison. In all my years working with family planning, the women who kill themselves do so for some other reason, so you have nothing to worry about.

Then what do I do? I said, still troubled. I can't truss her up like a pig and drag her to the hospital.

We may have to get tough with her, Gugu said, especially since it's your wife. Being my nephew is your bad luck, because if I let her go ahead, how am I going to deal with the masses? They'd be on me as soon as I opened my mouth.

I have no choice but to do as you say, I said. Should I bring members of my unit to help out?

I've already sent your unit a telegram.

Was it you who sent the first telegram?

Yes, it was me.

Since you knew early on that she was pregnant, why didn't you take care of it then?

I didn't know till I returned from attending two months of meetings in the county capital. That bastard Yuan Sai, she sputtered, all he ever gives me is trouble. Fortunately, someone reported him. That will save us trouble later on.

Will he be punished?

If I had my way, they'd shoot him! she said angrily.

I doubt that Renmei was the only one.

We have a handle on this. There's your wife, the wife of Wang Qi at Wang Clan hamlet, the wife of Jin Niu in Sun Family Village, and Wang Dan, Chen Bi's wife – she's the farthest along. There are another dozen or so in other counties, but they're not our concern. We'll start with your wife, and then the rest, one after the other. No one will get away.

What if they leave the province?

Gugu sneered. Even the magical monkey Sun Wukong could not escape from the Buddha's palm.

I'm in the army, Gugu, so Renmei should have the procedure. But Wang Dan and Chen Bi are farmers, and their first child was a girl. According to policy, they can have a second. She's so tiny that getting pregnant is always hard . . .

Gugu cut me off with a taunt: You haven't taken care of your own problem, so what are you doing speaking up for them? The policy is that they can have a second child, but only after the first child's eighth birthday. How old is their daughter, Chen Er?

It's only a matter of a few years, I said.

How glib that sounds, Gugu said sombrely. Just a few years early, but what if everyone was just a few years early? This would be a terrible precedent, it'd make a mess of things. Forget about other people. You've got problems of your own.

9

Gugu led a special family-planning team into our village. Her second-in-command was the deputy commander of the armed police bureau. In addition to Little Lion, the team consisted of half a dozen brawny militiamen. They arrived in a van equipped with a loudspeaker and a powerful caterpillar tractor.

But before the team entered the village, I knocked on my father-in-law's gate for the second time. This time he allowed me in.

You were in the army too, I said to him. There we do as we're told. Disobeying an order is not an option.

He mulled over what I said as he smoked a cigarette. If you knew she couldn't have another child, he said finally, then why let her get pregnant? How is she supposed to have an abortion so late in her pregnancy? What if she doesn't get through it? She's my daughter, the only one I have.

Don't blame me for this.

Then who should I blame?

If you're looking for someone to blame, look no further than that bastard Yuan Sai. He's already under arrest.

I'm telling you now that if anything happens to my daughter, I'll come looking for you and will put these old bones on the line.

My aunt says there's no problem. She says they've even done it at seven months.

Your aunt isn't a human being, she's a demon! my mother-in-law jumped in. How many lives has she destroyed over the past few years? Her hands are covered in blood, and when she dies the King of Hell is going to chop her into pieces.

What good does saying things like that do? my father-in-law said. This is men's business.

How can it be men's business? she asked shrilly. They want to push our daughter down to the gates of Hell. How is that men's business?

I'm not going to argue with you, Mother, I said. Tell Renmei to come out here. I need to talk to her.

Why are you looking for her here? She's a member of your family now and that's where she lives. What have you done to her? Give her back to me!

Hear that, Renmei? I said loudly. I had a talk with Gugu yesterday. I told her I planned to give up my Party membership and my commission and take up farming again so you can have the child. She told me I can't do that. That business with Yuan Sai has shaken things up all the way up to the provincial government, and county authorities gave her an order that all illegal pregnancies in her area had to be terminated.

We won't allow it! my mother-in-law shrieked as she flung a basin full of dirty water at me. What kind of society are we living in? Tell that slut of an aunt to come here and we'll have it out once and for all! She can't have babies, and seeing others have them makes her mad. She's jealous.

I left the house, drenched in filthy water.

When the work team van stopped outside my in-laws' house, every able-bodied villager showed up, including Xiao Shangchun, who'd suffered a stroke, and hobbled up, aided by a cane. Impassioned speech spewed from the loudspeaker: Family planning is a high priority, it impacts the nation's future and that of the people . . . it is essential for a country capable of implementing the four modernisations to control and improve the quality of its population . . . those with illegal pregnancies must not trust to luck to slip through the net . . . the people's eyes are bright. You can hide in caves or deep in a forest, but you will not get away . . . anyone who attacks family-planning personnel will be punished as counter-revolutionaries . . . anyone who subverts family planning by whatever means will be severely punished under Party and state law . . .

Gugu took the lead, followed by the deputy bureau chief, with Little Lion bringing up the rear. My father-in-law's door was shut tight. A couplet pasted on the gate read: *Our rivers and mountains have prospered for millennia/Eternal spring graces the fatherland*. Gugu turned and said to the crowd behind her, Without family planning, the face of the nation will change, the fatherland will collapse. Then where will we find prosperity for the millennia? Where will we seek an eternal spring? Gugu rapped the metal knocker and shouted in her characteristically raspy voice, Wang Renmei, did you really think you could fool me by hiding in the potato cellar by the pigpen? The county Party committee and the army have been alerted to your case, and you have set a bad example. There are two paths you can take from here: you can come out of there on your own and go with me to the health centre to terminate your pregnancy. Since you are so far along, we will accompany you, and our most experienced doctor will perform the procedure. Or you can be defiant, in which case the tractor will pull down the houses of your parents' neighbours on all sides, then pull down your parents' house. Your father will have to cover all your neighbours' losses. Even after that, we will still terminate your pregnancy. If it were someone else, I would treat her with kindness, but not you. Have you heard me, Wang Renmei? How about you, Wang Jinshan and Wu Xiuzhi? Gugu made a point of calling Renmei's parents by name.

Nothing stirred on the other side of the gate for a long moment. Then a young rooster crowed. My mother-in-law's voice was next: Wan Xin, you black-hearted, inhumane monster . . . a bad death awaits you . . . after you die, you'll have to climb a mountain of knives and boil in hot oil, your skin will be peeled, your eyes will be gouged out, and you'll burn from head to toe.

With a snicker, Gugu turned to the deputy militia chief. Go ahead, she said.

He had his men drag a long, thick cable up to the gate of the neighbour to the east and wrap it around an old scholar tree. With his hand on his cane, Xiao Shangchun bounded out of the crowd and jabbered at the top of his lungs: That's our family's tree! He tried to hit my aunt with his cane, but lost his balance in the attempt. So, this is your tree, Gugu said coldly. My apologies, but you seem to have chosen you neighbour poorly.

You're all local bandits . . . a bunch of Guomindang operatives . . .

The Guomindang curses us as 'Commie bandits', Gugu said with a cruel smile. Calling us local bandits shows you're not in the same league as the Guomindang.

I'm going to sue you people . . . my son works in the State Council.

Go ahead and sue, all the way to the top if you can manage.

Xiao Shangchun threw down his cane and wrapped his arms around the scholar tree. You can't pull my tree down, he said tearfully. Yuan Sai said that this tree carries the lifeblood of my family; if it flourishes, so does my family . . .

Gugu laughed. I wonder if Yuan Sai calculated when he'd be arrested.

You'll have to kill me first, Xiao bawled.

Xiao Shangchun, Gugu said sternly, what's happened to the ferocity you displayed when you were beating and making life miserable for people during the Cultural Revolution? Look at you, crying and snivelling like an old woman.

You can't fool me, I know you're exploiting your public office for personal gain . . . plotting revenge against me . . . it's your niece with the illegal pregnancy, so how can you pull down my tree . . .

Not just your tree, Gugu said. When it's down, we're going to pull down your gate arch, and then your house. Crying out here won't do you any good. You should go see Wang Jinshan. Gugu took the bullhorn from Little Lion and directed it at the crowd. All you neighbours of Wang Jinshan, listen carefully. In accordance with special regulations issued by the commune family-planning committee, since Wang Jinshan is shielding his daughter, who is maintaining an illegal pregnancy in defiance of the government, and insulting authorised workers, we will now pull down the houses of his neighbours on all sides. You can go to Wang Jinshan to recoup your losses. If you do not want your houses to be destroyed, now is the time to persuade him to have his daughter come out.

My father-in-law's neighbours erupted in a chorus of shouts.

Carry out the order, Gugu said to the deputy militia chief.

The caterpillar tractor roared into action, making the ground beneath our feet tremble.

The steel beast began to move, slowly picking up the slack in the cable, which sang out as it tautened. The leaves on the tree started to flutter.

Xiao Shangchun ran as fast as his limping leg would take him up to my father-in-law's gate, where he pounded like a madman. Wang Jinshan, you and your fucking ancestors are the scourge of your neighbours. You will not die well!

In his anxiety, his garbled speech inexplicably turned clear.

The only sounds on the other side of the gate were the heartbreaking howls of my mother-in-law.

Gugu raised her arm for the sake of the deputy militia chief and then made a chopping motion.

Step on it! the man shouted to the driver.

The roar of the tractor thudded against eardrums, the cable stretched taut enough to cut into the bark of the tree, from which sap oozed. Inch by inch the tractor moved ahead, sending blue smoke spurting into the sky from the vertical exhaust pipe up front. The driver, who was wearing blue canvas overalls, a white towel around his neck and a duckbill cap, kept looking back, biting his lip under a black moustache. He had the look of a model worker. The tree creaked as it began to list, such a sad sound. The cable had bitten deeply into the trunk, white wood showing as chunks of the bark broke off.

Get your arse out here, Wang Jinshan! Xiao Shangchun was pounding on the gate with his fists, hitting it with his knees, and butting it with his head. Now even my mother-in-law's sobs had stopped.

The tree leaned, farther and farther, its canopy of leaves fluttering to the ground.

Xiao Shangchun staggered over to the tree. My tree . . . my family's bloodline tree . . .

Roots were moving just below the surface.

Xiao Shangchun struggled back to my father-in-law's gate. Wang Jinshan, you son of a bitch, we've been neighbours, good ones, for decades, almost becoming relatives, and now you want to destroy us.

The roots were now exposed, like light yellow pythons, moaning as they felt the air. Some snapped in two, others grew longer and longer, all those underground pythons . . . The leafy umbrella swept the ground like a gigantic broom, willowy branches splintered as they bent down and raised eddies of dirt. The bystanders sniffed the air, which carried the smells of fresh soil and tree sap.

Wang Jinshan, I'll split my head open at your door, damn you! Xiao banged his head against the gate. We heard nothing, not because his head produced no sound, but because it was swallowed up by the roar of the tractor.

The tree was dragged a dozen metres away from Xiao Shangchun's house, leaving a gaping hole with torn roots where it had once stood. Children were already digging to find young cicadas.

My aunt announced through the battery-operated bullhorn, Next we will pull down Xiao Shangchun's gate arch.

People carried Xiao over to the side, where they pinched the spot beneath his nose and massaged his chest.

Neighbours of Wang Jinshan, take notice – Gugu spoke calmly – go to your homes to gather up your valuables. After we pull down Xiao Shangchun's house, we're coming for yours. I know this seems unreasonable, but lesser reason must give way to greater reason. And what is that? Family planning, controlling our population growth. I'm not afraid to be the villain, someone has to be. I know you all want me to die and go straight to Hell. Well, we Communists don't believe in such places, and materialists have nothing to fear. And I wouldn't be afraid even if there were such a place. Who would go to Hell if not me? Remove the cable from the tree and affix it to Xiao Shangchun's gate arch!

All my father-in-law's neighbours rushed in and began kicking and pounding on his gate. They threw bricks and tiles into his yard. Someone even brought over some dry corn stalks to stand up under the eaves. Wang Jinshan, he yelled, if you don't come out, we'll set your house on fire!

Finally the gate opened. Standing there was neither my father-in-law nor my mother-in-law; it was my wife. Her hair was a mess, she was covered in mud and dirt, and she had on only one shoe – the left. She'd obviously just crawled out of the cellar.

Gugu, she said as she walked up to my aunt, isn't it enough that I go with you?

I always knew that my nephew's wife had a profound understanding of right and wrong, Gugu said with a smile.

I have to give you credit, Renmei said. If you were a man, you could command an army.

Just like you, Gugu said. When you broke the marriage contract with the Xiao family back then, I knew you were an exceptional woman.

Renmei, I said, this has been hard on you.

Let me see your hand, Xiaopao, she said.

I reached out my hand, not knowing what she wanted with it.

She grabbed it and took a bite out of my wrist.

I didn't pull my hand back.

Dark blood seeped from two rows of teeth marks on my wrist.

She spat on the ground. You're making me bleed, she said spitefully, so I did the same to you.

I offered her my other hand.

She pushed it away. I don't want it, you taste like a smelly dog!

Xiao Shangchun had come to and was pounding the ground and bawling like an old woman: Wang Renmei, Wan Xiaopao, you owe me a tree . . . you have to pay me!

I'll pay you shit! my wife shot back. Your son rubbed his hands all over my breasts and kissed me on the mouth. That tree is payment for the theft of my innocence!

Ow! Ow! Ow! A bunch of half-grown youngsters shouted their approval of my wife's comeback.

Renmei! I called out angrily.

What are you bellowing about? She climbed into Gugu's car, stuck her head out the window, and said: He felt me through my clothes!

10

Chairwoman Yang of our unit's family-planning committee arrived. She was the daughter of a high-ranking military officer, a division commander. Her name was familiar, but this was the first time I'd seen her.

The commune leadership held a banquet for her; she asked that Wang Renmei and I attend.

Gugu dug up a pair of leather shoes for Renmei.

The banquet was held in a private room in the commune's dining hall.

I think I'll stay home, Xiaopao, Renmei said. I'm afraid of meeting high-ranking officials. Besides, this has been nothing to be proud of, turning the world upside down and all.

Gugu smiled. What's there to be afraid of? Even the highest official has only one nose and two eyes.

Chairwoman Yang invited Renmei and me to sit next to her at the table. Taking Renmei by the hand, she said cordially, Comrade Wang, I want to thank you on behalf of the army.

What I did was wrong, Madam Chairwoman, Renmei said, obviously moved. I caused you trouble.

I'd been afraid that Renmei would say something offensive, and was relieved to hear her speak with such civility.

My nephew's wife is a woman of high consciousness who became pregnant by accident and asked me to have the pregnancy terminated,

Gugu lied. Her frailty was the reason we waited so long to perform the procedure.

Young man, Chairwoman Yang said, it's you I need to criticise. All you male comrades are careless, hoping to be lucky not to impregnate your wives.

I nodded in agreement.

The Party secretary stood up, glass in hand. Join me in thanking Chairwoman Yang for taking time out of her busy schedule to instruct us on our work, he said.

I'm familiar with this area, she said. My father fought a guerrilla war here during the Jiao River campaign. His command post was in this very village. That's why I feel so comfortable here.

That pleases us a great deal, the Party secretary said. I hope the chairwoman will take a message back to our elderly leader, expressing our wish that he personally come to inspect our work one day.

Gugu stood up and held out her glass. Here's to you, Chairwoman Yang.

Chairwoman Wan is the daughter of a martyr, the Party secretary said. She followed her father into the revolution when she was still very young.

Chairwoman Yang, Gugu said, there is a bond between you and me. My father, who headed the Eighth Route Army's Xihai Hospital and was a student of Norman Bethune, treated Vice Commander Yang's leg wound.

Really? Chairwoman Yang stood up excitedly. My father is writing a memoir, and in it he mentions a doctor Wan Liufu.

My father, Gugu said. After he died, my mother and I lived for two years in the Eastern Jiao liberated area, where I played with a girl named Yang Xin.

Chairwoman Yang grabbed Gugu's hand as tears of excitement welled up in her eyes. Wan Xin, is that you?

Wan Xin, Yang Xin, two hearts. Isn't that what Chairman Zhong said?

Yes, it was him, Yang said as she wiped away the tears. I dream of you often, but I never expected to actually see you here.

As soon as I saw you I thought you looked familiar, Gugu said.

Come, everyone, the Party secretary announced, join me in congratulating Chairwoman Yang and Chairwoman Wan on their exciting reunion.

Gugu flashed me a signal with her eyes, which I immediately understood. I took Renmei's hand and went up to Yang. Chairwoman, I said, I owe you an apology for making it necessary for you to make a special trip here.

I'm so sorry, Chairwoman Yang, Renmei said with a bow. Don't blame Xiaopao for this, it was all my fault. I poked a hole in a condom when he wasn't looking.

Momentarily taken aback, Chairwoman Yang then laughed heartily.

My face was burning. That's nonsense, I said as I nudged her.

Yang took Renmei's hand and regarded her closely. Comrade Wang, she said, I like candid, open people. You're a lot like your aunt.

How could I be anything like Gugu? Renmei said. She's a loyal running dog of the Communist Party. She goes after anyone the Party sics her on.

That's rubbish! I said.

What do you mean, rubbish? It couldn't be more obvious. If the Party told her to climb a mountain of knives, that's what she'd do. If the Party told her to jump into a sea of flames, she'd do it.

All right, that's enough talk about me, Gugu said. There's more work to be done, and I have to dig in and do it.

Comrade Wang, Chairwoman Yang said, what woman doesn't love children? One, two, three, the more the better. The Party and the nation love children too. Take Chairman Mao, or Premier Zhou – aren't their faces wreathed in smiles when they see children? That sort of love comes from the heart. What is the revolution for anyway? In the end, it's for our children, so they can live rich, happy lives. Children are the nation's future, its treasure. But there's a problem. Without family planning, our children may not have enough to eat or clothes to wear or could be denied the chance to attend school. Family planning is about achieving great issues of humanity by denying minor ones. By putting up with a little pain and making a little sacrifice you are contributing to the nation at large.

I'll do as you say, Chairwoman, Renmei said. I'll do it tonight. She turned to Gugu. Gugu, she said, go ahead and cut out my womb while you're at it!

Again Chairwoman Yang laughed after a momentary pause of surprise. Everyone at the table laughed with her.

Wan Xiaopao, she said, pointing to me, I love this wife of yours. A very intriguing young woman. But there'll be no cutting out of wombs. You have to take good care of that, isn't that right, Chairwoman Wan?

My nephew's wife is very competent, Gugu said. After the procedure, I'll give her time to get back to normal before transferring her to the family-planning work group. Consider this a heads-up, Secretary Wu.

No problem, the Party secretary said. We want our best people working in the family-planning groups. Comrade Wang Renmei can achieve excellent results by citing her own experience.

Wan Xiaopao, what are your duties?

I'm in charge of sports and recreation.

How long have you been doing that?

Three and a half years.

Then you should be in line for promotion to deputy battalion commander, Yang said. That way Comrade Wang can move to Beijing as an army wife.

My daughter too? Renmei asked timidly.

Of course, the chairwoman replied.

But I've heard it's hard for an army wife to move to Beijing, that there's a quota.

Go home and work hard, Yang said, and leave everything to me.

I am so happy! Renmei said demonstratively. My daughter will be able to attend school in Beijing, she'll become a Beijing resident!

Chairwoman Yang sized Renmei up a second time. Make sure you take all precautions with the procedure, she said to Gugu. It has to be completely safe.

Don't worry about that, Gugu said.

11

Before she was wheeled into surgery, Renmei took my hand and looked down at the teeth marks.

I shouldn't have bitten you, she said apologetically.

That's all right.

Does it still hurt?

Hurt? No more than a mosquito bite.

You can bite me.

Please, I said. You're acting like a little girl.

She gripped my hand. Where's Yanyan?

At home with her grandparents.

Does she have plenty to eat?

Yes, I bought two bags of milk powder and two jin of butter cookies. I also bought some shredded pork and lotus meal. There's nothing to worry about.

Yanyan takes after you. You've got single-fold eyelids, mine are double.

I know. She should take after you, you're so much better-looking than me.

People say girls take after their father and boys take after their mothers.

Maybe so.

This one would have been a boy, I know that, I'm not joking.

The times have changed. Boy or girl, it makes no difference. I tried to sound casual. In a couple of years, you'll follow me to Beijing, and we'll find our daughter the best school there is. We'll raise her to be someone of distinction. A good daughter is better than ten troublesome sons.

Xiaopao . . .

What?

I wasn't naked when Xiao Xiachun touched me that time, really.

Don't be silly, I said with a laugh. I've forgotten that.

I had on a heavy jacket, a sweater underneath, and a shirt under that, and a . . .

And your bra, right?

I washed my bra that day, so I wasn't wearing it, but I was wearing an undershirt.

Okay, that's enough goofy talk.

He caught me by surprise when he kissed me.

So what? It was just a kiss, and you were going to marry him.

But I made him pay. I kneed him, and he squatted with his hands down there.

Oh, poor Xiao Xiachun, I joked. Why didn't you knee me when I kissed you?

He had bad breath, you don't.

What you're saying is we were fated to be married.

Xiaopao, I'm so grateful to you.

What for?

I'm not sure.

That's enough sweet nothings for now. You can talk later. Gugu stuck her head out the operating room door and waved to Renmei. You can come in.

Renmei grabbed my hand. Xiaopao . . .

There's nothing to be afraid of, I said. Gugu says it's a minor procedure.

When I get home you have to stew a whole hen for me.

Sure. I'll make it two.

She turned to look at me just before she walked into surgery. She was wearing my beat-up old grey jacket with the missing button. The thread hung loosely. The cuffs of her blue trousers were muddy. She had on the old leather shoes Gugu had given her.

My nose ached, my heart felt empty. From where I sat on the dust-covered corridor bench, I heard the clang of metal instruments inside and envisioned what they looked like, imagining the blinding rays of light; I could almost feel how cold they were. Children's laughter erupted in the yard behind the health centre. I stood up and looked out the window, where a three- or four-year-old boy playing with a pair of blown-up condoms was being chased by two girls about the same age.

Gugu popped out of the surgery, looking anxious.

What's your blood type?

Type A.

How about her?

Who?

Who do you think? Gugu's anger showed. Your wife.

Type O, I think.

Shit!

What's happened?

Gugu's smock was coated with blood, her face was ghostly white. My mind went blank

She went back inside and shut the door behind her. I tried looking through a crack in the doorway, but could see nothing. I didn't hear Renmei's voice, but I did hear Little Lion shouting into a telephone, ordering an ambulance from the county hospital.

I pushed open the door and immediately saw Renmei . . . saw Gugu with her sleeve rolled up and Little Lion drawing blood from her arm through a thick needle . . . Renmei's face was the colour of paper . . . Renmei . . . hang in there . . . a nurse pushed me back out of the room. Let me in there, I said, goddamn it, I want to be in there. People in white smocks came running down the corridor . . . a middle-aged doctor who smelled like cigarette smoke and disinfectant sat me down on the bench and handed me a cigarette. He lit it for me. Don't worry, he said, the county ambulance is on its way. Your aunt gave her

600 ccs of her own blood . . . everything's going to be fine . . .

The ambulance shrieks bored into me like snakes. A man in a white smock with a medical kit. A bespectacled man in a white smock with a stethoscope around his neck. Men in white smocks. Women in white smocks. Men in white smocks carrying a collapsible gurney. Some went into the surgery, others stood in the corridor. Their actions were brisk, but their faces looked calm. No one paid me any attention, no one even looked my way. The sour taste of blood filled my mouth.

The people in white smocks emerged listlessly from the surgery and stepped back into the ambulance, one at a time. The gurney went in last.

I burst through the surgery door and saw Renmei, hidden from me by a white sheet. Covered with blood, Gugu slumped in a folding chair looking crestfallen. Little Lion and the others stood around like wooden statues. The silence in my ears was broken by what sounded like buzzing bees.

Gugu, I said, didn't you say there'd be no problem?

She looked up, wrinkled her nose, her face ugly and frightening, and sneezed violently.

12

Sister-in-law, Elder Brother, Gugu said numbly in the yard, I'm here to apologise.

An urn with Wang Renmei's ashes stood on a table in the centre of the main room. There was also a white bowl filled with wheat seeds to support three sticks of incense. Smoke curled towards the ceiling. In my uniform, with a black armband, I sat beside the table holding my daughter, who had on mourning garb and frequently looked up at me to ask a question.

What's in the box, Papa?

I couldn't say anything as tears wetted the stubble on my face.

How about my mother, Papa, where is she?

Your mother has gone to Beijing, I said. We'll go see her in a few days.

Will Grandpa and Grandma go with us?

Yes, we'll all go.

Father and Mother were out in the yard sawing a willow plank in half. The plank was tied at an angle to a bench. Father was standing, Mother was seated. Up and down, back and forth the saw went – *shwa shwa* – with sawdust floating in the sunlight.

I knew they were sawing the plank in half to make a coffin for Renmei. Even though cremation had supplanted burial in our area, the state had yet to set aside a place to store funerary containers, and so the locals chose to bury them under a grave mound. If a family could afford it, a coffin was made for the ashes, and the container smashed. Poor families simply buried the container.

I saw Gugu standing out there with her head down. I saw the grief on my parents' faces and the mechanical repetition of their movements. I saw the commune Party secretary, who had come with Gugu, along with Little Lion and three commune cadres. They had brought fancy boxes of pastries and sweets, which they placed alongside the well opening. Beside the boxes was a damp cattail bag that gave off a strong odour. I knew the bag contained salted fish.

No one could have anticipated such a turn of events, the Party secretary was saying. Experts from the county hospital have determined that Chairwoman Wan followed all the appropriate protocols to the letter, and lifesaving attempts were carried out properly. Dr Wan even gave the patient 600 ccs of her own blood. We are deeply saddened and wish that more could have been done.

Are you blind? Father scolded Mother angrily. Can't you see that black line? The saw is a half inch off, and you should have seen that. Can't you do anything right?

Mother got to her feet, began to wail, and went inside.

Father threw down the saw and, with a bent back, walked to the water vat. He picked up the gourd ladle, tipped his head back, and drank, some of the water spilling down his chin to his chest, where it merged with the sawdust. He returned to the plank, picked up the saw, and recommenced sawing with a vengeance.

The Party secretary and cadres went into the house, where they bowed three times to Renmei's ashes. One of the cadres placed a manila envelope on the stove counter.

Comrade Wan Zu, the Party secretary said, we know that no amount of money can make up for the terrible loss this unfortunate incident has caused you and your family, and this five thousand yuan is merely a token of our respect.

Someone – apparently a clerk – said, Three thousand of this is public money. The additional two thousand was donated by Secretary Wu and several leading cadres.

Take it with you, I said. Please take it back. We don't need it.

I understand how you feel, the secretary said sadly, it won't bring her back, but the living have to continue on the revolutionary path. Chairwoman Yang telephoned from Beijing to express her sadness over Comrade Wang's death, to pass on her condolences to the bereaved family, and to inform you that your leave has been extended two weeks to give you time to take care of the funeral and matters at home before reporting back to work.

Thank you, I said. You may leave now.

The Party secretary and his retinue bowed once more to the funerary container and then walked out, still bent at the waist.

I gazed at their legs and at their backsides, some fleshy, some bony, and my tears flowed again.

A woman's wails and a man's profanities emerged from the lane, and I knew that my in-laws were coming.

My father-in-law was carrying a pitchfork. You bastards, he cursed, give me back my daughter!

My mother-in-law was making all sorts of wild gestures and bouncing on her bound feet, looking as if she was about to pounce on my aunt. But she fell before she could get there. She sat there beating the ground with both hands and howling. My poor daughter, why have you left us like that . . . how are we going to live without you . . .

The Party secretary stepped forward. We were on our way to your house, he said to my in-laws. What a tragic affair. This has saddened us deeply.

My father-in-law pounded the ground with his pitchfork handle. Come out here, Wan Xiaopao, you son of a bitch, he growled.

I walked up to him with my daughter, whose arms were wrapped around my neck, her face tucked up against my cheek.

Father, I said when I was right in front of him, you can take it out on me.

He raised his pitchfork, but his hands froze above his head. Teardrops dotted the grey stubble on his chin. His legs crumpled and suddenly he was kneeling.

But she was alive . . . He tossed the pitchfork aside and wept openly. As he knelt in the dirt, he said, She was so alive, but you people had to go and kill her . . . you evil people, aren't you afraid of heavenly retribution?

Gugu walked over and stood in front of my father-in-law, where she hung her head and said, Wang family parents, it's not Xiaopao's fault. You can blame me. Blame me for not being responsible enough, for not checking carefully to see that women of child-bearing age were properly fitted with intra-uterine devices, for not considering the possibility that the no-good Yuan Sai had the skill to remove an intra-uterine device, and for not sending Renmei to the hospital for the procedure. Now – she looked over at the Party secretary – I am prepared to accept punishment from my superiors.

What's done is done, the Party secretary said as he turned to my in-laws. We'll go back to decide the compensation you two deserve. But Dr Wan did nothing wrong. It just happened, a result of your daughter's unique physical constitution. Even going to the hospital would not have changed the outcome. In addition – the secretary raised his voice for the benefit of the people crowding into the yard and emerging from the lane – family planning is a national policy that cannot be changed because of an unfortunate accident. Women with illegal pregnancies should volunteer to have the pregnancies terminated. Anyone who is considering an illegal pregnancy or planning to circumvent family-planning policy will be severely punished.

It's your turn! my mother-in-law shrieked as she took a pair of scissors from her pocket and stabbed my aunt in the thigh.

Gugu pressed her hand against the wound to staunch the blood that seeped out between her fingers.

Commune cadres rushed up, pinned my mother-in-law to the ground, and wrenched the scissors out of her hand.

Little Lion crouched down beside Gugu, opened her medical kit and took out a bandage, which she wrapped around Gugu's leg.

Get on the phone, the Party secretary shouted, and send for an ambulance.

There's no need for that, Gugu said. Renmei's mother, I gave your daughter 600 ccs of my blood. Now our blood debt is paid in full.

Gugu's movements caused the blood to flow more freely than ever.

How could you, old woman! the enraged Party secretary said. You'll pay for it if anything happens to Chairwoman Wan.

The sight of all that blood must have frightened my mother-in-law. Once again she beat the ground and howled.

This is nothing to worry about, Renmei's mother, Gugu said. Even if I get tetanus and die, you're not responsible. I want to thank you for stabbing me. I can now cast off my burden and strengthen my beliefs – she turned to face the people drawn to the commotion and announced – Please pass the word to Chen Bi and Wang Dan to come to the health centre and ask for me. If they don't – she waved her bloodstained hand in the air – even if she hid in an underground tomb, I'll go dig her up!

BOOK THREE

BOOK THREE

Dear Sugitani Akihito sensei,

It's New Year's day, January first. It has been snowing since yesterday evening. The world outside my window is blanketed by white, and children are already out there playing boisterously. A pair of magpies is calling in the poplar tree in front of my house, chittering like they'd been pleasantly surprised.

My heart was heavy after reading your response, knowing that my letter had caused you to lose sleep and suffer physically. Your expression of sympathy has touched me deeply. You cried when you read the part where Renmei died; writing it had the same effect on me. I did not blame Gugu, she did nothing wrong. Even though she's expressed remorse more frequently in recent years, saying she had blood on her hands, that's history, and history is all about effects, not what caused them. One gazes upon China's Great Wall or the Egyptian pyramids without a thought to the blanched bones buried beneath these magnificent edifices. Over the past two decades China has resolved the problem of its population explosion by draconian measures, not only for the sake of the country's development, but as a contribution to humanity. When all is said and done, we live together on this tiny planet, with its finite resources. Once they're gone, they're not coming back, and seen from this perspective, Westerners' critiques of China's family-planning policies are unfair.

There have been significant changes in my hometown over the past couple of years. The new Party secretary is a young man in his late thirties with an American PhD, bold vision, and lofty goals. We've been told that he plans to develop the area on both sides of the Jiao River, and to that end, construction equipment has begun rumbling into the area. Within a few years, you won't be able to recognise the place, with all its changes. Much of what you saw when you were here will be gone. Whether these coming changes will work to the area's advantage or disadvantage is impossible to say.

I will include the third portion of material about my aunt with this letter – I'm embarrassed to call it a letter. I will, of course, keep writing. Your praise is all the encouragement I need.

Let me repeat our heartfelt invitation for you to visit us again at your convenience – maybe we should welcome you with the sort of treatment reserved for old and dear friends.

One more thing. My wife and I will soon retire and move back to our hometown. In Beijing we have always felt like outsiders. Not long ago, near the People's Theatre, we were pilloried for two hours by a pair of women who, we were told, had grown up in a Beijing lane, one of its famous hutongs, which cemented our desire to return to our roots. We don't expect the people back home to mistreat us like the people in big cities do. And maybe I'll be closer to literature there.

Tadpole
New Year's Day, 2004
Beijing

1

After dealing with Renmei's funeral and putting things in order at home, I rushed back to my unit. A month later I received a telegram informing me that Mother had died. I took the telegram to my superior and asked for more leave. At the same time I handed him a request to transfer to civilian life.

On the night of Mother's funeral, the yard was bathed in silvery moonlight. My daughter was sleeping on a rush mat laid out beneath the pear tree. Father was fanning her to keep the mosquitoes away. Katydids chirping on the bean trellis added to the sound of water flowing in the river.

You should find someone, Father said with a sigh. With no women in the family, this doesn't seem like a home.

I've sent in a request to return to civilian life, I said. So let's wait till I come back home.

Everything was going along fine, he said with another sigh, and look how it's turned out. I don't even know who to blame.

You can't blame Gugu, I said. She didn't do anything wrong.

I wasn't blaming her, he said. It was just our fate.

Without dedicated people like Gugu, I said, government policy would be impossible to implement.

What you say makes sense, but why did it have to be her? It broke my heart to see her get stabbed in the leg and bleed like that. She is, after all, my cousin.

Nothing we can do about that, I said.

2

According to Father, after my mother-in-law stabbed Gugu, the wound became infected and Gugu spiked a high fever that stubbornly hung on. Yet that did not stop her from leading a team to search for and arrest Wang Dan. The term sounds unduly harsh, but that's what they used.

Wang Dan's gate was locked and not a sound emerged from the other side. So Gugu told her team to break down the gate and enter the yard. Your aunt had to have been tipped off, Father said. She hobbled into the house, where she removed the lid from a pot on the stove and saw it was half filled with porridge. She tested it with her finger; it was still warm. She smirked. Chen Bi, Wang Dan, she announced loudly, either you come out on your own or I'll come get you, like dragging rats out of their hole.

Silence.

Gugu pointed to a wardrobe in the corner. Nothing but old clothes. Your aunt had people take out all the old clothes, exposing the bottom floor. She then picked up a rolling pin and pounded on it until a hole opened up. You can come out of there, guerrilla heroes, she said. Or do you want us to pour water in?

Chen Er, Wang Dan's daughter, was first out. Her face was streaked with dust, making her look like a temple demon. Not only did she not cry, she bared her teeth and giggled. Chen Bi was next. He hadn't shaved, his hair was curled, and he was wearing a vest that showed his chest hair; he was a sorry sight. A big man like that, Father said, and he immediately fell to his knees in front of your aunt and banged his head on the floor over and over, setting up a racket. His pitiful wails affected the whole village.

Gugu, dear, dear Gugu, I was the first child you delivered and Wang Dan is so tiny, won't you raise your noble hand and spare us . . . Gugu, our family will remember your mercy for generations . . .

Father said, People who were there said your aunt heard this with tears in her eyes. Chen Bi, she said, oh, Chen Bi, this isn't for me to decide. If it were, that would make it easy. I'd cut off my hand for you!

Please, Gugu, be merciful.

Chen Bi's daughter cleverly fell to her knees, just like her father, and banged her head on the floor.

Be merciful, she intoned, be merciful . . .

Right about then, Father said, Wuguan, who was part of the crowd, began glibly singing lines from the song 'Tunnel Warfare': Tunnel warfare/Hey, tunnel warfare/Thousands of brave fighters hidden below . . . tunnel warfare spread out over the boundless plain . . . If the Japs resist, we'll finish them off.

Your aunt wiped her darkening face. That's enough, Chen Bi. Now call Wang Dan out.

Chen Bi crawled up to your aunt on his knees and wrapped his arms around her leg. Chen Er copied him, wrapping her arms around the other leg.

Wuguan sang more of the song: Tunnel warfare spread out over the boundless plain . . . We'll cut them to pieces if they dare come here . . . Tie every man's tubes, practise birth control . . .

Your aunt tried to break free, but they refused to let go of her legs.

Then she realised something. Go down there! she ordered.

One of the militiamen climbed down into the hole, holding a flashlight in his mouth.

Another followed him down.

There's nobody here, came a shout from below.

Overcome by anger, Gugu toppled over and passed out.

That Chen Bi nearly put something over on your aunt, Father said. Remember that vegetable plot behind his house? Well, it had a well with a pulley, and that was the escape hatch for the tunnel. I don't know how Chen Bi managed such a big job, with all that dirt he had to get rid of. While he and Chen Er were tying up your aunt, Wang Dan had gone through the tunnel and pulled herself up by the pulley over the well. It couldn't have been easy, Father said, for that little slip of a woman, big belly and all, to climb up that rope to get away.

They carried your aunt over to the well. How could I be so stupid! she spat out angrily, accentuated by a stomp of her foot. How could I! Back when my father worked at the Xihai Hospital he led a team to dig just such a tunnel.

Your aunt passed out a second time. This time she was taken straight to the hospital. She came down with the same illness that had struck Bethune, and nearly died from it. She was a devoted Communist, and the Party reciprocated by treating her with an emergency supply of the finest and most expensive medicines.

After two weeks in the hospital she left on her own before her wound had completely healed. The incident weighed heavily on her mind. She said she wouldn't be able to eat or sleep until she'd gotten that child out of Wang Dan's belly. That's how strong her sense of responsibility was. Would you call someone like that human? Father sighed. No, she'd become a god or a demon.

Chen Bi and Chen Er were confined in the commune. There was talk that they were strung up and beaten, but that was just a rumour. When village cadres went to see them, they were being held in a room with a bed and bedding, a vacuum bottle and two glasses. Food and water were delivered to them. Their meals were the same as the commune cadres: steamed rolls, millet porridge, and whatever else was being served. Father and daughter gained weight and healthy complexions. They had to pay for their food, but Chen Bi had plenty of money from his business ventures. The commune checked with the bank to see just how much: it was thirty-eight thousand yuan! While your aunt was in the hospital, the commune sent a work team into the village, where they met with the local members and announced that all able-bodied villagers were to search for Wang Dan and would be paid five yuan a day, all to come out of Chen Bi's bank account. Some villagers said they wouldn't go, calling it blood money, but were told that if they refused, they would be *fined* five yuan a day. In the end, all seven hundred souls turned out. Three hundred of them searched the first day; when they returned home they were given their five yuan, making a total outlay that day of about eighteen hundred yuan. The commune also announced that whoever located Wang Dan and brought her home would be given a two hundred yuan reward. A hundred went to anyone who produced a viable clue. That turned the village into a frenzied mass, some clapping their hands from delight, others privately uncomfortable. Father said, I knew that some people coveted those rewards, but most only searched half-heartedly, making a turn or two around farmland and shouting: Come out, Wang Dan. If you don't, you'll be wiped out financially. After a few moments of that, they went back and worked their own plots. At night, of course, they went to get paid; they'd have been fined if they hadn't.

Didn't they find her? I asked.

How would they find her? Father said. Everyone felt she'd gone far away.

A little thing like that, with short steps and a big belly, how far could she have gone? I'll bet she was still in the village. I lowered my voice. She might have been hiding in her parents' home.

They didn't need you to point that out, Father said. Those people from the commune knew what they were doing. They wouldn't be happy until they dug down three feet in Wang Jiao's house. They even broke open the kang to see if maybe Wang Dan was hiding inside. I doubt there was a person in the village who'd have borne the responsibility of hiding her and not reporting. The fine was three thousand.

Could she have decided to end it all? Did they search the river and all the wells?

You underestimate that little woman. She was more intelligent than all the other villagers combined and had more ambition than the tallest man you could find.

You've got a point. I recall her pretty little face and her expressions, from crafty to headstrong. The problem was, she must have been seven months along by then.

That's why your aunt was so anxious. She said, Before it was 'out of the pot' it was just meat, and it needed to come out one way or another. But once it was out of the pot it was a human being, even if it had no arms and no legs, and was protected by national laws.

I conjured up an image of Wang Dan: two and a half feet tall, with a big belly, her delicate little head held high, a pair of thin legs in motion, a bundle over her arm, moving clumsily across a bramble-infested mountain road as she looked over her shoulder, tripping but getting back up, and running again . . . or seated in a large wooden basin, with an oversized stirring slat as her oar as she paddles breathlessly down river rapids.

3

Three days after Mother's funeral, according to custom, friends and family turned out to 'circle the grave'. There we burned paper replicas of horses and people, as well as a paper TV set. Mother's grave was only ten metres from where Renmei was buried. Bright green wild grass was already growing over her grave. I was told by a family elder to circle Mother's grave with raw rice in my left hand and unhusked millet in my right. Three counterclockwise revolutions were followed by three clockwise revolutions, during which I let the rice and millet drop slowly from my hands as I intoned: A handful of millet, a handful of rice, we send the dear departed to Paradise. My daughter followed me, tossing grain to the ground from her tiny hands.

Gugu took time out of her busy schedule to come. Little Lion, medical kit over her back, walked behind her. Gugu was still hobbling, and, in the months since I'd last seen her, she seemed considerably older. She knelt at the foot of Mother's grave and wailed. We'd never seen Gugu cry like that, and it shook us to our core. Little Lion stood off to the side, her eyes tear-filled. Women came up to console Gugu; they lifted her up by her arms, but the moment they let go, she fell back to her knees and wept even more bitterly. Affected by the display of Gugu's grief, women who by then had stopped crying fell to their knees and began to keen along with her.

I bent down to help Gugu to her feet, but Little Lion said softly, Let her cry. She's been holding this back for a very long time.

The look of compassion on Little Lion's face gave me a warm feeling.

When she finally stopped crying, Gugu got to her feet, dried her eyes, and said to me: Xiaopao, Chairwoman Yang phoned me to say that you want to leave the army.

Yes, I replied. I've already handed in a request.

Chairwoman Yang has asked me to talk you out of it. She's made arrangements to reassign you to the planning section, where you'll work directly under her, with a promotion to the rank of deputy battalion commander. She thinks highly of you.

That means nothing to me now, I said. I'd rather go back and collect manure than work in family planning.

That's where you're wrong, she said. Family planning is Party work, important work.

Phone Chairwoman Yang and thank her for her concern. But I'm coming home. I don't know how the very old and very young will get by if I don't.

Don't be so firm, she said. Give it more thought. You really should stay in the army. Fieldwork is hard on a person. Look at Yang Xin and then look at me. We're both involved in family planning, but she has a leisurely life and it shows, with her nice complexion and all. And me? Scurrying here and hopping there, blood one moment and tears the next, until I look like this.

4

I confess, fame and fortune meant a lot to me. Though I said I wanted to leave the army, when I heard that I could look forward to a promotion and that Chairwoman Yang regarded me highly, I wavered. Back home, when I talked it over with Father, he too thought that leaving was a bad idea. Years ago, your great-uncle healed an injury to Commander Yang's leg and cured his wife's illness, putting them in his debt. Now he's a high-ranking officer, and your future will be assured by having a connection with him. I voiced my objection to what Father was saying, but deep down that's what I was thinking. We were ordinary people, common citizens, and I could be forgiven for wanting to curry favour with people of power and influence, society's dragons and phoenixes. So the next time Gugu came to see me, my attitude had changed. And when she suggested a marriage between me and Little Lion, though I brought up Wang Gan's decade-long infatuation with Little Lion as an excuse, even that argument began to crumble.

I'm childless, Gugu said, and Little Lion has become like a daughter to me. She's a woman of fine character, has a heart of gold, and is fiercely loyal to me. How could I ever let her marry Wang Gan?

Gugu, I said, I'm sure you know it's now been twelve years since Wang Gan wrote that first letter to Little Lion. In that time he's written more than five hundred letters. He told me so. And that's not all. One of the ways he expressed his love for her was to report his own sister.

Of course, he reported Yuan Sai and Renmei too. How else would you have known about Yuan Sai's illegal removal of IUDs, and how else would you have known that Renmei and Wang Dan were pregnant in violation of family-planning policy?

The truth is, Little Lion never read any of those disgusting letters, since I intercepted every one of them. I told Postal Director Ma to send me all his letters.

But he helped you in your work, I said, ever since his father had his vasectomy. In this latest contribution, he handed you his own sister.

One absolutely cannot marry a person like that, she said angrily. How dependable can someone who would sell out his friends, even his own sister, over a woman be?

But he still helped you.

Those are two different matters. Remember this, Xiaopao, she said earnestly, a person can be anything, anything but a traitor. There is no reason, however lofty, that excuses that. From ancient times to the present, betrayers have always come to grief. That includes Wang Xiaoti. He may have been given five thousand ounces of gold, but I'm willing to bet that he will die badly. If you were to defect to the KMT today for five thousand ounces of gold, would you then defect to another political party that offered you ten thousand? So the more Wang Gan reports on others, the lower he is in my eyes, and in my heart he is nothing but a pile of dog shit.

But what if you hadn't intercepted his letters, Gugu? Is it possible that Little Lion would have been moved by what he wrote? Maybe even be married to him by now?

Impossible, absolutely impossible. She has lofty ambitions, and Wang Gan isn't the only one who's been smitten by her in recent years. There have been a dozen at least, including cadres and workers, but none has impressed her.

I shook my head. But, I said sceptically, she's not really very good—

Hah! Gugu replied. How short-sighted can you be! Some women look good at first glance, but the more you look, the more flaws you see. What about Little Lion? At first glance you'd think she isn't much to look at, but look long enough and you'll see just how attractive she is. You've probably never taken the time to do that, have you? I've spent my whole life around women, and I know exactly what makes a woman a prized creature. Do you recall the time you were just promoted to cadre status, how I tried to get you and her together? But you'd fallen for Renmei, and even though I opposed the match, given the freedom to marry whom one pleases in the new society, as your aunt I had no choice but to go along. Now, of course, she's left a void – don't get me wrong, I'm not happy she died and wish she'd had a long life – as the heavens have willed it, and the heavens have also willed that you and Little Lion be together.

Gugu, I said, no matter what you say, Wang Gan and I were childhood friends, and everyone – adults and children – knows how he feels. If I were to marry Little Lion, I'd drown under the spittle the masses would send my way.

You're wrong again, she said. His love for her is a one-sided affair, like a barber's carrying pole – only the pail on one end is hot. Little Lion never once expressed any interest in him. If she married you, it would be a case of 'the firebird knows which perch to choose'. Besides, this thing called love has nothing to do with loyalty among friends. Love is selfish. If Little Lion were a horse that Wang Gan had his eye on, then you could let him have her, no problem there. But Little Lion is a human being, and if you fall in love with her, you'll have to take her for your own. You've been out in the world for several years and have seen many foreign movies, so how can you be so inflexible?

Even if I said I'd do it, what would she—

Gugu interrupted me: You don't have to worry about that. She's been with me so long I know what she's thinking. I'll tell you the unvarnished truth: It's you she's in love with, and if Renmei hadn't left us, Little Lion would stay single all her life.

Let me think this over for a few days, Gugu, I said. The dirt on Renmei's grave is still damp.

Think what over? A long night brings many dreams. If Renmei's spirit is up there somewhere, she'll be clapping her hands in approval.

Why? Because Little Lion is a good woman, and it would be Renmei's good fortune for her daughter to have such a stepmother. Not only that, government policy would allow you and Little Lion to have a child, and I'd be wishing for twins. Xiaopao; you will have benefited greatly from misfortune.

5

The date for my wedding was set.

Gugu took care of the arrangements. I felt like a floating piece of rotting wood kept moving by gentle nudges.

Little Lion and I were alone together for only the second time when we registered to be married at the commune office.

Our first private meeting had been in the dormitory room shared by Gugu and Little Lion. It had been a Saturday morning. Gugu ushered us into the room and left, shutting the door behind her. A pile of dust-covered newspapers and a couple of books on obstetrics sat atop a three-drawer table between the two single beds. Bees swarmed around a dozen or so sturdy, pollen-laden sunflowers just outside the window. After pouring me a glass of water, she sat on her bed. I sat on Gugu's bed. The air carried the fragrance of hand soap. Soapy water half filled a Red Lantern washbasin. Gugu's unmade bed was an impossible mess.

Gugu is totally devoted to her work.

I know.

I feel like I'm dreaming.

Me too.

You know all about Wang Gan, don't you? He's written to you five hundred times.

Gugu told me.

Any thoughts about that?

Not really.

I've been married before and I have a daughter. Does that bother you?

No.

Do you want to talk this over with your family?

I have no family.

Later, she rode on the back of my bicycle to the commune offices. I had trouble controlling the bicycle over the bumpy road, only recently paved with shards of brick and tile. She sat with her shoulder pressed against my back. I could feel her weight. Some people ride well on the back of a bicycle, some don't. Renmei rode well, Little Lion did not. I was pedalling so hard the chain broke. My heart sank. That was a bad sign. Did it mean that now we would not grow old together? The broken chain lay on the road like a dead snake. I picked it up and looked around. We were surrounded by cornfields where women were spraying insecticide. The spraying machines hummed like air raid sirens. The women had draped plastic over their shoulders and were wearing hospital masks over their mouths and bandanas on their heads. It was brutally hard work, but the green mist rising above the cornstalks invested it with an almost poetic air. I thought about Wang Renmei. She'd been fearless. Unafraid even of snakes, she'd pick them up by their tails, much the same way I'd picked up the bicycle chain. She'd also sprayed insecticide after being dismissed from the school in the wake of her breakup with Xiao Xiachun. Her hair had reeked of insecticide. I don't have to wash it, she'd joked, since it'll ward off fleas and mosquitoes. But she did wash it, and I stood behind her and poured water over her head; she laughed the whole time. I asked what she was laughing about, which made her laugh so hard she knocked over the washbasin. I couldn't help but feel guilty as I thought about Renmei. I looked at Little Lion out of the corner of my eye. She was wearing a new, red-checked short-sleeve shirt with a turned-up collar and a glistening digital watch on her wrist. She was full-figured. She'd powdered her face with fragrant Pearl or another brand of face powder, which lessened the effects of acne.

We're still three li from the commune. I'll have to walk the bicycle.

We met Chen Bi outside the slaughterhouse gate. He was carrying Chen Er on his back.

He blanched when he spotted us. The look in his eyes made me ashamed. He turned his back on us.

Chen Bi! I decided to greet him.

Oh, I thought it was some big shot, he replied with biting sarcasm. He glared hatefully at Little Lion.

They let you out, did they?

The girl's sick, she has a fever, he said. To be honest, I didn't want to leave. The food inside was so good I could spend my life there.

Little Lion went up to feel Chen Er's forehead.

Chen Bi spun away.

Take her to the hospital for an IV, Little Lion said. Her temperature must be at least thirty-nine degrees.

Is that a hospital you're running? Chen Bi fumed. Or an abattoir?

I know you hate us, Little Lion said, but there's nothing we can do.

Nothing you can do? There's plenty you can do.

Chen Bi, I said, don't use your child to vent your anger. Come on, I'll go with you.

Thanks, pal, he said with a sneer, but I don't want to keep you from whatever it is you're doing.

Chen Bi . . . what can I say?

You don't have to say anything. I used to think you were a good guy, but now I know you're not.

Say what you like, I said as I stuffed some bills into his pocket. Now take her to the hospital.

Chen reached in, took out the money, and flung it to the ground. This is blood money!

He turned and walked off proudly with his daughter.

I gazed blankly at his back as he strode off. I bent down, picked up the money, and put it back in my pocket.

He's prejudiced against you both, I said.

He has only himself to blame, Little Lion said indignantly. Who can we pour our bitterness out to?

I was supposed to have had a letter from my unit to register for marriage, but Lu Mazi, the civil administration clerk laughed and said, No need for that. Your aunt has already talked to us. Wan Xiaopao, my son is a soldier in your unit, he said. He enlisted last year. He's a smart boy and is quick to learn. Keep an eye on him for me, okay?

I paused when I was about to put my fingerprint in the marriage register, because I was reminded of having done the same thing with Wang Renmei in the same register in the same room with the same Lu Mazi. I'd left a bright red print in the book. Ah! Renmei said, showing her happy surprise. It's a whorl!

Lu Mazi looked at me, then at Little Lion and said with a phoney smile, Wan Zu, you're a lucky man. You've managed to marry the commune's number one beauty. He pointed to the registry. Put your finger here. What are you waiting for?

Lu Mazi's comments sounded a lot like ridicule – in essence, that's what they were – Damn it, to hell with him. Okay, no more stalling! Life is short, I said to myself, and many things are determined by fate. Better to row with the flow than against it. Besides, things are too far along for me not to do it. What would that do to Little Lion? I've already ruined one woman's life; I can't ruin another's.

6

At the time I was under the impression that Gugu was so caught up in arranging the wedding that she'd forgotten about Wang Dan. I'd thought she might have relented a bit and would use the wedding as an excuse to let enough time to pass for Wang Dan to have her baby. I'd soon realise, though, that Gugu's sense of loyalty to her work had taken on maniacal proportions. She was obsessed with carrying out her tasks. I had no reason to doubt her good faith in bringing Little Lion and me together, for she was convinced that we were meant to be a couple. But her extravagant preparations for our wedding, her release of Chen Bi and his daughter from detention, and her announcement that the villagers no longer had to search for Wang Dan were all part of a smokescreen designed to lessen the vigilance of Wang Dan and whoever was hiding her. For Gugu it was a two-birds-with-one-stone strategy. What she hoped to achieve was to see a follower who was like her own daughter be married to her nephew and have a place to call home, and, at the same time, for Wang Dan to be taken into custody and the criminal foetus in her belly taken out and destroyed before it was too late. Using this sort of language to describe Gugu's work may seem inappropriate, but I can't come up with anything better.

On the morning before the wedding ceremony, I went to Mother's grave, as custom dictated, to burn some 'happy money'; ostensibly, I guess, to notify her spirit and invite her to the ceremony. After I lit the paper, a tiny whirlwind rose up and carried the ash in circles around the head of the grave. Of course I knew this was easily explained by laws of physics, but it unnerved me nonetheless. Mother's tottering image floated in my head and her wise, simple, meaningful words rang in my ears. Tears filled my eyes. I wondered what she would think about this marriage if she could talk.

The whirlwind abruptly left Mother's gravesite and moved over to the grassy area at the head of Renmei's grave. At that moment an oriole in a peach tree released a long cheerless call that nearly tore my insides apart. Peaches had ripened on the vast grove of trees; the two gravesites were in our family grove. I picked two red-tipped peaches, laid one before Mother's grave and threaded my way through the trees to Renmei's grave with the other. As I was leaving the house, Father said, Don't forget to burn some paper for her too.

I haven't had time yet, Renmei, I said silently, and I'm so sorry. But I won't forget you, I'll remember all the good things about you. Little Lion is a good person who will take good care of Yanyan. I won't stay with her if she doesn't.

After burning some paper at the head of her grave, I went up, laid down a sheet of paper, weighted it down, and set the second peach on it. Renmei, I said silently, though I know you are unhappy, I ask you with all my heart to come to my wedding with Mother. I'll put four steamed buns, some dishes of food, and that treat you thought at first had a medicinal taste, but then got addicted to – chocolate with liquor in the middle – on the altar table in the central room. The dead deserve our respect. Please enjoy the food!

On my way home from the graveyard, the path was lined with knee-high weeds; rainwater filled the ditches. Pear groves stretched south all the way to the Black Water River and west to the Jiao River. Growers were picking the ripe fruit, as three-wheeled tractors moved quickly down the broad road.

Wang Gan appeared in front of me, blocking my way, as if he'd popped out of the ground. He was standing there in a military uniform that was neither new nor old – the thought struck me that it was the uniform I'd given him the year before – and a fresh haircut. He was clean-shaven. Though slim as ever, he seemed especially energetic, having done away with his old slovenly look. His spirited appearance was comforting, though I couldn't shake an uneasy feeling.

Wang Gan . . . I tell you, in fact . . .

Wang Gan held his hands out and smiled, exposing his yellowed teeth. Xiaopao, he said, you don't have to explain, I understand, I really do, and I congratulate you both.

Old friend . . . all sorts of thoughts crammed my mind. I reached out to shake his hand.

He took a step backward. I've awakened from a dream. What they call love is really a sickness, and I've been cured of mine.

That's great. Truth is, you and Little Lion weren't a good match. All you have to do is pull yourself together and you can accomplish something big. And when that happens, you'll be able to choose an even more outstanding girl.

I'm a worthless man, and I owe you an apology. Did you see the ashes on Wang Renmei's grave? I'm the one who burned spirit paper for her. If I hadn't reported her, Yuan Sai wouldn't be in prison and your wife and baby would still be alive. I'm a murderer.

You're not to blame for any of that, I said.

I wanted to make myself feel better with some grand justification, like 'reporting an illegal pregnancy is the responsibility of all citizens' or 'it's all right to sacrifice family for the motherland', but they didn't make me feel better at all. I wasn't enlightened; I did it for my own selfish desires, in order to win Little Lion's heart. Because of that I developed terrible insomnia, and the minute I shut my eyes I could see Renmei coming with bloody hands to gouge out my heart . . . I don't think I have many days to live . . .

You're thinking too much, Wang Gan, I said. You did nothing wrong. You're not superstitious, so you know that when a person dies, that's the end of it. But even if a person's spirit lived on, Renmei would not hound you. She was a good woman of pure heart.

She absolutely was a good woman, Wang Gan agreed. And that

makes me feel even worse. Don't waste your sympathy on me, Xiaopao, and I don't deserve to be forgiven. I've been waiting for you today to ask a favour . . .

What is it, my friend?

Please have Little Lion tell Gugu that when Wang Dan climbed out of the well that day, she came straight to my house. She is, after all, my sister, and when she begged me to save her life and that of the child in her belly, even if I had a heart as cold and hard as steel, I couldn't help but be moved. I put her in a manure basket and covered her with dry wheat stalks and a hempen sack. Then I tied the basket to the back of my bicycle and rode out of the village. I was stopped and questioned by your aunt's hidden sentry, Qin He, at the head of the village. Your aunt really was born at the wrong time and engaged in the wrong occupation. She'd have been better suited to leading troops into battle. Of all the people I could have encountered, Qin He, your aunt's running dog, was the worst. I was willing to give up anyone for Little Lion, and he was ready to do the same for your aunt. He stopped me and asked where I was going. We'd seen each other in front of the hospital many times but had never exchanged a word; and yet, I could tell that he viewed me as a friend, since we suffered from the same malady. I'd come to his aid when he'd run afoul of Gao Men and Lu Huahua outside the Supply and Marketing Co-op restaurant. Gao, Lu, Qin, Wang – he was the Qin, I was the Wang – Northeast Gaomi Township's four morons came together on the street that day and put on a monkey show for the bystanders. You may not know it, my friend, but when someone is called a fool, even when he isn't one, it's amazingly liberating. I got down off my bicycle and stared at Qin He.

You must be going to market to sell a pig.

That's right, a pig.

I didn't see a thing.

He let me go. Two morons were of one mind.

Please tell Little Lion that I rode my sister to Jiaozhou and put her on a highway bus to Yantai, where she was to buy a ticket for a boat to Dalian, and from there take a train to Harbin. I'm sure you know that

Chen's mother was from Harbin, and he has relatives there. She took
plenty of money with her, and she's very smart. You know how clever
Chen Bi is. They had this all planned ahead of time. It's been thirteen
days, and Wang Dan has gotten to where she was going. Your aunt's
hand isn't big enough to cover the heavens. She can have her way with
things at the commune, but not in the rest of the world. My sister is
seven months pregnant, so by the time your aunt finds her, the child
will already have arrived. So your aunt can give up on this one.

Then why do you want me to tell them?

It's the only way I can gain salvation, and the only thing I can ask
of you.

All right, I said.

I really am a weak-willed person.

After marrying Little Lion, I should have lit a red candle and sat alone in front of it till daybreak as a means of expressing my remorse to Renmei and letting her know I missed her. But I only sat there till midnight before going to bed and embracing Little Lion.

It had rained heavily the day I married Renmei; a downpour also struck on the day I married Little Lion. Lightning crackled with blinding blue-white streaks, followed by deafening thunder and a cloudburst. The sound of sluicing water came from all directions; wet winds carrying the smell of mud and the stink of rotten fruit poured into the house through the windows. The candle sputtered briefly and then went out. That struck fear into me. A bolt of lightning lit up the sky for several seconds, time enough for me to see the bright lights in Little Lion's eyes. It turned her face a golden yellow. The blast of thunder sounded as if it were out in our yard and carried a scorched odour into the house. Little Lion cried out in fear and I held her in my arms.

I'd thought that Little Lion was hard as wood, never imagining that she could be as soft as a papaya. A full, round papaya from which juice oozes at the lightest touch. She had the texture of papaya and the same rich aroma. It would have been unfair to compare the new with the old, so I forced myself to keep my thoughts from getting away from me. But failed. When Little Lion and my bodies came together, so did our hearts.

Little Lion, I said shamelessly, in my eyes you and I make a better couple than Renmei and I did.

She covered my mouth with her hand. Some things ought not to be said.

Wang Gan asked me to tell you that thirteen days ago he rode Wang Dan to Jiaozhou, where she took a highway bus to Yantai, and from there went to the northeast.

Little Lion sat up. Another bolt of lightning lit up her face, which had turned from a look of passion to one that was sombre, even cold. She wrapped her arms around me and lay back down. He lied to you, she whispered. Wang Dan could not have gotten away like that.

Then, I said, does that mean you're letting her go?

That's not for me to say. It's up to Gugu.

Is that what she has in mind?

I doubt it, she said. If that's what she had in mind, she wouldn't be Gugu.

Then why haven't you taken any action? Don't you know she's already more than seven months along?

Gugu didn't pass on taking action. She has her people quietly making inquiries.

Have you found her?

Well . . . she hesitated briefly, then rested her head against my chest. I can't hide anything from you. She's in Yanyan's maternal grandmother's house, in the same hole Wang Renmei hid in.

What do you plan to do?

Whatever Gugu wants me to do.

What does she plan to do? The same as before?

She's not that dumb.

So then what?

Gugu has already had someone inform Chen Bi that we know where Wang Dan is hiding and that he is to tell the Wangs that if they don't send her out, the tractor will come tomorrow and pull down their house as well as those of her neighbours.

Yanyan's grandfather is a stubborn man. Will you really do that if he stands his ground?

Gugu's idea isn't to get the Wangs to send her out, but for Chen Bi to go in and bring her out. She promised him that all his property will be returned if he brings her out so the pregnancy can be terminated. Thirty-eight thousand yuan is a good reason to do as she says.

I heaved a long sigh. Why are you people so ruthless? Isn't killing Wang Renmei enough?

Wang Renmei had only herself to blame, Little Lion said coldly.

It seemed to me that her body suddenly went cold.

8

For days on end it was cloudy and drizzly; the roads were disrupted, keeping the buyers of our local peaches from getting through. Every family had picked fruit. Some went into baskets that piled up like a little mountain, keeping the rain off with plastic cloths, some were just stacked willy-nilly in the yard so the rain could do its damage. Peaches do not keep well; in previous years, the trucks had driven right into the groves, where the fruit was picked, weighed and loaded straight onto the trucks. The drivers didn't mind working all night so they could get on the road at first light and make deliveries many miles away. This year the heavens seemed to have decided to punish people who had enjoyed a succession of fine harvests by putting an end to clear days when the fruit ripened. With a series of heavy rains, moderate rains and drizzles, if the people chose not to pick the fruit, it rotted on the trees. If they did pick it, there was a glimmer of hope in waiting for the skies to clear, so the trucks could drive in and load up. But there were no signs of clearing on this day.

Our family only had thirty trees. Because Father was getting old, the trees were not well tended, yet they produced a modest harvest of nearly six thousand jin. We only filled sixteen baskets, due to a shortage of baskets, which we stored in a side room. The rest we simply laid out in the yard and covered with plastic cloth. Father kept going out in the rain to lift a corner of the cloth and check the peaches. And each time the cloth was raised our noses were hit by the smell of rotting fruit.

As Little Lion and I were newly married, my daughter stayed with Father. She ran after him every time he went out into the rain, carrying a little umbrella with animals printed on it.

She treated us with cool courtesy. She held her hands behind her back when Little Lion offered her sweets, but said, Thank you, Gugu.

Call her Mama, I said.

She glared at me, shocked.

She doesn't have to, she doesn't have to call me anything like that. People call me Little Lion – she pointed to the lion on her umbrella – so you can call me Big Lion.

Do you eat children? my daughter asked.

No, I don't eat children, Little Lion answered her. I protect them.

Father brought in some overripe peaches in his conical hat and peeled them with a rusty knife. He sighed.

Might as well eat the good ones, I said.

But these are money, Father said. The heavens don't care about us common folk.

Dad – this was the first time Little Lion had called him that, and it felt awkward – the government won't just stand by. They'll come up with something.

All the government knows is family planning, Father said with obvious resentment. Nothing else interests them.

The village committee loudspeaker sounded just then. Worried that he might miss something, Father ran into the yard to listen carefully.

The voice over the loudspeaker announced that the commune had made contacts in cities like Qingdao and Yantai, and that trucks had been sent to meet up at the Wu Family Bridge, some fifty li distant, to buy our peaches. The commune appealed to the people to deliver their peaches to the bridge by land and by water. The price would be less than half that of previous years, but it was better than letting them rot.

The village came to life as soon as the announcement ended. I knew that ours wasn't the only village to be energised, that the whole township had come alive.

We had a river, but not many boats. Every production brigade had been supplied with small wooden boats, but no one could find them after they were contracted to individual farmers for production quotas.

There's no disputing the fact that the masses possess enormous creative talent. Father ran over to the side building and took four large gourds down from the rafters, then picked up four pieces of timber, tied them together, and started building a raft. I took off my pants and shirt, and stood there in my underwear and a vest to give him a hand. Little Lion held an umbrella over me to keep me as dry as possible. My daughter was running around the yard with her little umbrella. I gave Little Lion a sign to hold the umbrella over Father, but he waved her off. He had draped a sheet of plastic over his shoulders and was hatless. A mixture of rain and sweat ran down his face. Old-time farmers like my father give their work their full attention; whatever they put their hand to, it is done accurately and powerfully, with no superfluous effort. The raft was swiftly completed.

The riverbank was a flurry of activity by the time we reached it with our raft. All those missing boats had miraculously reappeared. Dozens of rafts had been put in the water along with the boats. The rafts were fitted with gourds, inner tubes, and Styrofoam. Someone had even shown up with a large wooden basin. People were pouring out of the lanes with baskets of peaches, heading for the boats and rafts all tied to willow trees on the bank.

Dozens of draft animals were lined up on the riverbank, including mules and donkeys that were loaded down with full saddlebag baskets.

A commune cadre swam over and put on a raincoat, rolled up his pant cuffs, and held his sandals in his hand as he shouted instructions.

I saw a raft in front of ours that was a thing of beauty. Four thick China fir poles were tied together with rawhide into a tic-tac-toe grid. The centre was constructed of logs as thick as scythe handles, with four red, fully inflated inner tubes from a horse-drawn wagon. A dozen or more full baskets barely had any effect on the raft, testimony to the high quality flotation of the inner tubes. Vertical poles – one in each corner and a fifth in the centre – supported a light blue plastic tarpaulin as protection against both sunlight and rain. It was not the sort of raft that could be thrown together in a hurry.

Wang Jiao in a conical palm bark hat and a palm bark cape crouched in front of the raft like a fisherman.

Our raft, which could only hold six baskets, sat deep in the water. Father insisted on adding two more. All right, I said, but I'll go alone. You stay here.

He objected, probably out of concern that it was only my second day in the new marriage. Don't argue, Dad. Look out there and tell me if you see anyone else your age punting a raft.

Then you be careful.

Don't worry, I said. I may not be good at much, but I know what I'm doing on the water.

If it gets choppy, toss the peaches into the river, Father said.

Don't worry about that.

I waved to Little Lion on the riverbank, where she was holding Yanyan's hand.

She waved back.

Father untied the rope around the tree and tossed it to me.

I caught it, rolled it up, picked up my pole, and shoved off; the heavy raft moved slowly out onto the river.

Careful!

Be careful!

I punted fairly close to the riverbank, moving slowly.

The mules and donkeys kept pace with the water traffic, their loads weighing heavily on them, bells that had been draped around their necks by fastidious household heads ringing out crisply. Old folks and youngsters followed the burdened animals up to the head of the village.

There the river made a sharp bend and the flotilla entered a rapid flow. Instead of letting the current carry him forward, Wang Jiao, whose raft had been ahead of me, punted to the opposite bank at the bend, where the water was calmer, and the brush-covered bank was home to chirping cicadas. From the moment I saw his fancy raft, I'd had a bad feeling, and I was right to. Wang Jiao abruptly dumped his baskets into the water, where they floated lightly. They contained no peaches. He moved up close to the brush, where I saw Chen Bi jump onto the raft with his pregnant wife in his arms. Wang Gan followed, with Chen Er in his arms.

They quickly took down the plastic cloth canopy and turned it into a curtain as Wang Jiao picked up his punting pole and recaptured his glory days standing on the shafts of his cart and snapping a whip at his team, as impressive as ever. He stood straight and tall, proving that Gugu knew what she was talking about when she said his hobble and stooped carriage were all an act. And he'd only pretended to sever ties with his son, since at this critical moment they stormed the battlefield together. That aside, I instinctively wished them well, hoping they'd be able to deliver Wang Dan to wherever they planned to take her. Of course, when I thought about all that Gugu had invested in this affair, my sympathy rang somewhat hollow.

Wang Jiao's raft floated high and light on the water despite the weight of his load, and he outpaced the rest of us with ease.

Small wooden boats and rafts entered the water from both banks all along the river. By the time we reached Dongfeng Village, where Gugu's head had been clubbed bloody, hundreds of rafts and boats had formed a long dragon in the heart of the river sailing along with the flow.

I couldn't keep my eye off of Wang Jiao's raft, which, although it was far ahead of the rest of us, was still within sight.

His was the proudest raft on the river, not doubt about that. It was like a Hummer Predator in a line of ordinary sedans.

More than proud, it was mysterious. People who had witnessed what happened at the bend in the river obviously knew the identities of the secret passengers. People who hadn't, cocked their heads to get a glimpse behind the curtain, because no matter what else it might be shielding, it assuredly was not peaches.

As I think back now, the sight of Gugu's family-planning boat racing past us at full speed was indescribably thrilling. This was no longer the 1970 variety with its local-made motor. No, this was a white, streamlined speedboat with an acrylic windscreen on its semi-enclosed cabin. Once again Qin He piloted the boat, but he was now completely grey. Gugu and my bride, Little Lion, stood at the rear of the cabin, holding on to a railing, their clothes billowing in the wind. I viewed the sight of Little Lion's rounded breasts with mixed emotions. Four men sat behind the two women. The boat nearly swamped my raft and the eddies it created caused me to pitch and roll. Little Lion had to see me as they sped close by, but she didn't wave. The Little Lion of the few days after we were married had become a different person. A sense of unreality floated into my head; I felt as if I'd only dreamed the events of recent days. Little Lion's display of indifference spurred me to root for the fugitives: Hurry and get away, Wang Dan. Pole harder, Wang Jiao.

The speedboat cut through the flotilla on its way towards Wang Jiao's raft, ahead and to the right.

Instead of passing Wang Jiao, Gugu pulled up alongside and slowed until the sound of the engine virtually died out. No more than three metres separated the two craft. The speedboat gradually closed the gap, obviously in an attempt to force the raft to the riverbank. Wang Jiao stuck his pole against the side of the speedboat, thinking that would decrease the danger. But it had the opposite effect, pushing the raft farther out of the flow.

A man on the boat caught the plastic cloth with a pole functioning as a gaff and tore it with a loud ripping noise. A couple more twists brought everything that had been hidden into full view.

Wang Jiao swung his pole at the man on the boat, who warded off the blow with his pole. Wang Gan and Chen Bi picked up oars and began rowing for all they were worth, one on each side of the raft. Sitting between them was the pocket-sized Wang Dan, holding Chen Er in her left arm, the baby's head tucked into her armpit, and covering her rounded abdomen with the right. Her shrill cries broke through the din of battling poles and crashing waves: Gugu, have some mercy and let us go!

As the raft opened up space between it and the speedboat, Little Lion jumped in the direction of the raft but landed in the water. She did not know how to swim and began to sink almost immediately. Gugu shouted for someone to save her. Chen Bi and Wang Gan jumped at the chance to row with all their might, moving the raft out into the flow.

Rescuing Little Lion took a long time. The man with the pole reached out to bring her close to the side, but she grabbed his leg and pulled him into the water with her. He was a weak swimmer, so another man jumped in. Meanwhile, Qin He's piloting skills had seemed to vanish, to which Gugu reacted with rage. No one on the other boats or rafts was willing to come to their aid. But Little Lion was, after all, my wife, so I poled with all my might to get as close as possible. I nearly collided with a raft behind me and barely managed to keep from tipping over. Little Lion's head was surfacing less and less frequently, so I knew it was time to act. Abandoning the raft and the pole, I jumped into the river and swam as fast as I could to rescue my wife.

A question mark had risen in my mind at the moment she jumped into the river. Afterward, she boasted that she had detected the sacred smell of blood from a birthing woman and saw blood running down Wang Dan's leg. So she jumped – there is, of course, another explanation – a delaying tactic, risking drowning to buy time. She said she'd prayed to the river spirit: Wang Dan, hurry up and have your baby! Do it now! Once it's out in the world, it's a human life, a citizen of the People's Republic of China, protected as a flower of the motherland. Children are the nation's future. Of course, she added, my little trick didn't work on Gugu. She knew what I was doing from the get-go.

By the time we fished Little Lion and the family-planning cadre out of the river, Wang Jiao's raft had travelled at least three li. To top it off, the speedboat's engine had died, and Qin He dripped with sweat as he tried to restart it. Gugu flew into a rage. Little Lion and the waterlogged man were lying just inside the handrail, heads over the side, puking water.

Gugu jumped around furiously for a moment, but then abruptly grew calm. A sad smile creased her face, which was illuminated by a ray of sunlight that had broken through the cloud cover; it also lit up the turgid surface of the river and painted her with the look of an ill-fated hero. She sat down on the deck next to the cabin and said to Qin He, You can quit acting. All of you.

Qin He froze for a moment. Then he started the engine and the boat sped after Wang Jiao's raft.

As I thumped Little Lion's back I sneaked a look at Gugu, who lowered her eyes one moment and smiled the next. I wondered what was going through her mind. She was forty-seven years old, and it suddenly dawned on me that her youth was far behind her, that she was well into her middle years. And yet her weatherworn face had the sad look of someone much older. I thought back to all those times my now departed mother had said to me: What is a woman born to do? When all is said and done, a woman is born to have children. A woman's status is determined by the children she bears, as are the dignity she enjoys and the happiness and glory she accrues. Not having children is a woman's greatest torment. A woman without children is something less than whole, and she grows hard-hearted; a woman without children ages faster. Mother had Gugu in mind when she said that, but she'd never have said it in front of Gugu. Was Gugu getting old so fast because she was childless? At forty-seven, if she did find a husband, was a child even possible? And where was the man who might be that husband?

The speedboat easily caught up with Wang Jiao's raft, and as they drew near, Qin He slowed to nudge up close.

Wang Jiao stood at the back of his raft, pole in hand, ferocity written on his face as he took a fighting stance.

Wang Gan sat up front with Chen Er in his arms.

Chen Bi sat in the middle, holding Wang Dan in his arms, alternately crying and laughing. Wang Dan, he was shouting, have the baby, have it now. Have it and it's a living human being. Have it and they won't hound us any more. Wan Xin, Little Lion, you've lost. Ha-ha, you've lost!

Tears streaked the man's stubbled face.

The air was split by Wang Dan's screech, a terrifying, gut-wrenching cry.

The speedboat was right next to the raft. Gugu stood up and reached out her hand.

Chen Bi whipped out his knife and growled menacingly, Take that fiendish hand back.

This isn't the hand of a fiend, it's the hand of an obstetrician.

As my nose smarted, I suddenly realised what was happening. Chen Bi, I shouted, take Gugu aboard and let her deliver Wang Dan's baby!

I hooked his raft with my pole to let Gugu shift her stout frame over.

Little Lion jumped aboard after her, medical kit in her hand.

When they took out a pair of scissors and slit open Wang Dan's bloody trousers, I turned around, though I held on tightly to the pole behind me to keep the raft and speedboat from separating.

An image of Wang Dan floated into my head: she lies on the raft, her lower body blood-soaked, a tiny body with a big belly, looking like an angry, frightened dolphin.

The river roiled, day and night. The clouds parted, freeing the sun to send down bolts of light. The flotilla of rafts and boats rode downriver with its loads of peaches. My raft, now pilotless, actually followed the flow of water with them.

I was hoping expectantly, hoping amid the sound of Wang Dan's shrieks, hoping amid the pounding of the surf, and hoping amid the braying of animals on the bank.

A baby's first cries came on the air.

I spun around and saw Gugu holding a newborn, early-arriving baby in both hands. Little Lion was wrapping gauze around its middle.

Another girl, Gugu said.

Chen Bi, head down, was devastated, like a deflated tyre. He pounded his head with both fists. The heavens have abandoned me . . . The agony he felt was unmistakable. The heavens have abandoned me . . . five generations of the Chen family will end with me. I can't believe it!

What a scumbag you are! Gugu cursed him.

Even though Gugu sped Wang Dan and the baby back up the river in her speedboat, the mother could not be saved.

According to Little Lion, Wang Dan rallied just before she died, her mind clear for a brief spell. She had lost so much blood her face was like a sheet of gold foil. With a smile on her face, she mumbled something to Gugu, who bent down to hear what she was trying to say. Little Lion told me she did not hear what was said, but Gugu did. The gold pallor on Wang Dan's face faded to grey, her eyes were opened wide, though the radiance was gone. Her curled body looked like an emptied sack or a cast-off cocoon. Gugu sat beside Wan Dan's lifeless body, her head hanging low. A long time passed before she stood up, heaved a long sigh, and said, either to Little Lion or to herself: What was all that for?

Gugu and Little Lion cared for Wang Dan's baby, Chen Mei, until she was out of danger and healthy enough to go on living.

BOOK FOUR

Dear Sugitani sensei,

I find it hard to believe it's already been three years since we retired and moved back to Gaomi. Though the period has not been without its hardships, they have been more than offset by one very pleasant surprise. With fear and trepidation I read the high praise over the material on Gugu in the letter I sent. You said that a bit of reorganisation could turn it into a publishable novel, but I'm not so sure. First, publishers may not welcome a novel on this theme or topic. Second, if it is published, it could seriously upset Gugu. Though I have taken pains to show my respect, many painful episodes are still there for all to see. As for me, I am using this epistolary narrative form as a way to atone for my sins and find a way to lessen their impact. Your comforting remarks and reasoning have eased my mind considerably. Since writing can serve as an apology or an appeal for forgiveness, I will keep at it. And since writing must be sincere to make that appeal, that will be my goal.

Over a decade ago I said that writing must touch the most painful spots in one's heart as it records mankind's most unbearable memories. Now I believe that one must write things about which people feel most discomfited, about people's most uncomfortable conditions. The writer must put himself on the dissection table and under the microscope.

Twenty-odd years ago I boasted shamelessly: I write for myself. Writing for absolution is writing for myself, but only to a point; I think I ought to write for the people I hurt, and for the people who hurt me. I am grateful to them, because each time they hurt me I cannot avoid thinking about the people I hurt.

Sensei, I am sending you a packet of what I've been writing off and on over the past year. I think I'll stop writing Gugu's story and concentrate on a play with her as the central character.

Every time I see her she asks after you. She really and truly hopes you will visit again. She even wondered if you might have trouble affording a plane ticket, and she said I must tell you that she will buy one for you. Gugu added that there are many things she wants to say, but cannot bring herself to say to anyone. If you were to come, however, she'd tell you everything. She said she knows one of your father's deepest secrets, something she's never revealed to anyone. If it were to become known, it would shock you to your core. Sensei, I have a good idea what that secret is, but I'll wait till you return, so you can hear it directly from her.

Finally, while it has already appeared in the material I'm sending, I want to tell you anyway: though I am not that far from the age of sixty, I have recently become the father of a newborn infant! It makes no difference how this came about, Sensei, nor how much trouble will follow this child through life. I ask the blessing of a man of such noble standing, and hope that you would honour us by conferring a name on him.

Tadpole
October 2008, Gaomi

1

Gugu always impressed me as a woman of incredible audacity. There did not seem to be a person alive who frightened her, and there was nothing she was afraid to do. But Little Lion and I personally witnessed her frightened to the point of foaming at the mouth and passing out – over a frog.

It happened one April morning when Little Lion and I were to be guests of Yuan Sai and my cousin Jin Xiu, who had opened a bullfrog breeding farm. In the space of only a few years, Northeast Gaomi Township, a one-time backwater, had undergone a major transformation. Impressive white stone levees had been built on both sides of the river, and the green belts along the riverbanks had been beautified by the addition of rare flowers and exotic plants. Over a dozen residential developments, some with towers, and European-style villas, had sprouted on both banks. The area developed until it began to merge with the county capital, and was only a forty-minute car ride to the Qingdao airport. Korean and Japanese investors were building factories there, and most of our village had been given over to the Metropolitan Golf Course. Although the area's name had been changed to Chaoyang District, we still called it Northeast Township.

The distance from our community to the bullfrog farm was about five li; my cousin wanted to send a car, but we declined, preferring to take the riverside pedestrian path, where we passed young housewives pushing baby strollers. Their faces radiated health, their eyes shone, and the elegant aroma of expensive perfumes wafted from their bodies. The babies were sucking on pacifiers or sleeping soundly or looking around, eyes darting in lively fashion; they all emitted a sweet smell. Little Lion never missed asking these young mothers to stop so she could bend down and stroke the little babies' pudgy hands and tender, fair faces. Her expression proved her love of the little ones. As she stood in front of one blond, blue-eyed foreigner's stroller with a pair of twin babies in seersucker caps, she reached down, touched one and then the other, and said something under her breath as tears came to her eyes. I watched the mother smile politely as she grabbed hold of Little Lion's clothing: Don't dribble on their faces.

Little Lion sighed.

Why did I never notice how cute babies are before?

That just shows that we're getting old.

That's only part of it, she said. The quality of people's lives has improved now, and so has the quality of their offspring. That's what makes them so adorable.

We met some people we knew on the way, stopping to shake hands and chat, emotionally commenting on how old we've gotten and wondering where the decades had gone.

We saw a fancy cruise boat sailing slowly down the river; it looked like a floating old-style tower. Joyful sounds came across the water from women dressed in ancient costume, like characters in paintings, playing music and singing in the ship's cabins. A speedboat throwing up rooster tails of spray raced past and scared away all the gulls.

We were holding hands, a loving couple, though we were each thinking our own thoughts. She was probably thinking about children, all those lovely children; but what flashed through my mind were images of that frightful chase on this very river so many years before.

We crossed on the pedestrian walk of the recently completed cable bridge, on which BMW and Mercedes sedans were common sights. It was an elegant, gull-winged bridge that ended with the golf course to the right and the renowned Temple of the Fertility Goddess to the left.

A temple fair was in progress on that eighth day of the fourth lunar month. The temple grounds were packed with automobiles whose licence plates showed them to be from outlying counties, even a few from other provinces.

The spot had once been known as Fertility Goddess Village, its reputation gained from the temple that had stood there. As a child I'd gone there with my mother to burn incense; the image had stuck with me, though the temple had been torn down at the beginning of the Cultural Revolution.

The new Fertility Goddess Temple had a towering main hall with red walls and yellow tiles. On both sides of the crowded paved path peddlers of candles, incense sticks, and clay dolls hawked their wares to tourists.

Buy a doll here, buy a doll.

One of the peddlers, dressed in a yellow Chinese gown, head shaved, looked like a monk. He rapped a stick against his Buddhist temple block, known as a wooden fish, and sang out rhythmically:

> Buy a doll and take it home, a happy family you will soon be.
> Take one this year, raise one the next, soon Mum and Dad,
>   you will see.
> No finer dolls you'll ever find, all crafted from the finest clay.
> Lovely faces have all my dolls, eyes, noses, mouths of beauty.
> My dolls are most potent, sold to villages in eight counties.
> Buy one, you'll have a dragon; buy two, a dragon and a phoenix.
> Buy three for happiness, wealth, and a long life; buy four for
>   two pairs of officials.
> Buy five for five distinguished scholars; buy six, no, I can't give
>   you six or the wife will surely pout.

The voice sounded familiar, so I walked up to see. Just as I thought – it was Wang Gan.

He was trying to sell dolls to a gaggle of Japanese or Korean women.

I thought about taking Little Lion's hand and walking off to spare him the pain of what could only be an uncomfortable meeting for everyone. But she pulled her hand back and walked straight up to him.

No, I realised, she was going up to his stand of dolls. He was not overselling his dolls, which were indeed special. Those at other stalls were uniformly painted, boys and girls, all bright and all the same. Wang Gan's dolls were more understated; each was unique with individual expressions that ran the gamut from lively to peaceful, mischievous to naive, angry to joyful. One look told me they must have been made by Northeast Gaomi Township's master doll maker, Hao Dashou – Hao married my aunt in 1999 – who had for decades employed a unique sales approach for his dolls. What had led him to hand them over to Wang Gan? Wang pointed with puckered lips to the dolls and stalls to either side, then said in a soft voice to the women: Their wares are cheap, machine-produced, but mine are handmade by Northeast Gaomi Township's master craftsman, Qin He, who fashions them with his eyes closed. Perfectly lifelike and exquisitely fragile. Wang Gan picked up a doll with a petulant pout. Alongside Master Qin He's creations, Madame Tussaud's wax figures are mere figurines, he said. All creatures are born of clay, understand? The goddess Nüwa created humans out of clay, you see? Clay is invested with intelligence. Our Master Qin He uses clay dug from two metres deep in the Jiao riverbed, silt that is more than three thousand years old, cultural silt, historical silt. The silt is put out to dry in the sun and aired in the moonlight, soaking up the essence of the sun and the moon. After being broken down by a roller it is reconstituted with river water taken at daybreak and well water drawn as the moon starts its climb, to become clay, which he kneads for a while and pounds for a spell to form a nice round, doughy ball; only then does the creative process begin. I must tell you ladies that after each doll is made, Master Qin He pokes a tiny hole in the top of its head with a pointed bamboo strip, then pricks his middle finger and releases a drop of his blood into the hole. He seals the hole and places the doll in a cool, shady place for forty-nine days before applying paint, beginning with the eyes. These dolls are themselves spirits – don't let what I'm about to reveal frighten you, but at every full moon they dance to the music of flutes, twirling and clapping and laughing, the sound like speech emerging from a cell phone, soft yet clear. If you don't believe me, buy a few and take them home. If they don't come to life, bring them back and smash them here in front of my stall. But I doubt you will do that, for that releases its blood and you will hear it cry. After listening to Wang Gan's sales patter, the women bought two dolls each, which he packed in special gift boxes. His customers walked off happily. And then Wang Gan turned to greet us.

I think he knew we were there all along. He might not have recognised me, but there was no way he missed Little Lion, whom he had pursued with single-minded devotion for more than a decade. But he reacted with surprise, as if he'd just spotted us.

Aiya! It's you two.

How are you, my friend? I said. Haven't seen you in years.

Little Lion smiled and said something too soft for me to hear.

We exchanged a hearty handshake and cigarettes; I smoked the Eight Joys he handed me, he smoked the General I handed him.

Little Lion was busy admiring the dolls.

I heard you were back, he said. You can travel the world, but there's no place like home, it seems.

That's right, I said. A fox dies in the den where it was born, a leaf falls to the ground right below. But we're fortunate to be living in a new age. I hate to even think about how it was all those years ago.

We lived in cages back then, he said, either that or we were led around with leashes. Now we know what freedom is. You can do anything you want if you've got the money and it isn't illegal.

You're right. You've got quite a sales pitch, I said. I pointed to the dolls. Are they really as spirited as you say?

Do you think I'm just blowing smoke? He was dead serious. Every word is the sacred truth, with just a hint of acceptable exaggeration. Even the national media is allowed that.

I'm no match for you, I said. Did Qin He really make those?

Would I say he did if he didn't? That bit about flutes and dancing on a full moon, that was an exaggeration, but it's true that Qin He made them with his eyes shut. If you don't believe me, name the day and I'll take you to see for yourself.

So Qin He settled down here too, did he?

Who talks about settling these days? You live where it suits you. Wherever your aunt is, that's where you'll find Qin He. His kind of diehard loyalty is rare, no matter where you look.

Little Lion held up a lovely little doll with big eyes and a high nose, like a girl with mixed Chinese and European blood. I want this little girl, she said.

I began to sense something as I looked at the doll. Of course, I'd seen that face somewhere. But where? Who was it? Oh, my, it was Wang Dan's daughter, Chen Mei, the girl Gugu and Little Lion took care of for nearly six months, but then had to turn over to her father, Chen Bi.

I still recall the evening Chen came to our house to retrieve his daughter – it was on the night we sent the Kitchen God off to report on the family, not long before New Year's, with firecracker explosions and the smell of gunpowder in the air. Little Lion had filled out the paperwork to accompany me and had left her position with the commune health centre. I'd soon be taking her and Yanyan with me to Beijing. A two-room unit in a Beijing compound would be our new home. Father would not go with us, and was unwilling to move in to my older brother's home in the county capital. He wanted to stay where he was. Fortunately, my second brother had a job in the township, close enough to take care of him.

After Wang Dan's death, Chen Bi began to drown himself in liquor. He walked the streets, alternating between weeping and singing. People sympathised with him at first, but with the passage of time that turned to annoyance. Back when the pursuit of Wang Dan was on, Chen Bi's savings had been used to pay the villagers' wages. But after her death, most gave the money back to him. Additionally, the commune did not ask him to repay the money spent on him during his confinement. A conservative estimate put his savings at thirty thousand yuan, enough for him to spend on drink for several years. To all appearances, he had put out of his mind the child Gugu and Little Lion had taken to the health centre to fight for her life. In basic terms, his goal in subjecting Wang Dan to the dangers of a second pregnancy had been to produce a boy to carry on the family line, and when all the suffering and hardships in reaching that goal ended with the birth of another girl, he pounded himself in the head. The heavens have abandoned me! he wept bitterly.

Gugu named the child. Since she had a fresh, pretty face and a sister named Chen Er (Ear), she settled on Chen Mei (Eyebrow). Little Lion pronounced it to be a beautiful name.

Gugu and Little Lion thought seriously about raising the child on their own, but with the residence issue and the difficult procedures involved in adoption, when Chen Bi came and lifted her from Little Lion's arms, she still had no resident status. In accordance with the laws of the People's Republic of China, she did not exist, what is known as a 'bootleg kid'. How many of those there were at the time no one could say, but the number had to be astonishingly high. The bootleg kid residence issue was finally resolved in 1990 during the Fourth Census. The income derived from fining the masses for illegal births reached astronomical heights, but how much of that money actually made it into the national coffers is too tangled an affair for anyone to sort out. And the number of bootleg kids the masses have produced over the past decade or so is certainly another astronomical figure. The fine for such births is now ten times greater than twenty years ago, and when the next census rolls around, we'll see if the bootleg-kid parents can afford to pay the fines . . .

Back then, Little Lion's motherly instincts were in full bloom. She held Chen Mei, showering her with kisses, hardly ever taking her eyes off her, and I wouldn't have been surprised if she'd tried to nurse her, since her nipples looked funny – whether or not she could actually produce milk was hard to say, but such 'miracles' were said to have occurred. As a youngster I saw a play about a family in which the parents died tragically, leaving behind an eighteen-year-old daughter and her baby brother. Given no choice, she offered her virgin breasts to him, and in only a few days, milk oozed from her nipples. In the real world, such things are likely impossible these days. An eighteen-year-old girl with a nursing brother? Mother said it was common in old times for a woman and her mother-in-law to have children at the same time. Now? It could still happen. A girl in my daughter's college class has a newborn baby sister. Her father, a coalmine owner who hires migrant workers under slave-like conditions, was immeasurably wealthy. People like that live in luxurious villas in Beijing, Shanghai, Los Angeles, San Francisco, Melbourne and Toronto with their mistresses, who produce babies for them.

I pulled my thoughts back from where they were headed, like reining in a spooked horse. I thought back to the evening we were sending the Kitchen God off. I had just dumped a bamboo steamer full of dumplings into a pot of boiling water to the accompaniment of my daughter Yanyan, who clapped and sang a children's song about dumplings – 'Geese flying from the south splash into the river' – as Little Lion cooed to Chen Mei in her arms, when Chen Bi, in his worn-shiny leather jacket and cap with earflaps, sort of staggered into our yard. Chen Er was behind him, holding on to his shirt tail. She was wearing a little padded coat whose sleeves ended above her wrists, exposing hands red from the cold. Her hair looked like a bird's nest, and she was sniffling, probably from a cold.

You're just in time to eat, I said as I stirred the dumplings in the pot. Have a seat.

He sat on the threshold, his face illuminated by flames from the stove. His large nose looked like a turnip carved out of ice. Chen Er stood beside him, resting her hand on his shoulder, the light of fear in her large eyes that kept darting around curiously: from the dumplings roiling in the pot to Little Lion and the baby in her arms; then they alit on Yanyan, who held out a piece of chocolate. She cocked her head to look at her father, then looked up at us.

Take it, I said. She wants you to have it.

She reached out timidly.

Chen Er! Chen Bi snapped.

The girl jerked her hand back.

What's that for? I said. She's just a child.

Chen Er burst into tears.

I picked up a handful of chocolate and stuffed it into Chen Er's coat pocket.

Chen Bi stood up and said to Little Lion, Give me back my child.

She just stared at him. I thought you didn't want her.

Who said so? he growled. She's my flesh and blood, why wouldn't I want her?

You don't deserve her! Little Lion shot back. She looked like a sick kitten when she was born, and I'm the one who kept her alive.

Wang Dan went into labour so early because you were hounding her! If you hadn't she'd be alive today. You owe me a life!

Bullshit! Little Lion said. She should never have been pregnant in the first place. All you cared about was carrying on your line. You didn't give a damn if Wang Dan lived or died. Her death is on your hands!

How dare you say that! Chen Bi screamed. If you say it again I'll make sure your family has a terrible New Year's!

Chen picked a garlic press up off the counter and aimed it at the pot on the stove.

Have you lost your mind, Chen Bi? We've been friends since we were kids.

What good are friends in times like these? He sneered. Were you the one who reported that Wang Dan was hiding in your father-in-law's house?

That had nothing to do with him, Little Lion said. It was Xiao Shangchun.

I don't care who it was. All I know is, you have to give me back my child.

In your dreams! Little Lion said. I'm not going to let this child die at your hand. You have no right to call yourself a father.

You stinking hermaphrodites can't have kids of your own, so you won't let other people have theirs. When they do, you take them for your own!

Shut your stinking mouth, Chen Bi, I fumed. What's the big idea of coming to my house while we're sending off the Kitchen God and making a scene? Go ahead, throw it if you think you have the guts.

You think I won't?

Go ahead.

If you people don't give me back my child, nothing will stop me, not murder or anything, from getting what I want.

Father, who had been in his room, not saying a word, walked out. Good nephew, he said, for the sake of this bearded old man, who was your father's friend for so many years, put that garlic press down.

Then tell her to give me my child.

No one's going to take your child from you, but you need to talk this out with her, Father said. When all is said and done, if not for them, the child would have followed her mother.

Chen Bi threw the press to the floor and sat back down on the threshold, where he began to sob.

Chen Er patted his shoulder. Dad, she said through her tears, don't cry . . .

The scene was affecting me as well. I guess, I said to Little Lion, you should give her to him.

Don't even think that! she said. This child is a foundling, and I found her.

You shouldn't treat people like this, Chen sobbed. That's not how things are supposed to be . . .

Go call your aunt, Father said.

No need for that, Gugu said from just beyond the doorway, I'm right here.

I felt as if our saviour had arrived.

Stand up, Chen Bi, Gugu said. I was waiting for you to throw the garlic press into the pot.

Chen Bi obediently got to his feet.

Chen Bi, do realise you committed a crime?

What crime did I commit?

Child abandonment, Gugu said. We brought Chen Mei back with us, and kept her alive by feeding her millet porridge and powdered milk. For more than six months you didn't so much as come to see her. You're her biological father, that's true, but how have you met your responsibilities as a parent?

She's still mine, he muttered.

Yours? Little Lion asked fiercely. Call her and see if she responds. If she does, you can take her with you.

You're being unreasonable, and I won't argue with you. I was wrong, Gugu, I admit it. Now, give me my daughter.

We'll give her to you, after you go to the commune, pay your fine, and arrange her residency.

How much is the fine?

Fifty-eight hundred, Gugu said.

That much? I don't have that much.

You haven't got it? Gugu said. Then don't even think about taking the child.

Fifty-eight hundred! Fifty-eight hundred! That's more than my life's worth.

You can keep your life, Gugu said. And you can keep your money to buy liquor and food and even visit your whorehouses.

I don't do that! Chen protested angrily out of embarrassment. I'm going to sue you people. If I lose at the commune level, I'll go to the county, and from there to the province and even the Central Government if necessary!

And what if you lose at that level? Gugu asked contemptuously. Will you take your case to the United Nations?

The United Nations? Why not!

You're the man of the hour! Gugu said. You can get out of my sight now and come back for the child when you win your case. But I'm telling you, even if you do somehow win your case, you'll have to promise me in writing that you will bring her up well and you'll owe Little Lion and me five thousand yuan each as 'burden fees' for everything we did.

Chen Bi did not take Chen Mei with him when he left that evening, but once New Year's passed, on the sixteenth day of the new lunar year, the day after the Lantern Festival, he showed up with a receipt for the fine and left with Chen Mei. The 'burden fees' were just something

Gugu said in anger, and there was no need for him to pay them anything. Little Lion cried so hard she shook, as if her own baby had been taken from her. What are you crying about? Gugu scolded. If you want a baby that bad, have one!

But that only intensified her sorrow. Gugu rubbed her shoulders and said in a tone sadder than I'd ever heard, My life has already been settled, but your best days are ahead of you. Go on, forget about work for now, have a child and bring it back to show me.

After moving to Beijing, we tried hard to have a child, but Chen Bi's curse seemed to be working. Little Lion could not get pregnant. She was a good mother to my daughter, but I knew that Chen Mei was the one she pined for. And that was why she was holding a doll that was the spitting image of Chen Mei.

I want this one, she said to Wang Gan, but more to me than to him.

How much? I asked him.

What does that mean, Xiaopao? he asked, obviously miffed. Are you trying to offend me?

You've got me all wrong. You can't buy a doll without good faith, and how can you have that unless you pay for it?

You can't have good faith if you *do* pay for it, Wang Gan said softly. When you pay for one, what you've bought is a lump of clay. You can't pay for a child.

All right, I said. We're at the Binhe community project, number 902 in Building Nine. Come see us.

I will, he said. And I hope you have a son soon.

I shook my head and forced a smile. After saying goodbye to Wang Gan, I took Little Lion's hand and entered the temple's central hall, walking against the crowd of temple-goers on their way out.

Fragrant smoke curled out of the iron incense burners alongside an array of flickering red candles coated with wax drippings. Many women, some old and grizzled, others hibiscus fresh, some in tatters, others heavily bejewelled, an endless variety, each unique to herself, and all wearing expressions of devotion, were burning incense, lighting candles, and cradling clay dolls.

Forty-nine white marble steps led to the entrance to the towering central hall. I gazed up at the inscribed board beneath the swallow eaves over the entrance; it read: 'Moral Education for Children' etched in gold. Bronze bells hanging from the eaves rang out with each gust of wind.

Virtually every person who trod the marble steps was a woman with a doll, and I felt like a spectator as I mixed with the feminine crowd. Reproduction is so solemn yet so commonplace, so serious yet so absurd. I was reminded of that time in my childhood when with my own eyes I watched the 'Down with the Four Olds' struggle corps of the Number One County High School Red Guard faction come to tear down temples and destroy idols. They – boys and girls – picked up the Goddess idol and flung it into the river, accompanied by shouts of: Family planning is the only good path, the Goddess goes in the river to take a bath! Grey-haired old women lining the banks fell to their knees, and I wondered if their mutterings were prayers that the Goddess would come down in spirit to punish those unruly youngsters. Or were they asking the Goddess to forgive them for the sinful actions? No way to tell. 'Rivers flow east for thirty years, and west for the next thirty.' This is what proved the wisdom of that saying: a new temple had been built where the old one had once stood, and a golden idol now stood in the central hall. Not only did it carry on the cultural heritage, but it created a new convention; not only did it fulfill the people's spiritual needs, but it also was a great draw for tourists. The service industry was flourishing with visible economic growth, so better to construct a temple than to build a factory. My fellow townspeople and old friends all lived for and through the temple.

I gazed up at the idol: a face as round as the moon, hair like black clouds; thin brows that arched to her temples, eyes filled with compassion. She was cloaked in white, with jewels draped around her neck. A long-handled round fan in her right hand rested against her shoulder; her left hand lay atop the head of a child riding a fish. A dozen children in a variety of poses were arrayed around her. With lively expressions, filled with childish delight, the children were universally adorable, and all I could think was, the only people in Northeast Gaomi Township

capable of crafting such figures were Hao Dashou and Qin He. If Wang
Gan had been telling the truth, then the figures had to be Qin He's
handiwork, which led me to thoughts of comparing the white-clad
goddess with a youthful Gugu. The nine mats in front of the goddess
were filled by kneeling women who were in no hurry to give up their
spots; they kowtowed and they clasped their hands in prayer as they
gazed up at the goddess's face. Women also filled the space on the
marble floor behind the prayer mats, all with clay dolls laid out in front
of them, as they faced the goddess. Little Lion knelt on the floor and
banged her head loudly to demonstrate her devotion. Tear-filled eyes
were proof of her abiding longing for a child. I knew, however, that she
could never realise her dream of having one. Born in 1950, she was now
fifty-five years old and already post-menopausal, despite the fullness of
her breasts. I knelt alongside her and faced the goddess. People looking
at us would have assumed that the old couple on the floor was praying
for a child for their son or daughter.

Their prayers finished, the women stuffed money into the red
wooden box at the feet of the goddess. Those who gave little did so in a
hurry; those who gave more made a show of it. The offering completed,
a nun standing alongside the donation box handed each woman a red
thread to tie around her doll's neck. Two grey-cassocked nuns, one
on each side, eyes lowered, beat the temple blocks in their hands and
chanted prayers. One might think they saw nothing, but whenever
someone dropped a hundred yuan or more into the box, the wooden
fish sang out loudly, maybe to get the goddess's attention.

Since this was not a planned visit to the temple, we hadn't brought
any money, throwing Little Lion into a bit of a panic, so she slipped the
gold ring off her finger and dropped it into the box. The three loud beats
on the wooden fish sounded like the starter's pistol I'd heard at a race I'd
run in years before.

Minor goddesses stood in secondary halls to the rear: the Immortal
Goddess, the Vision Goddess, the Goddess of Sons and Grandsons, the
Typhus Goddess, the Mother's Milk Goddess, the Goddess of Dreams,
Peigu Goddess, the Goddess of Early Birth, and the Goddess of

Delivery. Women were on their knees praying in front of each of them, with nuns standing by to pound their temple blocks. When I checked the time by the sun, I told Little Lion we could come back tomorrow; she nodded reluctantly, and while we were on the temple path, nuns chanting in a little side building saw us off:

> *Benefactress, don't forget a longevity lock*
> *for your child!*
> *Benefactress, don't forget to buy a rainbow*
> *shawl for your doll!*
> *Benefactress, don't forget to buy cloud slippers*
> *for your doll!*

Since we had no money, we could only offer our apologies and flee.

The sun was high in the sky when we left the temple. My cousin called on my cell phone to get us moving. The grounds were like an anthill, with people scurrying back and forth; a little bit of everything was for sale for the hordes of shoppers. With no time to dawdle, we elbowed our way through the crowd to get to my cousin, who had parked his car just east of the temple grounds, at the entrance to the Sino-American Jiabao Women and Children's Hospital, whose grand opening was that afternoon.

We were too late for the ceremony, evidence of which – the shattered shells of firecrackers – was strewn across the ground. Baskets of flowers had been arranged at the gate, spread out like the wings of a phoenix. A pair of enormous balloons floated about the grounds, tied to an advertising banner. The building, a blue and white crescent-shaped structure, was intended to resemble a pair of embracing arms outstretched in silent elegance, a far cry from the flashy, ornamental Fertility Goddess Temple to the west.

We spotted Gugu at the same time as we caught sight of my cousin, in his suit and shiny leather shoes. People were picking flowers from the baskets and floral wreaths. Gugu was in the midst of that crowd, her hands filled with the stems of white, red, and yellow roses on the verge of blooming. We recognised her from the back. We'd have known her if she'd been in a crowd of thousands, all wearing identical clothing.

We saw a teenage boy hand her a package wrapped in white paper. As soon as she took it, he turned and ran off. When she peeled away the paper wrapping, she jumped in disbelief and cried out in fear. She reeled back and forth a time or two, then fell backward.

It was a big, black frog, which hopped away from her.

2

A phoney-looking security guard at the gate to the bullfrog farm gave my cousin a half-assed salute as the electric gate slid slowly open to allow his Passat entrance. Yuan Sai, the one-time fortune-teller and quack doctor, now CEO of the bullfrog farm, was waiting for us in front of a big, black sculpture.

It was supposed to be a bullfrog.

From a distance it looked like an armoured military transport truck. The following words were carved into the marble plaque at the base: Bullfrog (*Rana Catesbeiana*), Amphibian, Order Anura, Family Ranidae, Genus *Rana*, Derives its name from its bull-like croak.

A picture, take a picture, Yuan Sai greeted us. After that you can take a tour and then eat.

I studied the enormous bullfrog and was properly in awe. A jet-black back, jade-green mouth and golden eye sockets, it had algae-like wrinkled skin covered with warts; the gloomy gaze from its bulging eyes seemed to carry a message from the ancient past.

Xiao Bi, my cousin shouted, bring a camera! A willowy girl with red glasses wearing a long, striped skirt came running up with a heavy camera.

Xiao Bi, formerly an honours student from Qidong University's Art Department, is our office manager, my cousin informed us.

She's more than just beautiful, Yuan Sai said, she's exceptional in many ways. She can sing and dance and is a photographer and sculptor, among other talents. And, I might add, she can drink along with the best.

Mr Yuan likes to flatter people, Xiao Bi said as she blushed.

This classmate of mine is also a very special person, Yuan Sai introduced me to Xiao Bi. He was quite a runner in his youth, and we assumed he'd grow up to be a champion athlete, never expecting him to become a playwright. His name is Wan Zu, but everyone calls him Xiaopao. Now he goes by Tadpole.

Tadpole's my pen-name, I explained.

And this is Tadpole's wife, Little Lion. A specialist in obstetrics.

Little Lion, cradling her doll, nodded absent-mindedly.

I've often heard Yuan and Jin speak of you, Xiao Bi said.

The world's number one frog! Yuan Sai said.

It's Xiao Bi's creation, my cousin added.

I breathed an exaggerated sigh of admiration.

I'd be honoured if the respected Tadpole would tell me what he thinks of it.

We walked around the sculpture, and no matter where I stood I could feel its eyes on me.

After the pictures were taken, Yuan Sai, my cousin, and Xiao Bi accompanied us on a tour of the breeding pond, the tadpole pond, the metamorphose pond, the young frog pond, the feed preparation station, and the frog products workshop.

From that day forward, the image of the bullfrog-breeding pond has often invaded my dreams. Mate-seeking bull-like bellows from the inflated white throats of male bullfrogs spout from the murky surface of the pond, which is some four hundred square feet in size and three feet or so deep, drawing females slowly to them, their extended limbs afloat. Coupled frogs can be seen all over, moving across the surface, males on the females' backs, front legs holding on, rear legs constantly thumping her on the sides. The females eject transparent eggs to be fertilised by sperm ejaculated by the males. Frog fertilisation occurs outside the body – someone, either my cousin or Yuan Sai, said – with as many as ten thousand eggs laid by each female – they're so much more advanced than humans – and croaks fill the air above the pond, which is warmed by the April sun and gives off a nauseating stench. An arena for mating, it is also an arena for producing the next generation – we add stuff to the feed to increase the production of eggs – *wa wa wa* – frog croaks – *wah wah wah* – babies' cries . . .

With the croaking of frogs ringing in our ears, and visions of bullfrogs crammed into our heads, we were taken into a luxurious restaurant.

A pair of girls clad in pink would serve us.

Everything on today's menu comes from frogs, Yuan Sai said.

I picked up the menu and read the list of entrees: salt and pepper frogs' legs, fried frog skin, frog meat with green peppers, sliced frog with bamboo shoots, tadpoles in vinegar sauce, tapioca and frog's egg soup . . .

I'm sorry, I said, but I don't eat frogs.

Me either, Little Lion said.

Why? A surprised Yuan Sai asked. They're delicious. Why don't you eat them?

I tried to put the sight of those bulging eyes, sticky skin, and the cold, putrid smell out of my mind, but couldn't. I shook my head as I suffered.

Not long ago a Korean researcher succeeded in extracting a valuable peptide from the skin of frogs that is an effective antioxidant that eliminates free radicals, a natural anti-ageing compound, my cousin, Jin Xiu, said with a meaningful look. Naturally, it has a number of other fascinating effects, including drastically raising the odds of a woman giving birth to twins and more.

How about a small taste? Yuan Sai offered. Don't be a coward. You have no trouble with scorpions, leeches, worms or venomous snakes, so why not a bullfrog?

You haven't forgotten that my pen-name is Tadpole, have you?

Oh, that's right, Yuan Sai said to the serving girls. Clear the table and tell the chef to cook up a new meal – no frogs!

The new meal was served, the three rounds of toasts were completed.

How did someone like you come up with the idea of raising bullfrogs? I asked Yuan Sai.

The only way to make big money is to come up with new ideas, he said proudly as he blew a smoke ring.

How talented you are, I said, imitating the tone of a sitcom actor, with a sarcastic edge. You've been different ever since you were a child. Raising bullfrogs is fine, but doesn't it bother you to have to give up your arcane skills of removing nails from cows' stomachs and telling fortunes in the marketplace?

Tadpole, you stinker. Don't hit a man in the face in a fight and don't expose his shortcomings during a reprimand.

Not to mention using steel tongs to remove women's IUDs, Little Lion chimed in coldly.

Aiya, dear Sister-in-law, why bring that up? My awareness was at an all-time low then, and I was too soft-hearted, no match for women who caught me in their crazed demand to have children. A third reason? I was broke.

Would you do it today? I asked him.

Do what? He glared at me.

Remove an IUD.

To hear you say it, I have no memory. I'm a new man after those years in the reform-through-labour brigade. These days I walk the straight and narrow, earning a legitimate income. I wouldn't think of doing anything illegal, not even if you put a gun to my head.

We're a law-abiding, public-minded, municipally recognised and outstanding enterprise that pays all its taxes, my cousin said.

Little Lion had her hand on the clay doll throughout the meal.

That damned Qin He, Yuan said, is a bona fide genius. As soon as he started making the dolls, Hao Dashou was out of business.

Xiao Bi, who had sat by quietly with a smile, joined the conversation: All of Master Qin's creations are crystallisations of his emotions.

Are emotions really important in crafting clay dolls? Yuan Sai asked her.

Of course they are, she replied. Every artistic creation is the artist's child.

Then that big bullfrog must be your child. Yuan Sai pointed to the sculpture.

Not another word from the red-faced girl.

Your wife must really be fond of clay dolls, my cousin said to me.

It's not clay dolls she's fond of, Yuan Sai said. It's real babies.

Let's team up, Jin Xiu said excitedly. My cousin can join us.

You want us to be part of your bullfrog farm? I asked. Just looking at those things gives me goose bumps.

We don't farm bullfrogs exclusively. We also . . .

Don't frighten him away, Yuan Sai interrupted. Drink up. Remember how Chairman Mao educated the youngsters back then? Rural villages are the wide-open spaces, he said, where you can do what you want!

3

Wang Gan's comment that love is a sickness was a lesson he'd learned from personal experience. I found it almost incomprehensible that he could go on living after Little Lion married me, given his obsession over her and the bizarre direction it had taken over so many years. With that premise, Qin He's infatuation with Gugu must also be seen as a sickness. When she married Hao Dashou, Qin neither drowned himself in the river nor hanged himself; what he did was transfer his pain onto art, and a true popular artist was born, like a newborn infant emerging from clay.

Wang Gan went beyond not trying to avoid us by bringing up the subject of his obsession over Little Lion, talking lightly about it as if it had happened to someone else. I found his attitude comforting. A sense of guilt that had been concealed in my heart for years began to fade away, and that led to a rekindling of friendship, not to mention the birth of respect.

You might not believe me, he said, but when Little Lion walked barefoot along the riverbank, I followed her footprints on my hands and knees, like a dog, inhaling the smell of her feet as tears drenched my face.

You're just making that up, she said. She was blushing.

It's the absolute truth, Wang Gan insisted. If one word of that is a lie, may boils grow on the tips of my hair!

Did you hear that? Little Lion said. Instead of boils on the tips of his hair he should wish that his shadow would catch cold.

That's terrific, I said. Now I'll have to write you into my play.

Thanks, he said. You can include every idiotic thing the moron Wang Gan did. I'm a reservoir of material.

If you dare write me in, Little Lion said, I'll burn the manuscript.

You can burn the paper it's written on, but you can't burn the poetry in my heart.

Ah, here comes the bookish sentimentality again, Little Lion said. Wang Gan, I'm beginning to think I should have married you instead of him. At least you've gone down on your hands and knees to cry in my footprints.

No more of your world-famous jokes, please, Wang Gan said. You and Xiaopao are an ultimate match.

We must be, Little Lion said, since not even a glimpse of a child has appeared. If that's not an ultimate match, what is it?

All right, that's enough about us. How about you? Haven't you found anyone after all these years?

After I got over my sickness I discovered I really don't like women.

Have you turned gay? Little Lion joked.

I'm neither gay nor straight, Wang Gan said. I'm in love with myself. I love my arms, my legs, my hands, my head, my features, my internal organs, even my shadow. I often have a conversation with my shadow.

You must have contracted another sickness, Little Lion said.

Loving someone else exacts a price, but loving yourself doesn't. I can love myself any way I want to. I can be my own master . . .

Wang Gan took us to the house he shared with Qin He. A wooden plaque hung at the gate. The Master's Workshop, it said.

It was the building where livestock had been held during the commune era and one of my favourite places to play as a child. Back then the smell of horse and mule dung hung in the air day and night; there was a large vat alongside the well in the centre of the yard, and each morning, the livestock handler, a man named Fang, brought the animals out one at a time to drink, while his fellow tender, Du, poured water from the well into the vat. It was a large, well-lit space with a row of twenty feed troughs. The two larger troughs at the head were where the horses and mules were fed, while the shallow troughs inside were reserved for cattle.

As soon as I passed through the gate I was face to face with dozens of tethering posts; slogans on the walls were still visible, and the smell of the animals lingered.

They were going to tear the place down, Wang Gan said, but we heard that after an inspection, the authorities decided to leave traces of the commune for tourists, and so here it is.

Don't they need to raise livestock here? Little Lion asked.

I doubt it, Wang Gan said, then turned and shouted: Mr Qin, we've got guests!

There was no response as we followed Wang Gan inside; the feeding troughs were still there, so too were holes in the walls created by the animals' hooves, and dried cattle and horse dung. The oven where feed had been cooked and a kang just big enough for the six sons in the Fang family was there as well. I'd slept on it many winter nights when water froze before it hit the ground. Old Fang was too poor to own bedding for his children, so he stuffed dry grass into the opening beneath the kang to keep a fire burning; the bed got hot enough to fry an egg. His children slept like babies since they were used to the brick bed, but I tossed and turned all night long. Now a pair of quilts covered the kang, while the walls were pasted with New Year's posters of unicorns delivering babies and strolling ancient scholars. A thick wooden plank laid across two feeding troughs was a bench on which mounds of clay and clay-working tools sat; our old acquaintance Qin He sat on a bench behind the plank. He was wearing a blue smock whose sleeves and front were daubed with many colours. His white hair was parted in the middle, as before; his face was drawn like a horse, with a pair of large, deep melancholy eyes. When we approached him, he looked up and his lips moved, apparently a mumbled greeting. He then went back to studying the wall, his chin resting on his hands, as if deep in thought.

We held our breath, not daring to speak loudly and walking on tiptoes to keep the noise down so as not to interrupt the master's train of thought.

Wang Gan gave us a show of the master's handiwork. Unfinished dolls were drying in the cattle troughs. Dried dolls waiting to be painted were laid out on long boards against the northern wall. The children, in all their varieties, were waving to us from the cattle troughs, already lifelike, even before colours were added.

Under his breath Wang Gan said that the master sat trancelike like that every day, and sometimes didn't climb onto the kang to sleep at night. Yet, like a machine, he kneaded the clay at regular intervals, making sure it never stopped being soft and well formed. Sometimes he'd sit all day long without making a single child; but when he began, he worked remarkably fast. I sell the master's products and am responsible for his day-to-day living, Wang Gan said. At last I've found my calling, just as he's found his.

The master's needs are minimal. He eats what I place in front of him. Of course, I make sure it's the most nutritious food I can provide. He's the pride of the whole county, not just Northeast Gaomi Township.

I woke up late one night, Wang Gan said, and discovered that the master was not in bed. I immediately lit a lantern but didn't find him at his workbench or in the yard. Where could he be? I broke out in a cold sweat, thinking that something had happened to him, and what a loss that would have been for Northeast Township. The county chief has brought the heads of the cultural and tourism bureaus here on three separate occasions. You know who the county chief is, don't you? None other than the son of Yang Lin, the one-time county Party secretary who suffered so badly here and who had a tangled relationship with Gugu. Yang Xiong is a talented young man with penetrating eyes and neat white teeth, and who carries the smell of expensive cigarettes around on him. Word has it he studied in Germany. On his first visit he declared that the livestock-feeding building would not be torn down; the second time he invited the master to a banquet in town, but the master wrapped his arms around one of the tethering posts and held on like a man refusing to go in for a vasectomy; on the third visit, the county chief brought the master a plaque and a certificate proclaiming him to be a folk artist. Wang Gan reached into the cattle trough and brought out a gold-plated plaque and a certificate in a blue fleece cover to show us. Sure, he said, Hao Dashou has one of these plaques and a certificate, and the county chief also invited him to a banquet in town. He didn't accept the invitation either. He wouldn't have been Hao Dashou if he had. Well, these reactions had the county chief viewing the two Northeast Gaomi Township individuals in a new light. Wang Gan reached into his pocket for a stack of business cards, and selected three for us. See here, he said, he gives me one of these every time he visits. Lao Wang, he said to me, Northeast Gaomi Township has hidden talent just waiting to be discovered, and you're part of that. I'm a down-and-outer, I said, with a notorious record. Outside of an infamous romantic escapade, I've been a complete cipher. These days I get by hawking somebody else's clay dolls. Guess what he said to that? Anyone who can devote half a lifetime's energy to the pursuit of a romantic vision is a legendary figure in his own right. Your township has produced its share of unusual and eccentric people, and you're one of them. I tell you, the fellow's part of a new breed of officials, nothing like the ones we used to know. I'll bring you over to meet him the next time he comes to visit. He gave me the job of taking care of the master, responsible for safeguarding his welfare. So when I woke up in the middle of the night and couldn't find him anywhere, I panicked. What would I say to the county chief if something happened to the master? I sat in a sort of trance in front of the stove until moonlight flowed into the room. A pair of chirping crickets behind the stove invested the room with a sense of foreboding. Then I heard some chilled laughter emerge from one of the horse troughs. I jumped to my feet and looked down into the trough, where the master was lying on his back staring into the sky. The trough was too short for him, so he had to curl his legs yoga-fashion, while his hands were folded on his chest. He wore a peaceful look and a broad smile. I could tell he was fast asleep; the laugh was part of his dream. I'm sure you know that these geniuses, the pride of the township, all suffer from debilitating insomnia, and though I'm only half a genius,

I too suffer from insomnia. How about you two? Any sleep problems?

Little Lion and I exchanged a glance and shook our heads. No problems for us. We're snoring away as soon as our heads touch the pillow. I guess that proves we're not in the genius category.

Not everyone who suffers from insomnia is a genius, Wang Gan said, but all geniuses are insomniacs. Gugu's insomnia is known to everyone. In the deep of the night, when silence is king, you can sometimes hear the husky sound of someone singing out in the fields. That's Gugu. While she's out walking at night, Hao Dashou is home making clay dolls. Their insomnia is cyclical; it follows the waxing and waning of the moon. The brighter the moon, the worse their insomnia. They manage to sleep when the moon is on the wane. That's why our talented county chief named Hao Dashou's creations 'Moonlight Dolls'. He sent people from the county TV station to document the making of Hao Dashou's moonlight dolls with the moon shining overhead. You probably haven't seen that documentary, and there's no reason to beat yourselves up if you haven't. It was part of a series called *Uncanny Individuals of Northeast Gaomi Township*. Hao Dashou's moonlight dolls kicked off the series. Next came 'The Master in a Horse Trough', the third was 'An Uncanny Poet', and the fourth 'Singing amid a Chorus of Croaking Frogs'. If you want to see them, I'll have the station send over a DVD – the unedited version. I'll also suggest that they do an episode on you. I've already got a title: 'The Prodigal Son'.

Another glance passed between Little Lion and me. We both smiled. We knew that he'd drifted into an artistic mindset, and we saw no reason to call his attention to that. Why should we? Better to let him talk on.

After suffering from insomnia all those years, Wang Gan said, the master used the horse trough as his bed, where he slept the untroubled slumber of a baby, just like that infant that floated down the river in a wooden trough all those years before. My eyes filled with tears of emotion. Only an insomniac knows the agony of sleepless nights, and only an insomniac knows the joy of a good night's sleep. I maintained a silent watch over the trough, keeping my breathing shallow so as not

to startle the master out of his sleep. Gradually my tear-filled eyes grew
bleary, and a road seemed to open up before me, passing through lush
countryside where flowers bloomed in profusion, with a riot of colours
and a mist of uncommon bouquets, where butterflies flitted and bees
buzzed. A sound up ahead was calling to me, a woman's nasal voice,
somewhat muffled, but pleasantly intimate. The sound led me along.
I could see her lower body only: a nicely rounded bottom, long, shapely
legs, bright red heels, which left shallow footprints in the soft, wet mud,
so clear they provided perfect imprints of her soles. I followed behind her,
on and on, as if the narrow road would never end. Little by little I sensed
that I was walking side by side with the master, though I knew not when
or from where he had joined me. We followed the red footprints until
we reached a distant marsh, where the smell of mud and decay came to
us on the wind from somewhere deep inside. We stepped on clusters of
nut sedge and saw in the distance reedy marshes and patches of sweet
flag, plus many kinds of strange, nameless plants and flowers. The sound
of children's laughter and shouts came from deep in the marsh. The
woman with only her lower body visible shouted towards the marsh
in an alluring voice: Daguai, Xiaoguai, Jinpao, Yudai, repay kindness
with kindness, clear away debts owing and owed — Before she could
finish what she was saying, a jumble of little children, naked but for red
stomachers, came shouting out of the marsh; some had single braids
pointing to the sky, others had shaved heads, and the hair of still others
was formed into three tufts. The children seemed to be on the heavy
side, the marsh looked to be covered by a springy membrane on which
they ran, springing up with every step, like kangaroos. The boys and, of
course, girls surrounded the master and me, some holding on to our legs,
some jumping up onto our shoulders, some tugging on our ears, some
grabbing our hair, some blowing air on our necks, some spitting in our
eyes. We were wrestled to the ground by the boys and, of course, girls.
The boys and, of course, girls rubbed mud all over us, and, of course,
the boys did likewise to themselves . . . afterward, just how long after
I can't say, the boys and, of course, girls abruptly quieted down and sat
down and formed a semicircle, lying, sitting, and kneeling in front of us,

some propping their heads with their hands, some chewing their nails, and some with their mouths hanging open . . . all in all, a lively bunch in every imaginable pose. My god, they were posing as models for the master. I saw that he'd already started working. With his eyes fixed on one child, he picked up a handful of mud and began working it until the child came to life in his hands. Finishing one, he turned to another and repeated the process, over and over . . .

A rooster cry startled me out of my sleep. I discovered I'd fallen asleep next to the horse trough and had dribbled slobber on the master's clothing. Only by recalling a dream is an insomniac sure he's slept. The dream I just told you about was still right before my eyes, and that was proof that I'd slept. Wang Gan, who had suffered from insomnia for years had actually fallen asleep, which was worth celebrating with firecrackers. Even happier was knowing that the master had slept. The master sneezed and slowly opened his eyes. Then, as if something important had suddenly occurred to him, he hopped out of the trough. Dawn had just broken, and rays of colourful sunrise glided in through the window. He rushed to his workbench, uncovered the clay, tore off a chunk, and began kneading, kneading and twisting, twisting and kneading, until an impish little boy with a stomacher and a braid pointing to the sky materialised on the table in front of him. I was deeply moved, as the alluring voice of the woman resounded in my ears. Who was she? Who else could she have been? It was the merciful Fertility Goddess!

At this point in his account, Wang Gan's eyes glistened with tears, and I saw a strange lustre in Little Lion's eyes. She'd fallen under his spell.

Wang Gan continued with his story. I tiptoed out to get a camera and returned to take a picture of the master – no flash – as he worked in a sort of trance. Truth is, I could have fired a gun next to him and not snapped him out of it. The expression on his face kept changing – sombre one moment, playful the next, mischievous for a while, then bleak and lonely. It didn't take me long to discover similarities between the look on his face and that of the face of the child he was moulding. What I mean to say is, the master became the child he was fashioning in his hands. They had a flesh-and-blood bond.

The number of children on the master's workbench grew and grew. The boys and, of course, girls formed a semicircle facing the master, the exact formation I'd seen in my dream! I was astounded and ecstatic. And overwhelmed emotionally. Two people capable of sharing a single dream – 'kindred spirits through and through' is how the ancients described a man and a woman in love, but there was absolutely nothing wrong with using it to describe the master and me. We weren't lovers, but, as fellow sufferers, we enjoyed deep mutual empathy. After hearing me this far, you two ought to understand why all the dolls the master makes are unique, that no two are alike. Not only does he take real children as his models, he even takes them from his dreams. I don't have his talent, but I have a rich imagination and eyes that work like a camera. I can turn a child into ten children, a hundred, a thousand, and I can also shrink a thousand, a hundred, ten children down to a single child. I telepathically pass the dream images of children I've amassed in my head to the master, who then turns them into his artistic creations. That's how I'm able to say that the master and I are natural partners and that the finished products are joint creations. I don't say that to detract from his achievements. In the wake of my romantic episode, I was able to see through the ways of the world; wealth and position are like floating clouds to me. My reason for telling you this is to reveal the miraculous relationship between dreams and art and to help you understand that lost love is a wonderful asset, especially for creative artists. No one who hasn't experienced the bitter taste of lost love can ever lay claim to the highest levels of creative art.

All during Wang Gan's monologue, the master maintained a pose of resting his head in his hands, with no observable movement. It was as if he himself had become a sculpted figurine.

4

Wang Gan sent over a boy with a DVD of the TV series *Unique Individuals of Northeast Gaomi Township*. He was in bib shorts from which emerged long, skinny, Pinocchio-like legs and high-top boots that looked much too heavy for him. His hair was the colour of flax, his brows and eyelashes nearly white, his eyes blue-grey; one look, and you knew he had foreign blood. Little Lion ran in to scare up some treats for him. He stood with his hands clasped behind his back and announced in a thick Northeast Gaomi accent: He said you'll give me at least ten yuan.

We gave him twenty. He bowed and, with a whistle, ran downstairs. So we went to the window, where we sprawled against the sill and watched him clomp like a cartoon character on his way to the playground opposite our housing compound, where the funicular railcar hove in and out of view on its way up the mountain.

A few days later we ran into the boy while we were strolling by the riverbank. He was in the company of a tall Caucasian woman pushing a stroller and a little girl, obviously his kid sister. They were moving gingerly along on rollerskates, protected by a colourful plastic helmet and knee- and elbow-pads. A handsome middle-aged man walking behind them was talking on his mobile phone, speaking in a lilting South China Putonghua. Bringing up the rear was a big, fat dog with golden fur. I recognised the man right off as a renowned Peking

University professor and celebrated TV personality. When Little Lion bent over and all but buried her pudgy face in the blue-eyed baby, the woman smiled, a sign of good upbringing; the professor, on the other hand, reacted with a look of disdain. I reached down, grabbed Little Lion by the arm, and pulled her away from the stroller. She'd been so focused on the baby that the look on the professor's face had escaped her entirely. I nodded by way of apology, and he accepted my gesture with a slight nod in return. I had to remind her not to pounce on pretty babies as if she were Granny Wolf. These days children are like little treasures, I told her. All you ever look at are the babies, never at their parents' faces. Stung by the criticism, she first launched into a tirade against rich people, who have as many kids as they want, and Chinese men and women who marry foreigners, then have one baby after another. But self-pity and remorse set in for helping Gugu carry out the cruel, one-child family-planning policy, a harsh course of action that had led to a mass of aborted foetuses and, as a sort of heavenly retribution, made her sterile, unable to bear children. She told me to go marry one of those foreign girls and raise a brood of half-breed kids. I won't be jealous, Xiaopao, she said, not at all. Go find yourself a foreign girl, and have as many kids as you want, the more the merrier. I'll even help you raise them. By this time her eyes were glistening with tears and her breathing was rapid. Her breast heaved, filled with motherly love with no one to bathe in it. I had no doubt that if she were handed a child, her breasts would swell with milk.

That was how things were when I put Wang Gan's disk into the DVD player.

With the nasal strains of Shandong operatic speech – grating to the ears of outsiders, but capable of bringing tears to the eyes of locals – swirling in the air, the lives of my aunt and the sculptor Hao Dashou unfolded in front of our eyes.

I have to admit that, though I did not make it public, I had been personally opposed to Gugu's marriage. My father, my brothers, and their wives had shared my feelings. It simply wasn't a good match in our view. Ever since we were small we'd looked forward to seeing Gugu find a husband. Her relationship with Wang Xiaoti had brought immense glory to the family, only to end ingloriously. Yang Lin was next, and while not nearly the ideal match that Wang would have provided, he was, after all, a high-ranking official, which made him a passable candidate for marriage. Hell, she could have married Qin He, who was obsessed with her, and would have been better off than with Hao Dashou . . . we were by then assuming she'd wind up an old maid, and had made appropriate plans. We'd even discussed who would be her caregiver when she reached old age. But then, with no prior indication, she'd married Hao Dashou. Little Lion and I were living in Beijing then, and when we heard the news, we could hardly believe our ears. Once the preposterous reality set in, we were overcome by sadness.

This episode of the TV series, entitled 'Moon Child', was supposed to be about the sculptor Hao Dashou, though the camera was always on her, talking and gesturing as she welcomed journalists into Hao's yard and gave them a guided tour of his workshop and the storeroom where he kept his clay figurines, while he sat quietly at his workbench, eyes glazed over and a blank look on his face, like a dreamy old horse. Did all master artists turn into dreamy old horses once they reached the pinnacle of their artistry? I wondered. The name Hao Dashou was familiar to me, though I'd only met him a few times. After seeing him late on the night my nephew Xiangqun hosted a dinner to celebrate his acceptance as an air force pilot, years passed before I saw him again, and this time it was on TV. His hair and beard had turned white, but his complexion was as ruddy as ever; composed and serene, he was a nearly transcendent figure. It was during that program that we accidentally learned why Gugu had married him.

Gugu lit a cigarette, took a drag, and began to speak, sadness creeping into her voice. Marriages, she said, are made in Heaven. By this, I'm not promoting the cause of idealism for you youngsters, for there was a time when I was an ardent materialist, but where marriage is concerned, you must believe in fate. Just ask him, she said, pointing to Hao Dashou, who sat there like one of his sculptures. Do you think he ever dreamed of one day getting me as his wife?

In 1997, when I was sixty, she said, my superiors asked me to retire, whether I wanted to or not. I was already five years past the retirement age, and nothing I said would have made any difference. You know the hospital director, that ungrateful bastard Huang Jun, the son of Huang Pi from Hexi Village. Just who do you think dragged that little shit – they called him Melon Huang – out of his mother's belly? Well, he spent a couple of days in a medical school, and he came out almost as stupid as the day he went in – he couldn't locate a heart with a stethoscope, couldn't find a vein with a syringe, and had never heard the terms inch, bar and cubit when checking a patient's pulse. So who better to appoint as hospital director! He was admitted into the school thanks to my personal recommendation to Director Shen of the Bureau of Health. Only to be ignored by him when he was the man in charge. The wretched creature has two talents, and only two: playing the host, giving gifts, and kissing arse; and seducing, even raping, women.

At this point, Gugu thumped her breast and stomped her foot. What a fool I was, she said angrily, letting the wolf in the door. I made it easy for him to have his way with all the girls in the hospital. Wang Xiaomei, a seventeen-year-old girl from Wang Village, had nice, thick braids, a pretty oval face, and skin like ivory. Her lashes danced like butterfly wings, her eyes could talk, and anyone who saw her would believe that if film director Zhang Yimou discovered her, she'd be a hotter commodity than Gong Li or Zhang Ziyi ever were. Sadly, Melon Huang, the sex fiend, discovered her first. He rushed off to Wang Village, where, with a glib tongue that could bring back the dead, he talked Xiaomei's parents into sending her to his hospital to learn from me how to treat women's problems. He said she'd be my student, but she never spent a single day with me. Instead, the lecher kept her to himself as his daily companion and nightly lover. If that weren't bad enough, he even took her in the daytime; people had seen them. Then once he'd had enough fun with her, he went off to the county seat, where he hosted banquets for high officials with public funds, in the hope of being transferred to the big city. Maybe you haven't seen what he looks like: a long, donkey face with dark lips, bloody gums, and breath so bad it could fell a horse. Even with a face like that, he figured he had a chance of becoming assistant director at the Bureau of Health! So he dragged Wang Xiaomei along to drink and eat and entertain the officials, probably even offering her up as a gift for their pleasure. Evil! That's what he was, pure evil!

One day the wretch called me to his office. Other women who worked in the hospital were afraid to be in his office. But not me. I kept a little dagger handy, and wouldn't have hesitated to use it on the bastard. Well, he poured tea, smiled, and laid it on thick. What did you want to see me about, Director Huang? Let's get to the point.

Heh-heh. He grinned. Great Gugu – damned if he didn't call me Great Gugu – you delivered me the day I was born, and you've watched me grow into adulthood. Why, I could be your own son. Heh-heh . . .

I don't deserve such an honour, I said. You're the director of a big hospital, while I'm just an ordinary obstetrician. If you were my son I'd die from the honour. So, please, tell me what you have in mind. More heh-heh-hehing, before he got around to revealing the shameless reason he'd summoned me. I've made the mistake all leading cadres make sooner or later – through my own carelessness Wang Xiaomei got pregnant. Congratulations! I said. Now that Xiaomei is carrying your dragon seed, the hospital is guaranteed leadership continuity. Don't mock me, Great Gugu, I've been so upset the past few days I can't eat or sleep. Can you believe the bastard actually said he had trouble eating and sleeping? She's demanding that I divorce my wife, and if I won't she's threatened to report me to the County Discipline Commission. Really? I said. I thought having second wives was popular among you officials these days. Buy a villa, install her in it, and you've got it made. I asked you not to make fun of me, Great Gugu, he said. I couldn't go public with a second or a third wife. Besides, where would I get the money to buy a villa? Then go ahead and get a divorce, I said. He pulled that donkey face longer than ever and said, Great Gugu, you know full well that my father-in-law and those pig-butcher brothers-in-law of mine are violent thugs. They wouldn't hesitate to butcher me if they found out about this. But you're the Director, an official! All right, that's enough, Great Gugu. In your old eyes the director of a hospital in a piddling, out-of-the-way town is about as important as a loud fart, so instead of mocking me, why don't you help me come up with something! What in the world could I come up with? Wang Xiaomei admires you, he said. She's told me that many, many times. You're the only person she'll listen to. What do you want me to do? Talk her into having an abortion. Melon Huang, I protested through clenched teeth, I'll never again soil my hands with that atrocious act! Over the course of my life I've been responsible for more than two thousand aborted births, and I'll never do it again. Just wait until you're a father. Xiaomei is such a pretty girl, she's bound to present you with a lovely boy or girl, and that should make you happy. You go tell her that when the time comes, I'll be there to deliver the child.

With that, I turned on my heel and walked out of the office pleased with myself. But that feeling lasted only till I was back in my own office and had drunk a glass of water. My mood turned dark. No one as bad as Melon Huang deserved to have an heir, and what a shame it was that Wang Xiaomei was carrying his child. I'd learned enough from delivering all those children to know that a person's core – good or bad – is determined more by nature than nurture. You can criticise hereditary laws all you want, but this is knowledge based on experience. You could place a son of that evil Melon Huang in a Buddhist temple, and he'd grow up to be a lascivious monk. No matter how sorry I felt for Wang Xiaomei, I would not put ideas in her head; I simply couldn't let that fiend find an easy way out of his predicament. If the world had another lascivious monk, so be it. But in the end I helped her abort the baby she was carrying.

Xiaomei herself came to me, wrapped her arms around my legs, and dirtied my trousers with her tears and snot. Gugu, she sobbed, dear Gugu, he tricked me, he lied to me. I wouldn't marry that bastard if he sent an eight-man sedan chair for me. Help me do it, Gugu, I don't want that evil seed in me.

So that's how it was. Gugu lit another cigarette and puffed on it savagely, until I couldn't see her face for all the smoke. I helped rid her of the foetus. Once a rose about to bloom, Wang Xiaomei was now ruined, a fallen woman. Gugu reached up and dried her tears. I vowed to never do that procedure again, I couldn't take it any longer, not for anyone, not even if the woman was carrying the offspring of a chimpanzee. The slurping sound as it was sucked into the vacuum bottle was like a monstrous hand squeezing my heart, harder and harder, until I broke out in a cold sweat and began to see stars. The moment I finished I crumpled to the floor.

You're right, I do digress when I'm talking – I'm old. After all that chatter, I still haven't told you why I married Hao Dashou. Well, I announced my retirement on the fifteenth day of the seventh lunar month, but that bastard Melon Huang wanted to keep me around and urged me to formally retire but remain on the payroll at eight hundred yuan a month. I spat in his face. I've slaved enough for you, you bastard. You have me to thank for eight out of every ten yuan this hospital has earned all these years. When women and girls come to the hospital from all around, it's me they've come to see. If money was what I was after, I could have made at least a thousand a day on my own. Do you really think you can buy my labour for eight hundred a month, Melon Huang? A migrant worker is worth more than that. I've slaved away half my life, and now it's time for me to rest, to go back home to Northeast Gaomi Township. He was upset with me and has spent much of the past two years trying to make me suffer. Me, suffer? I'm a woman who's seen it all. As a little girl I wasn't scared of the Jap devils, so what made him think I was scared of a little bastard like him now that I was in my seventies? Right, right, back to what I was saying.

If you want to know why I married Hao Dashou, I have to start with the frogs. Some old friends hosted a restaurant banquet on the night I announced my retirement, and I wound up drunk – I hadn't drunk much, but it was cheap liquor. Xie Xiaoque, the son of the restaurant owner, Xie Baizhua, one of those sweet-potato kids of the '63 famine, took out a bottle of ultra-strong Wuliangye – to honour me, he said – but it was counterfeit, and my head was reeling. Everyone at the table was wobbly, barely able to stand, and Xie himself foamed at the mouth till his eyes rolled up into his head.

Gugu said she staggered out of the restaurant, headed for the hospital dormitory, but wound up in a marshy area on a narrow, winding path bordered on both sides by head-high reeds. Reflected moonlight shimmered like glass on the water. The croaks of toads and frogs sounded first on one side and then on the other, back and forth, like an antiphonal chorus. Then the croaks came at her from all sides at the same time, waves and waves of them merging to fill the sky. Suddenly, there was total silence, broken only by the chirping of insects. Gugu said that in all her years as a medical provider, travelling up and down remote paths late at night, she'd never once felt afraid. But that night she was terror-stricken. The croaking of frogs is often described in terms of drumbeats. But that night it sounded to her like human cries, almost as if thousands of newborn infants were crying. That had always been one of her favourite sounds, she said. For an obstetrician, no sound in the world approaches the soul-stirring music of a newborn baby's cries. But the cries that night were infused with a sense of resentment and of grievance, as if the souls of countless murdered infants were hurling accusations. The liquor she'd drunk, she said, left her body as cold sweat. Don't assume I was drunk and hallucinating, because as soon as the liquor oozed out through my pores, leaving me with a slight headache, my mind was clear. As she walked down the muddy path, all she wanted was to escape that croaking. But how? No matter how hard she tried to get away, the chilling *croak–croak–croak* sounds of aggrieved crying ensnared her from all sides. She tried to run, but couldn't; the gummy surface of the path stuck to the soles of her shoes, and it was a chore even to lift a foot, snapping the silvery threads that held her shoes to the surface of the path. But as soon as she put her foot down, more threads were formed. So she took off her shoes to walk in her bare feet, but that actually increased the grip of the mud, as if the silvery threads created suckers that attached themselves to the bottoms of her feet, so powerful they could rip the skin right off. Gugu said she got down on her hands and knees, like an enormous frog, and began to crawl. Now the mud stuck to her knees and calves and hands, but she didn't care, she just kept crawling. It was at that moment, she said, when an incalculable number of frogs hopped out of the dense curtain of reeds and from lily pads that shimmered in the moonlight. Some were jade green, others were golden yellow; some were as big as an electric iron, others as small as date pits. The eyes of some were like nuggets of gold, those of others, red beans. They came upon her like ocean waves, enshrouding her with their angry croaks, and it felt as if all those mouths were pecking at her skin, that they had grown nails to scrape it. When they hopped onto her back, her neck and her head, their weight sent her sprawling onto the muddy path. Her greatest fear, she said, came not from the constant pecking and scratching, but from the disgusting, unbearable sensation of their cold, slimy skin brushing against hers. They drenched me in urine, or maybe it was semen. She said she was suddenly reminded of a legend her grandmother had told her about a seducing frog: A maiden cooling herself on a riverbank one night fell asleep and dreamed of a liaison with a young man dressed in green. When she awoke she was pregnant and eventually gave birth to a nest of frogs. Given an explosion of energy by that terrifying image, she jumped to her feet and shed the frogs on her body like mud clods. But not all – some clung to her clothes and to her hair; two even hung by their mouths from the lobes of her ears, a pair of horrific earrings. As she took off running, Gugu sensed that somehow the mud was losing its sucking power, and as she ran she shook her body and tore at her clothes and skin with both hands. She shrieked each time she caught one of the frogs, which she flung away. The two attached to her ears like suckling infants nearly took some of the skin with them when she pulled them off.

Gugu screamed and ran, but could not break free of the amphibian horde. And when she turned to look, the sight nearly drove the soul out of her body. Thousands, tens of thousands of frogs had formed a mighty army behind her, croaking, hopping, colliding, crowding together, like a murky torrent rushing madly towards her. As she ran, roadside frogs hopped into the path, forming barriers to block her progress, while others leaped out of the reedy curtain in individual assaults. She told us that the loose-fitting black silk skirt she was wearing that night was being shredded by the sneak attack. Frogs that swallowed the strips of silk were thrown into a frenzy of cheek-scraping from choking before they rolled on the ground and exposed their white underbellies.

She ran all the way to a riverbank, where she spotted a little stone bridge washed by silvery moonlight. By then hardly anything remained of her skirt, and when she reached the bridge, nearly naked, she ran into Hao Dashou.

Thoughts of modesty did not enter my mind at that moment, nor was I aware that I'd been stripped naked. I spotted a man in a palm-bark rain cape and a bamboo coned hat sitting in the middle of the bridge kneading something that shimmered in his hands. I later learned he was kneading a lump of clay. A moon child can only be made from clay bathed in moonlight. I didn't know who he was, and I didn't care. Whoever he was, he was bound to be my saviour. She rushed into the man's arms and crawled under his rain cape, and when her breasts came into contact with the warmth of his chest, in contrast to the damp, foul-smelling chill of the frogs on her back, she cried out, Help, Big Brother, save me! She promptly passed out.

Gugu's extended narration called up images of frog hordes in our minds and sent chills up and down our spines. The camera cut to Hao Dashou, who still sat like a statue; the next scenes were close-ups of clay figures and of the little stone bridge, before returning to Gugu's face, focusing on her mouth as she continued her story.

I awoke to find myself on Hao Dashou's brick bed, dressed in men's clothes. He handed me a bowl of mung bean soup, the simple fragrance of which cleared my head. I was sweating after a single bowlful, and was suddenly aware that I felt painfully hot all over. That cold, slimy feeling that had made me scream was fading. I had itchy, painful blisters all over my body, I spiked a fever, and was delirious. But I'd passed an ordeal by drinking Hao Dashou's mung bean soup; I'd shed a layer of skin, and my bones ached dully. I'd heard a legend about rebirth, and I knew I'd become a new person. When I regained my health, I said to him: Big Brother, let's get married.

When she reached this point, Gugu's face was awash with tears.

The program continued with an account of how Gugu and Hao

Dashou together produced clay dolls. With her eyes closed, she said to Hao, whose eyes were also closed and who was holding a lump of clay in his hands: This child's name is Guan Xiaoxiong. His father is five feet, ten inches tall, has a rectangular face with a broad chin, single-fold eyelids, big ears, a fleshy nose tip, and a low bridge. His mother is five feet ten, has a long neck, a pointed chin, high cheekbones, double-fold lids, big eyes, a pointed nose tip, and a high bridge. The child is three parts father and seven parts mother . . . In the midst of Gugu's verbal portrait, Guan Xiaoxiong was born in Hao Dashou's hands. The camera zoomed in for a close-up. His features were crisp and clear, but he wore a hard-to-describe doleful expression that brought me to tears.

5

I accompanied Little Lion on a visit to the Sino-American Jiabao Women and Children's Hospital. She had wanted to work there, but had no one to open the door.

My first impression as we stepped into the lobby was that it looked more like an elite private club than a hospital. Cool breezes from the air-conditioning system took the bite out of a midsummer day. The background music was pleasant and relaxing, the fragrance of fresh flowers surrounded us. Inlaid in the wall facing us was the hospital's logo in light blue and eight oversized words in pink:

Say Yes to Life, Embrace Trust and Hope.

Two lovely young women in nurse's outfits with little white caps welcomed guests with broad smiles, bows and soft voices.

A middle-aged woman in a nurse's outfit, wearing a pair of white-framed glasses, walked up to us. May I help you, sir, madam? she asked cordially.

No, thank you, we're just here to look around.

She invited us into a waiting room to the right of the lobby. The room was furnished with a large wicker table and chairs, a simple bookshelf filled with glossy obstetrics-related magazines, and a tea table on which fancy brochures introducing the hospital were laid out.

After filling two glasses from a water fountain for us, she smiled and left us alone.

As I thumbed through the material, I came across the image of a middle-aged female doctor with a bright forehead, long curving eyebrows, friendly eyes, frameless glasses, white, even teeth and a beatific smile. A photo ID was pinned to her breast. Text above her left shoulder read: *The Sino-American Jiabao Women and Children's Hospital is the modern obstetrics hospital of your dreams. The cold atmosphere of other hospitals is absent here, replaced by warmth, harmony, sincerity, and a sense of family. You will experience true royal treatment* . . . text above her right shoulder read: *We abide strictly to the international medical standards set forth in the Geneva Convention of 1948, practising medicine with scruples and dignity. Our patients' health takes precedence over everything else, and we take pains to maintain patient confidentiality. We strive to protect the lofty reputation and noble traditions of the medical field* . . .

I sneaked a look at Little Lion, who seemed to be frowning as she skimmed a hospital brochure.

I turned the page. An obstetrician whose look inspired confidence was measuring the mounded, shiny abdomen of a pregnant woman. She had long lashes, a high nose bridge, lovely lips, and a ruddy face; absent was the gaunt, weary look of most pregnant women. A line of text across the doctor's arm and atop the woman's abdomen read: *We maintain the deepest respect for life beginning at the moment of conception.*

A man of medium build and thinning hair, dressed in brand-name casual wear, stepped briskly into the lobby. His self-assured airs and slight paunch told me that he was a person of position, if not a high official, then a man of wealth. Of course, he could have been both. He had his arm around a tall, slim young woman whose goose egg yellow silk skirt swished back and forth as she walked. My heart skipped a beat. It was Xiao Bi, the office manager at the bullfrog farm run by Yuan Sai and my cousin, the multi-talented Xiao Bi. I quickly lowered my head and held the brochure up to cover most of my face.

I turned to the next page, where, in the white space to the right and below a beautiful swollen abdomen, five naked infants sat in a row. Their heads were all turned to the left, a hint that someone off the page was playing with them. Round heads and puffy cheeks formed an adorable arc. Though their expressions were hidden, the arc itself formed an innocent smile. The hair on three of the heads was thin, the other two thick and full, black on two, golden yellow on one, and light yellow on the other two. All had large, fleshy ears, a sign of good fortune. Having their photographs in the brochure was a blissful sign of being favoured. They looked to be about five months old, barely able to sit up, their waists still sort of twisted. They were fat and round as little piglets, their protruding belly buttons visible under the folds of their arms. Their bottoms were flattened out, the two cheeks squeezed together, separated by a cute little crack. A dozen lines of text appeared to their left:

Our family-centred obstetrics services are tailored to communication between the pregnant woman, including those in labour, and our high quality medical team, with an emphasis on medical education.

The middle-aged man and Xiao Bi walked up to the front desk, where they spoke briefly to the receptionist before being led by an elegant woman to seats in a VIP area to the left of the lobby. They sat in brick red high-backed chairs behind a table with a vase of mauve roses. The man sneezed, and nearly made me jump out of my chair. It was a strange and distinctive sneeze, loud as an exploding detonator that triggered a memory. Could that be him?

Our doctors initiate detailed conversations with the pregnant woman and their family regarding the state of the woman's health, the state of the foetus, the mother's nutritional and exercise routines, and other concerns.

I desperately wanted to share my discovery with Little Lion, but she was too focused on the brochures, muttering as she read. How can they call this a hospital? Who can afford to stay in a place like this . . . With her back to Xiao Bi, she hadn't noticed their arrival.

Apparently concerned that they were too conspicuous, the man stood up, took Xiao Bi by the hand, and walked over to the coffee shop at the rear of the entry hall, separated by large pots of tortoise-shell bamboo, with their jade green leaves, and a potted banyan tree whose leafy branches nearly touched the ceiling. The wall behind a fireplace was papered in a red brick design. The coffee shop was equipped with a bar with a rack filled with brand name liquor. A young man in a black bowtie was brewing gourmet coffee whose fragrance blended with the floral perfume to produce a sense of nurturing.

The hospital is also equipped with a rehearsal room for women late in their pregnancy. Delivery options are discussed with doctors and nurses, based upon the pregnant woman's particular situation, and a mother-to-be classroom, all structured to enhance communications between hospital staff and patients, who are given unlimited opportunities to make their needs, concerns, and questions known.

He sat there with a cup of coffee, talking intimately with Xiao Bi. Yes, indeed, that's who it was. A person can change the way he talks, but not the way he sneezes. A person can turn single-fold eyelids into double folds, but the greatest plastic surgeon alive cannot change the look in a man's eyes. He was talking easily and laughing no more than twenty metres from me, totally unaware that a childhood friend was watching him. And as I watched, the wicked and merciless Xiao Xiachun, no longer with single-fold eyelids, separated himself from the body of the distinguished man.

It's hopeless! Little Lion said dejectedly as she tossed the brochure onto the table and leaned back. US-trained doctors, French-trained graduates, medical college professors . . . top medical group in the country . . . the only way they'd let me in here would be to clean the toilets . . .

We were from the same hometown, we lived in Beijing at the same time, and yet I hadn't seen him even once. I recalled how his father had paraded up and down the streets shouting, My son has been given a job at the State Council! after graduating from college. He spent several years in an office there before being taken on as the secretary to a bureau chief, and from there he took a post as deputy Party secretary somewhere. Then he left public office and became a real estate mogul worth billions . . .

The elegant woman who had greeted us located the two of them and led them out back somewhere. I shut the brochure I was reading. The back cover showed the hands of a doctor and a pregnant woman, all resting on her swollen belly. The text at the top read: *Mothers-to-be and their children are family to us. We provide the best treatment found anywhere. You will be able to soak up our atmosphere of sweetness and experience the blessing of total care and attention.*

In a complete funk as we left the hospital, Little Lion used every hackneyed political expression she could think of to excoriate these modern developments. I was too occupied with my own thoughts to pay attention to her. But her monotonous chatter started to bother me. All right, madam, enough sour grapes!

Rather than get angry with me, she just coughed up a bitter laugh and said, All a rustic doctor like me is good for is raising bullfrogs at Yuan Sai's farm.

We came back here to live in retirement, I said, not look for work.

I have to find something to do, she said. Maybe I can work as a live-in wet nurse.

Enough, I said. Say, guess who I just saw?

Who?

Xiao Xiachun. He changed his appearance, but I recognised him.

Impossible, she said. What would a rich man like him be doing back here? You must have mistaken somebody else for him.

If it had been my eyes, possibly, but not my ears. No one on earth sneezes like him. Then there were the look in his eyes and that laugh. He couldn't change those.

Maybe he's come back for another big investment, Little Lion said. I hear we're going to fall under Qingdao administration before long. When that happens, the price of land and houses will shoot up.

Now, guess who he was with?

How am I supposed to guess that, Little Lion replied.

Xiao Bi.

Who?

Xiao Bi, the girl at the bullfrog farm.

I see, she said. I knew she was a slut the minute I laid eyes on her. There's something unclean about her relationship with your cousin and Yuan Sai.

6

Little Lion found the bullfrog farm repugnant, and had little good to say about Yuan Sai and my cousin. But the day after we visited the Sino-American Jiabao Women and Children's Hospital, out of the blue she said: Xiaopao, I'm going to work at the bullfrog farm.

That was a shock. Her large face beamed with a smile.

Really. I'm not joking, she said soberly, the smile gone.

Those critters, I've been trying to drive the stubborn image of bullfrogs out of my head – after watching Gugu's TV documentary I think I developed a phobia of all frogs – and now you say you want to raise those critters?

There's no reason to be afraid of frogs, you know, since we have the same ancestors. Tadpoles and human sperm look about the same, and there isn't much difference between frog and human eggs. And there's more – have you seen human foetus specimens in the first three months, how they have a long tail? They're just like frogs in their metamorphic stage.

I could hardly believe what I was hearing.

Why does the word for frogs – *wa* – sound exactly like the word for babies – *wa*? This was a prepared speech. Why is the first sound a newborn baby makes an almost exact replica of a frog's croak? How come so many of the clay dolls made in Northeast Gaomi Township are holding frogs in their arms? And why is the ancestor of humans called Nü wa? Like the '*wa*' for frog. Doesn't that prove that our earliest ancestor was a frog, and that we have evolved from her? The theory that men evolved from apes is wrong . . .

As she went on and on I began to detect a conversational style used by Yuan Sai and my cousin, and I knew that she'd fallen under the spell of those two smooth talkers.

Okay, I said, if you're bored at home with nothing to do, you can give it a try. But, I added, trying to sound prophetic, I'm betting you'll pack it in within a week.

7

Sensei, even though I said I opposed Little Lion's plan to work at the bullfrog farm, deep down I was pleased. I am by nature someone who treasures his time alone; I like to go for solitary walks, when I can reflect on the past. And if there's nothing in the past that captures my fancy, I let my thoughts go where they will. Taking walks with Little Lion is something I need to do, and no matter how unpleasant it is to carry out such responsibilities, it's important to pretend I'm happy and excited to be doing them. Now things have taken a positive turn, since she leaves the house early in the morning to work at the bullfrog farm, getting there on a motorised bicycle she said my cousin had bought for her. I watch through the window as she primly motors down the riverside road, silently and effortlessly on the new ride. Once her figure disappears, I hurry down the stairs

Over a period of several months, I visited several communities north of the river. Traces of my travel could be found in woods, flower gardens, supermarkets big and small, a massage parlour run by the blind, a public fitness park, beauty salons, pharmacies, lottery stalls, malls, furniture stores, and the riverside farm products outlet. I took pictures everywhere I went with my digital camera, like a dog lifting its leg to leave its mark from place to place. I walked through fields and stopped at construction sites. Work on the impressive main buildings at some of the sites was finished, whereas work at other sites had not progressed beyond the foundation preparation, with no hint as to what was coming.

After taking in the sights on the northern bank, I turned my attention south. I could cross the high-arching suspension bridge, or I could let the flow of the river take me on a bamboo raft a dozen li or so all the way to Ai Family Pier. I usually walked; rafting seemed too risky for me. But when an accident snarled traffic on the bridge one day, I decided to take a raft and relive my experience of many years before.

My rafter was a young man in a Chinese-style jacket with cloth buttons. Just about everything out of his mouth was a buzzword in a heavy rural accent. His vessel was constructed out of twenty lengths of thick bamboo, with an upturned bow on which sat a painted dragon's head. A pair of red plastic stools was fixed to the deck in the centre of the raft. He handed me plastic bags to tie around my ankles to keep my shoes and socks dry. City folk, he said with a laugh, like to take off their shoes and socks. The women's little feet are as pale as whitebait fish, and they make a funny squishing sound when they dip in the water. I took off my shoes and socks and handed them to him. He put them into a metal box and said, half jokingly, That'll be a one yuan storage fee. Whatever you say, I replied. He tossed me a red life vest. You have to put that on, old uncle, or the boss will fine me.

When he poled us out into the river, rafters crouching on the riverbank cried out, Have a good trip, Flathead. Don't fall into the river and drown!

He skillfully poled us out into the river. No way, he said. If I drowned, your little sister would be a widow, wouldn't she?

We picked up speed out in the middle of the river, where I took out my camera and snapped shots of bridges and riverbank scenes.

Where are you from, old uncle?

Where do you think? I replied in my hometown accent.

You from around these parts?

Could be. Your father and I might have been schoolmates! His long, flattened head reminded me of a classmate from Tan Family Village. Flathead was what we'd called him.

That's possible, but I don't know you. May I ask what village you're from?

Just keep poling, I said. It's okay if you don't know me. But I know your parents.

The young fellow plied his bamboo pole expertly, turning to look at me from time to time, obviously trying to place me. I took out a cigarette and lit it. He sniffed the air. Unless I'm mistaken, old uncle, that's a China brand you're smoking.

He wasn't mistaken. Little Lion had given me a soft pack of China cigarettes, from Yuan Sai, she'd said. He'd told her they were a gift to him from some big shot. Yuan smoked Eight Joys only.

I took out a cigarette, leaned forward, and handed it to him. He leaned forward to take it, turned sideways to stay out of the wind, and lit it. He obviously loved the taste, as his face twisted into a slightly screwy expression I found sort of handsome. It's not everyone who can afford to smoke cigarettes like this, old uncle.

A friend gave them to me.

They had to be given to you. No one who smokes these ever buys them, he said with a grin. You must belong to the 'four basicallys'.

And what are those?

Your cigarettes are basically gifts. Your salary basically stays the same. You basically don't need a wife . . . I forget the fourth.

Your nights are basically filled with nightmares, I said.

That's not it, he said, but I really can't remember what the fourth one is.

Then don't worry about it.

It'll come back to me. Come take another ride tomorrow. I know who you are now, old uncle.

You do?

You must be Uncle Xiao Xiachun. Another of those strange laughs. My father said you were the most talented student in his class. You're the pride not only of that class, but the pride of our Northeast Gaomi County.

The man you're talking about really is the most talented. And that's not me.

You're just being modest, old uncle. I knew you were somebody special as soon as you stepped onto my raft.

Is that the truth? I asked with a smile.

Of course it is. Your forehead shines and there's a halo over your head. You're a very rich man!

Have you studied physiognomy with Yuan Sai?

You know old Uncle Yuan? He smacked himself on the forehead. How could I be so stupid? Of course you do, you were classmates. Uncle Yuan's talented too, but he's no match for you.

Don't forget your father, I said. I recall he can make a complete circle around the basketball court on his hands.

How hard can that be? he said with a note of contempt. All brawn and no brains. But you and Uncle Yuan know how to use your head. 'A thinking man rules others, a working man is ruled by others.'

You've got the gift of gab, just like Wang Gan, I said with a laugh.

Uncle Wang is gifted, but he walks a different path than you, he said. His triangular eyes narrowed. Uncle Wang pretends to be a fool as he rakes in the money.

How much can he rake in selling clay dolls?

Uncle Wang doesn't sell clay dolls, he sells art. There's a price for gold, old uncle, but art is priceless. Of course, next to you, Uncle Xiao, the little money Uncle Wang Gan makes is like comparing a pond and the ocean. Uncle Yuan Sai has a quicker mind than Uncle Wang, but he can only make so much from a bullfrog-breeding farm.

If his money doesn't come from the farm, where does it come from?

Don't you really know, old uncle, or are you teasing me?

I really don't know.

Old uncle, you're making fun of me. I thought anyone who reached your station in life knew every trick in the trade. Even a lowly commoner like me hears things, so how could you not know?

I've only been back a few days.

Okay, let's say you don't know. Since you're from around here, there's no harm in a foolish nephew like me prattling on to keep you from getting bored.

Go on.

The bullfrog farm is just a front for Uncle Yuan, he said. His real business is helping people make the other kind of '*wa*' – babies.

That shocked me, but I tried not to show it.

To put it nicely, it's a surrogate-mother centre. Not so nicely, he hires women to have babies for other women who can't have them.

People actually engage in that kind of business? I asked him. Doesn't that make a mockery of family planning?

Oh, old uncle, what times are you living in, bringing up something like family planning? These days the rich fine their way to big families – like the Trash King, Lao He, whose fourth child cost him 600 000. The day after the fine notice arrived, he carried 600 000 to the Family Planning Commission in a plastic knit bag. The poor have to cheat their way to big families. Back in the days of the People's communes, the peasants were tightly regimented. They had to ask for days off to go to market and needed written authorisation to leave the area. Now, you go where you want, no questions asked. They go out of town to repair umbrellas, resole shoes, peddle vegetables, rent basement rooms or set up tents at bridgeheads, and they can have as many babies as they want. Officials impregnate their mistresses – that needs no explanation. It's only public servants with little money and even less courage who toe the line.

If what you say is true, then the policy of family planning exists in name only.

No, he said. The policy is in place. Because that's the only way they can legally collect fines.

Well, then, let the people have their babies. Why go to Yuan Sai's surrogate-mothers centre?

You must be so caught up in your career, old uncle, you don't know what's going on around you. He smiled. The rich are supposed to have lots of money, but there aren't many like the King of Trash, who's so free with his money. For most people, the more they have the stingier they get. They want a son to inherit their riches, but not at the cost of a steep fine. So they hire a surrogate mother to get out of paying a fine. And most rich folks, the upper crust, are around your age, so when the man decides to try, he has to look somewhere other than his wife.

So take a mistress.

Of course, a lot of them do, sometimes more than one, but more common are men who are henpecked and hate being inconvenienced. They are Uncle Yuan's clients.

The sight of the little pink building that housed the offices of the bullfrog farm and of the golden halls of the Fertility Goddess Temple across the river gave me a bad feeling. I thought back to that recent morning after returning from a toilet visit at the health centre to an extraordinary bedtime drama with Little Lion.

You don't have a son, do you, Old Uncle? Flathead's son asked me.

I didn't answer.

It's not right for a special man like you not to have a son. You know that, don't you? It's actually a sort of sin. As Mengzi said: Of the three forms of unfilialness, not having an heir is the worst.

. . . After holding it in all night, I feel much better after relieving myself. I could use some more sleep, but Little Lion is getting frisky, and that hasn't happened in a long time . . .

You must have a son, old uncle. This isn't just about you, but for all of Northeast Township. Uncle Yuan has suggested many ways you could manage this, but a sexual surrogate is the best. The surrogate women are all beautiful, healthy, unmarried college graduates with terrific genes. You can stay with one until she's pregnant with your child. It's not cheap, at least two hundred thousand yuan. Of course, if you want the very best for your son, you can give her the most nutritious food and, if you're so inclined, a personal bonus. The greatest danger is that an extended period of living together could produce an emotional attachment, and what was only pretend could turn into something real, which in turn would affect your marriage. That's why I think your wife won't let you get away with this.

. . . She seems to be in the grip of passion, but her body is cold, and she's acting totally out of character. She wants to do it differently this time. What is it you want? I can see that her eyes are flashing in the morning light. She gives me a mischievous smile. I feel like abusing you. First, she puts a blindfold on me. What are you doing? Don't take it off – after years of bad treatment, today I want to get my revenge. Are you going to give me a vasectomy? She giggles – I couldn't bear to do that. I want you to enjoy this . . .

A woman caused a scene not long ago, young Flathead said. She wrecked Uncle Yuan's car. You see, her old man got romantically involved with his surrogate, and as soon as his son was born, he dumped her. That's why I'm sure your wife won't let you do it.

. . . She's really doing it to me, has got me hot and half crazed. She's putting something over it. What are you doing? Is this really necessary? No answer . . .

If all you want is a son, and you're not interested in tasting the forbidden fruit, I'll give you a money-saving hint. It's a well-kept secret that Uncle Yuan employs several inexpensive surrogates. They're scary-ugly, but they weren't born that way. They were beautiful once, by which I mean they have great genes. I'm sure you heard about that disastrous fire at the Dongli Stuffed Animal Factory, old uncle. Five girls from Northeast Township died in that fire. Three others survived the fire, but were terribly disfigured. Their lives ever since have been sheer agony. Uncle Yuan took them in out of the goodness of his heart, seeing that they had plenty to eat as well as a way to make a living and save up for old age. Naturally, they do their job without sexual contact. Your sperm is inserted into their uterus, and you take the child after it's born. They don't charge much – fifty thousand for a boy, thirty for a girl . . .

. . . She's made me howl. I feel like I've fallen into an abyss. She gently covers me and leaves . . .

Old Uncle, I recommend . . .

Are you pimping for Yuan Sai?

How could you even think of using an old term like that, old uncle? He laughed. I'm one of Uncle Yuan's professional associates, and I'm grateful to you, Uncle Xiao, for giving me the chance to make a little money. I'll give Uncle Yuan a call now. He steadied the raft and took out his cell phone. Sorry, I said, but I'm not your Uncle Xiao, and I don't need what you're selling.

8

Sensei, Little Lion and I had a fight a couple of days ago and, in the heat of the moment, I wound up with a bloody nose. Blood even stained the paper I was writing the letter on, which I decided to continue, even with a headache. When I'm writing my play I need to choose every word and craft every sentence with care, but a letter is a different matter. Anyone who knows a few hundred characters and has something to say can write a letter. Back when my first wife, Wang Renmei, wrote to me, she used drawings when she didn't know how to write something. Xiaopao, she'd say apologetically, I'm not an educated woman, and drawing is about all I can do. You are, too, I'd respond. Using drawings to 'say' what you mean is the same as creating new characters. Why don't I create a son for you, Xiaopao? she said. We'll create a son.

Sensei, after my conversation with the young Flathead on his raft, I nervously came to a conclusion that has troubled me a great deal: Little Lion, this woman who harbours an insane desire for a child, relieved me of my sperm and inserted it into the body of one of those deformed women. The image of countless little tadpoles encircling an egg floats into my mind, reminding me of my childhood, when we'd watch tadpoles in the shallows of the dried pond behind the village nibbling a water-soaked bun. The surrogate mother is none other than the daughter of my schoolmate Chen Bi, Chen Mei, in whose womb my child is growing.

I rushed over to the bullfrog farm, meeting a number of people on the way, some of whom waved to me, though I couldn't tell you the name of a single one. Through a crack in the automatic gate I caught my second glimpse of the frog sculpture and shivered from a clammy, menacing feeling, though maybe it was only a trick of memory. Six girls in colourful outfits were dancing in the square in front of the squat building, waving floral wreaths to the accompaniment of a man sitting off to the side playing a squeezebox. More than likely rehearsing for some sort of performance. Days of peace, sunlight and breezes, and nothing happened, so maybe it was something I had imagined. I needed to find a place to sit down and think hard about my play.

'Timid as a mouse when nothing is wrong, bold as a tiger when events are strong', and 'When your luck is good, it can't be bad; when your luck is bad, you've been had'. Those were lessons my father taught me. Old folks are usually a storehouse of warnings. Thoughts of my father reminded me that I was hungry. I was fifty-five, and though I mustn't refer to myself as old in front of my father, I was already more than halfway home and on a downward slide. There is nothing a man in the sunset of his life, someone who has retired early to return to live in his childhood hometown, needs to fear. That thought made me even hungrier.

I went into the Don Quixote, a little café next to the Fertility Goddess Temple square, a favourite haunt of mine since Little Lion went to work at the bullfrog farm. I took a seat by the window. Business was slow. This is like a reserved seat. The short, overweight waiter greeted me. Sensei, each time I sit at that table and gaze at the empty chair across from me, I dream that one day you'll be sitting in it and talking with me about the play I'm having so much trouble writing. There was a broad smile on the waiter's oily face, but a strange expression lay behind it. Maybe it was the look on the face of Don Quixote's retainer, Sancho Panza, that of a prankster, slightly unscrupulous, someone who likes to taunt people and is himself taunted. Hard to tell if he's lovable or hateful. The table is made of unvarnished Chinese linden, the grain marred by cigarette burns. It's where I've done much of my writing. Someday, maybe, when the play is a success, the table will become an object of literary lore. Then, anyone who sits at it to enjoy a drink will have to pay extra. If you could sit across from me, well, that would be super! Sorry, but literary figures tend to rely upon boastful fantasies as a stimulus for writing.

Sensei, the waiter gave the impression of bowing without actually doing so. Welcome, he said. The great knight Don Quixote's loyal retainer, Sancho Panza, here to serve you. He handed me a bill of fare in ten languages.

Thank you, I said. The usual. A margarita salad, a can of Little Widow Antonia stewed beef, and an Uncle Malik dark ale.

He waddled off like a duck. While I waited for my food I scrutinised the interior decorations. The walls are hung with a rusted helmet, a lance, and tattered gloves worn during a duel with a romantic rival, all symbols of celebrated battle skills, and certificates and medals for colossal achievements. Also on the wall are a remarkably lifelike deer's head, a pair of brightly feathered pheasants and some yellowed photos. Even though the decorations are imitations of a classical European style, the layout is not without its appeal. The bronze, life-size statue of a woman stands to the right of the entrance, her breasts rubbed shiny by human hands. I've kept my eye on it, Sensei, and every diner, male or female, brushes one of those breasts upon entering – The Fertility Goddess Temple square is always a hub of activity, and Wang Gan's hawking shouts are the loudest and liveliest. A new program has gotten underway recently, called Unicorns Deliver the Babies, ostensibly to return to traditions, whereas in fact it is the creation of a couple of workers at the municipal cultural centre. Though it's a patchwork scheme, neither domestic nor foreign, it has resolved the employment problem for dozens of people, which makes it worthwhile. Beyond that, Sensei, just as you have said, tradition starts out as artistic innovation. I've seen any number of similar programs on TV, hodgepodges of tradition, the modern, travel and culture, bustling with activity, bright and glitzy, radiantly joyful, friendliness that brings wealth. And, in line with your worries, the flames of war leave bodies strewn across the land in some place, while singing and dancing take place in others, along with debauchery. This is the world you and I live in. If there really were a giant who was as much larger than the earth as we are to a soccer ball, I wonder what he would be thinking as he circled the planet, where peace is followed by war, overabundance by starvation, droughts by floods . . . Sorry, Sensei, I've let myself get sidetracked.

The phoney Sancho brought me a glass of ice water and a plate of bread with a pat of butter, plus a little dish of virgin olive oil with garlic-infused soy sauce. Their bread is beautifully baked; everyone says it is. Dipping it in the sauce is a treat in itself, but that is followed by delicious entrees and soups – Sensei, you must come have a meal here; I guarantee you'll like everything about it – and the restaurant has a tradition, actually, more a 'custom' than a tradition: just before closing each night, the day's leftover bread – in a variety of shapes, colours and thickness – is placed in a willow basket at the entrance, free for anyone. Nowhere does it say that they should take only one loaf, but that's what everyone does instinctively. They stroll the grounds of the temple grounds with fresh loaves tucked under their arms or hugged to their chests – long or square, soft or fragrantly blackened, inhaling the fragrance of wheat, flax, almonds and yeast – their own bread. Sensei, this has always moved me deeply. I know, of course, that this may be an immoderate feeling, because I am painfully aware that the world is filled with people who lack clothes to wear and food to eat, plus some for whom survival is a constant struggle.

The margarita salad is a fresh, tasty dish with lettuce, tomato and endive. Who came up with such a romantic European name for a salad? One of my classmates, of course, and my first teacher's son – Li Shou. As I wrote to you in another letter, he was the most talented student in our group, and he should have been the one with a literary career, but that turned out to be me. He became a skilled doctor and had a brilliant future ahead of him until he gave it up and came back home to open this restaurant, which is a cross between Chinese and Western, or better described, one that is both Chinese and Western. The influence of literature on this old classmate of ours is evident in the name of his

restaurant and the dishes he serves. Opening a café called Don Quixote
in a place that has traces of both local and foreign influence was in itself
quixotic. He carries his success around his middle. Short to begin with,
all that weight makes him seem even smaller. He sits in the far corner
to watch me across the floor, and neither of us so much as waves to the
other. I sometimes sprawl across the table to scribble some impressions,
and he sits in a strange, leisurely pose, with his left arm over the back of
the chair, resting his chin in his right, for the longest time.

The waiter brought my order – Little Widow Antonia beef and
Uncle Malik dark ale – to the table. I took a drink, ate a bite, and slowly
savoured both as I gazed out the window at a sombre re-enactment
of a fairytale playing out in broad daylight: loud drumbeats and music
leading the way, followed by flags and banners, umbrellas and fans and
ostentatious outfits on extraordinary characters: a woman sitting atop
the unicorn, her face like a silver plate, eyes like bright stars, holding a
chubby pink infant. The Fertility Goddess always reminds me of Gugu,
though in reality, Gugu dresses in a baggy black robe, her hair is like
a bird's nest, and she has a laugh like an owl's hoot, a glassy look, and
incoherent speech; that effectively kills the illusion.

After being carried around the square, the goddess's flags lined up in
formation in the centre. The musicians put down their instruments to
allow an official in a high hat and crimson robe, holding a tablet in front
of his chest – his stature starkly reminiscent of a eunuch in an imperial
drama – to read from a yellow scroll: *Great Heaven and Sovereign Earth
produce the world's five grains; the sun, the moon and the stars nourish the
multitudes. In the name of the Jade Emperor, the Fertility Goddess brings a
sweet baby down to Gaomi. I hereby call the pious couple, Wang Liang and
his wife, to come forward for their baby* – but before the couple playing the
husband and wife received their son, a clay doll, it was snatched away by
a woman eager to have one of her own.

Sensei, though I console myself with many rationalisations, I am at
heart a coward, a little man who worries about nearly everything. Since
coming to grips with the reality that the girl Chen Mei is carrying my
child, a powerful sense of transgression has weighed me down. Gugu

and Little Lion took Chen Mei in as a baby, I even helped out by preparing formula for her. She is younger than my own daughter. One day, when Chen Bi, Li Shou and Wang Gan, all childhood classmates, learn the facts of what occurred, I will no longer be able to look any of them in the eye, even if I were to cover my head with a dog's pelt.

I thought back to my two encounters with Chen Bi since my return.

The first was on a snowy evening last year. Little Lion hadn't yet started work at the bullfrog farm, and we were strolling through the snow, watching snowflakes dance in the glare of golden yellow lights around the square. Firecrackers popped somewhere in the distance; it was getting to feel very much like New Year's. We were talking to our daughter, who was off in Spain. She said she and her husband were strolling the streets of Cervantes' hometown. I told her that by chance Little Lion and I were walking into the Don Quixote café, which evoked crisp laughter on the other end of the cell phone.

It's a small world, Papa.

Culture is everywhere, Sensei.

At the time we didn't know that Li Shou was the owner, but we sensed that whoever it was, he was no ordinary man. We liked the place as soon as we walked in. The simple, unadorned tables and chairs particularly impressed me. Covering the tables with clean, white, neatly starched tablecloths would have made it very European. But I agreed with Li Shou, whose later research showed that rural Spanish restaurants in Don Quixote's day did not use tablecloths. He added the gossipy comment that women back then did not wear bras either.

Sensei, I confess that when I saw that sculpture of the naked woman whose breasts were shiny from being rubbed, I reached out in spite of myself, which shows how sordid and yet open and candid I am. Little Lion shushed to stop me. What's that for? I asked. This is art. That's what all cultural degenerates say, she replied. The fake Sancho walked up with a smile, gave the impression of bowing without actually doing so, and said, Welcome, sir, madam.

He took our coats, scarves, and hats, and then led us to a table in the centre on which white candles floated in a dish filled with water.

We said we preferred another table by the window, where we could enjoy the sight of fluttering snow outside and observe the restaurant's décor at the same time. There at a table in the corner – the one that would later become my favourite spot – sat a man smoking. I knew who he was by the missing ring finger on his right hand. That and the big red nose. It was the once handsome Chen Bi, now bald on top, with hair hanging around his neck at the back, the way Cervantes had worn his. His face was gaunt, the cheeks sunken, probably a sign of missing molars. That seemed to magnify the size of his nose. He held the butt end of a lit cigarette to his lips with the thumb and two fingers of his right hand. The air filled with the strange odour of a burned cigarette filter. Two streams of smoke emerged from his wide nostrils. He had a glazed look, the typical sign of dejection. I wanted not to look at him, but couldn't help myself. My thoughts went to the sculpture of Cervantes on the Peking University campus, and I knew why Chen Bi was here. He was strangely dressed: a nondescript long coat and a white knitted, seersucker-like scarf around his neck; the only thing missing was a sword on his hip. Then I spotted one leaning against the wall, which led my eyes to chain-mail gloves, a shield, and a spear standing in the corner. I expected to see a dirty, scrawny dog at his feet, and there was one – dirty, but not scrawny. Cervantes was believed to be missing the ring finger of his right hand, but he did not go around carrying a spear and a shield – that would be Don Quixote – and yet the man had Cervantes' face. But then, none of us had ever actually seen Cervantes or, obviously, the fictional Don Quixote, so whether Chen Bi was made up to look like Cervantes or his fictional creation was an open question. My old friend's current situation saddened me. I'd heard of the tragedy that had befallen his two beautiful daughters, Chen Er and Chen Mei, once Northeast Gaomi Township's loveliest sisters. Chen Bi's ancestral background was a mystery, but it definitely included foreign blood, and they were thus spared the flat features of most Chinese. The classical description of beauty did not fit those two, who were camels in a herd of sheep, cranes in a flock of chickens. Had they been born into a rich family or in a more prosperous land, or even if they had been born into a poor family in some distant place, but had been fortunate enough to encounter a rich man, they might well have taken the world by storm. They left home and went south together, perhaps to seek such an encounter. I heard they both took jobs at the Dongli Stuffed Animal Factory, where the manager was a foreigner – whether or not he was a real foreigner was hard to say. If two beautiful, intelligent girls in an environment of luxury and dissipation had wanted to make a great deal of money and enjoy life, their bodies could have made that happen. Instead, they toiled in a factory workshop, enduring the life of common labourers, a life of brutal exploitation, and in the end, a fire that shocked the nation turned one of them to ashes and horribly disfigured the other. The younger girl survived only through the sacrifice of her sister. How sad, how tragic, how pitiful. This proved that they had not fallen into degeneracy, but had remained as pure as jade and as unspoiled as ice, a pair of good girls – I'm sorry, Sensei, I got carried away again.

Chen Bi's life had been one of incomparable sorrow. It seemed to me that by coming to the Don Quixote café to play the part of a famous dead man or a bizarre fictional character, his situation was much the same as that of the dwarf doorman at Beijing's Paradise Dancehall or the giant doorman at Guangzhou's Water Curtain Cave Bathhouse. They all sold whatever their body had to offer. The dwarf sold his pygmy stature, the giant sold his jumbo height; Chen Bi sold his nose. They were all in the same tragic circumstance.

Sensei, I recognised Chen Bi right off that night, though I hadn't seen him in nearly twenty years. I'd have recognised him if it had been a hundred years and in a foreign country. Naturally, I think, when we recognised him, he also recognised us. You don't need eyes to pick out a childhood friend; you can manage that with your ears – a sigh or a sneeze will do it.

Should I go up and say hello? Invite him to join us for dinner? Little Lion and I couldn't make up our minds. And I could tell from his look of indifference and the way he was staring at the buck's head on the wall, not even glancing out of the corner of his eye, that he couldn't decide if he should come over to our table. The memory of him coming to our house that year on the night we sent off the Kitchen God – Chen Er with him, wanting to take back Chen Mei – floated into my mind. A large man back then, he was wearing a stiff pigskin jacket. He'd threatened to toss our garlic press into the pot on the stove. He was breathing heavily and seemed ready to explode from frustration, like a raging bear. That was the last time we'd seen one another till this day. I'm sure we weren't alone in thinking about the past, that he was too. Truth be told, we never hated him; in fact, he had our deepest sympathies over his misfortunes. The main reason we did not go up and say hello to him was we couldn't decide how. Why? Because we were making it, as the locals said, and he wasn't. How does someone who's making it deal with a friend who isn't? We simply didn't know.

Sensei, I'm a smoker. It's a bad habit that encounters strict constraints in Europe, North America, even there in Japan, and makes us feel vulgar and ill bred. But not here, not yet. I took out a cigarette and lit it with a match. I love that brief burst of sulphur smell when striking a wooden match. Sensei, I was smoking Golden Pavilions then, a very expensive local brand. Two hundred yuan a pack, I'm told, which is ten yuan a smoke, while a jin of wheat sells for eighty fen. In other words, you'd have to sell twelve and a half jin of wheat to buy a single Golden Pavilion cigarette. Twelve and a half jin of wheat produce fifteen jin of baked bread, enough to meet a person's needs for ten days or more. But a single cigarette's life lasts no more than a few puffs. The resplendent cigarette packet reminded me of the Ginkakuji in your esteemed city of Kyoto, and I had to wonder if the Golden Pavilion had in fact been the model for the packet design. I knew how much my father detested the idea that I smoked this brand, but he limited his comment to: It's degenerate! I nervously tried to explain: I didn't buy these, they were a gift. His chilly response? That makes it obscene! I regretted telling him how much they cost, but that just shows how shallow and vain I was. How was I any different from the nouveau riche who parade their purchases of brand name products and crow about their new, young wives? But I couldn't throw away such expensive cigarettes over a single critical comment by my father. If I did, wouldn't that be even more degenerate? Golden Pavilions are enhanced with a special fragrance that produces intoxicating smoke. I could see that Chen Bi was getting fidgety. After sneezing loudly, over and over, he let his moody gaze move slowly from the stag's head – hesitantly, timidly, and tremulously at first, then eagerly, greedily, even a little menacingly – to us.

The man stood up at last, Sensei, and hobbled our way, dragging his sword as if it were a crutch. The light inside the café was muted, but bright enough to see his face. The complex expression created by the totality of his features and facial muscles is hard to describe. I couldn't be sure if he was looking at me or at the smoke coming from my mouth. I stood up so quickly the legs of my chair scraped the floor noisily. Little Lion stood up.

He stood in front of us. I stuck out my hand and pretended to be surprised to see him. He accepted neither my greeting nor my extended hand, keeping a respectable distance as he bowed deeply, then rested both hands on the handle of the rusty sword and said: Honourable Lady, Honourable Sir, I, the Spanish Don Quixote, knight of La Mancha, extend my deepest respect and humbly offer my unswerving desire to serve you.

Quit fooling around, Chen Bi, I said. Who are you pretending to be? I'm Wan Zu and this is Little Lion.

Honourable Sir, Respected Lady, for a loyal knight, no enterprise is more sacred than preserving peace and upholding justice, sword in hand.

Okay, pal, knock off the play-acting.

The world is a stage, one on which the same drama is played out every day. Sir, madam, if you could see fit to reward me with a cigarette, I will demonstrate my duelling skills.

I hastily handed him a cigarette and helpfully lit it for him. He took a deep drag, turning the end a bright red. He squinted and his face grew pinched, but then slowly smoothed out as smoke streamed from his wide nostrils. Seeing how relaxed and contented a cigarette made him both shocked and moved me. Though I'd been smoking for years, I wasn't a heavy smoker, which was why I could not relate to the effect of that cigarette on him. He took another drag, burning up most of the remaining tobacco. Those pricey cigarettes had an exceptionally long filter, which left little room for tobacco, a ploy to appease the wealthy users who were afraid of dying from smoking but found it impossibly hard to quit. Three puffs burned the cigarette down to the filter. I handed him the whole pack. He timorously looked to the right and left before snatching it out of my hand and stuffing it up his sleeve. His promise to demonstrate his duelling skills forgotten, he limped to the door as fast as he could manage, dragging his sword and one leg behind him, but before he got there, he reached into the willow basket and snatched up a baguette.

Don Quixote! You've panhandled another customer! the fat fake Sancho Panza shouted while he brought us two mugs of foamy dark ale. We looked out the window at the poor man dragging his rusty sword behind him, his gimpy leg leaving a long, flickering shadow, as he crossed the square and disappeared in the darkness. The apparently robust dog followed closely behind him. A pathetic-looking man with a dog that seemed to strut.

Damn him, the fake Sancho Panza said for our benefit, not quite apologetically and sort of showy. He's always embarrassing us by doing things behind our back, he said, and I want to apologise on behalf of my boss, sir, and you, madam. But I imagine you can't be overly upset about a knight cadging a few cigarettes or some small coins.

What do you . . . what kind of talk is that? I didn't like the way the fat man talked. Why talk like you're acting in a movie or stage play? You people hired him, didn't you?

I'll tell you the truth, sir, the waiter said. When we opened, the boss took pity on him and had him dress up like that so he and I could stand in the doorway to greet the customers. But he had too many failings. He was addicted to alcohol and tobacco, and when he needed a fix, he was incapable of doing anything else. Then there's that loathsome dog that never leaves his side. And sanitation means nothing to him. I take two showers a day, and while I might not be a feast for the eyes, my body odour can make people happy and relaxed. That is the standard an elite waiter should maintain. But the only time that guy got a wash was in a rainstorm. Customers turned up their noses when they smelled him. And there's more: he ignored the boss's orders to stop panhandling customers. I'd have canned a no-account bum like him, but my soft-hearted boss has given him chance after chance. He's incapable of changing, like a dog that eats shit. The boss gave him some money, hoping he'd stay away, but he was back as soon as it was gone. I'd have called the cops on him by now, but the boss is too kind to do that, so he gets away with things that hurt business. He lowered his voice. I later learned that he and the boss were in school together, but even a classmate shouldn't have to put up with that. Eventually, someone complained about Don Quixote's terrible body odour and the mangy dog's fleas. So the boss hired somebody to take him to a public bath and make sure he and his dog got a thorough cleaning. That became a policy: he was forced to take a bath once a month. Was he grateful? No, he cursed up a storm in the water. Li Shou, you son of a bitch, he'd shout, you've ruined this knight's reputation!

Sensei, after that night's dinner, Little Lion and I walked along the riverbank to our new house, feeling gloomy. It had been an emotional encounter with Chen Bi. The past was full of sad memories. Vast changes had taken place over the decades; things we'd never dared dream of had come to pass, and those we'd treated with inordinate seriousness had become laughable. We hadn't had a real conversation, but he and I were probably thinking the same thing.

Sensei, the next time I ran into him was in the district hospital. We'd gone there with Li Shou and Wang Gan. Chen had been hit by a police car, whose driver said witnesses would swear he was driving normally when Chen Bi ran out into the street – he was suicidal – followed by his dog. Chen was thrown into some roadside shrubs, his dog was run over. Chen had compound fractures of both legs and injuries to his arm and hip, none of them life-threatening. The dog, which had died for its master, was splattered all over the pavement.

The news of Chen Bi's accident came from Li Shou. The policeman was cleared of blame, but Li went to see someone in power and managed to get Chen a settlement from the station of ten thousand yuan. For injuries as serious as his, that was a pittance. I knew that Li's motive in having us classmates visit Chen in the hospital was to get help in paying Chen's hospital bills.

He was in Bed 9, next to the window of a twelve-bed ward. Lily magnolias blooming outside the window on that early May day sent a rich perfume into the ward. Even with the crowding, the ward was clean and neat; despite conditions that paled alongside Beijing and Shanghai hospitals, the improvements over the twenty years since the commune period had been substantial. Sensei, I had spent a week with my mother in the commune hospital, where the beds were home to hosts of fleas, the walls were blood-specked, and the air swarmed with flies. The thought alone makes me shudder. Both of Chen's legs were wrapped in plaster casts, as was his right arm. He lay in bed able to move only his left arm.

He turned his face to the wall when he saw us walk in.

Wang Gan relieved the awkwardness with his brand of comic chiding: How did this happen, eminent knight? Tilting at windmills again? Or duelling with a romantic rival?

You should have told me you were tired of living, Li Shou said. You didn't have to go looking for a police car.

He's faking it, Little Lion said, that's why he's not talking to us. It's all your fault, Li Shou, for turning him into a deranged individual.

He's not deranged, Li defended himself. He's a master at pretending.

Suddenly Chen burst into tears and lowered his head as far as it would go. His shoulders heaved; he scraped the wall with his good hand.

A nurse rushed into the room and gave us an icy stare. Stop that, Number 9, she demanded as she smacked the steel headboard.

He abruptly stopped crying and turned his head so we could see his face. He looked at us with a murky gaze.

The nurse pointed to a bouquet of flowers we'd laid on the nightstand and made a face as she sniffed the air. No flowers in the wards, she said sternly. Hospital policy.

Policy? Little Lion said. Not even Beijing hospitals have such a policy.

The nurse showed no interest in debating the issue. She turned to Chen Bi. Get your family over here to settle up, she said. Today's your last day.

What kind of attitude is that? I asked unhappily.

With pinched lips, she said, A workday attitude.

Is a humanistic spirit alien to you people? Wang Gan said.

I only work here. If you people are flush with humanistic spirit, then pay his medical bills. I think our director would reward each of you with a plaque that says: Model Humanist.

There was more Wang Gan wanted to say, but Li Shou stopped him. The nurse stormed out of the ward.

We exchanged glances, wondering what we should do. The treatment costs for injuries as serious as Chen Bi's were sure to be astronomical.

Why did you have them bring me here? Chen Bi asked accusingly. What the hell business is it of yours if I want to die? I'd have done so if you hadn't interfered, and I wouldn't be lying here suffering.

It wasn't us, Wang Gan said. The cop who hit you called for an ambulance.

If it wasn't you, he said with a total lack of warmth, then what are you doing here? Come to pity me? Give me sympathy? I don't need it. You can all leave, and take those toxic flowers with you – they give me a headache. Were you thinking of paying my hospital expenses? I don't need that either. I'm a formidable knight. The King is my good friend, so is the Queen. The paltry expenses for this hospital stay will come out of the national treasury. But even if the royal couple prefers not to settle up, I don't need your charity. Both my daughters are more beautiful than goddesses, their good fortune as vast as the Eastern Sea. If they do not sit on the Queen's throne, they will serve as the King's consort. They could buy this hospital with money that falls through their fingers.

Sensei, of course we understood what this crazy talk from Chen Bi was all about. He definitely was faking. In his mind he was clear as the surface of a mirror. Faking things can become a habit, and if you do it long enough, you can start sliding over the edge. We were on tenterhooks when we came to the hospital with Li Shou. We had no problem with taking along some flowers, some encouraging words, and a few hundred yuan, but to be responsible for a huge hospital bill, that would be . . . after all, we weren't blood relatives, and the way he was . . . now if he'd been a normal person . . . In the end, Sensei, though we were all principled, sympathetic individuals, we were just ordinary men, and nowhere near noble enough to bail a misfit out of a jam. So Chen Bi's crazy talk was intended to give us a face-saving way out. We all looked at Li Shou. He scratched his head and said, You just worry about getting better, Don. Since you were hit by a police car, they should be responsible for your hospital bill. If not, we'll think of something.

Get out, Chen Bi said. If I could use my arms, your stupid heads would taste my spear.

There was no better time to leave. We scooped up the flowers, which were spewing a low-grade fragrance, and were on our way out when the nurse walked in with a man in a white smock. She introduced him to us as the assistant director for finances, and us to him as Bed 9's visitors. He presented us with a bill totalling more than twenty thousand yuan, including emergency room treatment. He stressed the fact that this was their base cost; the normal computation would be much, much higher. Chen Bi was in full foul throat while this was going on: Get out of here, you profiteer, you and your exorbitant fees, you bunch of corpse-eating maggots. You mean nothing to me. He swung his good arm, banging it into the wall, and then felt around on the nightstand for a bottle, which he picked up and flung over to the bed opposite, hitting a critically old man who was getting an IV. Get out. This hospital is my daughter's and you're her hired help. One word from me and your rice bowl will be shattered.

Just as things were getting out of hand, Sensei, a woman in a black dress and veil walked into the ward. You'd know who it was without my telling you. That's right, it was Chen Bi's second daughter, the one who'd survived the fire at the toy factory, but was horribly disfigured.

Chen Mei drifted in like a spectre, the black dress and veil introducing mystery and a hellish gloom into the ward. The uproar came to an abrupt stop, like pulling the plug on a noisy machine. Even the stuffy heat turned to chill. A bird on the lily magnolia tree called out softly.

We couldn't see her face, or an inch of skin anywhere. Only her figure was visible, the long limbs of a fashion model. But we knew it was Chen Mei. Little Lion and I instinctively thought back to the infant in swaddling clothes of more than twenty years before. She nodded to us, then said to the assistant director: I am his daughter. I will pay what he owes you.

Sensei, I have a friend in Beijing, a burn specialist at the Number 304 Hospital, a man with the stature of an academician, who told me that the mental anguish burn victims experience may be worse than the physical pain. The intense shock and unspeakable agony of seeing their ruined faces in the mirror for the first time is nearly impossible to endure. Such people need incomparable courage to go on living.

Sensei, people are products of their environment. Under certain circumstances, a coward can be transformed into a warrior, a bandit can perform kind deeds, and someone too stingy to spend the smallest coin might part with a large sum. Her appearance on the scene and the courage it took shamed us, and that shame manifested itself in a willingness to spend our money on a good cause. Li Shou was first, and then us. We all said, Good niece Chen Mei, we'll take care of your father's expenses.

Thank you for your generous offer, she said unemotionally, but we have been in so many people's debt we'll never be able to clear the accounts.

Get out! Chen Bi bellowed. You black-veiled devil. How dare you palm yourself off as my daughter! One of my daughters is a student in Spain, romantically involved with a Prince, and will soon be married. The other is in Italy, where she has bought Europe's oldest winery, from where a ten-thousand-ton ship with the finest wine is sailing to China.

9

Sensei, I'm ashamed to say that I haven't even started to write the play you've been patiently waiting for. There's just so much material I feel a bit like the dog that wants to bite Mount Tai, but doesn't know where to start. When I'm thinking about the play, something related to the theme and rich with possibilities will crop up in my life and interrupt my train of thought. But what has made it especially hard is my inadvertent involvement in a very troublesome matter. I don't know how to extricate myself, or, more precisely, how to play the role expected of me.

Sensei, I think you've already guessed what that is. What I revealed to you earlier was not fantasy, but actual fact: Little Lion has admitted that she stole my tadpole-like sperm and implanted them in the body of Chen Mei, who is now carrying my child. That made my blood boil, and I slapped her hard out of uncontrollable rage. I know that was wrong, especially since someone who claims to be a playwright ought not to be guilty of such savage behaviour. But, I tell you, Sensei, I was out of my mind with anger.

After returning from my raft ride with Young Flathead, I did some investigating of my own. Each time I went to the bullfrog farm I was turned away by their security guards, so I tried phoning Yuan Sai and my cousin, but they both had new cell phone numbers. I demanded an answer from Little Lion, who just mocked me and called me crazy.

I printed out the surrogate mother details from the bullfrog company's website and took them to the municipal family-planning committee. They took my report, but nothing came of it. I next went to the police, where I was told this was not in their jurisdiction. I tried the mayor's hotline, and was told that my report would be on the mayor's desk. That's how it went for the next few months, Sensei, and by the time I finally got the truth out of Little Lion, the foetus in Chen Mei's belly was six months along. And so a fifty-five-year-old man was muddling along on the path to becoming another infant's father. Unless the dangerous and cruel ingestion of a drug ended the pregnancy, my fatherhood was a done deal. That is how, as a young man, I'd caused the death of my first wife, Renmei, the most painful thing I'd ever done, a sinful act for which I may never achieve atonement. Now, even if I harden my heart, Sensei, it won't make any difference, because I've been refused entry into the farm, and even if I managed to get inside, they wouldn't let me see Chen Mei. I'll bet there's a labyrinth of secret passages there, an underground maze, not to mention the probability, according to Little Lion and my own suspicions, that Yuan Sai and my cousin are underworld figures. If you push them, there's nothing they're incapable of – family or strangers, it wouldn't make any difference.

My slap sent Little Lion stumbling backward. She sat down hard and her nose bled. Not a sound from her for a long moment; instead of crying, she gave me a cold sneer. That was a good one, Xiaopao, she said, you thug! If that's what you're capable of, then a dog has eaten your conscience. I did this for you, she said. You have a daughter, but no son, and you should have an heir. I've long regretted not being able to give you a son, and having someone else bear your child is the only way I can make that up to you. A son will carry on your bloodline, extend your family for future generations. But instead of thanking me, you hit me. I'm crushed.

Then she cried, her tears merging with the blood from her nose, a sight that broke my heart. I was the one with the broken heart, but the anger rose in me again – for something this important, she should have told me.

I know you're unhappy over the sixty thousand yuan I spent, she said between sobs. You needn't worry, I'll pay that out of my retirement money. And you won't have to care for the baby, I'll do that. All in all, this has nothing to do with you. I read in the paper that they give a hundred yuan each time to sperm donors. I'll give you three hundred for being a donor, and you can return to Beijing. Divorce me if you want, or not. Either way, this has nothing to do with you. But, she wiped her face and said in the tone of a martyred warrior, if you're thinking of stopping the birth of this child, I'll kill myself in front of you.

Sensei, you have seen in my letters what kind of woman Little Lion is. When she was travelling all around with Gugu, encountering all sorts of people, she developed a disposition I'd have to call half heroic– half thuggish. The woman is capable of just about anything when she's provoked. It was up to me to find the best way to deal with this thorny problem, but with affection and reason.

The thought of inducing labour did cross my mind, but that gave me a cold, ominous feeling; and yet, it seemed to be the ideal solution. It was clear to me that money was the only reason Chen Mei would carry someone else's baby, so why not use money to solve the problem? That struck me as perfectly logical. The hard part was finding a way to see Chen Mei.

I hadn't seen her since that meeting in Chen Bi's hospital room. Her figure covered by a black dress, her face hidden behind a black veil, and her mysterious comings and goings convinced me that a world of mystery existed right here in Northeast Gaomi Township, a world populated by errant knights, psychics, and some who conceal their faces.

I thought back to a short time before, when I'd given Li Shou five thousand yuan to help pay Chen's hospital bill, and asked him to pass it on to Chen Mei. A few days later, Li returned the money to me, money Chen Mei refused to take. Maybe, I thought, she is carrying other people's babies to earn what she needs to pay her father's bill herself. Now my thoughts were going every which way – this is nothing but . . . damn you, Little Lion! All I could do was go see Li Shou, since he had the best mind among all us classmates.

We met in a corner of the Don Quixote café yesterday morning, when the square was crawling with people gathered to watch the performance of Unicorns Deliver the Babies. The fake Sancho Panza brought us two glasses of beer and wisely made himself scarce, his ambiguous smile a sign that he guessed what we were talking about. When I stammered my problem to him, Li Shou had a good laugh.

You're making fun of my bad luck, I said, showing my displeasure.

He held out his glass and clinked it against mine, then took a big drink. You call yours bad luck? he exclaimed. It's wonderful news. Congratulations! A son in old age, life's great joy!

Don't mock me, I said anxiously. I may have retired, but I'm still a public servant, and how am I supposed to deal with the organisation if I have another child?

Why talk about the organisation, or your job assignment, old friend? You're tying yourself up with your own rope. What you're looking at is, your sperm and an egg have come together to create a new life that will come crying into the world. The greatest joy in life is watching the birth of a child who carries your genes, because that is an extension of your own life —

The problem is, I cut him off, where will I go to get this new life registered?

How can you let a little matter like that bother you? That's all in the past. These days, there's nothing money won't buy. Besides, even if you can't get him registered, he'll still be a living human being, with all the rights every human being enjoys.

Enough, my friend, I came here for help and all I get is empty talk. Since I've been back I've discovered that all you people, educated or not, talk like stage actors. Where'd you learn that?

He laughed. We live in a civilised society, and in a civilised society everyone is an actor – film, TV, drama, crosstalk, sketch – we're all acting. Don't they say that all the world's a stage?

Please, no more crazy talk, I said. Come up with something. You don't want me calling Chen Bi father-in-law, do you?

What would happen if you did? Would the sun stop shining? Would the world stop spinning? Let me tell you something: Don't think the rest of the world is concerned about you or that everybody has their eyes on you. People have their own problems, and they couldn't care less about yours. Having a son with Chen Bi's daughter or a daughter with some other woman is your business. Nosey people spreading gossip is as transient as floating clouds. The primary issue here is, the child will be your flesh and blood and you're the big winner.

But me and Chen Bi . . . there's something incestuous about it!

Bullshit! There's no common blood, so where's the incest? And as far as age goes, that's even less to worry about. When an eighty-year-old man marries an eighteen-year-old, it's talked about like a fairytale. You've never even seen Chen Mei's body. She's a tool you're renting for a while, and that's all. In the end, my friend, don't worry so much, give yourself a break. Go get yourself in shape, so you can start raising your son.

You're wasting your breath, I said as I pointed to the fever blisters covering my lips. See that? I'm begging you, for the sake of an old classmate, take a message to Chen Mei to terminate the pregnancy. She'll still get the fee for carrying the baby, plus an additional ten thousand to make up for what it costs her physically. If she thinks that's not enough, I'll double the bonus.

What for? Since you're willing to spend that much money, wait till the child is born, then use it to get the child registered, and go be a proper father.

I won't be able to deal with the organisation.

You have too high an opinion of yourself, Li chided. I tell you, my friend, the organisation doesn't have time to worry about your piddling affairs. Just who do you think you are? Aren't you just someone who's written a couple of lousy plays no one has ever seen? Do you see yourself as a member of some royal family whose son's birth should be celebrated nationally?

A group of backpacking tourists popped their heads in at the entrance, and were immediately greeted by a smiling fake Sancho Panza. I lowered my voice. I'll never ask you for anything else as long as I live.

He folded his arms and shook his head to show there was nothing he could do.

Shit, damn you. You'll just stand by and watch me get buried alive, is that it?

You're asking me to commit murder, he said softly. At six months a foetus is ready to shout Papa through its mother's belly.

Will you help me or won't you?

What makes you think I can get in to see Chen Mei?

You can see Chen Bi at least. You can ask him to pass the word to her.

Seeing Chen Bi is no problem, Li said. He's out begging in front of the Fertility Goddess Temple every day. When the sun sets, he brings what he made here to buy liquor and pick up a loaf of bread. You can wait for him here or you can go looking for him there. But I hope you won't need to tell him, because you'll just be wasting your breath. And if you've got a bit of compassion in you, you won't add to his anguish with something like this. My experience over the past few years has concluded that the best way to solve a thorny problem is to quietly observe how it evolves and let nature take its course.

All right, then, I said, I'll let nature take its course.

When the child's a month old, I'll throw a party to celebrate.

10

I felt better after leaving the café. Why make such a fuss over something as common as the birth of a child? The sun was still shining, bird calls still filled the air, flowers bloomed, grass was still green, and breezes blew. In the square the Fertility Goddess ceremony was well underway, as women flocked to the temple amid the clamour of drumbeats and music, hoping to snatch a precious child out of the Goddess's hand. Everyone was passionately singing the praises of childbirth, looking forward to celebrating the birth of a child, while I agonised, worried and brooded over someone carrying my child. What that proves is: society didn't create my problem; I was the problem.

Sensei, I spotted Chen Bi and his dog behind a large column to the right of the temple entrance. Unlike the local mutt that wound up under the wheels of the police car, this was an obviously noble foreign breed with black spots all over its body. Why in the world would a dog with that pedigree choose to partner up with a vagrant? While it seemed to be a mystery, on second thought it wasn't so surprising. Here in developing Northeast Gaomi Township, it was common for the foreign and the domestic to come together, for good and bad to coexist, for beauty and ugliness to be indistinguishable, and for truth and falseness to look the same. Many faddish members of the nouveau riche could not wait to raise a tiger as a pet when the money was rolling in, and were anxious to sell their wives to pay off their debts when the money petered out. So many of the stray dogs on the street were once the costly playthings of the rich. In the previous century, when the Russian Revolution erupted, hordes of rich White Russian women were stranded in the city of Harbin, where they were forced to sell their bodies for bread or marry coolie labourers. They produced a generation of mixed children, one of whom could have been Chen Bi, with his high nose and sunken eyes. The spotted abandoned dog and Chen Bi appeared to belong to similar species. My thoughts were running wild. At a distance of a dozen metres or so, I watched the two of them. A pair of crutches rested beside him, a red cloth spread out in front. On the cloth, predictably, was a written plea for charity for a disabled man. From time to time, a bejewelled woman would bend down and place money – paper or a few coins – in the metal bowl. Every time that happened the dog looked up and rewarded the woman with three gentle, emotional barks. Three barks, no more, no fewer. The charitable woman would be moved, some to the extent of digging in her purse a second time. I'd given up my idea of paying him to talk Chen Mei into terminating the pregnancy and approached him now more out of curiosity than anything, wanting to see what was written on the red cloth – the bad habit of a writer. Here's what it said: *I am Iron-Crutch Li, come to the human world with a heavenly jade dog. My aunt the Fertility Goddess has sent me here to beg for alms. Your charity will reward you with a son, who will ride the streets as scholar number one.*

I assumed that the lines had come from Wang Gan, and that the calligraphy was Li Shou's, each using his unique talent to help an old classmate. He had rolled up the baggy cuffs of his pants to expose legs like rotten eggplants, and I was reminded of a story Mother had told me:

After Iron-Crutch Li became an immortal, one day there was no kindling at home for cooking, so his wife asked him: What shall we use for a fire? My leg, he said. With that he stuck one of his legs into the belly of the stove and lit it. The fire roared, water in the pot boiled, and the rice was cooked as his sister-in-law walked in and was startled by what she saw. Oh, my! she said, take care, brother-in-law, that you don't become a cripple. Well, he did.

After Mother finished her story, she warned us to be silent when confronted by miraculous sights and, under no circumstances, to show alarm.

Chen Bi was wearing a brick red down jacket that was grease-spotted and shiny as a suit of armour. The fourth lunar month, a time of warm southerly breezes and millet ripening in the far-off fields, was mating season for amphibians in distant ponds and, nearby, in the bullfrog breeding farm, where loud croaks were carried on the air. Girls and young women had changed into light satin dresses that showed off their curves, but our old friend was still wearing winter garments. I felt hot just looking at him, while he was curled up, shivering. His face was the colour of bronze, the bald spot on his head shone as if sandpapered. Why, I wondered, was he wearing a dirty surgical mask? To hide his nose from curious stares? My gaze recoiled as it met his, emanating from a pair of sunken eyes, and I turned to his dog, which was staring indifferently my way. Part of its left front claw was missing, as if sliced off by a sharp object, and that was when I knew that man and dog were united by common suffering. I also knew there wasn't a thing I could say to him, that all I could do was put some money in his bowl and leave. All I had on me was a hundred-yuan bill, meal money for lunch and dinner. But with no hesitation, I placed it in the bowl. He did not react, but his dog released three routine barks.

I sighed as I left them, walking a dozen steps before turning back for one last look. Subconsciously, I guess, I was wondering what he was going to do with the large bill I'd left, since the rest of the money in the bowl was small bills or change, crumpled paper and dirty coins. My pink bill was a real eye-catcher. I figured no one else would leave as much as I had, and thought he'd be moved by my act of generosity. Sensei, it really was a case of 'measuring the heart of a gentleman through the eyes of a petty man.' What I saw enraged me: a dark-skinned, fat boy in his teens ran out from behind the column, bent down in front of the full bowl, snatched up my hundred-yuan bill, and took off running. He was so fast that before I could react, he'd already run ten or fifteen metres down the alley alongside the temple, heading straight for the Sino-American

Jiabao Women and Children's Hospital. There was something familiar about the lazy-eyed boy. I knew I'd seen him somewhere, and then it hit me: it was the boy who'd handed Gugu a wrapped bullfrog at the opening of the hospital the year we returned, nearly scaring her to death.

Not even this unexpected turn of events got a reaction from Chen Bi. His dog growled a time or two, looked up at his master, and stopped. He lay his head down on his paws and quiet returned.

I couldn't help feeling the injustice of what just happened, not only to Chen Bi and his dog, but to me too. It was my money. I wanted to complain to the people around me, but they had other things on their mind, and the incident they'd witnessed was already forgotten, like a flash of lightning that leaves no trace. What that boy had done was unforgivable, undermining the township's reputation for honesty. What sort of breeding produced a boy like that, someone who would bully women, steal from the disabled, and other unconscionable acts? Even worse, I could tell by how expertly he'd managed his evil act that this wasn't the first time he'd stolen money from Chen Bi's beggar's bowl. So I took off running after him.

He was fifty metres or so ahead of me and had stopped running. He jumped up and broke a low hanging, leaf-filled branch off a roadside weeping willow and used it as a club on all sorts of things. He didn't so much as turn to look, knowing that the cripple and his lame dog would not come after him. Just you wait, you punk, *I'm* coming after you.

He turned into a riverside farmer's market, where a canopy of plastic turned everything inside a shade of green. The people were moving like fish in water.

A rich array of goods was available on a row of stalls in the shape of a winding arcade. Strange fruits and vegetables in a variety of colours and unusual shapes that even I, a peasant by birth, could not name, were displayed on many of the stalls. As I thought back to the times of scarcity, thirty years before, I could only heave an emotional sigh. Like a cart that knows the way, he headed straight to one of the fish stalls. I ran faster, while my eyes were drawn to the seafood stalls on both sides. The shiny salmon as big as piglets were Russian imports. The hairy

crabs, like oversized spiders, came from Hokkaido. There were South
American lobsters and Australian abalone, but the bulk of the seafood
was local – black carp, butterfish, croaker and Mandarin fish. Orange
salmon meat was laid out on a bed of ice, while the fragrance of roasting
fish wafted from one of the stalls. The punk was standing in front of a
roasted squid stall; he bought a skewer with the stolen bill and received
a wad of change. He raised his head, placed the tip of the skewer to his
lips, looking like the sword swallower who performed in the temple
square, and just as he was taking a tentacled strip, dripping with a dark
red sauce, into his mouth, I rushed up, grabbed him by the neck, and
shouted:

Where do you think you're going, you little thief?

He hunkered down and slipped out of my fingers, so I grabbed
him by the wrist as he swung the metal skewer of dripping squid at me.
I let go, and he slipped away like a river loach. But not before I had him
by the shoulders. He struggled, ripping his T-shirt in the process and
revealing skin as dark as black mackerel. Then he started crying – no
tears, just wolfish howls – and tried to stab me in the belly with the
skewer. I jumped out of the way, but the skewer got me in the arm. It
didn't hurt at first, nothing more than a stinging sensation. But the
sharp pain wasn't long in coming, along with dark blood. I clamped my
other hand over the wound and shouted:

He's a thief! He stole money from a crippled beggar!

With a roar, he rushed me like a crazed boar, murder in his eyes.
Sensei, I was terrified and frantically backed up, still shouting. And he
kept trying to stab me.

You owe me for a shirt! he yelled. Pay me for the shirt you ruined!

I can't bring myself to write all the words that came out of his mouth,
and I tell you, Sensei, I am mortified that Northeast Gaomi Township
has produced this sort of youngster. I picked up the first thing I could
see, a signboard on which the origins and prices of fish for sale were
written and held it as a shield to ward off the thief's attacks, each one
more vicious than the last; he had murder on his mind. The board took
the brunt of his skewer attacks, but I didn't pull my right hand away

quickly enough to avoid being stabbed. The blood flowed. Sensei, my mind was in turmoil, I simply didn't know what to do except retreat in the name of survival. I stumbled backward, and was nearly tripped up by baskets of fish and signboards more than once. If I'd fallen, Sensei, I wouldn't be writing you this letter. That savage punk would have pounced on me, resulting in either my death or serious injury and a life-or-death race to the hospital. Sensei, I don't mind admitting that I was scared to death, that my inherent cowardice rose to the surface at that moment. My eyes darted from side to side, hoping that the fish sellers would come to my rescue. But they just stood around, arms folded, watching – some indifferently, others with shouts of encouragement. Sensei, I'm worthless, clinging to life. Instead of raising a hand in defence, I let myself be victimised by a teenager. I heard a series of sobbing cries for help escape from my lips, like the pathetic yelps of a whipped dog:

Help me . . . help me . . .

The boy had stopped howling by then – he hadn't ever really cried – and was glaring, his eyes round as saucers, with hardly any white showing, the irises like a pair of fat tadpoles. Biting down on his lip, he glowered, paused briefly, then pounced again. Help me! I screamed as I raised the signboard, and was stabbed in the hand a second time . . . more blood . . . and another attack, and another. I kept screaming and backing up in a single-minded cowardly retreat, all the way out into the bright sunlight.

I threw down the signboard and took off running, still screaming for help. Sensei, I'm embarrassed to tell you about my pathetic exhibition, but I don't know who else I can divulge my sad tale to. I ran and ran, wherever my feet took me, my ears throbbing with shouts on both sides. I ran into the narrow street where light snacks were sold. A silver sedan was parked in front of a café. A black shop sign hanging in front of it was inscribed with two strange words: Pheasant Hen. Two women sat in the doorway, one big and fat, the other small and slim. They jumped to their feet, and I ran to them as if I'd seen my saviour, tripping and falling before I got there and ending up with a split lip and bleeding gums. What tripped me was a metal chain strung between two metal posts, one of which I'd knocked over. The women ran over, picked me up, and held me between them as they slapped and spat on me. But I was happy to see that the little punk had stopped chasing me. Then misfortune arrived, as the two women at Pheasant Hen stopped me from going anywhere. They said that when I knocked down their metal post, it fell onto their car and dented it. Sensei, there was a white ding on the car's boot, but one not caused by the falling post. Refusing to let me go, they called me terrible names, drawing a crowd. Sensei, the little one was the worst. She wasn't much different from the punk who was trying to kill me. She kept jabbing at me, damn near putting my eye out each time. Every word I uttered in my defence was drowned out by curses. Sensei, I wrapped my arms around my head and crouched down out of feelings of despair. The reason Little Lion and I had decided to return home was that we'd experienced something similar near the Huguo Temple in Beijing. It was at a restaurant called Wild Pheasant on a street near the People's Playhouse. As we walked up to read a poster in front of the playhouse we tripped over a metal chain connected to a red and white post, which fell to the ground, not even close to the rear of a white car parked there. But a young woman with hair dyed a golden yellow, a pinched face, and lips as thin as knife blades, who was sitting in front of Wild Pheasant, ran over to the car, spotted a white ding on it and accused us of causing it. With wild gestures, she tore into us verbally, using all sorts of Beijing gutter talk. She said she'd lived her whole life in that lane and had seen every kind of person there was. But what do you out-of-town turtles climb out of your burrows and come to the capital to do? Embarrass the Chinese people? Fat, and reeking of haemorrhoid cream, she charged me, fists swinging, and bloodied my nose. Young men with shaved heads and bare-chested old men stood by shouting encouragement and showing off as old-time Beijingers, insisting that we apologise and make restitution. Sensei, weak as always, I gave her the money and said I was sorry. When we got home, Sensei, we wept first and then decided to move back to Northeast Gaomi Township. Since this was our hometown, I didn't think I'd have to worry about being bullied here. But these two women were every bit as vicious as the woman on Snack Street in Beijing. What I don't understand, Sensei, is why people have to be so horrible.

But there was an even greater danger, Sensei: the predatory punk was coming at me. By now the squid was gone, making the skewer even more deadly, and that's when I realised that he was the son of the smaller of the two women, while her fat companion had to be his aunt. The survival instinct had me scrambling to my feet, and I knew it was time to put my asset – running – to work. After years of living in affluence, I'd forgotten what a fast runner I'd once been. It all came back to me now, when my life was threatened. The women tried to keep me from getting away, the punk was thundering his displeasure, and I began to howl like a cornered dog. With my face bloody, I bared my teeth to give them a momentary fright, since I'd seen a dazed look in the women's eyes with my first howls; I'd always been deeply sympathetic to women who had that look in their eyes. I took advantage of the moment to slip between two parked cars and ran off.

Run, Wan Zu, Wan Xiaopao the runner – fifty-five-year-old Wan Xiaopao was running as fast as he ever had. I ran like a madman down the street, passing the smells of frying chicken, raw fish, lamb kebobs, and some I couldn't name. My legs felt as light as grass, and every step bounced up as if the ground were a spring, which invested greater power in the next steps. I was a deer, a gazelle, a superman light as a swallow after landing on the moon. I felt like a horse, a fine Turkmenistan horse, a horse that steps on a flying swallow, powerful, unconstrained, no worries, no cares.

But in fact this powerful and unconstrained feeling was a short-lived illusion. The real situation was altogether different. I was gasping for breath, my throat was on fire, my heart was pounding like a drum, my chest had swelled up, my head felt as big as a bushel basket, my eyes pulsed black, and my veins seemed about to burst. The survival instinct was in control of my exhausted body; this was a true case of a last-ditch fight to live. Shouts of 'beat him' rose all around me. At first a bearded young man in a black tunic rushed me from the front, his green eyes flashing like fireflies on a mountain road late at night. At the moment his ghostly white hands reached out to grab me, my lips parted and I spewed a mouthful of dirty blood into his ghostly face, which immediately changed colour. He yelped in agony and his hands flew to his face as he crouched down. Sensei, I was filled with remorse, since I knew that he was justified in trying to block my way, that his action proved that he was highly moral and righteous, and spewing dirty blood was like a black Betta fish spewing its guts to ward off danger; I felt terrible about soiling his face and ruining his eyes. Had I been a more noble man, I'd have stopped, apologised, and asked for his forgiveness even with the tip of a knife in my back. But I didn't. Sensei, I have dishonoured your guidance. After that, several sanctimonious gentlemen stood by the side of the road also shouting 'beat him', but did not step forward, surely in fear of my unique blood-spewing skill. They threw half-finished Coke bottles at me, the symbolic colour of American culture, with its golden foam, but I knocked them out of my way.

Sensei, there had to be a conclusion to this. No matter how positive or negative an affair, it must reach a conclusion at some point. This chase and escape, in which right and wrong were totally jumbled, reached its end when my strength was exhausted and I collapsed in front of the Sino-American Jiabao Women and Children's Hospital. A shiny sapphire-blue BMW drove out of the tree-lined compound, where the fragrance of flowers hung in the air. My fallen state must have presented an awful sight to the occupants of the car – I was covered in blood, like a dead dog that's fallen from the sky. Startled at first, they were then struck by inauspicious notions. I knew that rich people tend to be highly superstitious. The degree of superstitious beliefs parallels the degree of wealth. I knew that their fatalistic beliefs outstripped those of poor people, and that their love of life was far greater. Nothing unnatural about that. The poor treat life as worth no more than a broken vessel; the rich treat it as a priceless porcelain bowl. My crumpled appearance in the path of their BMW was no less jarring than a stallion rearing up, eyes blazing and releasing a spine-tingling whinny. I felt just terrible. I'm sorry, I'm so sorry. I was racked by spasms as I tried to crawl out of the way, but, like an insect whose tail is pinned with a thumbtack,

I couldn't move. This reminded me of a prank I'd played as a youngster, even as an adult: I'd pin green insects to the ground or onto a wall by their tails to watch them try to get away, observing the struggle between their instinct to flee and bodies that would not do their bidding. I had been pitiless, actually enjoyed the spectacle. I'd been so much bigger and stronger than any insect, too big and too strong even for an insect to grasp my full appearance. To them I was a mysterious force that created disaster. They probably had no conception of the hand that had brought such evil down on them; their inkling did not extend beyond the thumbtack or the thorn. Now I'd tasted the suffering I'd inflicted on those insects. Little insects, I'm sorry, I am so sorry.

The driver honked his horn gently. A cultured, patient, decent man, obviously. Not a representative of the nouveau riche. If he had been, he'd have made it sound like an air-raid siren. If he'd been one of those, he'd have stuck his head out the window and bombarded me with filthy curses. Because he was a decent man, I tried even harder to crawl out of his way, but my body failed me again.

Seeing he had no choice, he got out of his car. He was wearing a soft yellow leisure suit with orange checks on the collar and sleeves. I vaguely recalled my time in Beijing when a friend who was an expert on famous brand products told me what this particular brand was called in Chinese translation, but I'd forgotten. I never could remember famous brands, which was probably a mental block, a complex psychological expression of loathing and jealousy by people towards their betters. That is much like the way I undervalue bread when compared to steamed buns, or fermented bean sauce over cheese. Rather than curse or kick me, the man shouted to the guard at the hospital entrance: Come here and carry him out of the middle of the road.

His order given, he squinted and looked into the sky to search for the sun and sneezed. The past came flooding into my head. Once again, the sneeze told me who it was: Xiao Xiachun, my one-time classmate, who had cast aside his official position to gain fabulous riches. Word had it that he'd caught a wave into coal for his first bonanza, then tapped into his carefully cultivated connections in officialdom to strike out in all directions and let the money roll in, until he was worth billions. I'd read an interview he'd given in which he actually spoke of eating coal as a child. He'd never eaten coal, I remember that clearly. As he'd watched us eating some, he'd studied the piece in his hand . . . Sensei, look at me, here I was, in dire straits, and I couldn't stop being trivial. I am beyond redemption.

One guard alone could not move me, so a second one came up, and each of them took an arm and, not too roughly, carried and dragged me over to a spot beneath the gigantic signboard just east of the hospital entrance. There they sat me upright with my back against a wall, where I watched classmate Xiao climb back into his car, proceed slowly across the speed bump, then turn and drive off. Here I should say I might have seen, but probably imagined, the lovely Xiao Bi, her long hair spilling over her shoulders, in the back seat of the car, a pink infant in her arms.

The crowd that was chasing me drew up. The two women, the little punk, and the young man whose face I covered with dark blood, plus all the ones who had thrown Coke bottles at me, craned their necks to observe me. Several dozen faces formed a hazy mosaic around me. The little punk still wanted to stab me, but was stopped from doing so by the woman who seemed to be the younger of the two. A professorial-looking man stuck two slender fingers under my nose to see if I was still breathing. I held my breath for the sake of self-protection. As a boy I once heard an old man who had returned to the village from Guangdong say that if you encountered a tiger or a black bear in the mountain forests, your best bet was to lie down, hold your breath, and pretend to be dead. Large predators share heroic qualities with humans: a valiant human will not attack a foe that has surrendered, a wild beast will only kill and eat living prey. Well, it worked, for the professor stood there speechless for a moment before turning and walking off. His action served as an announcement to the crowd: This man is dead! Even though, in their eyes, I was a criminal, the law did not give law-abiding citizens the right to beat a thief to death. So they got out of there as quickly as they could – better safe than sorry. The two women dragged the boy away from the scene. I exhaled, greatly relieved, and was suddenly aware of the dignity and honour the dead possess.

It must have been the guards who called the police, since they were the only ones who came to report what had happened when the police cars drove up, sirens blaring. Three policemen walked up and asked me how I was doing. They were all young, and their yellow teeth showed they were all from Northeast Gaomi Township. I got tearful, and before long was sobbing my story like a boy who's been victimised by a bully when he sees his father arrive. Only the cop with a growth between his eyebrows seemed to be listening to what I was saying. The other two were more intent on studying the signboard above me. When I finished, the first cop said: How do we know that what you've said is the truth? Go ask Chen Bi, I told him. The tallest cop said, without taking his eyes off the signboard, How do you feel? Want us to take you to the hospital?

I tried moving my legs. They were still working. Then I looked at the wounds on my arms and hands. They'd stopped bleeding. If you don't mind the bother, the cop with the growth on his brow said, you can come to the station with us and make a report. If it's too much bother, you can go home and rest up. That's it? I said. No who's right and who's wrong? There's right and there's wrong, he said, but we need proof, witnesses. Can you get that Chen Bi and those fishmongers to be witnesses? Can you be sure those two women and the boy would not turn around and accuse you? That kid, the grandson of the scoundrel Zhang Quan of Dongfeng Village, is a bad one, all right, but he is a child, and what do you think you can do to him? All right, I said, I'll just drop it, I lose – wisdom grows out of experience, and at my age a man should stay home and out of trouble, playing with his grandchildren and enjoying family life – thank you all, sorry to waste the nation's gasoline and wear down the nation's tyres, and cause you trouble. Are you mocking us, old sir? No, of course not, I wouldn't dare. I'm being truthful, absolutely sincere.

The two cops – one with the growth, the other very tall – turned to leave, but the third man – who had a wide mouth on a square face – kept staring at the signboard and had no interest in leaving. Let's go, Wang, Eyebrow Growth said. Has the sight of the babies paralysed you? Wide

Mouth responded with a note of approval, Cute, really cute! Eyebrow Growth teased, Then go home and give your seed to your wife. Can't, Wide Mouth said, she's barren. I can do the planting, but there'll be no sprouts. The tall cop joined the conversation: Don't put all the blame on her, he said. Go get checked. Maybe your seeds have all been fried. No way, Wide mouth said . . .

The banter continued as they climbed into their car and left me there under the signboard, depressed but resigned to my fate. What would I have gained by going to the station with them and making a report? Since the women were Zhang Quan's daughters – he had a third – Gugu was their enemy, and now I knew why the boy had scared her with that frog. He'd probably been coached by his mother or aunt as a means of avenging their mother, even though Gugu had not been responsible for her death. You can't be reasonable with people like that. To hell with it, I lose. No, God is testing me. So grin and bear it. I'm a strong-willed man, a playwright, and all these encounters and experiences constitute superb material. Important people become important by enduring the suffering and humiliation that defeats ordinary people. Examples like General Han Xin, who drank the cup of humiliation; or like Confucius, who endured hunger from Chen to Cai; or Sun Bin, who ate his own faeces . . . how can the little bit of suffering and humiliation I endured be mentioned in the same breath as that of those sages and ancient wise men? With that thought in mind, Sensei, I gained a sense of tolerance as my breathing returned to normal, my eyes lit up, and I felt my strength slowly return. Stand up, Tadpole, the heavens have bestowed great responsibilities on you. You must bravely accept suffering without complaint and with hatred towards no one.

I stood up, and though my wounds hurt, I was famished, my legs were rubbery, and I saw stars, I would not allow myself to fall back down. I thought there'd be people watching me, but there were none. Even the guards at the hospital entrance ignored me. This confirmed what Li Shou had told me. Thoughts of Li Shou reminded me of Chen Mei, in whose belly my child was growing. I felt different about that now than I had in the morning. I'd been hell-bent on forcing the death of the child, but no longer. I turned to look at the hospital signboard and the thought running through my head could not have been clearer: I want that child! I desperately need that child. He is a treasure sent down to me from the heavens, and is worth all my suffering.

Sensei, I want you to know that the signboard was etched with the enlarged photographs of hundreds of children, some laughing, others crying; some with their eyes shut, others open in a squint; some had both eyes wide open, others had one eye open and one eye shut; some were looking up, others were looking straight ahead; some were holding out both arms, as if reaching for something; the hands of some were balled into fists, as if they were unhappy; some were sucking on a fist, others had their hands over their ears; some were laughing with their eyes open, some with their eyes shut; some were crying with their eyes open, some with their eyes shut; some had no hair on their heads, others had a headful of black hair; some had soft, golden fuzz, others had sleek, shiny, velvet-like, flaxen hair; some had wrinkly faces, like little old men, some had fat faces with big ears, like little piglets; some had skin as white as glutinous dumplings, others were as dark as coal; some had puckered lips, as if angry, others looked like they were shouting; some were making sucking motions, looking to nurse, other pressed their lips together, cocking their heads, refusing to nurse; some were sticking out bright red tongues, others were sticking out pink ones; some had two dimpled cheeks, some had only one; some had double-fold eyelids, some had single-fold eyelids; the heads of some were round as balls, those of others long as gourds; the brows of some were thoughtfully furrowed, others had raised their eyes . . . in other words, their appearances and expressions varied widely, and each one was cute as could be. The promotional text informed me that these were pictures of every child born in the hospital in the two years it had been open, a bumper crop. This was truly a great undertaking, a noble one, and a sweet one . . . Sensei, I was deeply moved. As tears filled my eyes, I heard the call of a sacred noise, and experienced the most solemn feeling a human can know – the love of life; all other love, by comparison, is vulgar, low-class. Sensei, it was as if my soul had received a solemn baptism, and that I'd been given the chance to have all the sins of my past forgiven. Whatever the cause or the effect, I wanted to spread my arms to enfold this innocent new life sent to me by the heavens!

11

Sensei, my soul received a solemn baptism that day as I sat beneath the signboard etched with those hundreds of children's photographs. All my doubts, wavering, torment, beatings, humiliation, and being pursued were necessary steps in the process. Like the Tang monk Tripitaka, who encountered eighty-one trials on his trip to India for the Buddhist scriptures. A tortuous path leads to Nirvana; tribulations are essential for an understanding of life.

Back home I cleaned my wounds with alcohol and cotton swabs and drank some Yunnan powder steeped in liquor, which is particularly effective for bruises. The physical pain did not go away immediately, but my spirits were high. When Little Lion walked in the door I threw my arms around her and brushed her cheek with mine. Wife of mine, I said, thank you for creating my child. He has been nurtured not in your womb but in your heart. He is our very own child.

She wept.

Sensei, as I sit at my desk writing this letter to you I am pondering how I will raise this child. We are both nearly sixty, our bodies have begun their decline, and we should be looking for a nanny, someone experienced in the raising of a child, or a wet nurse, so that our child will taste mother's milk. My mother once said that a child raised on cow's or goat's milk lacks the smell of mother's milk. A child that grows and develops on cow's milk will be vulnerable to many dangers, and I wonder if the unprincipled merchants will actually stop their 'chemistry' experiments in the wake of the 'empty formula' and 'melamine formula' affairs. After the 'big-headed babies' and 'stone babies,' who knows what kind of babies will come next? Those people are now fleeing with their tails between their legs, like beaten dogs, trying to look as pitiful as possible. But before too many years have passed, their tails will be up in the air again, and they'll be concocting even worse formulas that will wreak damage on people. I know that mother's milk is the most precious liquid the world has to offer. The first lactated milk, known as colostrum, contains mysterious elements that, when distilled, are in essence a mother's love. I have heard of cases where parents have paid large sums of money to their surrogate mothers to purchase colostrum, and some have gone so far as to pay the surrogate to nurse the infant for its first month before taking it home with them. This is expensive, of course. Little Lion told me that the surrogate mothers company would not permit that. According to them, when a woman nurses an infant for a month, she develops an attachment to the child that creates serious problems.

Little Lion's eyes lit up as she said to me:

I'm his mother, and I'll produce milk for him!

Mother had told me stories about such things, but they seemed too far-fetched to believe. Maybe, I thought, a young woman who had previously borne and nursed a child might begin lactating again with the stimulation of a child's mouth and a heart filled with love, but no such miracle would visit Little Lion, a woman nearly sixty who had never been pregnant. If it did, it would be on a level beyond 'miracle'.

Sensei, I feel no sense of shame in writing about such things to you, a father who took a child the hospital told you had no chance of surviving and raised him. During that process you experienced many similar miracles. So I'm sure you know what I was feeling and have an appreciation for my wife's abnormal behaviour. Lately she's wanted to make love every night. She has gone from being a dried-up turnip to a honey peach, and this in itself is almost a miracle. I couldn't be happier. She reminds me each time: Tadpole, be gentle, take it easy, you don't want to injure our son. After we finish, she takes my hand and rests it on her belly. Can you feel it? He's kicking me. She washes her breasts every morning with warm water and gently tugs on her sunken nipples.

When we told my father that she was pregnant, ancient tears rolled down his ninety-year-old cheeks and his beard quivered.

Heaven has eyes, he said emotionally. Our ancestors have revealed themselves. The good shall be rewarded, Amita Buddha!

Sensei, we've made all the preparations for the baby, the best that money can buy. A Japanese stroller, a Korean crib, Shanghai disposable nappies, a Russian rubber infant's bathtub . . . Little Lion will not allow nursing bottles in the house. What if you don't have enough milk? I asked her. We should have one just in case. So we bought French bottles and some milk formula imported from New Zealand. But we weren't convinced that New Zealand formula was safe enough, so I suggested that we buy a milk goat and pasture it at my father's place. We could move into Father's house and feed our precious infant freshly squeezed milk every day. Cupping her breasts in her hands, Little Lion said unhappily:

I firmly believe that these could produce fountains of milk!

Our daughter phoned us from Spain and asked what we were doing to keep so busy. Yanyan, I said, I'm really sorry, but I have wonderful news. Your mother is pregnant. You're going to have a baby brother very soon. That was greeted with a moment of silence. Is that true, Papa? she asked. Of course it is, I said. But how old is Mama? she asked. Go online and you'll see that a sixty-two-year-old Danish woman just gave birth to a healthy pair of twins. My daughter was thrilled. That's wonderful! she said. Papa, congratulations to you both, hearty congratulations! Tell me what you need and I'll send it right away. We don't need anything, I said. We have everything we need. I don't care, my daughter said, I'm going to send you something, a gift from the heart of a big sister. Congratulations, Papa. A thousand-year-old sago palm has flowered, a ten-thousand-year-old dead branch has sprouted. You have created a miracle!

Sensei, I've always thought I owed a debt to my daughter, since I played a role in the death of her mother. Renmei died way before her time because of my concern over my so-called future, and the child she was carrying died with her. He'd be in his twenties now. No matter how I look at it, another son on the way is a comfort to me. In reality, this son will be that one. He'll just come twenty-odd years late. But he is coming.

I'm ashamed to tell you, Sensei, that my play won't be written till later. A bawling baby is much more important than a play. Maybe this is a good thing, because my thoughts up till now have been dark, have carried the stench of blood, are all about death and destruction, not life, despair not hope, and a play like that could only poison the viewers' souls, and that would make my offence even greater. Don't lose faith in me, Sensei. I will write that play. After my child is born, I'll pick up my pen and offer praise to the new life. I won't disappoint you, Sensei.

I went with Little Lion to see Gugu. It was a beautiful, sunlit day. Flowers were blooming on the scholar trees in her yard, while some had already fallen to the ground. Gugu was sitting beneath one of the trees, her eyes shut. She was muttering something. Flowers covered her thick, messy grey hair, around which bees were circling. Hao Dashou was seated on a stool in front of a limestone bench beneath the window. Given the title of county folk artist, he was moulding a lump of clay. He had a distant look in his eyes, almost trancelike.

This child's father has a round face, Gugu was saying, long, narrow eyes, a flat nose, thick lips and fat ears; his mother has a thin, oval face, almond-pit eyes with double folds, a small mouth, high nose bridge, and thin ears with no lobes. The child would take after his mother, but with a larger mouth, slightly thicker lips, bigger ears, and a nose bridge slightly lower . . .

As Gugu muttered her description, a clay doll took shape in Uncle's hands. After forming eyebrows with a pointed bamboo strip, he pulled back to take a look, made a few changes, then placed it on a plank in front of her.

Gugu picked it up, studied it, and said:

Make the eyes a little larger and thicken the lips.

He took it from her, made the changes and handed it back. His eyes lit up like lightning beneath his bushy grey brows.

With the doll in her hands Gugu held her arms out for a distant look, then brought them in close; a look of kindness spread across her face. Yes, that's it, she said, that's him. But then her tone changed as she spoke directly to the doll: This is you, you little sprite, you little debtor. Gugu destroyed two thousand eight hundred foetuses, and you're the last. With you, we have them all.

I laid a bottle of Wuliangye on the windowsill, Little Lion laid a box of sweets next to Gugu. Gugu, we said together, we've come to see you.

Like someone who has been caught making contraband, she was startled and jittery. She tried covering the doll with her sleeve, but couldn't manage. Then she stopped trying. I can't hide anything from you, she said.

Gugu, I said, we've watched the documentary Wang Gan sent us, and now we understand you and know what's in your heart.

I'm glad, she said as she stood up and carried the newest clay doll over to the eastern side rooms. Without turning around, she said, Follow me. Her large, shapeless figure in black created a mysterious tension in us. Father had said she hadn't been acting quite normal, so we'd seldom been to see her since our return. It was heartbreaking to see what a sad figure she'd become after the renown and influence she'd enjoyed as a younger woman.

A dank chill assailed our noses in the dim light of the building. Gugu pulled the chain on a hundred-watt bulb near the wall, bringing the room into sharp focus. Every window in the three rooms was bricked up. Latticed wooden racks fronted the eastern, southern, and northern walls, each little square occupied by a clay doll.

Gugu placed the doll in her hands into the last square on the wall, then stepped back, lit three sticks of incense on an altar in the centre of the room, fell to her knees, brought her palms together, and muttered prayerfully.

We hastily joined her on our knees, though I didn't know what I should be praying for. The lively images of the children on the signboard in front of the Sino-American Jiabao Women and Children's Hospital scrolled through my mind like a peepshow. I was feeling immense gratitude, shame and remorse, and fine threads of terror. I knew that by employing her husband's talents, Gugu was bringing to life all the children she'd stopped from being born. I guessed that was her way to assuage deep-seated feelings of guilt, and there was nothing wrong with that. If she hadn't done it, someone else would have. The men and women who defied the policy against multiple pregnancies could not escape a share of the responsibility for what happened. And if no one had done what she did, it is truly hard to say what China might be like today.

Her devotion completed, Gugu stood up and said, with a broad smile, Xiaopao, Little Lion, I'm glad you're here. I've fulfilled my desire. Take a good look around you. Every one of these children has a name. I've brought them all together here where they can accept my offerings. Once they have reached spiritual attainment they can leave for wherever they are fated to be reborn. Gugu led us past each of the squares and told us where the boys and girls went or were to go.

This girl, she said, pointing to a doll with almond-shaped eyes, and lips in a little pout, should have been born to Tan Xiaoliu and Dong Yue'e of Tan Family Village in August 1974, but I destroyed her. Now everything is fine. Her father is a wealthy farmer, her mother a resourceful woman, and together they invented a process of irrigating celery with cow's milk to produce a fresh vegetable that sells for sixty yuan a jin.

This boy, Gugu said as she pointed to a laughing doll with eyes reduced to a squint, should have been born to Wu Junbao and Zhou Aihua of Wu Family Bridge in February 1983, but I destroyed him. Now everything is fine. The little imp is flooded with good luck, reborn into the family of an official in Qingzhou Prefecture. Both parents are Party cadres, and his grandfather is high-ranking provincial official who is regularly seen on TV. Gugu has done well by you, you little imp.

These two sisters, Gugu said as she pointed to a pair of dolls in one of the squares, should have been born in 1990. Both parents had leprosy, and even though the disease had been stopped, they had claws for hands and demonic faces. Being born into a family like that was the same as being thrown into the bitter seas, and destroying them was their salvation. Now everything is fine. On the first night of 2000 they were born at the People's Hospital in Jiaozhou and became millennial babies. Their father is a renowned actor of Maoqiang opera, their mother owns a women's boutique. On New Year's day last year, the sisters appeared on a television program to sing the famous Maoqiang aria 'Zhao Meirong Observes Lanterns': Eggplant lantern, purple and neat/leek lantern, a messy treat/cucumber lantern, thorns all over/radish lantern, watery sweet/and then the crab lantern with buggy eyes/the hen lantern clucks as an egg lands at her feet . . . Their mother and father phoned to remind me to watch them on the Jiaozhou channel. I meant something to them. Pearly tears rolled down my cheeks.

Don't forget this one, Gugu said as she pointed to a cross-eyed doll. He should have been born into the Dongfeng Village home of Zhang Quan, but I destroyed him. It wasn't all my fault, but I bear some of the responsibility. In July 1995, the little imp was born to the second daughter of Zhang Quan, Zhang Laidi, in Dongfeng Village. Laidi came to see me. She already had two daughters, and another pregnancy would be illegal. Though her father had once cracked open my head, and there was a history of unpleasantness between us, I went ahead and returned to her the child that should have been born to her mother. He would have been her kid brother, and now he was her son. This is a secret that only I, and now you two know. You mustn't tell anyone. He is not a good boy. Knowing that Gugu is afraid of frogs, he once handed me one wrapped in paper and nearly scared me to death. But I don't hate him. In this mortal world, not a single person can be left out, not the good and not the bad . . .

The last square Gugu pointed to was the one in which she'd placed the doll after we walked in. Know who that is? she asked us.

There were tears in my eyes. Don't say anything, Gugu, I know who he is.

Gugu, Little Lion said, that child will be born soon. His father is a playwright, his mother a retired nurse . . . thank you, Gugu, I'm pregnant . . .

When you read this, Sensei, you will think I'm either crazy or dreaming. I admit there are issues with Gugu's mental state, and my wife had been yearning for a child for so long that she wasn't quite herself emotionally, so I ask for your compassion and understanding where they are concerned. Anyone burdened with feelings of guilt must find ways to comfort herself, as Xiang Lin Sao did in the Lu Xun story 'Benediction', a character who, as you know so well, offered a threshold for people to walk on to atone for what she considered her crimes. Clear-headed people were wrong to have laid bare her illusions, and should have given her hope, let her gain release, have no more nightmares, and live a life free of guilt. I have complied with their wishes, I even strive to believe in whatever they believe in. That seems like the proper thing to do. I know that people with scientific minds will laugh at me and that the moralists will criticise my decision, and that some of the more enlightened might even go public with their accusations, but none of that will change me. For the sake of the child and for the sake of Gugu and Little Lion, who had once been saddled with special work, I'm perfectly willing to muddle along the way I've been going.

Gugu had Little Lion lie down and expose her abdomen so she could listen with a stethoscope. When she was finished checking her, she placed her hands – hands that Mother had praised many times – on Little Lion's abdomen and said, Five months, I'd say. It sounds good, clear, and well positioned.

Past six months, Little Lion said with notable embarrassment.

Get up, Gugu said as she gently patted Little Lion's belly. Age could be an issue, she said, but I recommend natural birth. I don't favour caesarian sections. A woman whose child has not passed through the birth canal misses out on much of what a mother should feel.

I'm a little scared . . .

I'm here, so what's there to be scared about? She held up both hands. You need to place your trust in a pair of hands that have delivered ten thousand babies.

Little Lion grabbed hold of Gugu's hands and held them to her face, like a pampered little girl.

I trust you, Gugu, I do.

12

Great news, Sensei!

My son was born early yesterday morning.

Because my wife, Little Lion, was well past the prime age for a first pregnancy, even the doctors at the Sino-American Jiabao Women and Children's Hospital, reputedly holders of PhDs from British and American medical universities, refused to be in attendance during her labour. Naturally, we thought of Gugu. Old ginger is still the spiciest. My wife trusted no one more than Gugu, whom she had assisted in countless births and who had witnessed Gugu's composure during many crises.

Little Lion went into labour when she was working the night shift at the bullfrog-breeding farm. By rights, she should have been at home resting at that stage in her pregnancy, but she stubbornly refused to take that advice. When she walked through the marketplace, preceded by an enormous belly, she was the recipient of idle talk and of envy. People who knew her greeted her with: Dear Sister-in-law, why aren't you home in bed? Brother Tadpole is a cruel man! What's the big deal? she'd reply. When the fruit is ripe it drops on its own. Farming wives routinely have their babies in cotton fields or in groves of trees. It's the pampered women who have all the problems. Old-time practitioners of Chinese medicine share her views. People within earshot mostly nod their heads in agreement. Hardly anyone voices a different opinion to her face.

When the news reached me I rushed over to the breeding farm, where Yuan Sai had already sent my cousin to fetch Gugu, who arrived in a white surgical gown and mask, her messy hair tucked into a white cap. The look of intense excitement in her eyes reminded me of an old packhorse. A woman in white led Gugu to a secret delivery room, while I drank tea in Yuan Sai's office.

A black leather, high-backed chair rose up behind a burgundy-coloured desk the size of a ping-pong table in the centre of the office. A stack of books on the desk was, surprisingly, topped by a little red Chinese flag. Even a bandit can be a patriot, my friend, he said sombrely, anticipating my question.

He poured tea into the special service and said proudly, This is Da Hong Pao, a fine tea from Mount Wuyi, and while it may not be the gold standard, it is of such high quality that I won't serve it even for the county chief. But I'm serving it to you to prove I have style.

Noticing that I wasn't paying attention, he said, There's nothing to worry about when I'm in charge. Nothing can go wrong. We don't normally ask your aunt to come over. She is Northeast Gaomi Township's patron saint. When she's on the scene, the results can be stated in eight words: Mother and son doing fine, everyone is happy.

After a while I fell asleep on the leather sofa and dreamed of Mother and of Renmei. Mother was dressed in shimmering satin clothes and was leaning on a dragon-headed cane; Renmei had on a bright red padded jacket and green trousers, absolutely countrified yet still lovely. A red cloth bag was slung over her left shoulder, a yellow knit sweater peeking out from the opening. They were pacing the hallway, Mother's cane making an unhurried clack on the wooden floor that filled me with anxiety. Won't you sit down and take it easy, Mother? I said. Pacing back and forth, you two, is putting everyone on edge. She sat on a sofa, but only for a moment before taking to the floor, where she sat in the lotus position. Sitting on a sofa, she said, makes it hard to breathe. Renmei, looking timorous, hid behind Mother like a shy little girl. Every time I looked her way, she avoided my eyes. She took the sweater out of her bag and opened it up; it was no bigger than the palm of my hand. That's just about the right size for a doll, I said. I measured the baby in me to make it the right size, she said as she blushed. That drew my attention to her belly, which was noticeably swollen. The slightly mottled skin on her face proved she was pregnant. The child in there can't be that small, can it? I asked. Her eyes reddened. Xiaopao, she said, ask Gugu to let me have this baby. Have it right now, Mother said as she banged her cane on the floor. I'm here to protect you. An old woman's cane hits a debauched monarch on high and traitorous officials below. An ugly death awaits anyone who tries to stop me. She tapped a button on the wall, and a hidden door slowly opened. The room inside was bright as a sunlit day, revealing an operating table covered by a white sheet, on either side of which stood two people in surgical gowns and masks; Gugu was at the head of the table, also in white and wearing rubber surgical gloves. When Renmei entered and saw what awaited her, she turned to run, but Gugu reached out and stopped her. She cried like a helpless little girl. Xiaopao, she called out to me, in the name of our long marriage, help me . . . As sadness penetrated my heart, tears fell from my eyes. With a sign from Gugu, the four women – nurses apparently – picked Renmei up, placed her on the operating table and, working together, removed her clothes. I looked down and saw a tiny red hand between her legs. The little thumb was touching the tips of the last two fingers, leaving the first two fingers to form the international 'V' sign: Gugu and the others burst out laughing. When she'd gotten that out of her system, Gugu said, That's enough horseplay. You can come out now. A little baby began slipping out, looking around as it emerged, like a sneaky little critter. Taking aim, Gugu grabbed it by the ear, wrapped her arm around its head, then pulled with all her might. I want you out of there! There was a loud pop and an infant, covered with blood and a sticky substance lay in Gugu's hands . . .

I woke up with a start, feeling cold all over. My cousin walked in with Little Lion, who was holding swaddling clothes, from which husky cries emerged. My heartiest congratulations, my cousin said softly, you have a son.

My cousin drove us to my father's village, which had already been incorporated into a metropolitan district. As I wrote in a previous letter, it is a village that retains its cultural characteristics on orders from our county chief – now promoted to mayor – with the early Cultural Revolution style of buildings, slogans painted on the walls, revolutionary signs at the head of the village, loudspeakers mounted on poles, an open spot for bringing the production brigade together . . . dawn had broken, but there was no one on the streets, only some early morning buses speeding along with a few ghost-like passengers, and some street sweepers, with everything but their eyes covered, raising clouds of dust with their brooms on the pedestrian paths. I desperately wanted to see the baby's face, but the look on Little Lion's face – more sombre than a pregnant woman, weary, and overjoyed – nipped that thought in the bud. A red bandana was wrapped around her head, her lips were chapped as she held the baby close to her and kept burying her face in the blankets, either to look at her baby or to inhale his smell.

We had already moved everything the baby would need to Father's place, mainly because it was so difficult to find a milk goat, and Father had arranged to buy milk from a villager named Du. They were raising a pair of milk cows that together produced a hundred jin of milk every day. Father made it clear that they were not to add anything to the milk they sold us. Grandpa, the villager said, if you don't trust us, you can come milk them yourself.

My cousin pulled up and parked outside my father's gate. He was waiting for us. With him were my second sister-in-law and some young women, probably nephews' wives. Second Sister-in-law grabbed the baby as the young women carried Little Lion out of the car and into the yard, and from there into the room we'd prepared for her convalescence.

Second Sister-in-law opened the bundle to let Father set eyes on this late arriving grandson. Wonderful, he said over and over, tears in his eyes. And when I saw the dark-haired, ruddy-faced infant, my heart filled with emotions, my eyes with tears.

Sensei, this child helped me recapture my youth and my inspiration. While the gestation and birth might have been more difficult, more torturous than most, and while issues concerning his status might create some thorny problems, as my aunt said, Once it's seen the light of day, it's a life and will become a legal citizen of the country, entitled to all the rights and benefits of the country. If there is trouble, that is for those of us who permitted him to come into the world to deal with. What we have to give to him is love, nothing more.

Sensei, tomorrow I will spread out some writing paper and complete the laboured birth of this play. My next letter will include a play that might never see the stage:

Frog.

BOOK FIVE

BOOK FIVE

Dear Sensei,

I finally finished the play.

So many things in real life are tangled up in the story told in my play that when I was writing I sometimes could not tell if it was a true-to-life record or a fictional work. I finished it in a period of five days, like a child who can't wait to tell his parents what he's seen or thought. I know it's a bit of an affectation to compare myself to a child, but that is exactly what I was feeling.

This play ought to constitute an organic part of my aunt's story. Though some of the incidents did not actually occur, they did in my mind, and that makes them real to me.

Sensei, I used to think that writing could be a means of attaining redemption, but when the play was finished, instead of lessening, my feelings of guilt actually grew more intense. Although I can trot out an array of rationalisations to absolve myself of responsibility for the deaths of Renmei and the child in her womb – my child, too, of course – and place the blame on Gugu, the army, Yuan Sai, even Renmei herself – that is what I did for decades – now I understand with greater clarity than at any other time that I was not just the chief culprit, but the only one. For the sake of my so-called 'future', I sent Renmei and her child straight to Hell. I tried to imagine that the child carried by Chen Mei was the reincarnation of the unborn child, but that was nothing but self-consolation. It served the same function as Gugu's clay dolls. Every child is unique, irreplaceable. Can blood on one's hands never be washed clean? Can a soul entangled in guilt never be free?

I long to hear your answers, Sensei.

Tadpole
3 June 2009

Frog

A PLAY IN 9 ACTS

Dramatis Personae

GUGU, *a retired obstetrician, in her seventies*

TADPOLE, *playwright, Gugu's nephew, in his fifties*

LITTLE LION, *one-time assistant to Gugu, Tadpole's wife, in her fifties*

CHEN MEI, *surrogate mother, in her twenties, a fire victim with a disfigured face*

CHEN BI, *Chen Mei's father, Tadpole's elementary schoolmate, a vagrant in his fifties*

YUAN SAI, *Tadpole's elementary schoolmate, Bullfrog Company boss, secretly engaged in a 'surrogate mother company', in his fifties*

COUSIN, *Jin Xiu by name, Tadpole's cousin, Yuan Sai's subordinate, in his forties*

LI SHOU, *Tadpole's elementary schoolmate, restaurant owner, in his fifties*

STATION CHIEF, *police officer in his forties*

WEI YING, *policewoman, a recent police academy graduate, in her twenties*

HAO DASHOU, *a folk artist, Gugu's husband*

QIN HE, *a folk artist, Gugu's admirer*

LIU GUIFANG, *Tadpole's elementary schoolmate, manager of the county guesthouse*

GAO MENGJIU, *Gaomi County Chief during the Republic of China era*
YAMEN CLERKS
HOSPITAL SECURITY GUARD *and* HOSPITAL SECURITY SUPERVISOR
TWO MASKED INDIVIDUALS IN BLACK
TV CAMERAMAN, FEMALE JOURNALIST, *and* OTHERS

Act I

Sino-American Jiabao Women's and Children's Hospital compound. An impressive gateway, suggestive of a government office. The hospital marquee hangs above and to the left of the marble-faced main door.

To the right stands a sign the size of a billboard etched with hundreds of baby pictures.

A security guard in a grey uniform stands stiffly to the left of the gate, welcoming or sending off each luxury automobile that enters or leaves the compound with a crisp salute. His action is comically, laughably exaggerated.

A full moon shines brightly on the backdrop, behind which emerges the sound of exploding firecrackers; an occasional burst of fireworks lights up the backdrop.

SECURITY GUARD: (*takes out his cell phone, reads a text message, and laughs*) Tee-hee.

The security supervisor slips out through the gate.

SUPERVISOR: (*standing unnoticed behind the security guard, says sternly in a low voice*) What's so funny, Li Jiatai? (*feels something land on his foot*) Where did all these frogs come from at this time of year? What are you laughing at?

SECURITY GUARD: (*startled, nervously snaps to attention*) Reporting, sir, the earth is getting warmer, the greenhouse effect. What's funny? Nothing . . .

SUPERVISOR: If nothing's funny, what are you laughing at? (*shakes the foot on which the frog rests*) What's going on here? Is another earthquake on its way? I asked you what's so funny.

SECURITY GUARD: (*seeing there's no one around, says with a laugh*) Sir, this joke is really funny . . .

SUPERVISOR: I've told you people, no texting!

SECURITY GUARD: Reporting, sir, I'm not texting. I'm just reading a few text messages.

SUPERVISOR: What's the difference? If Department Head Liu saw you, you could kiss your rice bowl goodbye.

SECURITY GUARD: So what? I've been thinking of packing it in anyway. The boss at the bullfrog breeding farm is my uncle. My mother has asked her cousin to get her husband to hire me at the farm . . .

SUPERVISOR: (*impatiently*) Okay, that's enough. All this uncle-cousin-husband talk has me going in circles. You might not care about your rice bowl because you've got an uncle you can rely on, but I need mine to survive. So while you're on duty, no reading text messages and no answering your phone.

SECURITY GUARD: (*snaps to attention*) Yes, sir!

SUPERVISOR: Be careful.

SECURITY GUARD: (*snaps to attention*) Yes, sir! (*can't keep from laughing*) Tee-hee . . .

SUPERVISOR: Have you been drinking dog piss, or did you dream you were marrying a rich woman? What the hell are you laughing at?

SECURITY GUARD: I'm not laughing at anything . . .

SUPERVISOR: (*sticks out his right hand*) Hand it over!

SECURITY GUARD: What?

SUPERVISOR: Your cell phone, that's what.

SECURITY GUARD: I promise I won't use it again, sir. Okay?

SUPERVISOR: Shut up! Are you going to hand it over or aren't you? If you don't I'll report you to the department head.

SECURITY GUARD: I'm involved in a romance, sir, and I need my cell phone.

SUPERVISOR: When your father was involved in a romance, he didn't even have a telephone and he managed to win over your mother, didn't he? Make it snappy!

SECURITY GUARD: (*reluctantly hands over his cell phone*) I didn't mean to laugh, but the message was just so funny.

SUPERVISOR: (*plays with the phone*) I want to see just what it was that had you laughing so hard . . . 'In an effort to produce a champion sprinter, the National Athletic Commission ordered a marriage between men's hundred-metre-dash gold medallist Qian Bao and women's distance gold medallist Jin Lu. When Jin Lu's pregnancy had reached full term, she delivered a baby in the hospital. Qian Bao asked the doctor: Is it a boy or a girl? The doctor replied, I couldn't tell. It ran off as soon as it was out.' You laughed at that old joke? I've got a couple of good ones here. (*He takes out his cell phone, but before he starts reading, he realises what he's doing and stuffs both phones into his pocket.*) Tonight's the Mid-Autumn Festival. Department Head Liu said we have to double our vigilance on special holidays.

SECURITY GUARD: (*sticks out his hand*) My phone!

SUPERVISOR: I'm keeping it for now. You can have it back when you're off-duty.

SECURITY GUARD: (*pleading*) This is a holiday, sir. Families are having happy reunions, enjoying moon cakes, setting off firecrackers, gazing at the full moon, falling in love, but not me. I'm stuck here like a pole, and you're taking even the pleasure of exchanging text messages with my girlfriend from me.

SUPERVISOR: That's enough. Stand your watch, keep your eyes and ears open, and stop all suspicious individuals at the gate.

SECURITY GUARD: Oh, come on. Don't pay attention to Big Head's nonsense. Who wants to come to a hospital on special days? Even crooks celebrate holidays.

SUPERVISOR: Stop clowning around! Is this some kind of game to
    you? (*lowers his voice secretively*) On New Year's a terrorist gang
    entered the (*unintelligible*) Maternity Hospital and snatched eight
    babies as hostages . . .

SECURITY GUARD: (*soberly*) Oh . . .

SUPERVISOR: (*mysteriously*) Are you aware that a certain someone's
    mistress is in the hospital to have a baby?

SECURITY GUARD: (*cocks his ear to listen attentively*)

SUPERVISOR: (*softly, secretively*) Get it? Remember, a black Mercedes
    and a green BMW are his cars. Be sure to give them snappy
    salutes coming and going. No sloppy behaviour!

SECURITY GUARD: Yes, sir! (*reaches out*) Now can you give me back my
    cell phone?

SUPERVISOR: No, absolutely not! This is a special night. Not only is
    Boss Jin's wife expecting to deliver, but Party Secretary Song's
    daughter-in-law is due as well. A black Audi A-6, licence 08858,
    keep your eyes open for it.

SECURITY GUARD: (*unhappily*) Those pricks sure know how to pick the
    right day! My girlfriend told me that the moon tonight will be
    the brightest and roundest in the last fifty years. (*gazes into the sky*)
    When is the moon full? I ask with a glass in my hand. We toast
    the heavens with wine . . .

SUPERVISOR: (*in a mocking tone*) Oh, please! If you've memorised
    everything from school, what are you doing as a security guard?
    (*suddenly alert*) What's that?

*Chen Mei, dressed in black, a black veil covering her face, enters carrying a
tiny red sweater.*

CHEN MEI: (*swaying from side to side, as if drunk*) My baby . . . my
    baby . . . where are you? Mummy's coming for you, where are
    you hiding?

SECURITY GUARD: Her again. She's crazy.

SUPERVISOR: Go chase her away.

SECURITY GUARD: (*stands up straight*) I cannot leave my post.

SUPERVISOR: I'm ordering you to chase her away.

SECURITY GUARD: I am a sentry.

SUPERVISOR: Your duty station extends to fifty metres on either side of the gate.

SECURITY GUARD: If anything suspicious occurs in the vicinity of the gate, the guard on duty is required to man his post and stop suspicious individuals from entering, then report immediately to his superior. (*He takes his walkie-talkie from his belt.*) Reporting, sir, a suspicious individual to the right of the main gate. Request backup.

SUPERVISOR: Damn you!

Stage lights focus on a spot in front of the signboard.

CHEN MEI: (*points to the baby photos*) Baby, my baby, Mummy's calling you. Can you hear me? Are you playing hide-and-seek with Mummy? Not letting her find you? Hurry, you naughty thing, you little angel, come out so Mummy can nurse you. If you don't, a puppy will take Mummy's milk from you . . . (*points to one of the photos*) You want my milk? No, you can't have it. You're not my baby. My baby has double-fold lids and big eyes. You're squinting . . . you want my milk too? But you're not my baby either. My baby has nice, apple red cheeks, but your face is sallow . . . you definitely aren't mine, my baby is a boy, a pudgy little boy, but you're a little girl, and girls aren't worth anything. (*alertly*) Fifty thousand to bear a boy, only thirty thousand for a girl. You bastards, with your feudal preference for boys over girls, your mothers were girls, weren't they? Your grandmothers . . . If everyone had boys and no girls, the world would end, wouldn't it? All you high officials, you intellectuals, you great thinkers, how can you not know something as simple as that? What's that, you say you're my baby? You little rascal, the smell of my milk has you drooling, hasn't it? (*sniffs*) You can't fool me, you rascal, go dream someplace else. I'm telling all of you, you could cover my face with a blindfold, or you could put my baby in the middle of a thousand babies, and I could find him with my nose alone. Didn't your mothers tell you that every baby has its own smell? If you're hungry, go find your mummy. Oh, that's right, you charmed children don't call them 'niang', you call them 'mama' and you don't say 'nursing', you say 'drinking mother's milk'. What's that? Your mama has no milk? How can someone with no milk be a mama? All your talk about moving forward, to me it's going backward, so far backward that children don't have to arrive via the birth canal and breasts no longer have to produce milk. You people have turned your job over to cows and goats. Children who grow up on cow's milk give off a bovine smell, and those who grow up on goat's milk smell like them. Only children who grow up on mother's milk have a human smell. If you think you can buy my milk, you have another thing coming, not if you came up with a mountain of gold. My milk is for my baby . . . hurry, come to Mummy. If you don't, these children will take my milk from me. See how hungry they are, see all those open mouths? They're hungry because their mamas sold their milk for cosmetics for their faces and perfume for their bodies. They are not good mamas. All they care about is showing themselves off. Their babies' health means nothing to them . . . be a good little baby and come to Mummy . . .

SUPERVISOR: (*stands at attention and salutes*) Madam, this is a maternity hospital. The patients and their babies need peace and quiet, so please leave at once and stop creating a scene.

CHEN MEI: Who are you? What are you doing here?

SUPERVISOR: We're security.

CHEN MEI: What does security do?

SUPERVISOR: We maintain social order and are responsible for the safety of institutions like schools, businesses, post offices, banks, markets, restaurants, bus and train stations, and more.

CHEN MEI: I know you! (*mad laughter*) I know who you are, you're

Yuan Sai's bodyguards, the ones people call watchdogs.

SUPERVISOR: I'll not stand for such insults. Without us, there would be anarchy.

CHEN MEI: You're the ones who stole my baby! I'd know you even without your surgical gown and mask.

SUPERVISOR: (*alarmed*) Watch what you're saying, madam. If you're not careful I'll sue you for slander.

CHEN MEI: Did you really think you could hide your identity from me by changing clothes? That putting on a uniform would make you a decent person? You're one of Yuan Sai's dogs. Wan Xin, that witch, delivered my baby, let me have one look . . . (*painfully*) no, not even a single look . . . they covered my face with white cloth, I wanted to see my baby, just one look, but they took my baby away without letting me have a look . . . but I heard my baby cry, crying for me, he wanted to see me too. Is there a child on earth that doesn't want to see his mother? But they snatched him away from me. I knew he was hungry, he wanted to nurse, you people don't know how precious the first drops of colostrum are to a baby, you thought I was uncultured, and didn't know things like that, but I do, I know everything. I sent all the finest elements of my body up to my breasts, including the calcium in my bones, the oil in my marrow, the protein in my blood, and the vitamins in my flesh. My milk would ensure that my baby would not suffer from colds, diarrhoea or fevers, would grow fast and strong, and would be handsome, but you people took my baby away before he had a drop of my milk. (*goes up and claws at the supervisor*)

SUPERVISOR: (*flustered*) You've got the wrong person, madam, take my word for it. Round-cheeked or square-faced Yuan, it makes no difference, I don't know who he is.

CHEN MEI: Of course you'd say that. You thieves, you gangsters, you steal children to sell them, a pack of devils. You may not know me, but I know you. Wasn't it you people who gave me sleeping pills after you stole my baby, and when I woke up told me he was stillborn? Wasn't it you people who flashed a skinned cat in front of my eyes and told me it was my baby's dead body? After stealing my baby, you cheated me out of my fee, you said a live birth was worth fifty thousand, but my baby was stillborn, so you only gave me ten thousand, and after taking my baby, you tried to steal my milk. You came with a bowl and a baby bottle to squeeze first milk out of my nipples, saying each gram was worth ten yuan. You bastards, that milk is for my baby. Ten yuan? I wouldn't sell it for ten thousand!

SUPERVISOR: I'll ask you one more time to leave, madam. If you don't, I'll have to call the police.

CHEN MEI: The police? Good, call them. That's exactly who I want to see. The people's police love the people. Can they ignore people who lose children?

SUPERVISOR: No, they can't. They'll even help you find a lost dog, let alone a child.

CHEN MEI: That's good. I'll go find a policeman.

SUPERVISOR: Good idea, do it now. (*points out the way to go*) Straight ahead, then right at the traffic light. The Binhe precinct station is next to the dancehall.

A car drives up from the hospital, horn blaring.

CHEN MEI: (*briefly dazed, then comes to*) My baby, they're taking my baby away in that car. (*rushes towards the car*) Give me my baby, you thieves!

The supervisor tries to stop her, but she is uncommonly strong and shoves him away.

SUPERVISOR: (*exasperated*) Stop her!

The security guard rushes up and wraps his arms around Chen Mei as she tries to block the car's way. She struggles. The supervisor comes up to help the guard restrain Chen Mei. Her veil is torn loose in the struggle, revealing a horribly disfigured face destroyed by fire. The guard and supervisor recoil in horror.

SECURITY GUARD: My god!
SUPERVISOR: (*spots frogs that have been flattened by the car's tyres and people's feet*) Shit! Where did all these damn things come from?

Curtain

Act II

Green lights turn the stage into a gloomy underwater world. The entrance to a cave at the rear is moss-covered. The croaks of frogs and wails of babies emerge from the cave. A dozen bawling babies hang down from above the stage, limbs flailing.

A pair of workbenches for making clay dolls has been placed at the front of the stage.

Hao Dashou and Qin He sit behind the benches in lotus position creating clay dolls.

Gugu crawls out from the cave. She is wearing a baggy black robe, her hair is uncombed.

GUGU: (*as if reciting from memory*) My name is Wan Xin, I am seventy-two years old, and have been an obstetrician for fifty years. Though I am retired, I am anything but idle. I have been in attendance at the birth of nine thousand eight hundred and eighty-three babies. (*She looks up at the babies hanging above the stage.*) You children, I love to hear the sound of your crying. It makes me feel alive and real. Not hearing you cry makes Gugu feel empty inside. There isn't another sound anywhere to match that of your crying. It is Gugu's requiem. I only wish there had been tape recorders around back then to record the sounds of your crying as you were born. Gugu would play those sounds every day while she was alive and have them played at her funeral when she died. What wonderfully moving music the sound of nine thousand eight hundred and eighty-three babies crying together would make. (*totally carried away*) Let your crying move Heaven and Earth, let it deliver Gugu into Paradise . . .

QIN HE: (*gloomy*) Be careful their crying doesn't send you down to Hell!

GUGU: (*wanders lightly among the babies hanging above the stage like a fish swimming spryly through the water, lightly spanking their bottoms as she passes among them*) Cry, my darlings, cry! Not crying means there's something wrong with you, crying means you're healthy.

HAO DASHOU: Crazy!

QIN HE: Who is?

HAO DASHOU: I am.

QIN HE: It's okay to say you're crazy, but not me. (*self-importantly*) Because I am Northeast Gaomi Township's most famous clay-doll artisan. Though some may disagree, they're welcome to their opinion. Where making things out of clay is concerned, I am the world's number one. People have to learn how to promote themselves. If you don't treat yourself like someone special, who will? The dolls I create are objets d'art, each valued at a hundred US dollars.

HAO DASHOU: Did you all hear that? That's what you call shameless! When I was making dolls out of clay you were crawling on the ground scrounging for chicken feed. I was designated a master folk artist by the county chief himself. And what are you?

QIN HE: Comrades, friends, did you hear that? Hao Dashou, you're not shameless, you're too thickheaded to even feel shame, you're deranged, you're obsessive-compulsive. After a lifetime of making clay dolls, there isn't one that can be called finished. You make one, then destroy it. The next one will be the one, you tell yourself. You're like the bear in the cornfield picking ears and discarding

them. Comrades, friends, take a good look at those hands. Hao
Dashou, Big-Hands Hao? Those aren't hands, they're frog claws,
duck's feet, webbing and all . . .

HAO DASHOU: (*angrily throws a lump of clay at Qin He*) You're full of
shit, *you're* deranged. Get the hell out of here!

QIN HE: Make me!

HAO DASHOU: This is my house.

QIN HE: Can you prove that? (*points to Gugu and the hanging children*)
Can she? Can they?

HAO DASHOU: (*points to Gugu*) Of course she can.

QIN HE: Prove it.

HAO DASHOU: She's my wife.

QIN HE: Prove it.

HAO DASHOU: We're married.

QIN HE: Got any proof?

HAO DASHOU: We've slept together.

QIN HE: (*deeply hurt, holds his head*) No – you're a liar, you're lying to
me. I gave up my youth for you, you promised you wouldn't marry
anyone, not ever!

GUGU: (*looks daggers at Hao*) Why are you provoking him? We agreed.

HAO DASHOU: I forgot.

GUGU: You forgot? Let me remind you. I told you back then that I'd
marry you, but only if you accepted him as my kid brother, and
that you'd put up with his outbursts, his foolishness, his crazy talk;
and that you'd supply his room, board and clothing.

HAO DASHOU: And let him sleep with you?

GUGU: Deranged, you're both deranged.

QIN HE: (*points angrily at Hao*) He's deranged, not me.

HAO DASHOU: Make as much noise as you want, be as angry from
embarrassment as you want, it won't make any difference. You can
raise your fists above the trees, cherries can spray from your eyes,
you can grow horns, birds can fly out of your mouth, you can grow
pig's bristles all over your body, and none of those will alter the
fact that you're deranged. That is etched in stone.

GUGU: (*mocking*) Is that language you learned from Tadpole's little drama?

HAO DASHOU: (*points to Qin He*) Every two months you have to check in to the Ma'er Shan Asylum for a three-month stay. They put you in a straitjacket and a sedative regimen; if that doesn't work, they use electric shock therapy. When they finish with you, you're skin and bones and glassy-eyed, like an African orphan. Your face is covered with flyspecks, like an old wall. You finally escape, but are never out more than two months. Tomorrow or the day after, you have to go back there again. (*deftly imitates the sound of an ambulance siren. Qin He trembles and falls to his knees*) When you go in this time, you'll not come out again. If they let you out with your manic condition, you would introduce an element of disharmony into harmonious society.

GUGU: That's enough!

HAO DASHOU: If I were a doctor, I'd lock you up for good and use a cow prod till you foamed at the mouth, till your body was racked by spasms, and you went into such deep shock you'd never come out of it. But if somehow you did, you'd have no memory.

Qin He wraps his arms around his head as he rolls on the ground and releases horrifying shrieks.

HAO DASHOU: Braying like a donkey and rolling on the ground are paltry skills. Go on, keep rolling. Look, your face is getting longer. Your ears are getting bigger. Feel them yourself. You're becoming a donkey. A donkey turns a millstone, round and round and round. (*Qin He crawls on the floor, his rump raised, as he mimics a donkey turning a millstone*) Right, that's it, you're a fine donkey. After you mill two pecks of black beans, mill a bushel of sorghum. A good donkey doesn't need blinders, because a good donkey doesn't nibble at the grain on the millstone. Do a good job and your master will treat you well. I've got your feed already prepared, just waiting for you.

Gugu goes up to stop Qin He, but he bites her hand.

GUGU: Damn you, you don't know what's good for you!

HAO DASHOU: I've told you you've got no business here. You go take care of the children. Make sure they're not cold or hungry. But don't let them eat too much either or get too warm. Like you've always said: Children are best comforted by keeping them slightly hungry and a little cold. (*turns to Qin He*) Why have you stopped? You lazy donkey, do I have to use a whip on you?

GUGU: Stop abusing him, he's not well.

HAO DASHOU: *He's* not well, I think *you're* not well!

Qin He collapses on the stage, foaming at the mouth.

HAO DASHOU: Get up, you can stop playing dead. This isn't the first time you've played that game. I've seen it many, many times. If you think you can scare me with that, you're mistaken. Even a stinkbug knows how to play dead. What you need to do is really die. Do it now, don't wait another minute.

Gugu rushes up to help Qin He. Hao Dashou gets up and stops her.

HAO DASHOU: (*painfully*) My patience has run out. I'm not going to let you save him like that . . .

Gugu moves left, Hao follows; Gugu moves right, Hao follows.

GUGU: He's not well. In the minds of us doctors there are two types of people, healthy and sick. If he'd hit my mother yesterday and was struck by illness today, I'd put aside my hatred and treat him to the best of my ability. If his brother had an epileptic seizure while he was raping me I'd push him off and try to save him.

HAO DASHOU: (*abruptly stiffens and lowers his voice to say painfully*) You finally admit that you had illicit relations with the two brothers.

GUGU: History is like that, the history of thousands of years of
civilised society. Those who acknowledge history are history's
materialists. Those who deny it are history's idealists.

*Gugu sits beside Qin He and wraps him in her arms like a baby. She rocks
him and sings an indistinguishable song.*

GUGU: My heart breaks when I think of you . . . I cry but without
tears when I think of you . . . I want to write but cannot find your
address . . . I want to sing but cannot recall the words . . . I want
to kiss you but cannot find your lips . . . I want to hold you but
cannot find your body . . .

*A child in a green stomacher embroidered with a frog, his head as clean as
watermelon rind, emerges from the dark cave entrance at the head of an
army of frogs (played by children) in wheelchairs, on canes, their front legs
wrapped in gauze. The boy shouts* Collecting debts! Collecting debts! *The
frogs behind him produce a guttural chorus.*

*Gugu lets out a shrill scream, runs away from Qin He and dodges the child
and the frogs.*

*Hao Dashou and the suddenly alert Qin He block the attack of the green boy
and frogs; Gugu leaves the stage in their protection. The green boy and frogs
take up the chase offstage.*

Curtain

Act III

A police station waiting room. One table only, with a telephone. Certificates of merit and citations adorn the wall.

A policewoman named Wei sits behind the table, gesturing to Chen Mei to take the chair on the other side. Chen Mei is still all in black, with her veil.

WEI: (*prim and proper, sounds like a student*) Have a seat, visiting citizen.

CHEN MEI: (*illogically*) Why aren't there two big drums at the entrance to the main hall?

WEI: Drums? What for?

CHEN MEI: That's what they used to have, so why don't you? Without drums how are the common people supposed to announce their complaints?

WEI: You're talking about the yamens of the old, feudal society. In a socialist society those things have been discarded.

CHEN MEI: Not in Kaifeng Prefecture.

WEI: Did you see something like that in a TV series? Magistrate Bao sat in Kaifeng Prefecture.

CHEN MEI: Take me to see Magistrate Bao.

WEI: Citizen, you are in the public waiting room of the Binhe Road police station. I am Duty Officer Wei Ying. Tell me what you've come for. I'll record it and open a case file, then I'll report to my superior.

CHEN MEI: Only Magistrate Bao can resolve a problem as great as mine.

WEI: Citizen, Magistrate Bao isn't in today, so tell me what your problem is, and I will be sure to relay it to the magistrate. How's that?

CHEN MEI: Do I have your word?

WEI: You do. (*gestures to the chair*) Have a seat.

CHEN MEI: This common woman dares not sit.

WEI: If I say sit, you sit.

CHEN MEI: This common woman thanks you.

WEI: Would you like a glass of water?

CHEN MEI: This common woman dares not.

WEI: Citizen woman, let's stop the TV drama, all right? What's your name?

CHEN MEI: This common woman's name was Chen Mei, but Chen Mei died, or shall we say, she is half dead, half alive. So this common woman does not know her name.

WEI: Are you making fun of me, Citizen? Or are you expecting me to play your games? You are in a police station, where that sort of thing is not allowed.

CHEN MEI: I once had the loveliest eyebrows in all of Northeast Gaomi Township, and that is why my name was Chen Mei, Eyebrows Chen. But they're gone now . . . and not just my brows (*shrilly*) but even my lashes and my hair! So I no longer have the right to be called Chen Mei.

WEI: (*a sudden realisation*) Citizen woman, if you don't mind, would you remove your veil?

CHEN MEI: No!

WEI: If I'm not mistaken, you were a victim of the Dongli Stuffed Animal Factory fire.

CHEN MEI: How clever of you.

WEI: I was a student at the police academy at the time, and I saw TV reports of the fire. Those capitalists have hearts of stone. I felt so sorry for what happened to you, but if you are looking for compensation, you need to go to the courts. Either that or go see the city's Party committee or government. You could even take your case to the media.

CHEN MEI: Didn't you say you knew Magistrate Bao? He's the only one who can give me justice.

WEI: (*with forced resolve*) All right, let's hear it. I'll do everything within my power to take your case to my superiors.

CHEN MEI: I want to charge them with the crime of stealing my child.

WEI: Who stole your child? Take your time. Just tell me what happened. I think you need a drink of water. You're getting hoarse. Water will help. (*pours a glass of water and hands it to her.*)

CHEN MEI: No water for me. I know that's just an excuse so you can see my face. I hate my face and hate for others to see it.

WEI: I'm sorry, but that wasn't my intention.

CHEN MEI: I have only looked in a mirror once since the accident. I hate mirrors, hate anything that gives reflections. I was going to kill myself after I'd paid off my father's debts, but I've changed my mind. If I killed myself, my baby would starve to death. If I killed myself, my baby would be an orphan. I hear my baby crying. Listen . . . he's cried himself hoarse. I want to nurse him, my breasts have swelled up like balloons about to pop. But they've hidden my baby someplace . . .

WEI: Who are *they*?

CHEN MEI: (*casts a watchful glance at the door*) Frogs, bullfrogs as big as pot lids, always croaking, vicious frogs, frogs that eat children . . .

WEI: (*gets up and shuts the door*) Don't worry, big sister, these walls are soundproof.

CHEN MEI: They know all the tricks, and they conspire with officials.

WEI: They don't scare Magistrate Bao.

CHEN MEI: (*gets out of the chair and kneels*) Magistrate Bao, the injustice to this common woman is as deep as the ocean. Please see that justice is done.

WEI: You may speak.

CHEN MEI: Reporting. This commoner is Chen Mei, a resident of Northeast Gaomi Township. Her father, Chen Bi, greatly favours boys over girls. Years ago, when he wanted a son, he forced my

mother into an illegal pregnancy, but the secret was exposed. He
hid her here and there, until they were chased and caught on the
river. My mother had her baby – me – and then died. My father
was disappointed to have a second daughter. He abandoned me at
first, then took me back, but because I was born illegally, he was
fined five thousand eight hundred yuan. From then on he took to
drinking, and when he was drunk he beat his daughters. When
we could we two went south to work in a Guangdong factory to
pay off our father's debts and hope for a brighter future. My sister,
Chen Er, and I were known as great beauties who could make our
fortune if we wished to leave the path of virtue. But we refused
to give up our chastity and modelled ourselves after the lotus that
emerges from the mud and remains pure. But there was a terrible
fire that claimed my sister's life and ruined my face . . .

Wei dries her eyes with a tissue.

CHEN MEI: My sister died trying to save me . . . why did you do that,
    Sister? I'd rather be dead than live a life like someone who is
    neither human nor demon.
WEI: Those horrid capitalists. They should all be rounded up and shot.
CHEN MEI: They're not so bad. They gave us twenty thousand for my
    sister and paid all my hospital bills plus fifteen thousand. I gave it
    all to Father. Dad, I said, this is for the fine you paid when I was
    born plus twenty years' interest. I no longer owe you anything.
WEI: Your dad is not a good man either.
CHEN MEI: Good or bad, he's still my dad, and you're out of line saying that.
WEI: What did he spend the money on?
CHEN MEI: What else? Food, drink, cigarettes, till it was all gone.
WEI: A degenerate man, no better than a pig or a dog.
CHEN MEI: I told you not to talk about him like that.
WEI: (*self-mocking*) I was just following your lead.
CHEN MEI: Eventually, I went to work at the Bullfrog Company.
WEI: I'm aware of that company, it's quite famous. I hear they're

working on making a high-end skin care product out of frog skins.
If they're successful, they'll own the global patent.

CHEN MEI: They're the ones I'm charging.

WEI: Tell me.

CHEN MEI: Raising bullfrogs is just a screen. Their real business is
making babies.

WEI: Making babies, how?

CHEN MEI: They've hired a bunch of young women to get pregnant for
rich men.

WEI: Are you kidding me?

CHEN MEI: There are twenty hidden rooms in their compound, each
with a woman, married, engaged, or single, ugly and pretty, some
getting pregnant through sexual activity, others not.

WEI: What are you saying? What's pregnant by sexual activity and
what's not?

CHEN MEI: Please, no false innocence. Do you not know about things
like that? Are you a virgin?

WEI: I honestly don't know.

CHEN MEI: Sexual activity means that men sleep with the women, like
any couple, and stay with them till they get pregnant. No sexual
activity means they take the man's sperm, put it in a syringe, and
insert it into the woman's womb. Are you a virgin?

WEI: Are you?

CHEN MEI: Of course I am.

WEI: But you just said you've had a baby.

CHEN MEI: I've had a baby, but I'm still a virgin. They had their fat
nurse squirt a syringe filled with sperm into my womb so I
became pregnant and had a baby, but I've never slept with a man.
I'm a chaste woman, a virgin!

WEI: Just who are the *they* you're talking about?

CHEN MEI: I can't tell you that. If I did they'd kill my baby . . .

WEI: Was it that fat person at the bullfrog breeding farm? The one
called, what's his name . . . right, Yuan Sai.

CHEN MEI: Where's Yuan Sai? He's the one I'm looking for, you bastard, you cheated me, you all got together to cheat me. You told me my son was stillborn. You showed me the corpse of a skinned cat and said it was my baby, a modern-day re-enactment of the leopard cat and prince story. You used that to cheat me out of some of my fee and to see that I wouldn't have any thoughts of looking for my baby. I didn't care about the money, money means nothing to me. When I was in Guangdong, a Taiwanese boss was willing to pay a million to spend three years with me. But I wanted a baby, the finest baby in the world. Magistrate Bao, you must help me seek justice.

WEI: Did you sign a contract with them to be a surrogate mother?

CHEN MEI: Yes. They gave me a third of the fee up front. The rest was to be paid when the baby was born.

WEI: That could be a problem. But let's not worry about that. Magistrate Bao will sort everything out. Go on.

CHEN MEI: They said the contents of the syringe came from a very important man, with excellent genes, a genius. They said he'd stopped smoking and drinking for half a year, and ate a whole abalone and two sea cucumbers every day, all to guarantee the birth of a healthy baby.

WEI: (*sarcastically*) What he wanted was an investment.

CHEN MEI: All he wanted was to father a perfect child. They told me he'd seen a photo of me before my face was ruined, and believed that I was a mixed-race beauty.

WEI: If money means nothing to you, why be a surrogate mother?

CHEN MEI: Did I say that money means nothing to me?

WEI: Just a moment ago.

CHEN MEI: (*reflects*) Now I remember. My father was in the hospital because of a traffic accident and I became a surrogate to earn enough to pay his bills.

WEI: You are a true filial daughter. A father like that would be better off dead.

CHEN MEI: I thought that too, but he was still my father.

WEI: That's why I say you're a filial daughter.

CHEN MEI: I knew my baby wasn't stillborn, because I heard him cry . . . listen . . . he's crying again . . . my baby has never tasted his mother's milk . . . my poor baby . . .

The station chief opens the door and enters.

STATION CHIEF: All this crying and carrying on. If you've got something to say, say it. Don't cry.

CHEN MEI: (*kneels*) Magistrate Bao, please seek justice for this common woman . . .

STATION CHIEF: What's that all about? Ridiculous.

WEI: (*under her breath*) Chief, this could be a monumental case. (*hands him her notebook; he scans what she's written*) It could involve a prostitution ring and child trafficking!

CHEN MEI: Magistrate, please save my child!

STATION CHIEF: All right, Citizen Chen, I'll take your case and be sure to pass it on to Magistrate Bao. Go home and wait to hear from us.

Chen Mei leaves.

WEI: Chief.

STATION CHIEF: You're new here, so you don't have a handle on what's going on. That woman was disfigured in the fire at the Dongli Stuffed Animal Factory. She hasn't been right in the head for years. We all feel sorry for her, but there's nothing we can do.

WEI: Chief, I saw . . .

STATION CHIEF: What did you see?

WEI: (*embarrassed*) She's lactating.

STATION CHIEF: That must have been perspiration. You're new to this post, Wei. In this profession we have to remain vigilant and keep from being overly sensitive.

Curtain

Act IV

The stage is set as in Act II.

Hao Dashou and Qin He sit at their benches making dolls.

A middle-aged man in a wrinkled grey suit and red tie, a fountain pen in his pocket and a briefcase under his arm enters quietly.

HAO DASHOU: (*head down*) What are you doing here again, Tadpole?

TADPOLE: (*flatteringly*) You're a wizard, Hao Dashou. You knew it was me just by the sound.

HAO DASHOU: Not the sound, the smell.

QIN HE: A dog's sense of smell is thousands of times keener than a man's.

HAO DASHOU: Was that meant for me?

QIN HE: Did I say that? I was only talking about a dog's sense of smell.

HAO DASHOU: That *was* meant for me. (*quickly twists the clay in his hand into the image of Qin He's face, shows it to Tadpole and Qin, then flings it to the floor*) I've just flattened a face that knows no shame!

QIN HE: (*taking up the challenge, twists a clay replica of Hao's face, shows Tadpole, then flings it to the floor*) I've just flattened an old dog!

TADPOLE: Hold your temper, Uncle Hao, you too, Uncle Qin. Stop it, both of you. The two images you just created were works of art.

What a shame to flatten them.

HAO DASHOU: Butt out! Be careful I don't make you, then flatten you.

TADPOLE: Make one of me, I beg you. But don't flatten it afterward. When my play is finished, I'll put that on the cover.

HAO DASHOU: I already told you that your aunt would rather watch ants climb a tree than read your trashy play.

QIN HE: Why are you writing plays instead of working in the field? If you actually manage to write your play, I'll eat this ball of clay.

TADPOLE: (*modestly*) Uncle Hao, Uncle Qin, Gugu is getting old and her eyesight is failing. I wouldn't dare ask her to read it herself. I plan to read it to her and to you at the same time. I'm sure you both know Cao Yu and Lao She. Well, they both went to the theatre to read their plays to actors and directors.

HAO DASHOU: But you're not Cao Yu, and you're not Lao She.

QIN HE: And we're not actors, and we're definitely not directors.

TADPOLE: But you are characters in my play! I worked hard to enhance your images. You'll be sorry if you don't listen, but if you do, and there are parts you're unhappy with, I can change them. Otherwise, the play will be staged and will be published as a libretto, and then it will be too late for you to do anything about it. (*suddenly sad*) I've worked on this play for ten years and have gone through everything I owned. I even sold off the rafters in my house. (*with his hands on his chest, he coughs painfully*) For the sake of this play, I smoked cheap tobacco, and when I had none of that, I smoked the leaves of locust trees – countless sleepless nights, deteriorating health, my very life drained, all for what? Fame? Fortune? (*shrilly*) No, and no! For Gugu's love, to give permanent recognition to Northeast Gaomi Township's very own goddess. If you won't listen to me read, I'll kill myself in front of you.

HAO DASHOU: Who are you trying to scare? How do you plan to do it? Rope? Poison?

QIN HE: It actually sounds slightly moving. I think I'd like to hear it.

HAO DASHOU: You can read your play if you want to, but not in my house.

TADPOLE: First and foremost, this is Gugu's house; only after that is it
    yours.

Gugu crawls out from the cave.

GUGU: (*lazily*) Who's talking about me?
TADPOLE: It's me, Gugu.
GUGU: I know it's you. What are you doing here?
TADPOLE: (*hastily opens his briefcase and takes out a manuscript; reads
    quickly*) Gugu, it's me, Tadpole from Two Counties Village. (*Qin
    and Hao exchange puzzled looks*) Yu Peisheng is my father, Sun
    Fuxia is my mother, I was one of the 'sweet potato kids' and the
    first child you ever delivered. You also delivered my wife, Tan Yu'er.
    Her father is Tan Jinhai, her mother is Huang Yueling . . .
GUGU: Stop there. You've changed your name to be a playwright? And
    your date of birth? Your parents, the name of your village, and
    your wife?

*Gugu wanders among the babies hanging above the stage, stopping from
time to time to lower her head in thought or to beat her breast and stomp
her feet. Then she stops and whacks the bottom of one of the babies, making
him cry. She does the same to all the others, and now they are all crying.
Surrounded by all that noise, she begins to jabber nonstop, and the crying
gets less intense.*

GUGU: Listen to me, you sweet potato kids. I'm the one who brought
    you all into the world. And not one of you made it easy on me.
    For fifty years Gugu has delivered babies, and cannot rest even
    now. During those fifty years, Gugu did not enjoy more than a
    few hot meals or a few good nights' sleep. Bloody hands and a
    sweaty body soiled by babies' bodily waste, and you probably think
    that a village obstetrician has an easy life. In the eighteen villages
    that make up Northeast Gaomi Township, is there even one of
    the more than five thousand thresholds I've not stepped across?

Is there one of your mothers or wives whose dusty belly I haven't seen? And it was me who tied off the tubes of those weasels you call fathers. Some of you are now high-ranking officials; others have gotten rich. You can be willful before the county chief and insolent in the mayor's office, but around me you have to act like gentlemen. When I think back to those days, the way I see it, I should have castrated every one of you little studs and saved your wives a peck of trouble. Quit smirking and straighten up. Family planning has an impact on the national economy and the people's livelihood, and it is of the greatest importance. Don't bare your teeth at me, you're just wasting your time. Keep them or lose them, it's not up to me. Men are no damned good. Know who said that? You don't? You really don't? Well, neither do I. All I know is, men are no damned good, but we can't do without you. It's all part of God's plan. Tigers and wild hares, sparrow hawks and sparrows, flies and mosquitoes . . . we need them all in this world. I've heard there's a tribe in the African jungle that lives in the trees. They make their nests in the trees, where the women lay eggs and perch on branches to eat wild fruit. The men cover their backs with leaves and sprawl on top of the eggs for forty-nine days, when the infants break through the shells, jump out, and start climbing the tree. Do you believe that? You don't? Well, I do. Gugu once delivered an egg as big as a football, placed it at the head of the kang for two weeks, and out jumped a fat little baby, fair-skinned and pudgy. I named him Hatchling. Unfortunately he died of encephalitis. He'd be forty years old today, and would be a great writer. When, as a baby, he was given a choice of things to grab, he chose a writing brush. When there is no tiger on the mountain, the chimp is king. Hatchling died, giving you the chance to be a writer . . .

TADPOLE: (*with great respect*) Gugu, your words are like poetry. You are more than a wonderful woman's doctor; you are also a natural playwright. The words tumble out of your mouth ready-made for the dramatic stage.

GUGU: What do you mean by tumbling out of my mouth? Every
    word Gugu says is carefully considered. (*points to the manuscript in
    Tadpole's hand*) Is that your play?

TADPOLE: (*modestly*) Yes.

GUGU: What's it called?

TADPOLE: *Wa.*

GUGU: Is that '*wa*' as in '*wawa*' for babies or '*wa*' as in '*qingwa*' for frogs?

TADPOLE: For now it's the '*wa*' in '*qingwa*', but I can change it later to
    the '*wa*' in '*wawa*' for babies, or in 'Nüwa', the goddess who created
    mankind. After she populated the earth with people, the character
    for frogs symbolised a profusion of children, and it has become
    Northeast Gaomi Township's totem. Frogs appear as creatures of
    veneration in our clay sculptures and our New Year's paintings.

GUGU: Is it possible that you are unaware of my fear of frogs?

TADPOLE: Analysing Gugu's fear of frogs is the central aim of my play.
    After reading my play, the complexities will be unravelled, and you
    may find that you no longer fear frogs.

GUGU: (*reaches out*) Then hand me your manuscript.

Tadpole respectfully hands the manuscript to Gugu.

GUGU: (*to Qin He and Hao Dashou*) Which of you is going to take this
    manuscript out and burn it?

TADPOLE: Gugu, that's ten years of blood, sweat, and tears.

GUGU: (*flings the manuscript into the air, pages flying everywhere*) I don't
    need to read it. One sniff tells me what kind of fart you've just laid.
    With what little knowledge you possess, do you really think you
    can figure out why Gugu is afraid of frogs?

*Tadpole, Qin He, and Hao Dashou scramble across the stage fighting over
pages.*

GUGU: (*caught up in nostalgic thoughts*) On the morning you were born,
    Gugu was down by the river washing her hands, when she saw a

tight mass of tadpoles in the water. It was a year of drought, and there were more tadpoles than the water could accommodate. That got me thinking that no more than one out of ten thousand of them would become frogs; the others would become part of the muddy riverbed. Just like a man's sperm, except for them, only about one in ten million penetrates the egg to make a child. Gugu was reflecting that a mysterious connection exists between tadpoles and humans in the propagation of species. So when your mother asked me to give you a name, Tadpole was the first word out of my mouth. A good name, your mother said, a perfect name. Tadpole. Children with debased names are easy to raise. Tadpole, you could not ask for a better name.

Tadpole, Qin He, and Hao Dashou stand quietly, listening, each with sheets of paper in his hand.

TADPOLE: Thank you, Gugu!

GUGU: Sometime after that, *People's Daily* introduced the 'Tadpole contraceptive method', urging ovulating women to swallow fourteen tadpoles in the privacy of their own rooms to forestall pregnancy. But not only did it not prevent pregnancy, the women who used the method gave birth to frogs.

HAO DASHOU: Stop there. Say any more and your illness will act up again.

GUGU: Act up? Not me. They're the ones who were sick, those who ate frogs. They made women go down to the river and cut the heads off frogs, then skin them, like taking off a pair of pants. Their thighs were like a woman's. That's when my fear of frogs was born. Their thighs were just like a woman's.

QIN HE: Those who ate frogs all paid a price for swallowing them, because they carried parasites that travelled up to the women's brains and turned them into idiots. In the end, their facial expression was the spitting image of a frog.

TADPOLE: This is an important plot. Those who ate frogs all turned into frogs. And Gugu became the heroic protector of frogs.

GUGU: (*painfully*) No. The blood of frogs is on Gugu's hands. Without being aware of it, Gugu was tricked into eating meatballs made of chopped frog. Like the story your great-uncle told of King Wen of Zhou, who was unaware that the meatballs he ate were made from the chopped flesh of his son. When King Wen fled from Chaoge, he lowered his head and retched several meatballs, and when they landed, they turned into rabbits, which sounded to him like 'son's bits'. When I came home that day, I had an upset stomach that rumbled with a strange guttural sound, nauseating and intolerable. So Gugu went down to the river, lowered her head, and retched a bunch of little green things, and when they landed in the river they turned into frogs.

The boy in the green stomacher crawls out of the cave, followed by an army of crippled frogs. Collecting debts! *the boy cries out.* Collecting debts! *The frogs behind him produce an angry guttural chorus.*

Gugu shrieks and passes out.

Hao Dashou catches her and pinches the groove beneath her nose, the philtrum.

Qin He drives off the boy and the procession of frogs.

Tadpole scoops up all the sheets of paper.

TADPOLE: (*takes a red invitation out of his pocket*) Gugu, I know exactly why you are afraid of frogs. I also know all the ways you've tried over the years to atone for what you view as your sins. Truth is, you've done nothing wrong. Those chopped-up frogs are illusions you created. Gugu, it was you who made the birth of my son possible. So I have laid out a grand banquet for you (*turns to Hao and Qin*) and the two of you.

Curtain

Act V

Night. Lamplight shining in from the side turns the stage a golden yellow.

Chen Bi and his dog are curled on the ground beneath a thick column in a corner of the Fertility Goddess Temple. The dog can be played by an actor. A few paper notes and some coins lie in a chipped begging bowl in front of Chen and alongside a pair of crutches.

Chen Mei, all in black and wearing a black gauzy veil, drifts onto the stage.

Two men in black, also wearing black gauzy veils, follow her onto the stage.

CHEN MEI: (*howls*) Baby . . . my baby . . . where are you . . . my baby . . . where are you . . .

The two men in black draw close to her.

CHEN MEI: Who are you? Why are you all in black and why have you covered your faces? Oh, I get it, you are also victims of the terrible fire.

FIRST MAN: Yes, we too are victims.

CHEN MEI: (*alert*) No. The victims of the fire were all women, and you are unmistakably men.

SECOND MAN: We are victims of another fire.

CHEN MEI: I'm sorry to hear that.

FIRST MAN: Yes, you can be sorry.

CHEN MEI: Are you in pain?

SECOND MAN: Yes, we are.

CHEN MEI: Have you had skin grafts?

FIRST MAN: (*puzzled*) Skin grafts, what's that?

CHEN MEI: They take unburned skin from your buttocks, your thighs, and other spots and graft it onto the burned areas. Did you really not have any?

SECOND MAN: Yes, yes, we have. Skin from our buttocks has been grafted onto our faces.

CHEN MEI: Did they graft eyebrows?

FIRST MAN: Yes, yes they did.

CHEN MEI: Did they use hair from your head or pubic hair?

SECOND MAN: What? Pubic hair can become eyebrows?

CHEN MEI: If the scalp has been burned, they have to use pubic hair. It's better than nothing, but if you don't even have that, then you must go without, like frogs.

FIRST MAN: Yes, that's it, we must go without, like frogs.

CHEN MEI: Have you seen yourselves in a mirror?

SECOND MAN: Never.

CHEN MEI: We burn victims fear nothing more than mirrors, and hate nothing more as well.

FIRST MAN: That's right. We smash every mirror we see.

CHEN MEI: That's a waste of time. You can smash mirrors, but you can't smash storefront windows, or marble surfaces, or reflecting pools; most of all, you can't smash the eyes that see us. Those eyes react with fear and avoidance; children cry, people call us monsters and demons. Their eyes are our mirrors, so you can never smash all the mirrors, and our best strategy is to hide our faces.

SECOND MAN: Right, so right, and that's why we cover our faces with gauzy veils.

CHEN MEI: Have you ever thought of killing yourselves?

SECOND MAN: We . . .

CHEN MEI: From what I know, five of the girls who were injured in the
    fire have committed suicide. They killed themselves after looking
    in a mirror.

FIRST MAN: Mirrors killed them.

SECOND MAN: That's why we smash every mirror we see.

CHEN MEI: I considered killing myself, but I changed my mind.

FIRST MAN: Always choose life. A demeaned life is better than the
    best death.

CHEN MEI: I stopped thinking about dying once I became pregnant,
    when I felt a new life moving inside me. I considered myself to be
    an ugly cocoon with a beautiful life growing inside, and that when
    it emerged, I would become an empty cocoon.

SECOND MAN: Well spoken.

CHEN MEI: But the baby was born, and I did not become an empty
    cocoon and die. I discovered that I was in love with life. I wasn't
    dried up, I wasn't withering. No, I was fresh and radiant. There
    seemed to be a moist quality to the tight skin of my face, my
    breasts filled with milk . . . the birth of my baby gave me a new
    life . . . but then they took my baby from me . . .

FIRST MAN: Come with us. We know where your baby is.

CHEN MEI: You know where he is?

SECOND MAN: We came looking for you for one reason – to help you
    go to your baby.

CHEN MEI: (*excitedly*) Thank the heavens. Take me there now, take me
    to see my baby.

The men in black try to spirit Chen Mei off the stage.

*Like an arrow off the bow, Chen Bi's dog jumps up and attacks First Man,
biting him on the left leg.*

*Chen Bi also jumps up and moves across the stage on his crutches, stops,
supports himself on one crutch and beats Second Man with the other.*

The men in black break free of Chen Bi and his dog and flee to the edge of the stage, where they draw daggers. Chen Bi and his dog stand together.

Chen Mei stands downstage, forming a triangle with Chen Bi and his dog.

CHEN BI: (*roars*) Let my daughter go!

FIRST MAN: You old derelict, you drunk, you scoundrel, you old beggar, how dare you claim her as your daughter!

SECOND MAN: You say she's your daughter. Call her and see if she responds.

CHEN BI: Mei . . . my poor, suffering daughter.

CHEN MEI: (*coldly*) You've mistaken me for someone else. I'm not who you think I am.

CHEN BI: (*agonising*) Mei, I know you hate your dad. I let you down, I let your sister down, and I let your mother down. Your dad caused you all great pain. Your dad is a sinner, a good-for-nothing, a man stranded on the line between life and death.

FIRST MAN: Is that what you call a confession? Is there a church nearby?

SECOND MAN: There's a newly renovated Catholic church twenty li east of here, following the river.

CHEN BI: Mei, your dad knows they tricked you. Your dad's old friends have cheated you, and I'm going to help you get justice.

FIRST MAN: Step aside, old man.

SECOND MAN: Come with us, Miss. We promise you'll get to see your baby.

Chen Mei walks towards the men in black. Chen Bi and his dog block her way.

CHEN MEI: (*angrily*) Who are you to block my way? I want to go see my baby, don't you know that? He hasn't had a drop of milk since the moment he was born, and if he doesn't eat soon, he'll starve, you know that, don't you?

CHEN BI: Mei, you hate me, I understand that. You say you're not my daughter, I can live with that. But don't go with them. They sold your baby, and if you go with them, they'll throw you into the river to drown, then make up a story that you threw yourself in. They've done that before, and more than once.

FIRST MAN: I think you've lived long enough, old man. You can't smear us like that.

SECOND MAN: How can you spout such rubbish? Murderous, ugly butchery like that does not exist in our society.

FIRST MAN: You've been watching too many videos in roadside shops.

SECOND MAN: You're delusional.

FIRST MAN: You've turned socialism into capitalism.

SECOND MAN: Turned good people into bad ones.

FIRST MAN: Turned good will into donkey's guts, pure malice.

CHEN BI: You're the donkey's guts, cow parts, filth vomited by cats and dogs, the dregs of society.

SECOND MAN: How dare he accuse us of being the dregs of society! You're a pig that feasts on piles of garbage. Do you know what we do?

CHEN BI: Of course I do. I not only know what you do, but what you've done.

FIRST MAN: I think we ought to invite you down to the river for a cold bath.

SECOND MAN: Tomorrow morning, people who come to burn incense and choose dolls will discover that the old beggar that asks for alms in front of the temple is not around. Even his crippled dog will be missing.

FIRST MAN: No one will care.

The men in black attack Chen Bi and his dog. The dog is killed, Chen is knocked down. They are about to stab Chen to death when Chen Mei rips off her veil to expose a hideous face; her shriek terrifies the two men, who leave Chen Bi and run off.

Curtain

Act VI

An enormous round table, set for a meal, sits in the yard of a peasant's house. At the rear of the stage, a banner proclaims: 'Celebration of Jin Wa's first month'.

Tadpole, dressed in a glossy silk Chinese-style jacket embroidered with the words 福 (good luck) and 壽 (long life), greets guests at the gate.

Tadpole's elementary school classmates Li Shou and Yuan Sai, plus Tadpole's cousin, enter, each intoning pleasantries and the traditional words of congratulations.

Gugu, in a deep red gown, enters in the company of Hao Dashou and Qin He.

TADPOLE: (*welcoming*) We're glad you've come, Gugu.

GUGU: How could I not come when the Wan family has a new son?

TADPOLE: It is only through the efforts of Gugu that Jin Wa has come to the Wan family.

GUGU: You flatter me. (*looks around, smiles*) No exceptions. (*The others seem puzzled.*) Except for these two (*points to Hao and Qin*), all of you here came into being with my two hands. I can tell you how many warts there are on all your mothers' bellies. (*laughter all around*) Why aren't you people seated?

TADPOLE: Who would dare sit down before you?

GUGU: Where's your dad? Have him come out and take the seat of honour.

TADPOLE: He's been a little under the weather the past few days, so he's gone to my sister's to get over it. He said to give you the seat of honour.

GUGU: I cannot refuse.

EVERYONE: It's only right.

GUGU: Tadpole, you and Little Lion are both over fifty, and you have a bouncing baby boy. While that won't get you into the – it's Guinness, right? – the *Guinness Book of World Records*, it's the first time in my five decades of delivering babies. That makes this a joyous occasion.

The other guests join in, some saying Joyous occasion, *others saying* A miracle.

TADPOLE: All thanks to Gugu's medical genius.

GUGU: (*emotionally*) In her youth, Gugu was a dyed-in-the-wool materialist, but now, an old woman, she's grown increasingly idealistic.

LI SHOU: There ought to be a place in the history of philosophy for idealism.

GUGU: Hear that? There's a big difference between the educated and the uneducated.

YUAN SAI: We know nothing about idealists and materialists, we're all coarse people.

GUGU: There may be no ghosts and spirits in the real world, but divine retribution definitely exists. For Tadpole and Little Lion to be blessed with a son in their fifties proves that the Wan family had built up considerable merits in past lives.

COUSIN: Gugu's medicine also helped.

GUGU: Sincerity can work miracles. (*turns to Tadpole*) Your mother lived a miserly life, but things are better for your generation. You have plenty of money, and now this joyous addition. It's time to change and show some generosity.

TADPOLE: You needn't worry, Gugu. Though we have no camel's hump or bear's paw, there is more than enough meat, fish, and fowl here for everyone.

GUGU: (*examines the table*) Seven plates and eight bowls, that looks like plenty. But what about liquor? What's there to drink?

TADPOLE: (*reaches under the table and takes out two bottles of Maotai*) Maotai.

GUGU: Real or fake?

TADPOLE: I got it from Liu Guifang, manager of the municipal guesthouse. She guarantees it's real.

LI SHOU: She's an old classmate.

YUAN SAI: It's the old classmates you have to watch out for.

GUGU: Her, she's the second daughter of Liu Baofu in Liu Family Village. Also one of mine.

TADPOLE: I pointed out that relationship to her. With care and respect she took these bottles out of her safe.

GUGU: She'd be embarrassed to give you fake Maotai for me.

Tadpole opens the bottle and offers Gugu the first taste.

GUGU: It's excellent. The real thing, no doubt about it. Now, pour it for everyone.

Tadpole pours glasses for everyone.

GUGU: Since I've been given the seat of honour, I'll start the ritual. For this first glass, we thank the leadership of our Communist Party, which has freed us all from poverty, led us to wealth, liberated our thoughts and brought us a good life, and that is what guarantees a fine future. What do you say, everyone, did I get it right?

The crowd shouts its agreement.

GUGU: Empty the first glass!

Everyone drinks.

GUGU: For the second glass we thank the Wan family ancestors for
    accumulating so many merits that their sons and grandsons live
    comfortable lives.

Everyone drinks.

GUGU: For this third drink we turn to the reason we are here, to
    celebrate the birth of a son late in life to Tadpole and his wife
    Little Lion.

They all raise their glasses and shout congratulations.

*Liu Guifang and a pair of helpers enter with cardboard boxes, followed by
TV journalists and cameramen.*

LIU GUIFANG: Congratulations!
TADPOLE: My old classmate, what are you doing here?
LIU: I came for a celebration drink. Am I not welcome? (*She shakes
    hands with the people around the table and exchanges pleasantries,
    saving Gugu for last.*) Gugu, you've recaptured your youth.
GUGU: That makes me an old witch.
TADPOLE: We couldn't get you here with an invitation, but here you
    are. What is all this stuff? I don't want you to go broke.
LIU: I'm just a cook, what's there to go broke? (*points to the boxes*)
    I cooked this myself for you. Fried yellow croaker, pork-skin jelly
    and large steamed buns. Tell me what you think of my cooking
    skills, everyone. Gugu, I've brought a bottle of fifty-year-old
    Maotai especially for you to show my respect.

GUGU: It's not every day you drink fifty-year-old Maotai. Last New Year's, one of the high officials in Pingnan city had his daughter-in-law give me a bottle. When the cork was pulled, the room was suffused with its special aroma.

TADPOLE: (*uneasily*) And who are these people, old classmate?

LIU: (*drags the female reporter up*) I forgot to introduce everyone to Miss Gao, who works for the municipal TV station, hosting and producing the program *Aspects of Society*. Miss Gao, this is Uncle Tadpole, the playwright who has fathered a son late in life, a remarkable feat. And she (*the woman in the role of reporter is dragged over to Gugu*) is our Northeast Gaomi Township's sainted Gugu, which is what we call her no matter how old or young we are. She has ushered everyone here, from one generation to the next, into the world.

GUGU: (*takes the reporter's hand*) What a charming girl you are. One look at you and I can picture what your father and mother are like. In the past, it was family status that determined whether or not a match was appropriate. Now I'm in favour of looking at genes before family status. Good genes are what guarantee the birth of intelligent, healthy babies. With bad genes nothing works.

REPORTER: (*signals the cameraman to film*) Gugu is right in step with the times.

GUGU: Hardly. But in my dealings with people in all fields I manage to pick up some modern terms and ideas.

TADPOLE: (*softly to Liu Guifang*) This isn't something we should broadcast, is it?

LIU: (*softly*) Miss Gao is going to marry into my family soon. There is stiff competition among TV stations these days, fighting over information, material and ideas, and I need to help her.

REPORTER: Gugu, why do you think Uncle Tadpole and his wife were able to have a child so late in life? Is it because of their good genes?

GUGU: Most definitely. They both have good genes.

REPORTER: Do you think that one of their genes might be a tad better than the others?

GUGU: You need to have a better understanding of genes before you can ask that question.

REPORTER: Do you think you can explain what genes are in terms that our viewers can easily understand?

GUGU: Genes are life, genes are one's fate.

REPORTER: Fate?

GUGU: Flies can't get into an egg that isn't cracked. Do you understand?

REPORTER: Yes.

GUGU: People with bad genes are like cracked eggs, and their offspring will be born with cracks. Understand?

LIU: (*to Gao*) Why don't you let Gugu take a moment to have a drink. You can ask Uncle Tadpole. This is Uncle Yuan Sai, and this is Uncle Li Shou. They were all classmates of mine, and they know everything there is to know about genes. You can interview each of them. (*pours a glass for Gugu*) Here's to Gugu's health and a long life, may you always look after our Northeast Township's children!

REPORTER: Uncle Tadpole, I know you were born in 1953, which makes you fifty-five this year. At that age, country folk are already grandparents, but you have just fathered a son. Can you tell us how you feel about that?

TADPOLE: Last month, seventy-eight-year-old Professor Li of Qidong University celebrated the one-month anniversary of his son and visited his hundred-and-three-year-old father, elder Professor Li, in the hospital. Did you read that?

REPORTER: Yes.

TADPOLE: A man is at his prime in his fifties. The issue is with women.

REPORTER: Would it be all right to interview your wife?

TADPOLE: She's resting. She'll come out to toast our guests in a little while.

REPORTER: (*holding the microphone in front of Yuan Sai*) Chairman Yuan, now that your friend Tadpole has become a father at his age, are you itching to do the same?

YUAN: What an interesting phrase, itching to do the same. I may be itching, but not to do the same. I doubt that I have particularly good genes. I have two sons, and one's as big a drain on me as the other. If I had another, I doubt that the results would be any better. Then there's my wife, whose soil has seriously hardened. If I planted a sapling, in three days it would be a cane.

LI SHOU: Why not let your mistress do it?

YUAN SAI: How can you say things like that at your age, my friend? We're upright, highly moral individuals who don't get involved in ugly affairs like that.

LI SHOU: Ugly affairs? It's all the rage these days, a new wave, gene improvement, aiding the poor and lending a helping hand to the weak, fuelling domestic demand and furthering development.

YUAN SAI: Stop right there. If that gets out, they'll be coming after you.

LI SHOU: Ask them if they dare broadcast that.

REPORTER: (*smiles without answering, turns to Gugu*) Gugu, I hear that you have developed a 'return to spring' elixir that will restore a post-menopausal woman's youth.

GUGU: Many people say I have a potion that can change the sex of a foetus. Do you believe that?

REPORTER: I'd rather believe it than not.

GUGU: There's a god if you believe there is, and if you don't, it's just an unpainted clay idol. That's just how people are.

TADPOLE: Miss Gao, you and your station colleagues are welcome to join us at the table. You can continue interviewing after you've had something to drink.

REPORTER: No, you go ahead. Just pretend we're not here.

LI SHOU: How are we supposed to do that with you people walking around while we're drinking?

REPORTER: You can – pretend we're not people, pretend we're – whatever you want.

YUAN SAI: Guifang, you were my idol during our school days, so I have to raise my glass to you.

LIU: (*clinks glasses with Yuan*) Here's to the success of your bullfrog breeding farm and the early arrival of your Jiaowa Skin Care product in the market.

YUAN SAI: Don't change the subject. I want to tell you how besotted I was with you back then.

LIU: Stop being foolish with your false display of affection. Everybody knows there's a harem of beautiful women in Chairman Yuan's bullfrog farm.

REPORTER: (*takes advantage of the pause to speak into her microphone*) Ladies and gentlemen, today's *Aspects on Society* program focuses on a joyous event in Northeast Gaomi Township. On the fifteenth of last month, the famous playwright Tadpole, a recent retiree who has returned home to write, and his wife, Little Lion, both now in their fifties, were blessed with the birth of a healthy, lively, pudgy son . . .

GUGU: Bring the baby out to show everyone.

Tadpole runs off the stage.

LIU: (*glares at Yuan and says under her breath*) Enough nonsense. You'll make Gugu unhappy.

Tadpole enters with Little Lion, a towel around her head, the swaddled baby in her arms.

The cameraman films away.

The guests applaud and shout their congratulations.

TADPOLE: Let Gugu see him.

Little Lion takes the baby up to Gugu, who pulls back the blanket to see him.

GUGU: (*with emotion*) A fine boy. A truly fine boy, with excellent genes. So good-looking that if he'd been born during feudal times, he'd be the top scholar at the civil service examination.

LI SHOU: Why stop there? He could be Emperor.

GUGU: What is this, a bragging contest?

REPORTER: (*puts the microphone in front of Gugu*) Did you deliver this baby, too, Gugu?

GUGU: (*tucks a red envelope into the swaddling clothes. Tadpole and Little Lion try to refuse the gift, but Gugu waves them off*) This is the custom. Your aunt can afford it. (*to the reporter*) Fortunately, they trusted me. She was past the normal child-bearing age, and she's under a lot of pressure. I told her to go to the hospital to 'slice open the melon', but she said no, and I supported her in her decision. Only a woman who delivers a baby through the birth canal knows what it means to be a woman and how to be a mother.

While Gugu is being interviewed, Little Lion and Tadpole show the baby to all the guests, each of whom tucks a red envelope into the swaddling clothes.

REPORTER: Will he be the last baby you deliver, Gugu?

GUGU: What do you think?

REPORTER: I hear that women in Northeast Gaomi Township aren't the only ones who revere and trust you, that many pregnant women come to you from Pingdu and Jiaozhou counties.

GUGU: I was born to work hard.

REPORTER: I've heard that there's a magic power in your hands, and that all you have to do is place them on a pregnant woman's abdomen to greatly lessen their pain. Even their worries and their fears evaporate.

GUGU: That is how myths are born.

REPORTER: Gugu, please show us your hands. We'd like to get a couple of shots of them.

GUGU: (*sarcastically*) The people need their myths. (*turns to the guests*) Know who said that?

LI SHOU: A great person, by the sound of it.

GUGU: I said it.

YUAN SAI: Gugu just about qualifies as a great person.

LIU: What do you mean, just about? Gugu *is* a great person.

REPORTER: (*sombrely*) These two ordinary hands brought thousands of babies into the world.

GUGU: It was also these two ordinary hands that sent thousands of babies straight to Hell. (*empties her glass*) Gugu's hands are stained with two kinds of blood, one fragrant, the other fetid.

LIU: Gugu, you are our Northeast Township's Living Buddha. The closer we look the more the Goddess in the Fertility Temple looks like you. They made her in your image.

GUGU: (*drunkenly*) The people need their myths.

REPORTER: (*holds the microphone in front of Little Lion*) Can we hear some of your thoughts, madam?

LITTLE LION: About what?

REPORTER: Whatever you like. How you felt when you discovered you were pregnant, for instance. Or how it felt to be pregnant, or why you insisted that Gugu be there when it was time . . .

LITTLE LION: Discovering I was pregnant was like a dream. How could a woman in her fifties, two years past menopause, suddenly become pregnant? As for my feelings during my pregnancy, it was roughly equal between joy and worry. The joy came from the knowledge that I was going to be a mother. I worked as an obstetrics doctor with Gugu for more than a decade, helping her bring many babies into the world, but never having one of my own. A childless woman is less than complete, someone who cannot look her husband in the eye. That has all been resolved now.

REPORTER: What about the worry? What worried you?

LITTLE LION: Mainly thoughts of my age, afraid I might give birth to an unhealthy baby. Next I was worried that I might need to have a surgical birth. Of course, when I went into labour, Gugu laid her hands on my abdomen, and my worries vanished. After that I had only to do what Gugu said to deliver my baby.

GUGU: (*drunkenly*) Washing the fetid blood away with the fragrant blood . . .

Chen Bi enters on crutches.

CHEN BI: What kind of people do not invite a grandpa to his grandson's one-month anniversary?

The guests are astonished.

TADPOLE: (*thrown into a panic*) I'm sorry, old friend, truly sorry. It completely slipped my mind . . .

CHEN BI: (*mad laughter*) Did you just call me old friend? Ha ha. (*points to the baby in Little Lion's arms with a crutch*) Normal courtesy demands that you get down on your hands and knees and kowtow to me three times and call me 'Esteemed Father-in-law', doesn't it?

YUAN SAI: (*goes up to stop Chen Bi*) Come with me, Chen, old fellow, I'll buy you a good meal at the famous King of Abalone and Shark's Fin restaurant.

CHEN BI: Get out of my face, you shameless piece of shit. Do you really think you can shut me up with some stinking seafood? That's not going to happen. Today is a big day in my grandson's life, and I'm not going anywhere. I'm staying here to have a celebratory drink. (*sits down and spots Gugu*) Gugu, your mind is like a spotless mirror. You took care of all our Northeast Gaomi Township babies. You knew whose seeds would not sprout and whose soil would not grow grass, so you borrowed seeds and soil, you replaced beams with rotten timbers, you used Chencang as a decoy, you deceived the heavens to cross the ocean, you sacrificed the plum to preserve the peach, you let someone get away in order to capture, you killed with a borrowed knife . . . you have used all the thirty-six stratagems from *The Art of War*.

GUGU: You used only two – you made a sound in the east and attacked from the west, and you escaped like a cicada sloughing off its skin. I nearly fell for your tricks back then. Half the foetid blood on my hands (*holds them to her nose to smell*) you put there.

LI SHOU: (*pours a glass for Chen*) Have a drink, old Chen. Drink up.

CHEN BI: (*tosses down the glassful*) Young classmate, you're a fair man. Come reason this out for us —

LI SHOU: (*doesn't let Chen finish; refills his glass*) Only the heavens know about fairness. Drink up. Here, use a bigger glass.

CHEN BI: Are you trying to get me drunk? You're wrong if you think liquor will shut me up.

LI SHOU: Of course I'm wrong. No one can outdrink you. We're drinking real Maotai today, and you don't want to waste the opportunity, right? Down the hatch!

CHEN BI: (*tips his head and drains the glass, breathes heavily as tears begin to fall*) Gugu, Tadpole, Little Lion, Yuan Sai, Jin Xiu – I, Chen Bi, have fallen as low as a man can fall. Is there a single person among the fifty thousand residents of the eighteen villages in Northeast Gaomi Township as pitiful as me? I ask you, is there? No, there isn't, no one is as pitiful as me. But you, all of you, have ganged up to bully me, a cripple. I guess that's all right, since I'm not a good person and never have been. Bullying me is like heavenly retribution. But you shouldn't take advantage of my daughter. Chen Mei, a girl you have all watched grow up, the prettiest girl in all of Northeast Gaomi Township, she and her sister, Chen Er, who together could have married into the imperial family as queens or royal consorts, but . . . it's all my fault . . . retribution . . . my daughter carried your child (*angrily points at Tadpole*) to earn enough to pay off my debts. But you, my old classmates, all you uncles and elders, all you playwrights, all you big bosses, conspired to fabricate a story that her baby was stillborn. You cheated her out of her forty-thousand-yuan fee. The heavens are only three feet above your head. Why doesn't God open his eyes to see how these terrible people are riding roughshod over us . . . turn on your camera, TV people, shine a light on us all – me, her, them – for all your viewers . . .

LIU: Everyone says nobody holds his drink as well as you, old Chen. So why are you spouting all this nonsense after only two glasses?

CHEN BI: You're a shrewd woman, Liu Guifang. When the guesthouse went private, you became a big boss overnight. You're now worth millions. I begged you to find a job for my daughter, even if it was tending a fire in your kitchen, but you chose not to be generous, saying you were in the process of downsizing and that the door to charity was hard to open. But . . .

LIU: I was wrong, old friend, and I'll take care of Chen Mei. It's only one more mouth to feed, isn't it? I'll take her under my wing, how's that?

Yuan Sai, Jin Xiu, and others try to 'escort' Chen Bi out of the yard.

CHEN BI: (*struggles*) I still haven't seen my grandson. (*takes out a red envelope*) Grandson, your granddad may be poor, but ethical codes must be followed. I have prepared a red envelope for you . . .

While Yuan Sai and the others manhandle Chen off the stage, Chen Mei, all in black, enters to the astonishment of everyone present. There is total silence.

CHEN MEI: (*sniffs the air in exaggerated fashion, softly at first, but builds in intensity*) My baby, my darling, I have picked up your sweet-smelling, pungent scent. (*feels her way up close to Little Lion, like a blind person, just as loud cries emerge from the swaddling clothes*) My baby, my good, little baby, you have never tasted your mother's milk, you must be starving. (*She snatches the baby away from Little Lion and dashes offstage. The guests, stunned by the act, do not know what to do.*)

LITTLE LION: (*opens her now empty arms*) My baby (*in real despair*), my little Jinwa . . .

Little Lion runs after Chen Mei, followed by Tadpole and others. Chaos onstage.

Curtain

Act VII

Scenery changes constantly on a large screen at the rear of the stage. A busy street one moment, a crowded marketplace the next, followed by a public park, where people are practising Tai Chi, carrying bird cages and playing the two-stringed erhu. The changing scenery denotes the places she passes in Chen Mei's getaway.

As Chen Mei runs with the baby, she speaks her heart to him.

CHEN MEI: My little darling, Mummy has finally found you . . . she'll never let you go again . . .

Little Lion, Tadpole, and many others are chasing her.

LITTLE LION: Jinwa . . . my son . . .

Some of the time, Chen Mei is alone onstage, running and looking over her shoulder, at other times she shouts to people she passes: Help, save me, save my baby.

Some of the time, she and the people chasing her are on the stage together. Chen Mei shouts to people on the street: Help, save us! *Little Lion and the others shout to the people ahead:* Stop her. Stop that baby stealer, stop that madwoman!

Chen Mei stumbles, clambers to her feet, stumbles again, gets up again.

The fast, lively, shrill music of an opera fiddle together with a baby's cries form a background from when the curtain goes up till the curtain falls.

Curtain

Act VIII

The TV drama Gao Mengjiu *is being filmed.*

The main hall of a county yamen during the Republican era. Though there are signs of reform, it basically follows the old patterns. The words 'justice' and 'integrity' are carved into a signboard hanging above the hall. One scroll to the side of the signboard proclaims: 'Wind, then rain, then the blue sky'. Its mate on the other side proclaims: 'The civil, the martial, and the barbaric'. A large shoe rests on an altar in the centre of the hall.

Gao Mengjiu is in a black tunic and top hat, a watch chain looping out of his breast pocket. Yamen clerks stand straight on both sides of the stage, each holding a long red and black 'fire and water' club, but they are dressed in modern black tunics, a comical effect.

The director, cameraman, and sound technician move around busily.

DIRECTOR: Take your places. Ready – action!
GAO MENGJIU: (*picks up the shoe and bangs it on the table*) Oh my, oh
    my . . . What a nuisance! (*sings*) Magistrate Gao is in his hall to
    try a case: two families, Zhang and Wang, have a dispute over
    land. Zhang is in the right, and so is Wang. Both families have
    a claim, and I must settle the dispute. My name is Gao Mengjiu

from Weibaodi county in the Tianjin municipality. I joined the army in my youth under Field Marshal Feng Yuxiang, performing outstanding service in battles north and south. Marshal Feng selected me to be his guard battalion commander. One day, Marshal Feng spotted a soldier under my command parading around town in dark glasses, a prostitute on his arm, and censured me for lax discipline. I was so embarrassed at having fallen short of the marshal's expectations that I tendered my resignation and returned to my native home. In the nineteenth year of the Republic, 1930, Gao's fellow townsman Han Fuju, Governor of Shandong, respectfully and repeatedly invited me to take up an official position. I could not refuse the request of a fellow officer, so was sent to Shandong, first as a provincial representative, then as head of Pingyuan, Qufu, and, as of this spring, Gaomi counties. The people here are cunning and stubborn, crime is rampant, gambling is ubiquitous, opium is a scourge, and public order is non-existent. After taking office, I boldly instituted reforms, stamped out criminal activity, promoted filial behaviour, and travelled incognito, resolving difficult cases. (*softly*) Of course, not everything went smoothly, as is always the case for one who is not a sage. And even sages make mistakes from time to time. The local gentry families presented me with a pair of scrolls, with 'Wind, then rain, then the blue sky' on one and 'The civil, the martial, and the barbaric' on the other. Well written. Extremely well! They also came up with a nickname for me: Gao the Second with Shoe-soles. The origin of this moniker came from my proclivity to use the soles of shoes across the faces of criminals and harridans. (*sings*) In troubled times an official must employ severe punishments/Answering brutality with brutality/Use clever schemes to exterminate bandits/A shoe sole is the tool of an upright magistrate. I say, all you clerks —

YAMEN CLERKS: Yes, sir!

GAO MENGJIU: Is all in readiness?

YAMEN CLERKS: It is.

GAO MENGJIU: Call for the plaintiffs and defendants.

Chen Mei, baby in her arms, stumbles onto the stage.

CHEN MEI: Magistrate Bao, please help me gain justice.

Little Lion, Tadpole, and the others enter, one after the other.

The actors playing Zhang and Wang are among the crowd as they enter.

DIRECTOR: (*frustrated*) Cut! Cut! What's going on here? This is a
　　mess. Where's the stage manager?
CHEN MEI: (*falls to her knees at the front of the stage*) Magistrate Bao,
　　please help me gain justice!
GAO MENGJIU: My name is Gao, not Bao.
CHEN MEI: (*amid the sound of the baby's cries*) Magistrate Bao, I lay an
　　odd grievance at your feet for impartial justice.

*Yuan Sai and the cousin take the director aside and say something to him that
others cannot hear. The director nods his head. Yuan's comment to the director
can barely be heard:* Our company will donate a hundred thousand.

The director walks up to Gao Mengjiu and whispers something to him.

The director signals to the cameraman and others to continue filming.

*Yuan Sai walks up to Tadpole and Little Lion and speaks to them in hushed
tones.*

GAO MENGJIU: (*picks up the shoe and bangs it on the table*) Citizen at the
　　front of this hall, hear me. I will today be extraordinarily generous
　　by deciding an additional case. Tell me your name, your residency,
　　what charges you bring, against whom, all in complete truth. If I
　　hear one false note, do you know how I will deal with it?

CHEN MEI: I do not.

YAMEN CLERKS: (*in unison*) Woo-wei!

GAO MENGJIU: (*takes hold of the shoe and bangs it on the table*) If there is one dishonest word, I will use this shoe on your face.

CHEN MEI: Now I know.

GAO MENGJIU: Tell me everything.

CHEN MEI: Hear my report, Your Honour: My name is Chen Mei, I am from Northeast Gaomi Township. I lost my mother when I was a girl and grew up alone with my older sister. We took jobs at a toy factory, where there was a fire that killed my sister and destroyed my face . . .

GAO MENGJIU: Remove your veil, Chen Mei, and let me see the damage.

CHEN MEI: I cannot remove it, Magistrate Bao.

GAO MENGJIU: Why not?

CHEN MEI: With it on I am human, if I remove it I am a demon.

GAO MENGJIU: When I decide a case, Chen Mei, I follow the letter of the law. With that veil over your face, how am I supposed to know you are who you say you are?

CHEN MEI: Will you tell them all to cover their eyes, Your Honour?

GAO MENGJIU: Cover your eyes, all of you.

CHEN MEI: I will let you see, Magistrate. It is a bitter life I lead!

Chen Mei puts the baby down, removes the veil, and covers her face with both hands.

Gao makes a sign to the front of the hall. Little Lion rushes forward and picks up the baby.

LITTLE LION: (*sobs*) My darling, Jinwa, my little Jinwa, let Mama take a look at you . . . Tadpole, come look, what's wrong with Jinwa . . . that crazy woman has killed my baby!

CHEN MEI: (*screams and madly rushes towards Little Lion*) My baby . . . Your Honour, she has stolen my baby . . .

The yamen clerks stop her.

Gugu slowly enters.

TADPOLE: Gugu is here.

LITTLE LION: Gugu, tell me what's wrong with Jinwa.

Gugu pinches and rubs the child in places. The baby cries. Tadpole hands Little Lion a nursing bottle. She puts the nipple in the baby's mouth. The crying stops.

CHEN MEI: Don't let her feed my baby, Your Honour. That milk is toxic. I have milk, Your Honour . . . I'll squeeze some out for Your Honour if you do not believe me.

Chen Bi and Li Shou enter.

CHEN BI: (*pounds a crutch on the floor*) Fairness, I demand fairness!

GAO MENGJIU: (*sorrowfully*) Cover your face, Chen Mei.

CHEN MEI: (*terrified, she grabs the veil and covers her face*) I have frightened you, Your Honour. I am so sorry.

GAO MENGJIU: Chen Mei, your case has fallen into my hands, so I must get to the bottom of it.

CHEN MEI: Thank you, Your Honour.

Tadpole and Yuan Sai try to bundle Little Lion off the stage.

GAO MENGJIU: (*bangs his shoe on the table*) Stop right there! No one leaves until I have handed down my judgement. Watch them, yamen clerks.

The director gives a sign to Gao, who pretends not to have seen it.

GAO MENGJIU: Chen Mei, you insist that the baby is yours. Then I ask you, who is the father?

CHEN MEI: He is a high official, a rich man, a powerful man.

GAO MENGJIU: No matter how high, how rich, or how powerful, he must have a name.

CHEN MEI: I do not know his name.

GAO MENGJIU: When were you married?

CHEN MEI: I have never been married.

GAO MENGJIU: Oh, a child out of wedlock. Then when did you and he . . . in bed?

CHEN MEI: I do not understand, Your Honour.

GAO MENGJIU: Ah! When did you sleep with him? What do they say – make love? Understand?

CHEN MEI: I have never slept with a man, Your Honour, I am a virgin.

GAO MENGJIU: Ah! Now I *am* confused. How could you be pregnant and have a baby if you have never slept with a man? Are you ignorant of basic biological knowledge?

CHEN MEI: Your Honour, every word of what I say is the truth (*points to the group that includes Little Lion*) With a syringe they . . .

GAO MENGJIU: A test tube baby.

CHEN MEI: No, not a test tube baby.

GAO MENGJIU: I understand. It's the sort of artificial insemination they use for livestock.

CHEN MEI: (*on her knees*) Please, Your Honour, pass your fair judgement. I wanted to have this baby at first to earn enough to pay my father's hospital bills, then drown myself in the river. But death stopped being attractive once I became pregnant and felt him moving around inside me. There were other women like me, but who hated the children they were carrying. I loved mine. My disfigured face and scarred body itch and hurt on rainy, overcast days, and on hot dry days, my wounds crack and bleed. It was hard to carry my baby to term, Your Honour. I suffered miserably, but by being careful I was able to have a successful delivery. But those people lied to me, saying my baby was stillborn. I knew he wasn't dead, so I searched and searched until I found him. I don't want

the surrogate fee, a million, ten million, I don't care, I just want my
baby. Please, Your Honour, make them give me my baby . . .

GAO MENGJIU: (*to Tadpole and Little Lion*) Are you legally married?

TADPOLE: For more than thirty years.

GAO MENGJIU: And all that time you had no child?

LITTLE LION: (*unhappily*) What would you call him, if not a child?

GAO MENGJIU: You look to me to be in your fifties, am I right?

LITTLE LION: I knew you'd ask that. (*points to Gugu*) This is our
Northeast Gaomi Township's doctor of obstetrics, who has
delivered thousands of babies and has cured many women of
infertility. Who knows, maybe you yourself were one of her babies.
She will testify for me, since she was with me throughout my
pregnancy to the birth of my baby.

GAO MENGJIU: I have long been familiar with Gugu's reputation. You
are a local sage, someone who enjoys universal respect and whose
words carry great weight.

GUGU: I delivered that child.

GAO MENGJIU: (*asks Chen Mei*) Did she deliver your baby?

CHEN MEI: They blindfolded me in the delivery room, Your Honour.

GAO MENGJIU: This case is difficult to adjudicate. We will need DNA
results.

*The director goes up to whisper something to Gao, who has words with him
under his breath.*

GAO MENGJIU: (*sighs, then sings*) Strange case, strange case, a very
strange case – putting old Gao in a difficult place – to whom does
the child belong – an ingenious plan has come to me. (*steps down*)
Hear me, everyone, since your case has fallen into my hands,
I must turn make-believe into real life and make my judgement!
Yamen clerks!

CLERKS: Yes, sir!

GAO MENGJIU: If anyone disputes my judgement, use a shoe on their
face.

CLERKS: Yes!

GAO MENGJIU: Chen Mei, Little Lion, each of you tells a convincing
story, and I cannot choose one over the other. Therefore, I must
ask Little Lion to give the child to me for now.

LITTLE LION: I won't . . .

GAO MENGJIU: Yamen clerks!

CLERKS: (*in unison*) Woo-wei . . .

*The director whispers to Tadpole, who nudges Little Lion and indicates she
should hand the baby to Gao Mengjiu.*

GAO MENGJIU: (*softly as he looks down at the baby*) A fine baby for sure.
No wonder the two families are fighting over him. Hear me, Chen
Mei, Little Lion, I cannot decide to whom the child belongs, so
I must ask you to try to take him from me. Whoever wrests the
child from my hands gets him. A messy case deserves a messy
resolution. (*holds the child over his head*) Now!

*Both Chen Mei and Little Lion rush up and grab hold of the baby, who
begins to cry. Chen Mei wrests him away and holds him to her breast.*

GAO MENGJIU: Yamen clerks, take the child away from Chen Mei and
arrest her.

The clerks take the baby from Chen Mei and hand him to Gao.

GAO MENGJIU: Audacious Chen Mei, you falsely claimed that the baby
was yours, yet you did not hesitate to wrest him out of my hands,
something a real mother would not do. When Little Lion heard
the baby cry, her motherly instincts would not let her do anything
to harm her child, and she let go. Magistrate Bao settled a similar
case centuries ago. The one who let go was the true mother. With
this precedent, I award the child to Little Lion. For trying to take
another's child and lying in court, I ought to sentence Chen Mei

to twenty lashes with a shoe sole. But in view of your disability, I mercifully withhold punishment. Leave this court!

Gao Mengjiu hands the baby to Little Lion.

Chen Mei shouts and struggles, but is stopped by the clerks.

CHEN BI: Gao Mengjiu, you are a muddled judge.
LI SHOU: (*nudges Chen*) Let it be, old friend. I have already talked with Tadpole and Yuan Sai, who have agreed to give Chen Mei a hundred thousand yuan.

Curtain

Act IX

Gugu's yard, same scene as Acts II and IV.

Hao Dashou and Qin He are still making clay dolls.

Tadpole, manuscript in hand, stands to the side.

TADPOLE: *(intones loudly)* If someone were to ask me to name
   Northeast Gaomi Township's predominant colour, without
   hesitation I would respond: Green!

HAO DASHOU: *(grumbles)* What about red? Red sorghum, radishes, the
   red sun, red jackets, red peppers, apples . . .

QIN HE: Yellow earth, droppings, teeth, yellow weasels, everything
   yellow but gold.

TADPOLE: If someone were to ask me to name Northeast Gaomi
   Township's predominant sound, I would proudly respond: the
   croak of frogs.

HAO DASHOU: What's there to be proud about?

QIN HE: The cry of a baby is worth being proud about.

TADPOLE: The croak of a frog, like the heavy lowing of a young cow,
   like the sad bleating of a young goat, like the crisp sound of a
   hen when she lays an egg, like the loud and mournful sound of
   a newborn infant . . .

HAO DASHOU: How about a barking dog, a mewing cat, a braying donkey?

TADPOLE: (*angrily*) Are you two messing with me?

QIN HE: In my view, your play is messing with you.

GUGU: (*coldly*) Did I really say the things you just read?

TADPOLE: The Gugu in the play said them.

GUGU: Is the Gugu in the play me? Or isn't it?

TADPOLE: It is and it isn't.

GUGU: What does that mean?

TADPOLE: It's a common principle in art. Like the dolls they make, modelled after real life but enhanced by their imagination and creativity.

GUGU: Are you really planning to stage your play? Aren't you afraid of the trouble it could cause, since you've used people's real names?

TADPOLE: This is just a draft, Gugu. In the final version I'll use all foreigners' names. Gugu will become Aunt Maria, Hao Dashou will be Henry, Qin He will be Allende, Chen Mei will be Tonia, Chen Bi will be Figaro . . . even Northeast Gaomi Township will become the town of Macondo.

HAO DASHOU: Henry? Interesting name.

QIN HE: I think I should be Rodin or Michelangelo, since their work resembles mine.

GUGU: Tadpole, play-acting is play-acting, reality is reality. I think that you – no, I have to include myself – we all treated Chen Mei badly. My insomnia has returned in recent days. All those crippled frogs that damned little devil brought out come to disturb me at night. Not only can I feel their chilled, slimy skin, but I can even smell their cold stench . . .

HAO DASHOU: Those are illusions brought on by your nervous condition, nothing but illusions.

TADPOLE: I understand how you feel, Gugu, and the way we dealt with this has weighed heavily on me. But I don't know how else to deal with it. No matter how you look at it, Chen Mei was insane, a madwoman with a hideous, disfigured face, and giving the baby to her would have violated our responsibility to the child. Not only that, I was the child's biological father, albeit a reluctant one. If his mother had gone off the tracks emotionally and could not even care for herself, then the father would have had to assume child-raising duties. Even the People's Supreme Court would have made that determination. Am I right or not?

GUGU: Maybe she would have been fine if we'd given her the baby. Miracles can happen when you put a woman and child together.

TADPOLE: We couldn't take the chance, not with the child's wellbeing in the balance. People with mental problems are capable of anything.

GUGU: People with mental problems can still love children.

TADPOLE: But her love could have harmed the child. Gugu, don't beat yourself up this way. We've already done everything compassion and humanity dictate. We gave her twice her original fee and got her admitted into a hospital for treatment. Even Chen Bi was not short-changed. If one day her mental health is restored, and the child is old enough, when the time is right, we'll reveal all this to him — even if that will be painful for him.

GUGU: I want you all to know that I've been thinking about death a lot recently.

TADPOLE: I don't want to hear such crazy talk, Gugu. You're barely seventy years old. Though it's an exaggeration to say you are the noonday sun, it's not flattery to say that you're the sun at two or three in the afternoon, a long way from darkness. Besides, the people of Northeast Gaomi Township cannot live without you.

GUGU: I didn't say I wanted to die, not as long as I'm in good health, have a good appetite, and can sleep at night. Who would? But sleep has become a problem. Everyone else is sound asleep in the middle of the night, everyone but me and that owl in the tree. The owl stays awake to hunt mice. What about me?

TADPOLE: You can take a sleeping pill. Lots of important people are troubled by insomnia, and that's how they deal with it.

GUGU: Sleeping pills don't work with me any more.

TADPOLE: Try Chinese herbs.

GUGU: I'm a doctor, and I'm telling you, this isn't physical. The day of reckoning has arrived. All those avenging ghosts have come to settle accounts. At night, when all around is quiet and the owl begins to hoot in the tree, they come. Coated in blood, they wail and moan, accompanied by those frogs with missing legs and claws. Cries and croaks swirl together and cannot be distinguished, one from the other. They chase me around the yard. I'm not afraid of being bitten, what frightens me is their slimy skin and the cold stench they produce. Tell me, what things have frightened me at any time in my life? Tigers? Panthers? Wolves? Foxes? I have never been afraid of animals that frighten others. But the ghosts of those frogs petrify me.

TADPOLE: (*to Hao Dashou*) Should we invite a Daoist priest to do an exorcism?

HAO DASHOU: She's giving you an actor's lines.

GUGU: When I can't sleep, I think back over my life, starting with the first child I delivered all the way to the last. They all play in my head, like a movie. I don't think I've done an evil thing ever in my life . . . but those . . . was that evil?

TADPOLE: That's hard to say, Gugu, but even if they were, you were not responsible. Don't blame yourself, Gugu, and don't feel guilty. You're a hero, not a sinner.

GUGU: I'm not? Really?

TADPOLE: If the township residents voted for the best person, you would get the most votes.

GUGU: Are my hands clean?

TADPOLE: Not just clean, but sacred.

GUGU: When I can't sleep, I think of how Zhang Quan's wife died, and Wang Renmei, and Wang Dan . . .

TADPOLE: You didn't kill them, it wasn't you.

GUGU: Did you know that Zhang Quan's wife uttered some last words?

TADPOLE: I didn't know that.

GUGU: 'Wan Xin,' she said, 'you will die a terrible death.'

TADPOLE: That bitch had no right to say that.

GUGU: Did you know that Renmei uttered last words as well?

TADPOLE: What did she say?

GUGU: She said, 'I'm cold, Gugu.'

TADPOLE: (*agonisingly*) I'm cold, too, Renmei.

GUGU: Did you know that Wang Dan said something to me before she died?

TADPOLE: No.

GUGU: Do you want to know?

TADPOLE: Of course . . . but . . .

GUGU: (*in high spirits*) She said, 'Thank you for saving my baby's life, Gugu.' Did I really save her baby's life?

TADPOLE: Of course you did.

GUGU: Then I can die in peace, right?

TADPOLE: Don't say that, Gugu. What you should say is you can sleep in peace and keep living well.

GUGU: A sinner cannot and has no right to die. She must live on, to suffer torment, to be like a fish frying in a pan, like medicine boiling in a pot of water, all for the sake of atonement. Only when that is complete, is she free to die.

A large black noose drops from above the stage. Gugu goes up, stands on a stool, sticks her head through the noose, and kicks the stool over.

Hao Dashou and Qin He do not look up from their doll making.

Tadpole picks up a knife, rights the stool, jumps up onto it, and cuts the rope in two.

Gugu drops to the stage floor.

TADPOLE: (*props up Gugu*) Gugu! Gugu!

GUGU: Am I dead?

TADPOLE: I guess you could say that. But people like you don't really
die.

GUGU: Then I've been reborn.

TADPOLE: Yes, you can say that.

GUGU: Are you all okay?

TADPOLE: We're fine.

GUGU: The baby too?

TADPOLE: He's doing beautifully.

GUGU: Has Little Lion begun to lactate?

TADPOLE: Yes.

GUGU: Lots of milk?

TADPOLE: Lots and lots of it.

GUGU: What does it look like?

TADPOLE: Like a fountain.

Curtain

(Finis)